The Summer of Good Intentions

A Novel

WENDY FRANCIS

Author of THREE GOOD THINGS

THREE SISTERS WITH SUITCASES FULL OF SECRETS
SPEND A SUMMER BY THE SEA IN THIS
POIGNANT, COMPELLING NOVEL SO REAL THAT
YOU'LL BE SHAKING THE SAND OUT OF THE PAGES.

"Love in all of its messiness is written with convincing thoughtfulness and insight, each flawed character beautifully and realistically portrayed. Feel the sand between your toes as you explore the special bonds of sisterhood and family in what promises to be one of the best books of summer." —KAREN WHITE, author of *THE TIME BETWEEN*

"Wendy Francis has created both a family and a story I did not want to leave. These three sisters on a summer vacation display the strong ties that can both hurt and heal a family. Filled with the sweet briny air of Cape Cod, this extraordinary tale shows that, together, we can weather all the seasons of life." —PATTI CALLAHAN HENRY, author of *THE STORIES WE TELL*

"I was immediately engrossed by this story of three adult sisters who share their own bonds, heartbreak, and challenges. So much more than a beach read, this very real, poignant, and funny novel will make you look at your own family in fresh, new ways." —LEE WOODRUFF, author of *THOSE WE LOVE MOST*

"A lovely summer read. Wendy Francis deftly explores the bonds of sisterhood and the complexity of family relationships." —WENDY WAX, *USA TODAY* bestselling author

"WENDY FRANCIS IS A WONDERFUL WRITER." —LUANNE RICE

Praise for *Three Good Things*

"A toothsome tale . . . a debut as light, sweet, and fluffy as Danish pastry dough. Culinary romance lovers—fans of Sharon Boorstein, Susan Mallery, and Deirdre Martin—will devour it."

—*Library Journal*

"Like gossip over morning coffee in the kitchen . . . warm and comforting."

—*Kirkus Reviews*

"*Three Good Things* is a flavorful tale of sisters and second chances, fresh starts and sweet surprises. Wendy Francis has written a rich debut, sure to delight the lucky readers who discover her here."

—Barbara O'Neal, **author of** *The All You Can Dream Buffet*

"There are so many good things to say about *Three Good Things*. It's a warm, witty, and wise story of sisters on their journey through love and life. Wendy Francis's new novel is as delicious as the kringles made in Ellen's bakeshop."

—Susan Wiggs, **author of** *The Beekeeper's Ball*

"Wendy Francis's *Three Good Things* is as sweet, rich, and comforting as a Danish kringle, spiced with lots of good surprises."

—Nancy Thayer, **author of** *Nantucket Sisters*

"A lovely story about people you wish were your next-door neighbors. I wish, too, the kringle shop were next door, because I loved the mouthwatering descriptions of its treats. Curl up with this book, along with a cup of tea and a kringle (what else?) and lose yourself in a world you won't want to leave after you turn the last page."

—Eileen Goudge, **author of** *The Replacement Wife*

Also by Wendy Francis

Three Good Things

The Summer of Good Intentions

WENDY FRANCIS

Simon & Schuster Paperbacks

New York   London   Toronto   Sydney   New Delhi

Simon & Schuster Paperbacks
An Imprint of Simon & Schuster, Inc.
1230 Avenue of the Americas
New York, NY 10020

First Simon & Schuster trade paperback edition July 2015

SIMON & SCHUSTER PAPERBACKS and colophon are registered trademarks of Simon & Schuster, Inc.

For information about special discounts for bulk purchases, please contact Simon & Schuster Special Sales at 1-866-506-1949 or business@simonandschuster.com.

The Simon & Schuster Speakers Bureau can bring authors to your live event. For more information or to book an event contact the Simon & Schuster Speakers Bureau at 1-866-248-3049 or visit our website at www.simonspeakers.com.

Interior design by Lewelin Polanco

Manufactured in the United States of America

10 9 8 7 6 5 4 3 2 1

Library of Congress Cataloging-in-Publication Data
  Francis, Wendy.
    The summer of good intentions : a novel / Wendy Francis.—First Simon & Schuster trade paperback edition.
        pages ; cm
    1. Sisters—Fiction. 2. Family secrets—Fiction. 3. Domestic fiction. I. Title.
PS3606.R36535S86 2015
    813'.6—dc23
                                                                    2014040902

ISBN 978-1-4516-6642-7
ISBN 978-1-4516-6643-4 (ebook)

For my mom and dad,
both gone too soon

The mess is holy. . . . There is beauty in what is.

—DANI SHAPIRO

JULY

Maggie

The salty Cape air blew in through the window, and Maggie listened to the steady thump of blinds hitting the windowsill. The spot next to her in bed was empty, the sheets dimpled. Mac must have already gotten up to fetch the paper and coffee at the Blueberry Bagel down the road. It was one of her favorite things about their annual month on the Cape: iced coffee waiting for her on the kitchen counter when she managed to pull herself out of bed. For eleven months of the year, she was the one in charge, responsible for waking the kids, making sure they were dressed before they climbed on the bus, packing their lunches, ferrying the twins to dance, soccer, drama, and entertaining baby Luke. Of course, Luke was no longer a baby. He'd be entering kindergarten in the fall.

But in July everything shifted. Mac was home, and at last, Maggie had some precious time to herself when she could sit in the sun or nurse a glass of wine after dinner, looking out over the ocean without a care. Or, at the very least, she could *pretend* she didn't have a care. In July, Mac turned off his scanner, and the office knew better than to bother him unless a case turned up that only his expertise could unriddle. Maggie had understood it wouldn't be easy being married to a Boston cop when she walked down the aisle fifteen years ago, but she wasn't prepared for the constant worry of whether her husband would return home at the end of his shift. The worry had nearly driven her crazy during the first years of their marriage, but then the twins were born and a whole new host of concerns emerged. Her fears about Mac had faded to a low-grade hum that played in the background of her days. On the Cape, however, for this one precious month, the family had Mac all to themselves. *Safe* was all she could think. Happy was what she felt.

She rolled over and felt the heat drifting in like sheets on a breeze. The sun pooled on the wide plank floors of the master bedroom. The house was quiet. Either Mac had taken Luke, her usual first riser, to the coffee shop with him or Luke was still asleep like his sisters. They'd arrived last night—a jumble of bags, canvas totes, coolers, and inflatable water toys—as the sun was starting its descent in the sky. The drive, normally an hour and a half, had unspooled into nearly three with the vacation traffic. The kids' iPads and I Spy had entertained them for the first hour, but eventually the children had whined with impatience. Maggie could hardly blame them.

They inched their way through the Hingham merge, where traffic always slowed, then past Marshfield and Duxbury. The giant wind turbine spun up ahead, a towering white knight in the evening sky. When at last they reached the Sagamore Bridge, she silently thanked the heavens. Greeting them, as it did each summer, was a sign from the Samaritans that asked in bold letters, ARE YOU DESPERATE? with a number to call posted underneath. It always gave her a perverse chuckle. How did they know, Maggie wondered, that carloads of parents were ready to jump off the bridge at this precise moment?

The shock of verdant green that met the eye as they topped the bridge surprised her each July. On either side of the canal, blue and purple hydrangeas dotted the roadside and swayed in the cool evening breeze, as if waving to them in greeting. In this final stretch, Maggie exhaled and finally allowed herself to enjoy the familiar mix of humanity around them. Rickety pickup trucks packed with lobster crates rode bumper-to-bumper with expensive convertibles on their way to catch the last ferry to the Vineyard or Nantucket. Plenty of SUVs, like theirs, were loaded to the top for a summer's escape.

In some ways, the house on the Cape felt more like home to Maggie than their rambling Victorian on Boston's South Shore. The summer house, where she and her sisters had been coming since they were little girls, held some of her most precious memories: fireworks on the beach, late-night s'mores, her first kiss, her first heartbreak, and the day she and Mac were married under a big white tent on the sand. Her dad had been down in May for a general check of the place, but a musty smell, coupled with something sweet, like air freshener, greeted them when they pushed open the front door. Maggie pulled back the heavy curtains and threw open the windows in the common area, then shooed the kids upstairs to do the same. She tugged the dusty sheets off the couches and hung them on the deck to air. Eventually the lights flickered on (though it was always a wild card as to whether the electric company had actually *turned on* the electricity on the date they'd requested) and the water began gurgling up through the pipes. *Ah, summer,* she thought. *At last.*

The Cape house was cozy, manageable. A common room filled with well-worn couches opened onto a deck with stairs that led directly down to the beach. An antique chest of drawers housed the board games played over the years—battered boxes of Yahtzee, Monopoly, Life, all with missing pieces. Upstairs was a modest master bedroom, a guest room with a double bed, and the kids' room, with three bunk beds and barely passable rows in between. The kitchen, with its 1950s linoleum floor, was stuck in time, but Maggie thought it charming, especially the wallpaper with its happy yellow roses. From the kitchen, she could see the dining area, where a long wooden table served as both their supper table and late-night game console, scattered initials carved into it from when they were young. Coming here was like falling into the arms of a comfortable, familiar lover.

She'd had a slight scare, though, when she flicked on the down-stairs bathroom light last night and discovered the bottom window transom broken, a few pieces of glass punched out. A swirl of dark dots lay splattered across the white tile floor like chicken pox. She bent down to touch them, then pulled her hand away. Was it blood? Dried blood?

"Honey? Can you come here?" she called out. *Had someone broken in? Were they still in the house?* Her thoughts raced to the kids upstairs. Mac arrived to investigate.

He checked the window, the blood on the floor. Peeked in the medicine cabinet, still flush with Tylenol and cold medicine. "I don't think we had an intruder," he said, reading her mind. She appreciated his use of the past tense. *Had.* "If we did, there would be more glass on the inside." He tried opening the window, but the sash was jammed. "When did you say your dad was down again?"

"In May?" She grabbed her cell phone and punched in Arthur's number. At first, her dad had pretended not to know what she was talking about. "What? A window? Where?" But after Maggie described the damage, he grew frustrated. "Why didn't you say the *bathroom* window? Yes, yes, that was me. Broke the damn thing trying to open it. Forgot to call Jay." Jay was the family's handyman on the Cape.

"Okay, I'm just glad someone didn't break in. We'll get it fixed. Are you all right? It looks like you might have cut yourself."

"Of course," Arthur said curtly. "Pricked my hand on the glass. No big deal."

But the conversation had nagged at her last night.

"Don't you think it's weird about my dad and the window?" she asked Mac in bed. He was nearly asleep, weary from the long drive and a few double shifts the week before.

"Weird?" he mumbled from his pillow.

"Like he didn't want to admit he broke it."

"Maybe he was embarrassed. Or maybe he forgot. He's not getting any younger, you know."

But it wasn't like her dad to let something like a broken window go. That he'd let it sit unattended for two months was almost unthinkable. Maybe, she reasoned, he felt silly when it happened and then guilty about not getting it fixed. She decided to let it slide. *This was her month not to worry!* Besides, she felt guilty herself for not checking on the house all spring. She could hardly jump on Arthur for having done just that.

She stretched her body down to her toes and fingertips, arms out at the sides. Today they would put in the dock. The pieces to it lay under a tarp in the backyard, and every year on the first day of vacation, they assembled the various sections that hooked together like enormous Lego blocks. Jess and her family would be arriving later this afternoon, and between the four adults—Mac, Maggie, Jess, and Tim—they'd manage during low tide to lay out piece by piece the modest dock that provided a jumping-off point for the kids all month. For Maggie, putting in the dock marked the official start of summer.

She thought back to when she and her sisters were kids, how she and Jess would race to be the first ones in the water as soon as the car pulled into the driveway (they'd insist on wearing their bathing suits for the ride down). She could almost smell the scent of lavender in their freshly dried beach towels. Honestly, where had the time gone? Her parents had been so happy then. And life so much simpler. Now everything was endlessly complicated. Virgie lived on a different coast. Jess was drowning in her responsibilities as a high school principal. The sisters hardly got a chance to see each other outside of their one idyllic month on the Cape. And Arthur and Gloria had been divorced going on a year and a half now.

Yes, life was more complicated, Maggie thought. And probably in no small part because she was a mother herself now. But July was her month to relax. *Que sera, sera.* It was one of her mother's favorite sayings at the beach house, so much so that the words hung on a plaque in the front hallway. Right next to ABSOLUTELY NO WHINING! VIOLATORS WILL BE CHARGED 5 CENTS.

Maggie kicked her feet under the sheets. This summer would be just like old times. She could feel it. She would make sure of it.

Only a handful of things waited on her to-do list to ready the house for her sisters: a quick dusting downstairs, fresh sheets on the beds, and a run to the corner market to pick up a few items (they'd already packed the car full with staples, like cereal and chips). For supper tonight, they should have something that would appropriately mark the start of vacation. Perhaps a fresh sea bass or some haddock.

She slipped into her shorts and a white T-shirt (her uniform during the summer) and a pair of pink flip-flops. Every summer, each child got a new beach pail stuffed with a towel and flip-flops. This, too, had become part of the Herington tradition (a summer without new flip-flops would hardly count as summer at all!). The one year she'd neglected to buy them in advance, Maggie and the girls had raced out to the nearest shop and paid three times the price she typically shelled out at Target. She hadn't forgotten the flip-flops since.

She stood at the bathroom sink and splashed cool water on her face, relieved to see the water gush from the old spigot. Last night, when the water had trickled out, she'd worried that the pump from the well wasn't working properly. But any kinks seemed to have resolved themselves overnight. She traveled down the hall and poked her head into the kids' room. Their duffel bags lay unopened on the floor, their clothes from yesterday strewn across the room like tossed cards. Luke was gone, but the girls still slept sprawled on top of blue cotton quilts. Only eleven, they looked so angelic when they were sleeping, their long corn-silk hair splayed across their pillows. Some days, Lexie (the girl who would surely push Maggie to the edge) already acted like a teenager, full of snide comebacks and rolling eyes. Last night she'd announced that the Cape was "boring" and insisted on asking why they couldn't do something different. As if every child were lucky enough to have a summer house to visit!

Maggie headed downstairs just as Mac and Luke burst through the front door.

"Mommy, we saw a raccoon!" Luke cried.

"You did?" Maggie grabbed the iced coffees from Mac and gave him a kiss. She cast a wary glance his way, as if to say, *Raccoons? Already?* They were a nuisance, varmints as far as she was concerned. They would have to be sure to keep the trash covered this year.

"He was pretty big," Mac confirmed as he set the bagels and newspaper on the kitchen counter. "About the size of a bear, wouldn't you say, buddy?"

Luke opened his mouth, about to object, then caught his dad's drift. "Maybe not a bear, but at least a pig. Definitely a *big* pig."

"Uh-oh." Maggie laughed. Luke had become strangely obsessed with pigs in the last year. He drew parades of pigs, had a collection of stuffed pigs, knew all sorts of random facts about them. For example, the world's largest pig weighed six hundred pounds. Maggie prayed it was just a phase. He tugged on her shorts. "Mama, can we go swimming now?"

"In a little bit, hon. Let's wait for the girls to wake up, okay?" She sipped her coffee and skimmed the headlines. "I need to run to Sal's to pick up a few things anyway."

When Luke started to protest, Mac interrupted his whining.

"C'mon, buddy. We haven't even had breakfast yet. Let's go sit on the deck and eat our bagels." With a wink, he coaxed Luke outside.

Maggie finished her coffee, grabbed her wallet and backpack, and headed out to the shed. A rusty padlock hung on its latch. She twirled the numbers, the code memorized by heart, and pulled open the door, searching for the rickety three-speed that she rode each summer. It took a moment for her eyes to adjust before spying the Schwinn in back. Carefully, she navigated a path around a wagon, a line of terra-cotta pots, a Hula Hoop. A plastic baby swimming pool rested against the bike. Only last summer, Luke had liked to splash around in it when the ocean waves grew too strong. Would he still use it this summer, or had he gotten too big? she wondered. She moved the pool over so that it listed against a wall, then brushed the cobwebs off the bike's handlebars. Slowly, she inched the bike out of the shed, careful not to knock loose the wicker basket, and added a few puffs of air to the tires before hopping on.

Her dad used to ride this very Schwinn when Maggie was little. And, at the thought of Arthur, her stomach tightened again. Was it possible that the last time they'd seen him was over Christmas at their house in Windsor? She shook her head as if to clear a foggy memory. But no, that was right. They hadn't seen her dad for six months. She knew Virgie called Arthur every Sunday, but Maggie had let even her phone conversations with him slide. They were uncomfortable, odd little exchanges where she struggled to fill the space with stories about the kids. She always hung up feeling deflated and disappointed, as if she should be a more interesting daughter and Arthur a more engaged grandfather.

And now, this most recent conversation had gotten her mind spinning.

Arthur had sounded, well, *off.* She couldn't think of better way to describe it. As if he couldn't imagine why she'd be calling him in the first place or what on earth she was talking about when she mentioned the window. Perhaps she'd woken him or caught him in the shower? Whatever the reason, it was unsettling. She'd feel better, she told herself, once he was here and she could lay eyes on him.

Yes, it would be good for everyone to fall back into their summer routines: the kids swimming till their eyes stung from the salt water while the adults shared a cocktail or two on the deck. Maybe this would be the year Luke dove off the dock (he'd gotten so close last summer!). And maybe the twins would master the backflip. In the top kitchen drawer of the summer house, Maggie kept a spiral notebook for recording just such milestones and funny quotes from the kids, updating it each July. *The first summer the twins rode their bikes without training wheels! Lexie swam out to the jetty and back. Luke walked across the kitchen all by himself!* She'd always meant to transfer the scribbles to an electronic file, but there was something pleasing about seeing first her handwriting and then the girls', their tilted capital letters giving way to more precise lowercase, then loopy cursive. On the front, Sophie had scrawled, *The Book of Summer*.

Maggie was looking forward to catching up with her sisters, maybe playing a few rounds of poker or gin rummy. And thank goodness Arthur and Gloria were coming for separate weeks this year. After a tense summer last July when everyone tiptoed around them both, the wounds of the divorce still raw, Maggie had made certain that her parents were slotted for different weeks this time. *Maggie McNeil at your service!* she had thought, as she toggled back and forth between them on the phone. *Let me pencil in your reservation!*

She followed the soft curves of the bike path, the sun warming the back of her neck. Sweeping ferns lined either side, and every so often a honeysuckle or a cape rose poked its head out. Maggie threw her hands in the air like a child and shouted, "Heeeello, summer!" No one was around. She could be carefree and thirteen again. How she'd imagined this feeling a thousand times, nurtured it as if it were her own exquisite orchid, in the depths of winter. The thought of the

Cape house was the only thing that made Boston winters bearable, with loads of laundry to do and the kids climbing the walls. *Just wait,* she'd tell herself. *Before you know it, you'll all be back at the summer house.*

Eventually, the dirt path turned to pavement and wound past the charming post office (white with blue trim), the town library, an ice cream shop, a handful of quaint shops, and at last, Sal's Market. Maggie leaned her bike against a post. Like everything else in town, Sal's looked more or less the same and still sported its cherry red door and gray cedar shingles.

When she swung open the screen door, four tidy rows of supplies greeted her along with the smell of basil and an assortment of freshly picked produce, including fat, gorgeous blueberries and strawberries the size of walnuts. She gathered up a wire basket, threw in two pints of berries and a clutch of basil, and began combing the aisles for the items on her list. She pulled a carton of farm eggs and milk from the refrigerated section, then headed to the deli and fish counter. A small line had formed and Maggie took her place behind a woman in a faded pink sundress and floppy straw hat. *Probably a year-rounder,* she thought wistfully. When it was her turn, she stepped up and grinned at Sal, who was busily wiping the counter. A white deli hat sat perched on top of his sandy curls, and his butcher's apron already reflected a swift morning's business. When he glanced up and saw her, his face beamed.

"Maggie, girl! Welcome back! I was wondering if you all would get in this week."

She tugged a stray piece of hair behind her ear. She loved that Sal never failed to make her feel like a pretty teenager all over again. "Thanks, Sal. It's good to be back. You know we wouldn't miss July down here if we could help it."

"I always know it's summertime when the Herington girls are back. The whole gang with you?"

"You bet." Maggie eyed the specials on the blackboard behind
him: STRIPED BASS; BLUEFISH; SCUP; TUNA; HADDOCK; HALIBUT; COD.

"Well, you'll have to bring those gorgeous girls by the store. And
Luke! How old is he now?"

"Just turned five," Maggie confirmed. "Kindergarten in September."

"Wow." Sal's face softened. "They grow up fast, don't they?"
Maggie nodded. "Are your sisters headed in, too?" She grinned. She
knew that Sal had a soft spot for Virgie.

"Yep. Jess should be here today with her family. Virgie gets in on
Wednesday."

Did Sal's face light up just a tad or was it Maggie's imagination?
He cleared his throat. "That's terrific. So, what can I get you today?"

"How's the striped bass?"

"Delectable, as always." He reached to pull a few fillets from a
tray. "How many would you like?"

Maggie did the quick arithmetic in her head for her family
and Jess's. "A baker's dozen? And a pound of ham and turkey each,
please."

"You got it." He tugged off a sheet of waxy paper and tossed the
fillets on it, then sliced the deli meat and wrapped it all in a tidy bundle. "Enjoy." He handed it over. "Say hi to everyone for me."

"Thanks. Will do, Sal." She made her way over to the checkout
counter, taking a quick inventory of her basket to make sure nothing
would be too heavy to lug back on the bike, and paid. She was stuff-
ing the groceries into her basket outside when a familiar voice called
out: "Maggie, is that you?"

Maggie turned and smiled. "Gretchen! How are you? I almost
didn't recognize you."

Gretchen had been coming to the Cape for summers nearly as
long as Maggie and her sisters. She and her husband had two kids,
and occasionally the families would get together for a beach day

and cookout. Maggie noticed that her friend had gone blond this summer.

Gretchen ran her hand through her hair self-consciously. "I know. A bit of a shock, right? But I needed something to get me through middle age." Maggie laughed as she leaned in to give her friend a hug. "It looks great. How are the kids?"

"Good," said Gretchen. "Really good. Except for the times when I want to strangle them, of course. Jasper is eight going on four, and Anna is fifteen going on twenty."

Maggie hopped on her bike. "I know what you mean. Lexie and Sophie are in those fun 'tween' years." Gretchen groaned sympathetically. "We'll have to get together. How long are you here for?"

"Three weeks," answered Gretchen. "We head back for the kids' camp in August."

"Give me a call on my cell." Maggie waved over her shoulder. "We don't have a landline at the house anymore."

"What?" Gretchen called after her in mock surprise. "You finally got rid of that vintage rotary phone?" Maggie grinned. Gretchen's summer house was nothing like hers. A colonial with five bedrooms and three baths, it was a restored sea captain's mansion that they'd bought when the market was down. There was nothing "camp-like" about it, but Maggie knew that was how her friend liked it. If she couldn't find luxury living along the beach, Gretchen wouldn't have deigned to come to the Cape in the first place.

Sparrows chirped in the old oaks and pines that flecked the town square. Maggie inhaled as she rode along, a mix of salt and pine stinging her nose, and felt curiously free. Only a few summers ago she'd fretted she would never escape the days of diapers and binkies and then potty training with Luke. And that cumbersome car seat! It drove her crazy, how Luke would howl about the seat belt cutting into his chest. Until one day, she glanced in the rearview mirror and saw all three kids buckled into their seats, the diagonal strap crisscrossing

Luke's shoulder, and Luke uncomplaining. *A small miracle!* There were so many milestones like these, Maggie thought. They seemingly happened overnight after she'd waited forever for them to occur.

She pulled up to the house and parked the bike. When she stepped inside, all was quiet, the girls still asleep. She set the groceries on the counter and wandered onto the deck, shielding her eyes from the sun with her hand. *There.* About a quarter mile down the beach, she could make out the profiles of Mac and Luke. She let herself out the gate and went down the steps to the boardwalk, the sea grass tickling her calves as she pulled off her flip-flops. At the shore line, the icy cold water lapped at her toes, but she knew from years of summers that it would grow warmer as the day went on. She was about to call out to them, but something stopped her.

On the horizon, white fleecy clouds hung in a sky that was colored a perfect robin's-egg blue. The bright sun danced on the water. Above her, gulls dipped and soared, calling out to one another. Maggie inhaled the salty air and dug her toes deeper into the sand. She was searching for the right word to describe the shimmering world before her. Then it came to her: *hallowed.* This was hallowed ground, the place that gave her the most peace, her own private retreat.

Each summer, she resolved to toss out her to-do lists, lengthy spools that ran through her mind like ticker tape most days of the year. After years of self-recrimination, she'd resigned herself to the fact that she liked things to be just so. *Type A,* Mac called her. *But in a way that I love,* he reassured. But was it really so bad? So what if there were individual cubbies for the kids in the mudroom? So what if the kitchen in Windsor had a whiteboard with the children's activities detailed in color-coded marker? And her linen shelves were methodically labeled: GIRLS' SHEETS, LUKE'S SHEETS, M&D SHEETS, PILLOWCASES, EXTRA BLANKETS?

She kept things organized. She kept the family running. They needed her.

But on the Cape, there was no need for such charts. Because everything was already as it was supposed to be. *Que sera, sera.* And if anything *were* amiss, if Arthur, for instance, *was* acting a little odd, well, it would be righted at Pilgrim Lane. That was what the summer house was for. Standing on the beach, she was also struck with the realization that *this* was the place (*the summer house, of course!*) to tell Mac what she'd been dreaming about the last few months, an idea she desperately hoped he'd be open to. Time would tell.

Slowly she lifted her right leg up, toe pointing toward her knee, and swept her arms above her head. Her Tree Pose. She pressed her fingertips together and inhaled, willing her body to remain balanced on one foot. *Yes,* she thought. She could feel some of the tension slipping away, feel her heart opening to the possibilities of summer.

Until, that is, Lexie shouted from the deck, "Mom! Sophie took my towel!" Followed by a wail, which Maggie was quite certain came from Sophie.

2

Virgie

Virgie watched Thomas pace back and forth across Larry's office, his gestures growing more animated by the minute. It wasn't hard. Larry had raised the blinds that divided the glass window of his office from their cubicles. When they were on the outside, looking in, the journalists joked it was because Larry wanted to keep an eye on them. But when someone else was on the inside with Larry, looking out, it was a different story. A closed door with the boss meant a colleague was getting fired, being promoted, or being handed a coveted story. Whatever it was, it rarely meant good news for those outside the fishbowl.

Virgie was playing Candy Crush on her computer, pairing colored jelly beans while she snuck looks. She had a pretty good idea of what was happening. Thomas had been itching for a big story for months and had stumbled upon the same one she had: Liz Crandle, a prominent Seattle attorney, was accusing a partner at her firm of sexual harassment. Allegedly, the partner had offered more compliments on her breasts than her legal briefs. The story probably meant a gazillion dollars in a settlement since it was evident the firm was eager for the whole mess to disappear. But Virgie had an "in" and Larry knew it. She and Liz bought their morning coffee at the same shop down on the pier. They'd exchanged hellos a few times, even commiserated over bad hair days together. Virgie was pretty sure she could scoop an exclusive before the other local stations got wind of it.

She shook the tingles out of her hands. Lately, all the caffeine she'd been drinking was giving her the shakes. She knew she had to quit, but her job demanded constant focus. If she ever wanted to get promoted to anchor desk, she couldn't afford to miss a beat. It felt like ages since she'd had a good night's sleep; insomnia had become her new bed partner. Of course, some of that sleep deprivation was due to Jackson, and she felt herself flush at the thought. *Jackson, Jackson, Jackson.* She wanted to write his name in big, loopy letters on her notebook as she had done with her high school boyfriends. She and Jackson had been dating for only three weeks, but Virgie couldn't stop thinking about him. It was almost refreshing to be dating in her thirties; there was no need to play it coy. No wondering whether the object of her affection would call. *No games, no secrets,* they'd told each other on their third date. And Virgie had thought, *Finally, someone who gets me.*

As if Jackson had felt his ears burning, her cell phone chimed with a text. *Dinner tonite?*

She picked it up off her desk. "Yes!" She began to text back immediately, before downgrading the exclamation point to a period. Then: *Where?*

A minute later, his reply: *Romeo's? Seven?*

She smiled. Romeo's was a cozy little Italian place perched on a corner with a view of Elliott Bay. Chic without being pretentious. She texted back: *Perfect. See you then.* She and Jackson had dined there once before, when Virgie pronounced the scallops and fettuccini worth dying over. That and the enormous decanters of wine that sat on each table easily made it her new favorite place.

She checked her watch. Already 3:30 and she was still waiting for Larry to tell her the story was hers. What was taking him so long to break the news to Thomas? She wanted to get a four-mile run in before dinner. She looked up at Larry's office. *Any minute now.* Thomas stood at the door, his hand resting on the handle. A moment later, he exited and cast a glance her way before hurrying toward his cubicle. If Virgie had read the vibes right, the story was all hers.

Larry stood in the doorway of his office. "Virgie, can I talk to you for a minute?" She tried her best to act surprised. A few colleagues smiled and gave her a thumbs-up. Larry was a smart guy. He knew better than to hand a sexual harassment story to a male reporter. It should be a woman—someone who would be sympathetic, someone whom Liz Crandle would want to spill her heart out to. Heck, Virgie even knew what kind of coffee she liked. Actually, it was tea. Chai tea, extra foam. Virgie was already considering where the interview should take place. Liz's home? Or maybe she should suggest a more neutral setting. Perhaps the coffee shop.

She shot Larry an assured smile and breezed into his office. She was glad she was wearing her red Jimmy Choo pumps since now they would be forever linked to the day she'd caught her big break.

Larry shut the door behind her and gestured to a chair across from his desk. "Have a seat." He cleared his throat and shuffled the papers on his desk.

"What's up?" She aimed to sound cavalier.

"Listen, I know you're keen on the Liz Crandle story—" he began.

"That's right," she interrupted. "We get coffee at the same place. I'm sure I could get an exclusive with her before KCB swoops in." KCB-TV was their archrival. KCB's newscasters were sharp, slick reporters, and they'd been beating up her station in the ratings for the past five years.

"I'm sure you could." Larry hesitated. "But it turns out that Thomas's brother-in-law is running buddies with Miss Crandle. He's already made the case to Liz as to why she should talk to Thomas."

Virgie felt a tickle in her throat and coughed. "You're joking, right?"

Larry shook his head. "I'm afraid not. I'm sorry. I wanted to give this one to you, but Thomas is having none of it. He refuses to step aside."

A flush of anger flickered up her neck. She could feel red splotches blooming on her skin. "You don't really think Liz is going to confide everything to a *guy* about this story, do you? That's just bad judgment."

"You're probably right. But she seems to have made up her mind. I have to at least give Thomas a shot."

Virgie stood up, clasping her notebook tightly. She didn't want to turn around and face her colleagues, who were undoubtedly watching *her* through the glass now.

"This was my story, Larry, and you know it." She frowned when her voice cracked.

"I'm sorry." He took off his glasses and rubbed his eyes. "I'll make it up to you. You'll get the next big one."

"Right." She couldn't help herself, the sarcasm cutting through the air, even though they both knew that Larry could fire her on the spot.

"Virgie," she heard him begin, but she couldn't stay in his office a moment longer for fear she might say something she'd regret. She marched back to her desk, her skin burning. She jammed her notebook and cell into her gym bag, shut down her computer, and told her assistant that she was heading home to review notes for a story. It was a lie, but no one would miss her today; it wasn't as if she had an anchor spot on the six o'clock news after all. She was only in charge of her show, *Verbatim with V,* which ran twice a week. It was mostly fluff, but it got her face time on the air.

The elevator pinged down twelve floors, Virgie cursing under her breath. To be honest, she didn't care that much for the Crandle story, but it smacked of high ratings, the kind that got producers' attention. She knew if she did the story right, it would be a feather in her broadcasting cap. *Well, screw you, Larry,* she thought. She winged through the revolving door into the bright, sunny day. If her boss was too big an idiot to see what a bad call this was, then the station didn't deserve her. She fantasized about who else she might work for in the Seattle area. Maybe Channel 7? PBS? Surely, they didn't play favorites like this. But something else was bothering her.

She couldn't tamp down the feeling that Larry had passed her over for another reason. Maybe he was afraid that the story would hit too close to home. More than once, he'd tried to convince Virgie to go out with him; more than once, she'd declined. Maybe he worried talking to Liz would get her thinking about her own workplace environment. Of course, that was preposterous. Virgie knew Larry was harmless in the way that most overweight, balding, forty-something men were. Virgie wasn't threatened by her boss in the least.

Only in the sense that he held the keys to her career.

As she walked along Twelfth Avenue, she realized that the day had settled into a beautiful warm afternoon. Bright red begonias blossomed in storefront window boxes, and a mild breeze floated off the water. When she first moved here, seven years ago, she'd worried about the rain. She thought maybe she was one of those people who needed sunshine to be happy. And while it was true that Seattle had more gray than sunny days, the summers had turned out to be surprisingly pleasant. She'd quickly fallen in love with the place and its clean streets, its environmentally conscious people, its tie to the San Juan Islands.

Her phone chimed in her bag, and when she retrieved it she saw Jackson's text: *Can't wait. Ah, Jackson,* she thought. *Sometimes you just make the world a better place.*

At the club, she changed into her workout clothes and headed for the treadmill. It felt good to let her mind wander as she ran. If she wasn't going to be Seattle's most successful news journalist, she reasoned, at least she could be its fittest. She still had her figure from college, tall and lean. She drank an ungodly number of green toxic-looking shakes for breakfast; she used more skin creams than should be allowed; she whitened her teeth every few years; she got Botox injections like the best of them. After all, thirty-five could be said to be past your prime if you were a woman in the news industry. On television. Not the same for gray-haired wise men like Peter Jennings or Walter Cronkite. But Virgie wanted to be the next Barbara Walters, the next big thing.

Too bad she got thwarted at every big break.

Gradually, her breath found its way into an easy rhythm. She thought ahead to a few days from now and felt a stab of giddiness. *Just her and her sisters at the summer house!* And their families, of course. She'd get to play with her nieces and nephews, get tipsy with Maggie and Jess, beat Mac and Tim at cards, soak up the sun. She hadn't invited Jackson. It felt premature. And, yet, a part of her was disappointed that he wasn't coming. If he joined her, Virgie wouldn't be the odd girl out for once, the single sister. Maggie and Jess had always shared the impenetrable, maddening bond of twins. Plus, they were eight years older than Virgie. And now that they both had their own families, the gap between their lives and Virgie's single life seemed even bigger, deeper. A chasm.

Would they like Jackson?

Probably, though they wouldn't take him seriously. *Just another one of Virgie's guys,* they'd think. Virgie imagined them shooting judgmental glances at each other across the dinner table. Everyone knew Virgie was married to her career. Even as a little girl, she'd loved playing newscaster, reporting her school's daily news at the dinner table. Maybe one day she would want a family, but not now, and certainly not like Maggie and Jess had done it. Maggie and Mac had gotten married soon after college, and once the kids arrived, Maggie's life had revolved solely around them.

And then there was Jess. *Poor Jess*, as Virgie thought of her, practically one word: *poorjess*. As far as she could tell, Jess's life was a mess. Every time Virgie called, Jess was either coming from or going to work. The kids were constantly shouting in the background. And Tim (such a bland guy when Jess first married him) had not, alas, turned out to be any more interesting over the years. And, honestly, how interesting could an accountant be? Like warm milk, Tim was comforting at first but turned sour when left to sit too long. No, Virgie had learned from her sisters' mistakes. She would marry when the time was right, when *the guy* was right.

She pounded out four miles, then showered and dried off. In the mirror, she could see the jeweled flecks of cellulite where her toned thighs used to be. The small creases hovering above her nose, once obvious only when she scowled, had become deeper, permanent fixtures. Even the parentheses around her mouth had grown more pronounced in the last few months. Unlike the women she read about in magazines who claimed to have worse self-images than were actually warranted, Virgie had the opposite problem: she had an inflated self-image. She thought she looked better than she actually did. *Shit*.

She'd have to book her next Botox appointment soon.

She got dressed, dried her hair, and quickly applied a faint blush and mascara. She wasn't going to let a few jiggly bits and lines stop her today. She had Jackson to meet! How he had managed to make his way into her heart so soon and so easily, she couldn't fathom. He was a little bit geeky after all—a nurse who could perform metric conversions in his head. Not one iota like the guys she usually dated, a sea of bankers and stockbrokers with egos that matched the size of their wallets. But that's what made Jackson so refreshing. She didn't have to get dolled up to see him. She could just *be,* and it felt strangely, wonderfully liberating.

She walked the few short blocks across town and ducked over to the street with Romeo's. When she got a glimpse of Jackson through the restaurant's paned glass doors, she smiled. There was his tousled brown hair, his tanned skin, his khaki pants, and a blue shirt that she knew without looking highlighted his blue eyes, a shade of seaglass, above a slightly hooked nose. Just seeing him made her relax, a tight coil sprung.

As she drew closer, he turned to her and his smile lit up. He pushed open the door and said, "Right on time. I like that in a woman."

"Hi there, stranger," she said, though it had been fewer than twelve hours since they'd been curled up together in her bed. His hand touched her on the back, gently guiding her forward, and sending a small shiver up her spine. The bad taste of the afternoon's events began to slip away. In fact, she didn't know if she'd even bother telling Jackson how shabbily Larry had treated her. Why spoil an otherwise promising evening? They followed their hostess to a table in the back near a window looking out over the bay. The evening sun glinted off the water in slender shards of light.

"Ah, perfect," Jackson said, pulling out her chair. Virgie was thinking exactly the same thing as she sat down and unfolded the crisp white napkin in her lap.

For a few hours at least, she could stop worrying about what she didn't have and enjoy what she did.

3

Jess

Jess placed a folded pair of Superman underpants on the laundry pile as Tim walked into the family room. She was finishing packing for the trip tomorrow. A crime show played on the television, and a glass of white wine sat on the coffee table. After much pleading to stay up late, the kids were finally tucked into bed and asleep.

Even though she knew it wasn't necessary, Jess still lay down with Teddy at bedtime, waiting for his short breaths to register the slow, even cadence of sleep. She couldn't help it; she loved their late-night talks before he drifted off. Tonight everything had centered on what they would do at the Pilgrim house, as he called it. Now that he was four, he could anticipate his time on the Cape, and excitement radiated from his small body like sound waves. He worshiped Luke especially, who was a year older and, therefore, the ultimate of cool.

Seven-year-old Grace had fallen asleep first tonight, exhausted from a day of swimming with her friends. Her curly brown hair spilled over her pillow. She and Teddy still shared a room, but Jess knew that sooner or later they would need to clear out the home office and reconfigure it into a bedroom for Grace. Right now the kids were so close, it was as near perfect as it would ever be. It made her wish that she could freeze time, keep her children right where they were.

She sipped her wine and watched while a forensics officer culled evidence at a crime scene. Somewhere, on the periphery, she registered that Tim had sat down next to her, a beer in hand. Had he sighed as he sank into the worn red cushions?

"Finished packing?" he asked, without making a move toward the pile of rumpled clothes in the basket.

"Almost," she said. "Just a few more things I had to wash." She focused on the show, not looking at him. In the past year, Jess had given up trying to get her husband to help. After nine years of marriage, she'd begun to suspect that Tim was not her soul mate after all. If someone asked her to put her finger on when things started to go wrong, she would be hard-pressed to say. The troubles in her marriage felt like a snowball that had been building over the last year, a hard icy little ball that had turned into a boulder tumbling downhill. They had tried counseling, but each session only succeeded in pushing her husband further away. Tim didn't think their marriage was unraveling. In his mind, Jess was making a big deal out of nothing. He worked hard; she worked hard; they had two great kids. *The American Dream.* When she pointed out that they hardly spoke to each other anymore, he stared at her blankly. Their therapist removed her glasses and pinched her nose, as if listening to them gave her a headache.

And so now, more often than not, they left Post-it notes for each other. It began as a way of communicating when their schedules required hurried exchanges. She would hand off the kids to Tim as she headed out to night school for her master's. On the refrigerator, she would leave notes: *Brush kids' teeth; don't forget bedtime story; put wash in dryer, please!* But when graduate school ended, the Post-it notes continued and the *pleases* and *thank yous* fell away. "Why do you and Daddy leave so many notes for each other?" Grace asked over dinner one night when Tim wasn't home. Jess was torn. Should she tell the truth and say that she and Daddy communicated best by Post-its, or should she pretend it was a game? She opted for the latter.

"We like to leave little messages. Like a treat. You know, like when I put a note in your lunch box that says 'I love you.'" But even Grace appeared unconvinced, her delicate eyebrows arched into tiny upside-down Vs.

How had it come to this? Jess asked herself this question often, maybe twenty times a day. She'd be talking with a student about her failing grades and suddenly a little alarm would go off in her head: *Warning! Marriage in trouble!* She never thought they would be one of those couples who needed therapy. It had taken arm-twisting, cajoling to get Tim to the counselor, and after eight sessions, the therapist admitted even she couldn't help until Tim was willing to admit there was a problem. Tim rested his hands in his lap, his fingers tightly steepled. And so they'd tabled the discussion. *To be continued,* thought Jess.

Now when she cast a glance his way, she saw that her husband's shirt strained against his waistband, his belly plunging over. On nights when he missed dinner, he was more often than not out with his buddies, drinking. His sandy blond hair, which had been thick when they first met, had thinned considerably. And while it had never bothered Jess before that her husband was on the shorter side, it did now. It was as if his body had grown out of proportion, a lop-sided tree, his top heavier than the bottom.

Sometimes she wondered if she gave him a little push, would he topple off balance?

That Tim did little to ignite passion in her these days could hardly be considered a fault. Married couples, she understood, eventually reached a certain comfort level where emotions found their balance, like groundwater settling at its natural level. When she first met Tim in a bar in South Boston, he had been sweet, handsome, a cut above the rest. The two big dimples that danced on either side of his grin immediately caught her eye. He told her he'd majored in literature, but his day job was accounting. She was charmed. A literature major who made money? It struck her as a win-win: they could discuss Shakespeare while they counted their hundreds in bed! The courtship sparked quickly. Was it because she'd never had a serious boyfriend in college? Or was she simply flattered that someone was finally interested in her and not in her more beautiful twin, Maggie?

Of course, Maggie was married by then. But still.

They married in Boston's Trinity Church on a balmy spring day with three hundred guests in attendance. Jess's mom had spent two years planning and organizing, right down to the lavish bouquets of white calla lilies that arched like swans' necks across the aisles. Jess's wedding would *not* be the slipshod affair that Maggie's had been, if their mother had anything to say about it. Maggie and Mac had insisted on a small, informal family gathering at the Cape house, and Gloria Herington seemed to interpret her oldest daughter's decision as a personal slight. Well, she'd made up for it in spades when it came to planning Jess and Tim's big day.

Lately, though, Jess felt a distinct prick of dissatisfaction whenever she shared a room with her husband. There was such a vast disconnect between the way she had imagined her life would be—one filled with passion, heady discussions, a surplus of cash—and the way it had turned out. Sometimes it startled her, and she felt sick to her stomach. She couldn't recall the last time Tim had picked up a book or suggested they see a movie. His desk at home was a mountain of spreadsheets. Where were the trips to the museum or the symphony? The dinner parties with friends? The vacations they'd dream up on lazy Sunday mornings in bed, the paper strewn about the sheets after they'd made love?

"You talked to Nancy? They're moving out the end of the month." Tim interrupted her thoughts.

Jess sighed. "Yes. It's too bad. They're good kids."

Tim sipped his beer. "We'll have to find some new tenants."

"Yes." Her voice grated. She understood why the couple who lived upstairs, both students at Northeastern, was moving out. They needed to live closer to campus. But the news delivered earlier this morning had dropped like a plate on her foot. It would fall to Jess to find new tenants—and soon. One more thing to add to her never-ending to-do list. Add it to the microwave that still awaited fixing. And the ice dispenser in the fridge that made little clicking noises but no ice.

She longed for a free night when she could climb up to their bedroom, crawl into bed, and read for an hour uninterrupted. No laundry to fold, no bills to pay. The truth of it was, though, that by the time Teddy fell asleep, Jess was completely drained. And while school work always slowed down during the summer months, Jess still had responsibilities. There was a small group of summer students that needed tending to and a host of discipline and scheduling issues that inevitably crept up.

"So, how was your day?" Tim asked.

She knew she should count it as a victory that her husband was asking her this one small question, a question he'd been unable to ask her over dinner because he was not yet home. That it was not written on a Post-it note. She considered giving a thoughtful reply, but then stopped herself. They were beyond that. To tell him that, at work, she'd had to break up a fight between two girls and only barely missed getting punched herself, seemed beside the point. Or, to tell him the sillier, but equally depressing thought that she'd noticed her thighs were touching again, which surely meant she'd gained back all the weight she'd struggled to lose last fall, was similarly out of the question. No, they were beyond that. Tim didn't expect a real answer.

"Fine," she said instead. She shook out his cotton button-down shirt, advertised as wrinkle-free in the catalog but irritatingly crinkled in her hands now.

"Mmm," he uttered.

"I thought we could shoot for leaving around ten tomorrow morning. What do you think?" She was trying her best to act civil, normal. She was hoping against all hope that she might get her marriage back this vacation. That something would change in her, in Tim. *Something.* A magic spell, perhaps, that the sun and the beach air might cast upon them, melting the deep freeze of their marriage.

"Sure." He rested his feet on the coffee table and reached for the clicker. *Did the man really have nothing to do before they left tomorrow for two weeks of vacation?* Jess studied her to-do list, which had at least ten uncrossed items on it.

"Could you put a hold on our mail before we go?" She paused. "You can do it online."

"Sure." His eyes stayed on the television.

She regarded his bare feet on the table. They were a pasty white, even a few weeks into summer. And they were pudgy. Her husband had developed pudgy feet. Unlike her sister's husband, Mac, who seemed to grow more robust with each passing summer, Tim appeared to sink more deeply into himself, a mollusk without a shell.

"Thanks. I'm putting a check mark next to 'hold mail' on my list," she pronounced. She grabbed her felt pen and made an elaborate checking motion, as if willing Tim to get up and turn on the computer to accomplish this one simple task.

"Mind if I change the channel?" he asked instead.

It took every ounce of will not to shout, *Please just do this one thing so I don't have to think about it!* But she managed to get out, "Sure. Go ahead," through clenched teeth. He would do it on his own time. She gathered up the rest of the laundry and hoisted the basket on her hip. With the other hand she picked up her wineglass, the amber liquid sloshing a touch over the rim, and indelicately licked the edge.

"Think I'll head up. Pack the kids' last things. Get myself packed."

"Sounds good." Tim didn't look up. If she quizzed him on what she'd just said, she doubted he would know.

How was it, she wondered, that she could be principal of a school, in control of her teachers, her students, her budget, and yet at a total loss when it came to her own marriage?

She knew neither Maggie nor Virgie was a huge fan of Tim. For years she had defended her husband's quiet ways, his seeming lack of enthusiasm for doing anything other than sitting on the couch and watching sports at the beach house. But not this year. She'd had enough. Of course, Virgie was a fly-by-your-skirt kind of girl, flitting from one relationship to another. She was hardly a paragon of good relationship advice. But Maggie and Mac were good together. Maggie, who could sometimes seem to read Jess's mind, would have sage words.

As Jess climbed the stairs, she heard the familiar jingle of her cell phone, which lay on the bed where she'd thrown it when she got home. She picked it up. It was a text. From Cole. Again. *Can I see you?* Jess sighed.

She deleted the text and tossed her phone back on the bed.

4

Arthur

"Arthur, are you there? It's me, Gloria."

Arthur paused and stared out the window. Of course, he was here. He was picking up the phone, wasn't he? What a silly thing to ask. The better question was, *Why was his ex-wife calling him at seven-thirty in the morning?*

"I'm here, Gloria," he said. "Good morning. Is everything all right?" He tried to recall the last time they'd spoken. Maybe two weeks ago?

"Well, I was having my morning coffee, and I thought I'd share the most astonishing thing that happened," she said.

Arthur waited. Whenever his ex-wife called, he was torn between gratitude that she still wanted to talk to him and renewed surprise that she was now living in Boston, a bustling metropolis a hundred-plus miles away. He poured himself a cup of coffee and added the cream.

"So," Gloria resumed. "I was sitting by my kitchen window, when a coyote appeared in my courtyard, and I thought, *How odd!*

You never see a coyote in the city, certainly not this close. Do you suppose it's rabid? It probably is, right? Do you think I should call the animal control folks? I'd hate for someone to get bitten. You see these things on the news, but you never think they're going to happen to you. What do you think I should do?"

In their forty-six years of marriage, Arthur had grown accustomed to Gloria's penchant for thinking matters through out loud, as if she were jotting down all the possibilities on a public whiteboard. He remembered finding it an endearing trait.

"Where is it now?" he asked. He heard a shuffle in the background—Gloria, he presumed, going to peek out the window again.

"Oh, I don't know. It's not there anymore. Do you suppose it ran off into someone else's yard?"

"It's probably rabid if it's out in daylight," agreed Arthur. "You should call animal control to give them a heads-up. I wouldn't go outside till they get there."

"Right, that's exactly what I was thinking." He could hear Gloria's nails clicking on the kitchen countertop, as if she was right there in their, rather *his,* kitchen.

"All right then. I guess I better get going?" he said, though he regretted the way it came out sounding like a question, as if he were seeking Gloria's permission to hang up.

"Yes, I wouldn't want to keep you," she said hurriedly. "Thank you, Arthur. Toodle-oo!" The phone went silent in his hands.

Arthur placed the receiver back on the hook and wondered if he shouldn't have been more assertive about the whole coyotes-can-be-dangerous idea. He didn't think Gloria would try to outfox the animal, but the woman could be bold, recklessly so. For a moment, he considered calling her back and telling her he was serious about staying inside until they'd caught the predator. But then he shook his head at his own foolishness. They were divorced, for Pete's sake! Gloria could handle things on her own now.

Wasn't that what she'd been trying to tell him when she first slid the divorce papers across the dinner table one night, one line signed, the other still awaiting a signature? *His.*

He crossed the kitchen and pulled the eggs out of the fridge. The shuffle of his slippers on the floor rang in his ears. It was a discouragingly familiar sound. He could now admit to himself that his days and nights were lonely without Gloria. Five hundred and fifty days without her by his side. That she had up and left him still took him by surprise, as if someone had shaken him and hung him upside down, then righted him and demanded he walk a straight line that he couldn't quite discern. Some mornings he rolled over in bed to fold an arm around her warm body, only to remember that she was no longer his, no longer slept beside him. He didn't need to worry about his sour morning breath making her turn away.

Whenever she called, she sounded breathless, as if she couldn't possibly talk fast enough to cover all her exciting news. When she finally paused to ask how Arthur was, it felt only partly sincere. She might make the obligatory inquiry about his new book, but he surmised that she thought his life's work—writing—to be one big joke. It pained him to think she'd never expected him to amount to much in the first place. He had always thought—or was the right word *assumed?*—that Gloria was as content as he was in their small coastal town, that she loved Maine's rocky beaches and its small-town feel. That she anticipated spending their retirement years doing pleasant things together, such as reading, and gardening, and hiking.

All those years of being mistaken. It tired him just to contemplate it. He cracked the eggs in the pan, poured in the milk, and with his knife, speared the yellow, shiny yolks that reminded him of melting suns.

Gloria always filled him in on the girls and the grandkids—in that way, at least, she was good. The twins were busy with sports, a fact that made him proud, and Luke was always saying something funny to make him laugh. His ex-wife made a point of writing down the grandkids' little quotes so she could remember to tell Arthur. Things like Teddy saying "the trees are leaking" on a rainy day, or Grace wanting to know if God and Santa were friends.

Well, he would see his grandkids soon enough. On Saturday! He couldn't wait to get to the summer house and wrestle with them, maybe shoot some hoops with the boys. He enjoyed kicking back a few beers with Mac, who'd always struck Arthur as a stand-up guy, a good match for Maggie. Jess's husband, on the other hand, was a different story. If anyone asked Arthur, his middle daughter had married a bit of a nincompoop.

But, of course, no one ever did. Except for Virgie, his baby.

She cared what her old man thought, and at the idea of her, Arthur's heart performed a little pirouette in his chest. *His girl.* Funny how he thought of only Virgie that way. She was so much like her mother in personality, all color and flash, but she'd followed in Arthur's footsteps by becoming a journalist, a writer, and that made him exceedingly proud. He wasn't supposed to have favorites, but damn it, Virginia was a good kid.

He pushed the runny scrambled eggs onto a plate and carried them out to the deck to cool, then returned to pour himself another cup of coffee. He leaned against the counter and sipped. It seemed he was forgetting something, but he couldn't recall what. Had he talked to Maggie last night? He thought that he had, a conversation skimming the edges of his memory. But it hadn't been about next week. What was it again? He searched his mind, turned back to the phone as if it might offer a clue. Then he saw it: the sketch of a window on the notepad sitting on the counter. The broken window. He was supposed to call Jay to get it fixed. Or was it Maggie? It didn't matter. He picked up the phone and dialed, waiting until the answering machine clicked on.

"Hullo, Jaybird. It's Arthur here." He paused, cleared his throat.

"Listen. Maggie and the kids are down at the house, and there's a broken window in the downstairs bathroom. It would be super if you could stop by and fix it. I'll be there on Saturday and will pay you back in beers." The machine cut him off before "beers," but he knew Jay would understand. It was their standard barter.

It irked him that he'd let such a thing go. As he walked back to the deck with his coffee and paper, he tried to remember what he'd been doing at the summer house. When he sat down, the fork suspended over his plate, he was struck with instant recall. A small scar snaked across his right hand, starting at the fleshy, soft indent below the index finger and traveling down around his thumb. The skin had caught on the glass when it cracked. Arthur had been trying to let in fresh air, but the next thing he knew, his hand was bleeding like crazy. No wonder he'd forgotten to call about the window! He'd cut the hell out of his hand and had to go search for bandages in the upstairs cabinet. He'd been so focused on cleaning up the blood in the upstairs sink that he'd completely forgotten about the window. At the time, he had worried he might need a stitch, but the wound healed up okay.

He took a bite of his eggs, soggy and lukewarm. It was hard to make good eggs, he reflected. Gloria must have had a secret recipe, where she got the ratio of eggs to milk just right. He swallowed, dissatisfied. The weather stain he'd applied a few years ago was wearing thin on the deck railings, light specks of wood poking through the varnish, as if the deck had a bad case of eczema. He was struck with a pang, almost physical in his side, by a single word: *ephemeral. Everything was so goddamned ephemeral.*

He lifted his eyes above the railing and could see the morning light playing on the water, small waves lapping at the shore. Corpulent clouds tumbled across a radiant sky. He didn't understand how Gloria could abandon such beauty. Hadn't she looked forward to more mornings like this, discussing the day's headlines, going for walks on the beach to a breakfast shanty where they could enjoy egg sandwiches still warm in their tinfoil? He sipped his coffee and thought to himself with a hint of bitterness: *Apparently not.*

When he replayed it in his mind, though, he couldn't honestly say why his wife had left. Perhaps he could have been more attentive, but it was strange to think that this had become an issue after forty-some years, the kids grown. No, he thought that Gloria had become a different person in the last year and a half, that she was going through a belated midlife crisis at sixty-five. He'd read about such things in the paper, heard about them at the store or the library when he bumped into friends. Jack Connelly had bought himself a Mercedes convertible and gotten hair plugs. A few years back, Keith Jefferson sold his car dealership and moved his whole family to Arizona. These things happened. He just never expected they would happen to him, by proxy.

He glanced at the newspaper headlines, then looked out on the water again, where the morning light frolicked on the waves as if in an Impressionist painting, perhaps a Monet or a Renoir. If Gloria were here, he thought with a small smile, they could debate it together. A gull swooped down to grab a fish and sailed off, the thing squirming in its beak, and Arthur felt momentarily sorry for it. The thought *ephemeral* seized him again. He took a few more sips of coffee, got up, tucked his paper under his elbow, and carried his half-eaten eggs back to the kitchen as he followed a path through the maze of piles lining his living room. It was hell without Gloria to pick up after him. Carefully, he smoothed out his paper atop the large stack that already stood by the front door. Someday one of the stories would make good fodder for his writing, a plot line lurking in the headlines.

As he turned, he spied his trash gator leaning against the couch. When he'd first seen the contraption online, he'd been struck by its apparent genius. A tool that allowed a person to pick up litter without having to bend over—*Imagine!* By pressing a slick little handle at the top, he could control the small pincher claws at the bottom.

He'd even paid for the expedited two-day delivery. When the new toy arrived, Arthur had traveled all over the house, practicing picking up socks, a stray Kleenex, the *TV Guide*.

But its real purpose was to help him rid the beach of its litter on his morning walks. Each day Arthur would set out and find the sand littered with junk. It annoyed him that people felt free to sully such splendor. Most days there were abandoned beer bottles, chip bags, candy bar wrappers, even a spoiled condom. But every so often he stumbled upon a forgotten sweater, a discarded wallet with a few damp bills tucked inside, a necklace with a broken clasp, a left-behind leather sandal. Precious things worth saving. Maybe the owners of the various objects would return one day, he reasoned, and tell him how grateful they were that Arthur had saved what others might consider trash.

He grabbed his wide-brimmed hat from the closet and ambled down to the beach. Already he could feel the heat on his back. The bitter taste of coffee and eggs lingered in his mouth, and he momentarily regretted not having gargled with mouthwash. He'd stop further down the beach and reward himself with something sweet, maybe a Danish and a cool lemonade, at one of the kiosks. It was just the carrot to entice him along for the distance.

Arthur dug the gator into the sand, using it as his walking stick for balance, and looked ahead. *Always put your eyes on your destination,* he used to tell the girls. *It will help you remember where you're going and why.* It was sound advice, he thought.

Then he set off, imagining a stranger's gratitude as he began his search for treasure, eyes wide open.

5

Maggie

"Hello?" Jess's voice rang through the hallway. "Anybody home?"

Maggie was in the kitchen fixing sandwiches for lunch while the kids played Monopoly, biding their time till their cousins arrived. Even though Maggie had begged them to hold off swimming until after lunch, both Lexie and Sophie were already in their swimsuits. Putting the dock in the first day of summer was a tradition, as was the kids' sticking their toes in the water at the same time.

Luke and the twins beat her to the door. "Aunt Jessie!" the girls yelled while Luke tackled his cousin in a bear hug.

"Hiya, Sis." Maggie embraced her twin. "Girls, give your poor aunt a break," she warned as each tugged on Jess's arms. Maggie bent down to kiss her niece and nephew. "I swear you guys have gotten bigger since the last time I saw you. When was it? Two weeks ago?"

"Something like that," Jess said. "Same goes for you three." She hugged the girls and Luke. "But not you, of course." She turned to Maggie. "You look exactly the same."

"Thank goodness," Maggie said, and they shared a laugh.

A minute later, Tim came up the front steps, bags hanging off his shoulders and a large cooler in his hands.

"Where's Mac when I need him?" he joked. "Hi, everyone. You got the place all set up for us?" He leaned in to peck Maggie on the cheek.

"Mac went for a quick run. He should be back any minute." Maggie held the door open for her brother-in-law. "Here, come on in. Girls, help the kids with their bags upstairs. You, too, Luke."

"Then can we go swimming?" Lexie pleaded. Maggie eyed Jess to gauge whether she was ready to let the kids go in the water so soon, but Jess just shrugged.

"After you eat lunch, I don't see why not."

"Yay!" The kids bounded up the stairs with their backpacks and suitcases. Maggie pointed Tim toward the kitchen and helped her sister with the bags.

"Come on," she said, as she showed Jess upstairs. "There are fresh sheets on all the beds. The towels are washed and in the linen closet, so help yourselves. The water has been a little touch and go, but I think the pump is working now. Let me know if you guys have any problems with it, okay?"

When they reached the guest room, Jess smiled.

"What's so funny?" Maggie demanded.

"I love how you play house here, as if we're the boarders coming to stay at your bed-and-breakfast. You know we've been here a few times ourselves, right?"

Maggie felt her cheeks color. Here she was prattling on about things her sister already knew. "I'm sorry. I just want to make sure everyone feels at home."

"And we do," said Jess. "Thank you. The place looks great." Maggie watched as her sister scanned the guest room. A vase of pink roses that she'd clipped from the backyard this morning rested on a small side table. On top of the bed lay a crisp white comforter, capped with oversize pillows. On either side of it were built-in bookcases, filled with titles like *Gift from the Sea* and *A Field Guide to the Atlantic Seashore*. Maggie flopped down on the comforter and watched as her sister transferred clothes from her suitcase.

"Ooh, that's pretty," she said when Jess went to hang up a light blue sundress with delicate white daisies twirling across it. "When can I borrow it?"

"Don't even," Jess teased. Fortunately, Maggie reflected, Jess's sense of style had evolved for the better over the years. When they were growing up, she'd always wanted to borrow Maggie's clothes. Not because she liked them more, but simply because Jess never took the time to shop for herself. She was too busy saving the world with Habitat for Humanity or some other humanitarian group. Funny how the tables had turned, Maggie thought. She couldn't recall the last time she'd gone clothes shopping. For herself, that is.

"Hey, I forgot to mention," she said now. "We've closed off the downstairs bathroom till Jay can fix the window."

"What?" Jess stopped and turned.

"The window in the downstairs bathroom is shattered," Maggie explained. "We thought someone had broken in, but when I called Dad, he fessed up to it. Cracked the glass trying to open it. He forgot to ask Jay to fix it when he was down in May."

"Was Dad okay?"

"He claimed to be. Said he grazed his hand on the glass."

"Huh." Jess seemed to consider this while she resumed unpacking, arranging multiple tubes of sunscreen on the bureau in a neat little row. "Did you get Dad the iPad?"

"Yes," Maggie said, unable to hide the quiver of excitement in her voice. She was quite proud that she'd thought of this particular gift for their father, who had turned seventy-two a few weeks ago. Though Arthur had said he didn't want any presents, Maggie thought he'd protested a bit *too* much. Which was why she'd rallied her sisters to chip in on this newest electronic gadget. It was a useful present for a writer, she thought—one that even her father, so difficult to please, might actually like.

"That's great. Thanks. Dad will love it."

Maggie sat up and swung her feet to the floor. "Well, I'll let you get settled while I finish up the sandwiches. I'm sure the kids are eager to go swimming."

Back in the kitchen, Tim sat at the table, eating a turkey and cheese sandwich. His green eyes peered out from behind little wire-rim glasses. He was, Maggie decided, looking more and more like an accountant every year.

"Oh, I was saving those for the kids," she said without thinking.

"Oops." Tim got out through a mouthful of bread. "Sorry."

"That's all right." Maggie backpedaled. "I can make some more. In fact, that's what I came to do!" She reached for the butter knife and slathered mayonnaise onto a slice of whole wheat. There was no need to start off on the wrong foot with her brother-in-law. Initially, Maggie had thought Tim a good match for her more tightly wound sister. But in recent months, Jess had hinted that things had gotten tense at home. When Maggie inquired about what was going on, Jess had said, *Nothing. That's the problem.* Apparently, Tim had "checked out" from the family. Maggie couldn't say she was entirely surprised (to her eyes, Jess did all the work), but if it was true, she was sad for her sister. *All marriages go through stages,* she counseled. Jess and Tim would work things out, and life would get back to normal.

Just then, the kids breezed into the kitchen, their beach towels draped over their shoulders, looking like little conquerors. "Look at you all," Maggie exclaimed and clapped her hands together. "So grown up." She felt tears spring to her eyes, but Lexie stopped her in her tracks. "Mom, don't start. It's so embarrassing," she said before dropping into a chair.

"Sorry." Maggie turned to Tim. "Sometimes I feel like time is getting away from us, you know? Our babies growing up so fast?" She glanced at him for corroboration, but her brother-in-law stared at her, clueless. She sighed and had just begun passing out sandwiches when Mac arrived, soaked in sweat.

"Hey, there! How you doing, man? Sorry about the sweaty paw." He went over to shake Tim's hand. Mac's face was ruddy, his hair matted on his forehead. At six foot four, her husband was a big guy, barrel-chested, and looked the part of a cop. But he'd added a few pounds over the years, and she knew he was trying to shake them this summer.

Tim gripped his hand and slapped Mac on the shoulder. "Good to see you. You're looking buff."

"Always trying." Mac high-fived the kids and snuck a sandwich off the tray.

"Ooh, Daddy, you *smell*," cried Lexie as she got up and tossed her water bottle in the trash.

"Lexie McNeil!" Maggie pointed to the blue recycling box sitting next to the trash can. She was willing to let certain things slide at the summer house, but not the recyclables. With an eye roll (her daughter's favorite move of late), Lexie transferred the bottle to the blue box. *This* was the child Maggie was hoping to connect with this vacation? She had promised herself she would try to be patient with Lexie, but things were off to a dismal start.

"Duly noted," Mac said now. "I'll hop in the shower and then we can get the dock in."

When he headed for the stairs, he nearly collided with Jess, who had changed into her bathing suit. Black straps peeked out from underneath a pink cover-up. Jess was staring down at her cell phone, tiny frown lines hovering above her nose.

"Guess what," she said, looking up. "That was Mom. She wants to come down to the house on Saturday. *This* Saturday. To the *Cape* house," Jess clarified when they all stared at her blankly. "For a week," she tried again.

"But she can't," Maggie began, then caught herself. The kids were watching. "I mean, we won't have enough room, at least not until later this month." Maggie realized this probably sounded cruel, but she and Gloria had already discussed it. Their mother would come down for a day visit when Virgie, the kids, and Jess were all here. Then she'd return and stay for a week at the end of July, when the house had more room. Plus—*and it was a big plus*—their dad was due at the Cape house on Saturday. There was no way on earth that Maggie was going to have both her parents sleeping under the same roof. She could see it now, her mother constantly nagging Arthur, Arthur taking it in stride. Maggie would climb the walls.

"That's the thing," Jess continued. "Mom is staying at a bed-and-breakfast. She's already booked the room."

"You're kidding." Maggie couldn't hide her surprise. Gloria typically came to her first with such requests, yet she'd performed a neat little balletic twirl around Maggie's tightly crafted schedule of houseguests. Perhaps that was precisely why her mother hadn't approached her first. She knew her oldest daughter (because Maggie *had* been born three minutes and forty-two seconds before Jess) would insist she stay at the summer house while she figured something else out for Arthur. Could it be that her mother was developing an altruistic side, one that put other people before herself? Maggie thought it unlikely.

"And, get this." Jess cast around the room. The kids were chattering away again, but Jess whispered anyway. "She's bringing someone."

"Someone? As in a friend or as in a date?" Maggie needed clarification.

"I think it might be a date." Jess grinned conspiratorially. "Some guy named Gio. She said she'd met him in her dance class."

Maggie burst out laughing. The whole idea was absurd. Their sixty-five-year-old mother hitting on someone named Gio while she danced the tango?

"Hey, don't judge. He could be nice. Besides, Mom's been looking for a companion. Another senior citizen who can dance might be perfect for her."

Maggie shook her head. She couldn't believe it. Her vision of a calm, relaxing time at the summer house was growing hazier by the minute.

"Good old Gloria," Tim chimed in. "That woman does *not* let grass grow under her feet. You gotta love her." He got up and reached into the fridge for a beer. "Don't mind me, I'm going to enjoy the view until dock duty calls."

Maggie's head was suddenly in a tailspin, trying to do the math. *Could* they accommodate everyone here after the Fourth? Virgie would arrive on Wednesday. Her dad would be here on Saturday as well. Already, they had nine people sleeping under the same roof. She planned to put Virgie in the kids' room, which would fill up all three sets of bunk beds. Tim and Jess were in the guest room; herself and Mac in the master. When her dad came, he would stay on the pull-out couch downstairs. He'd always favored that bed for some reason, though Maggie found it stiff as plywood.

But if Gloria came, that would change the dynamic altogether. Maggie would have to kick Jess and Tim out of the guest room and let Gloria sleep there. But then where to put Gio, assuming he came along? And Jess and Tim? In sleeping bags in the living room next to her dad? That was preposterous. The thought of her friend Gretchen and her sea captain's mansion flitted through her mind. Surely, Gretchen had some extra space. But Maggie was loath to impose. What kind of friend asked another friend to put up her mother and her mother's paramour at her house?

No, her mom was right, Maggie could see that now. There was

simply no room for Gloria and her special friend at the summer house. Somehow it surprised her; this house was cozy but had always had ample room for them when they were growing up.

And what about Arthur? Her dad would be heartbroken if he saw their mother with another man. Should she warn him? Tell him not to come?

Only one day into vacation, and already it was getting complicated. She felt hot, slightly dizzy, and went upstairs to change into her bathing suit. What she needed, she decided, was to go for a long, soothing swim. She'd help with the dock and then, stroke by stroke, swim away from the chaos. Somehow the right path would reveal itself, effervescent bubbles pointing the way in the cool, refreshing water.

6

Jess

"Can I interest you in a strawberry smoothie?" Maggie snuck up beside Jess with a chilled glass in her hand. She set down a bowl of chips and passed Jess the drink.

"Oh, yes, please. What's in it?"

"Vodka," Maggie said, sitting down next to her, her hair still wet from her swim. "And a few strawberries, of course." Jess laughed.

After a good two hours, the pier was in—and Jess was spent. Their gang wasn't in its twenties anymore, and putting in the dock was hard work. At one point, Mac had gotten the level, and anyone could see that the last two sections weren't quite even. But by then, nobody cared. It was good enough. Now when she gazed out at the dock, she could discern the slight crook toward the end, where Teddy and Luke took turns jumping off. In their life jackets, the boys bobbed up and down like plump orange marshmallows in the water, while the girls drifted lazily on their rafts. *Ah, summer.*

When they'd pulled up to the house earlier today, Jess felt as if she'd traveled to two continents and back since the last time she'd slept at Pilgrim Lane. She nearly cried to hear the gate creak open and see the cheery daisies on the porch steps, each clump blooming like multiple exclamation points in the terra-cotta pots. "You're here!" they seemed to shout. It was as if the summer house had stayed frozen in time while her own life had been spinning out of control.

Tim, of course, had forgotten to place a hold on the mail last night, and Jess was furious. But as soon as she stepped foot in the summer house, she could feel the tremors of anger floating up from her body, hot little orbs of light. Suddenly, it seemed silly to get worked up about a thing as small as holding the mail. Maybe she *was* overstressed, a point that Tim liked to make whenever she came down on him.

Jess lowered her drink to the beach table, grabbed a tube of sunblock, and squeezed a dollop into her palm, the scent of coconut rushing over her.

"Mmm . . . that smells delicious," said Maggie. "Like I could eat it."

Jess smiled. "Be my guest."

"I was beginning to think summer would never get here," Maggie admitted.

Jess leaned back in her chair. "Me too. This winter felt impossibly long." They'd had record-breaking snowfall in Boston, and as the snow piled up outside, she'd felt more and more like a prisoner in her own home. Then Cole had arrived, like a tender crocus hiding in the flower beds fronting her porch. The fact that she had kept Cole a secret from Maggie all these months amazed her. And yet where to begin? There was so much more she had to explain about her marriage falling apart before she could get to Cole. But she couldn't be sure that Maggie, her twin, her best friend, would take her side. She thought of describing Cole's warm laugh, his funny stories, how he surprised her by kissing her at the kitchen sink one night, how soft his lips were and how she could feel actual back muscles through his shirt.

She considered trying to explain to Maggie how, when your husband becomes a stranger, when he no longer seems interested in talking to you or making things better in your marriage, it is surprisingly easy to fall for someone else. Even now that the fling had run its course (Jess had ended things over lattes in Harvard Square just days before vacation), would her sister understand? Maggie's moral compass was strong; the mention of Jess's affair might cause it to crack.

"So?" Maggie turned to her, as if reading her mind. "Tell me everything. I want to know." Her voice dropped an octave. "How are things with you and Tim?"

As much as Jess wanted to tell, she felt slightly ambushed. She couldn't get into it right now with Tim and the kids in front of them, could she? She would need a few more smoothies for that. "They've been better?" She hoped her voice sounded breezy, cavalier.

"Mommy, watch me!" Teddy called out from the edge of the dock.

Jess lifted her eyes and watched as he performed a cannonball that ended in a deafening, triumphant splash.

"I honestly don't know where to begin," she said now and waited for Teddy's head to reappear above the water.

"Oh, hold that thought," Maggie said. "I forgot the salsa. I'll be right back. And when I come back you'll tell me everything?" She pushed up from her chair.

"You bet," said Jess. She gave a thumbs-up as Teddy pulled himself up on the dock and glanced back at her for approval. *Summers are so easy,* she thought. All she needed to do was make sure the kids were slathered in sunblock.

By the time Maggie returned, however, Grace and Teddy were begging Jess to come in the water. And she couldn't say no, not on the first day of vacation. She glanced over at Tim, who appeared to be deep in conversation with Mac. *Of course.* She grabbed a chip and dipped it in the homemade salsa. "Delicious," she proclaimed. Then she shook her head and apologized to her sister: "Duty calls."

Maggie groaned. "All right. But you're not off the hook. I've got you for days," she said as she sat back down. "I want to make sure everything is perfect between you two."

Jess laughed and tugged off her cover-up before tiptoeing across the hot sand. *If only it were that easy*, she thought. She waved to the kids, then dove in, swimming away from thoughts of Cole, infidelity, and her broken marriage.

After a few hours, the children's skin had turned a bright shade of pink despite multiple applications of sunscreen, and Jess insisted everyone head inside. Grudgingly, the kids tromped upstairs to change out of their bathing suits and then tromped back down to hang them on the deck (it had taken years to teach them this, as opposed to flinging their wet suits on the floor). While Maggie started on dinner preparations, Jess swept up the fresh trail of sand that snaked across the living room floor. Sophie and Grace lay on the couch swapping rubber bands for their bracelet looms. Lexie's head was bent over a Harry Potter novel. And Luke and Teddy were sprawled across the floor, engrossed in their electronic games.

In the kitchen, Jess found Maggie shucking the corn that she and Tim had picked up from a roadside stand on the drive down. "How can I help?" she asked.

"There's not much to do." Maggie pushed a stray hair from her forehead with the back of her hand. "Mac's grilling the fish. If you wanted to make the caprese salad, you could. Stuff's in the fridge."

Jess pulled out the items from the crisper and shut the fridge door with her knee. She set the tomatoes, mozzarella, and basil on the counter and glanced over at her sister, who was dropping the husked corn into boiling water. How did Maggie manage to make everything look so effortless? she wondered. Even in shorts and a T-shirt, her sister was radiant, pulled-together looking. Jess's hair was full-out frizzy, and she looked exactly how she felt: in desperate need of a shower.

"Here," Maggie said, handing over a paring knife without looking up. Her sister was also possessed with a preternatural gift for anticipating everyone's needs before they even knew they needed anything. Sometimes Jess thought the two of them must have had a tug-of-war in utero in which Maggie had whipped her butt, stealing all the good genes. As a teenager, Jess had hated the fact that she was the "ugly twin." Jess's hair was a fine, medium brown like Arthur's, while Maggie's was wavy and blond. People found it difficult to believe that they were twins (unlike Sophie and Lexie, who were identical, save for a delicate brown birthmark on Sophie's neck). Whenever anyone mentioned the two in tandem, they would mention Maggie first, and it had been that way since Jess could remember. *Maggie and Jess.* And so, Jess was accustomed to thinking of herself in this manner, as if an invisible cord stretched between them, Maggie leading the way.

Gradually, Jess had come to understand that she wasn't ugly, just not as beautiful as her twin. She would never be as dazzling as Maggie. That was okay, though. She was Teddy and Grace's mom. She was a high school principal. She was successful by her own lights. She was, apparently, still attractive enough to win a man's heart. And at the thought of Cole, she felt a splash of guilt wash over her. Was it possible, she wondered as she cut into the tomatoes, that it wasn't all her fault? If Tim were invested in their marriage, even one cent, would she have let another man kiss her? She laid out the mozzarella, sprinkled the basil, and then drizzled olive oil over the salad. Would she have continued to let him kiss her?

But she'd kissed Cole back, fair and square. She'd been eager for his visits. Hell, she'd *encouraged* him, running her hands up and down his back, through his hair in her kitchen while the kids slept upstairs. She shivered, remembering. No, she couldn't absolve herself. The only thing she'd done right in the whole mess was to break it off.

"Fish is ready!" Mac called from the deck, an announcement quickly followed by the scampering of the kids' feet.

Jess poured herself a glass of ice water as Maggie plucked the steaming corn from the pot. "Can you grab the butter?" she asked before heading outside with the platter of corn. On the deck, the kids were seated at their own small table, a plastic folding table that she and Maggie had discovered during a Christmas Tree Shops outing several summers ago. The adults were gathered at the main picnic table. Jess hesitated a moment, searching for a place to sit. When she realized there was only one space left, she sat down next to her husband.

"This smells heavenly." She held out her plate for Mac, who dropped a generous fillet onto it. "Thank you." She cut into the flaky white fish and twirled it on her tongue, savoring the pop of lemon, the buttery goodness of it. "Wow," she said after a moment. "There's nothing better than the catch of the day, is there?"

"I couldn't agree more," said Mac.

For a while, everyone ate in silence, a summery web of contentment spun around them. The sun, with splashes of brilliant pink and orange, was dropping on the horizon in a dazzling display. Then Grace told a knock-knock joke, scattering the quiet, and the kids returned to chattering. Yes, this was summer. This was what she'd been waiting for. It was almost perfect.

When Tim reached out to hold her hand, Jess instinctively pulled it away. She couldn't have been more surprised. But after a moment she placed her hand back on top of his. The roughness of his skin, the curvature of his hand, was at once foreign and familiar.

And she let her hand sit there for a while, as if trying it on for size, only lifting it finally to reach for the butter for her corn.

7

Virgie

Jackson always smelled like soap, clean and inviting. Whenever she got a whiff of a similar scent, Virgie thought of him. It was almost Pavlovian. The teenage girl sitting next to her on the plane must use the same brand. What was it? Ivory? Zest? Virgie guessed her fellow traveler was probably fifteen or sixteen, her earbuds firmly in place while she thumbed through the July issue of *Seventeen*. Virgie peered over her shoulder, pretending not to. Most of the celebrities in the magazine were people she didn't even recognize. *Damn, she felt old.*

She glanced out the window at large, frothy clouds that reminded her of the foam on a milk shake. It felt good to be leaving the office behind. When the flight attendant stopped the metal cart beside her row, Virgie ordered a Diet Coke with lime.

"No limes," the attendant said unapologetically and snapped open a can of soda. "Here you go." She efficiently handed over the can, a cup of ice, and a package of pretzels.

"Thanks," said Virgie, secretly wondering when flight attendants had gotten so snarky. Maybe this one was just having a bad day.

Virgie knew the feeling. She sipped her drink and closed her eyes. The Liz Crandle story had aired yesterday, and Virgie was miffed that Thomas had actually done a crackerjack job with it. He'd managed to make Liz sound both wronged and sympathetic. Personally, Virgie doubted she could have done it any better. *Whatever,* she told herself. When she got back from vacation, she was going to figure out a Plan B. Maybe switch to a new station, where she'd have a more direct route to the anchor desk.

She was also trying her best not to feel guilty about not inviting Jackson to the summer house with her. Not that he'd acted upset about it when she kissed him good-bye at the airport. But she'd had her reasons. She ticked through them now:

1. She didn't want to scare him off. Inviting Jackson to join her on vacation was like inviting him to a family wedding. It had *serious* written all over it. And they'd been dating only a few weeks.

2. Meeting the entire Herington clan all at once could be intimidating for even the most devoted of boyfriends. Her father had vetoed several of her high school and college beaus, and it was no secret that Arthur didn't suffer fools gladly.

3. There was something sacred about the Cape house. All those memories. Bringing Jackson there would be like granting him access to her family's personal Narnia, a wardrobe transformed into their own magical world. Did she want him to know her that well so soon?

4. And what if—though it seemed impossible—Jackson didn't like it? What if he didn't adore the summer house the way she did? She didn't think she could love a man who didn't grasp the charm of the house's pocked wooden floors, its slightly cracked plaster ceilings, and creaky beds. She felt like a mother, oddly protective of it.

No, it was better if Jackson didn't see the house yet. Besides, she needed to warm her sisters up; they hardly knew the first thing about him. She'd only mentioned him in passing to Maggie when they were confirming the details of her arrival the other night. "I've met someone new," she said.

"Really!" Maggie sounded happy for her, not at all surprised. "Is he coming with you?" That was a typical Maggie comment, focused on the practicalities, what needed to be done. Virgie could almost hear the wheels spinning in her sister's mind on the other end: Would she need to put Virgie in the guest room now, as opposed to bunking her with the kids? Did the summer house have enough sheets? Would they be grilling for one more?

"Don't worry, Mags," she said. "It's only me this time."

"Oh, okay." Maggie sounded almost disappointed, and Virgie imagined her crossing off *Extra sheets?* on her list. "Another time then."

"Yes," agreed Virgie. "I'd love for you to meet him. Assuming it lasts." She heard her sister's light, good-natured laugh on the other end.

"Fair enough." And then they quickly moved on to her flight information, when she'd be touching down in Boston and was Virgie sure she didn't want one of them to drive up to get her at the airport?

"No, thanks. Not necessary. I'm renting a car. I'm a big girl, remember?" When Maggie relented at last, Virgie was glad. It was easier this way.

She eased her seat backward. When she removed her thumb from the button, though, a sticky residue clung to it. She dug into her purse for antibacterial lotion and rubbed it into her hands. Whenever traveling on assignment, Virgie carried a tube of it with her, and she was grateful for it now. There were so many gooey, germ-infested places where a girl could put her hands. If journalism had taught her one thing, it was that the world was not a safe place, and Virgie did her best to guard against whatever it chose to throw her way.

Gradually, the release of a much-needed vacation began to set-tle over her, like a gentle fog softening the edges of her discontent. Maybe Miss-No-Smiles had taken pity on her and slipped something into her soda. *Be kind, for everyone you meet is fighting a hard battle,* she told herself. That is, right before the girl sitting beside her shifted in her seat and accidentally smacked Virgie in the calf with her foot, sending a spiral of pain up her leg.

"Ouch!"

"Oh! Sorry," the girl said.

"That's okay. These seats are awful." Virgie rubbed her leg and forced a smile. The girl gave her a look, but Virgie couldn't tell if it was because she was interested in talking or because she thought Virgie was a nutcase.

"Are you from Boston?" Virgie tried.

"Not exactly," She removed an earbud. "I go to school outside of the city."

"Oh? Whereabouts?" Virgie thought she looked awfully young to be flying out for college.

"Exeter." The girl was nothing if succinct. "I'm helping with summer school."

"That's supposed to be a great prep school. Do you like it?"

"It's all right."

"I'm from Maine, but I went to Vassar." Virgie paused to see if there was any response. "In Poughkeepsie," she added. "New York."

"Cool." The girl turned back to her magazine and replaced her earbud. But Virgie felt distinctly uncool. Her seatmate clearly wasn't interested in striking up a conversation. Shouldn't she be pumping Virgie for information about college? But, then again, Virgie hadn't thought that far ahead when she was in high school either. All she'd cared about was boys, one boy, in particular. Seth Laraby, a soccer player who spoke fluent French. His parents had worked abroad when he was young, and Seth had gone to private school outside of Paris. She hadn't thought about Seth in years.

She stared out the window and twirled the ice in her soda. She wondered if Sal would be around this summer. Of course, he'd be working at the store, but would he be dropping by the house like last summer, bringing her small treats? They'd had on-again, off-again flings over the summers, but they were getting a little old for that. Virgie had Jackson now—she couldn't exactly be cavorting around with another guy on another coast. Maybe Sal had met someone serious, too.

She readjusted her shoulder pillow (another item she never traveled without) and closed her eyes. This would be the summer of relaxation, not romance. At least for her. If anyone needed romance, it was her dad. Each Sunday night when she checked in with him, she would ask if there were someone new in his life, perhaps a dinner partner? But Arthur just laughed. "Honey, you know I'm too old to get back out there," he said.

"But, Dad, you're not." Virgie recalled their conversation last week. "There are tons of senior women out there, online even, who are looking for someone. You should check out the dating sites. You don't have to get married. Just go out to dinner!"

Her father let out a heavy sigh. "*Senior* women," he said. "That has an appealing ring, doesn't it?"

"You know what I mean," she chided. "Don't knock it before you try it."

"Perhaps I will one of these days." But they both knew that he didn't really mean it.

It would be good to see Arthur in person. It had been too long since she'd laid eyes on her dad last Christmas, when they'd all gathered at Maggie's house in Windsor. Even then, he'd seemed smaller to her, as if his clothes had outgrown him. She worried about him, asked him if he was eating well and asked her sisters if Dad didn't seem lonely, maybe a little depressed? But Maggie and Jess told her

she was being silly. Dad was the same as he ever was. A lovable cur-
mudgeon till the very end.

The thing was, Virgie loved Arthur like crazy. And she was pretty
sure he felt the same way about her. She'd always been her daddy's
little girl, while Jess and Maggie had insisted on forging their own
paths. Everything Virgie did was meant to impress Arthur, even her
career in journalism. When she won an Edward R. Murrow Award
for reporting, Arthur was the first person she called. When she got
promoted to doing the personal interest stories, *Verbatim with V*
(which Virgie closed every Tuesday and Thursday night with "And
there you have it, word for word, with Virginia Herington"), Arthur
had flown out to treat her to dinner and toast her as the "daughter
most like me." Virgie had nearly burst with pride. She thought back
on that moment, how special it had been, how much she still wanted
to make Arthur beam.

Before long, the flight attendant's voice came back on over the
intercom, announcing they would be landing soon. Virgie shook the
fog from her head. She must have drifted off to sleep. She glanced
down at her empty glass and crumpled bag of pretzels and passed
them over to the aisle. Earbuds Girl was still reading her magazine.
Virgie righted her tray and pulled out her phone to double-check
her car reservation. *Sweet.* The black Mini Cooper convertible she'd
ordered was waiting for her.

She imagined herself racing down Route 3, tunes blasting, her
long hair blowing in the wind. On how many trips to the Cape in
the family station wagon, wedged between her sisters in the back,
had she imagined her grown-up self traveling along the same route?
Being able to do this one delicious thing was a bold check mark off
her bucket list. As the plane began its descent, she felt her stomach
plunge and she gripped the armrests, digging her fingers in for support. Soon the whoosh of air and the sound of luggage tumbling
overhead made her squeeze her eyes shut, as it did every time.

"Ouch!" cried the young woman sitting next to her. Virgie opened her eyes as the plane came to a halt. When she glanced down, she saw that she was clutching the poor girl's hand in a vise, her knuckles a bright pink. As with so many things in Virgie's life lately, she'd had no idea.

8

Arthur

On Tuesday and Wednesday afternoons, Arthur set out for the local library, a tan building that sat on a craggy ledge overlooking the water. He could walk to it, a fact that appealed to him immensely. Aside from his house, the library was, perhaps, his favorite place on earth. Unlike his house, it was orderly, books meticulously arranged by category and then alphabetically by author's last name. Theoretically, he was here to man the front desk. He checked out patrons' selections, answered the rare question, and shelved the returns. But, in reality, there was little for him to do in the afternoons, at least until the rush of schoolchildren broke through the doors at three-thirty. Then they would race through the main entrance, pulling off their backpacks, and fling themselves onto the beanbags in the children's section. As much as Arthur loved to see a youngster pick up a book, the children's section with its noise and bustle was not for him. He found it unnerving.

But now, in the summer months, not even the schoolchildren broke the quiet. He had lived in this small coastal town most of his married life, and so the majority of patrons were, at the very least, acquaintances. It pleased him that he could greet people by their first names before they handed him their cards. He made a point of it. Lately, though, some of the names escaped him, people's faces that he'd known for twenty years. He blamed it on the fact that he was occupied with the new book he was writing and that all he could think of were its main characters—Inspector Larson, Claire Dooley, and Rita Wigglesworth.

Sometimes when he peered into a patron's face, Arthur would see flashes of his characters. His old pal, Eleanor, for instance, had a hawk-like, pointed face, not unlike that of Rita Wigglesworth. And the bulbous nose of Hank Sellers, a regular who checked out every Agatha Christie novel and penciled editorial suggestions in the margins (Arthur knew this because he checked the books before and after Hank borrowed them), reminded him of Claire Dooley's nose. Arthur wondered if his patrons influenced the physical attributes and mannerisms of his characters or was it the other way around?

Often he would scribble notes on the little sheets of paper meant for writing down call numbers. He detailed things he wished to include in his new book. Sometimes he would become so immersed in his note-taking that he forgot where he was, and a patron would have to clear his throat a few times before getting Arthur's attention. He was always quick to apologize. But everyone knew that he volunteered at this job. He couldn't be expected to take it too seriously. For that, they would need to ply him with free whiskey.

On this Wednesday before the Fourth, the library was particularly quiet. Arthur felt as if he was working in a velvet-lined jewelry box, the very kind that housed the diamond ring he'd presented to Gloria on bended knee forty-six years ago. It was three-carat, and he'd saved diligently until he could afford it. It was exactly what Gloria wanted. They'd gone window-shopping in the diamond district in Boston, a street of stores now called Downtown Crossing that had once housed places where a person had to ring a buzzer to gain entrance to a vaulted store at the top of the stairs. There, a helpful but aloof salesman waited, as if the purchase of a diamond that day made little difference to him.

Arthur remembered the day like it was yesterday. It was a December afternoon, and a light snow fell on the Boston Common while he and Gloria idled along, admiring the Christmas lights that were draped like colorful scarves across the trees. They held hands, Gloria's snug in her mittens, hand-knitted blue things with little strings attached at the ends. He'd teased her that they were like a schoolgirl's, until she told him that her mother had given them to her last Christmas and that he'd better be quiet if he knew what was good for him. He'd always liked that about her. She could give him a hard time and he'd just love her more. Their futures were ripe with possibility then. Arthur planned to finish grad school and then teach American literature. Gloria couldn't wait to have children. They debated how many children were enough. How many were too many? They agreed that three seemed the perfect number.

When they turned down Washington Street, the dancing Christmas Bears in the Jordan Marsh window greeted them. They pointed out sweaters and hats that might make good gifts for friends. When they crossed the street to the jewelers' side, Arthur suggested they climb the stairs to the diamond shop to look at rings "just for the hell of it." He was trying to act glib, but he was as nervous as a kid suited up for his first football game. Arthur knew his soon-to-be fiancée well enough to understand that the only ring that would suit her finger would be one that she'd have a say in.

In truth, he was itching to propose. There was no other girl for him. They giggled when the buzzer let them in and a pale salesman welcomed them at the top of the stairs only to point them through another locked door. Arthur joked it was like entering a jail cell, but Gloria shushed him. "Oh, come on," she said. "Marriage isn't that bad, Arthur, is it?" And she squeezed his hand before they crossed into a room that quite literally sparkled with diamonds.

As soon as she saw it, Gloria knew the exact ring she wanted: a bright, twinkling diamond, nearly translucent with dazzling blue sapphires on either side, sitting in a gold band. Arthur had to hand it to her. The ring was exquisite.

"That's the best of the bunch, no question," he agreed. "Here, try it on for fun, why don't you?" he said, ignoring the annoyed look of the salesclerk behind the counter, who had to unlock the case to reach the ring. But he did so, if a bit grudgingly. Did the man really think he was bluffing here? Arthur wondered.

When she slipped the ring on, small *Oh!*s escaped from them both. Not only because it dazzled so elegantly on her slim finger but also, Arthur suspected, because of all that it suggested. A life for two people, for *them,* forever. Arthur grew light-headed and went to grab a seat. The jeweler, suddenly kind, fetched him a glass of water and joked that it happened all the time. Grooms got sticker shock while the women started planning the wedding in their heads.

When they left the store, Gloria teased him that if they ever did get married, Arthur would need a stiff drink before heading into the chapel. But she didn't understand. For Arthur, it was exactly the opposite. It wasn't that he was getting cold feet or felt sick about paying such a princely sum for a ring. Rather, a vision of him with Gloria, her long blond hair tied up in a loose bun, holding hands in a row with their children—and this he had envisioned quite clearly, though Gloria would never believe it—three girls, twins and a younger daughter, swept across his field of vision.

And he was floored. Floored by the sheer gorgeousness of that image, as if it were a premonition of all the good that his life ahead held. It had momentarily blinded him, struck him off his feet.

Of course, they'd had a good laugh about it. Gloria joked he didn't need to get her that *exact* ring if it was too expensive. Something similar would be fine, so long as it meant she was tied to him. It was, perhaps, the kindest thing she ever said to him.

When he opened the velvet box at Anthony's Pier 4 over raspberry cheesecake and coffees, it housed the very ring she'd slipped on. "Yes!" she exclaimed, throwing her arms around him, and Arthur was filled with a certainty that his life was proceeding precisely as it should.

Gloria, he thought now, with a pang.

He checked the books on the to-be-shelved cart and saw only a handful. Circulation always fell during the first weeks of summer, when the entire town was either hosting company or traveling. Arthur picked up a few titles, mostly gardening books and a weight-loss book promising results in one week. He hadn't seen Gloria since Christmas, when the whole family had gathered at Maggie's house. His ex-wife had burst through the front door, stomping snow from her boots, and an image of her on the day that they'd gone ring shopping, the snow drifting down, had flashed before him unexpectedly. He'd actually bent over and clutched the back of a chair.

Her hair was different now, cut into a bob that swept just above the shoulder, and she'd gone lighter, a blond color that still managed to look natural. She wore a sharp lavender suit. Arthur had always admired that Gloria never stooped to wearing holiday sweaters or pins like so many older women did. That frigid Christmas Day, she carried bags stuffed with presents that she let fall to the floor when the grandchildren ran to hug her. She smiled at Arthur and he smiled back while Mac helped remove her coat. The scent of gardenias, Gloria's signature perfume, floated through the room. Arthur hoped that perhaps the smile meant something, perhaps she wanted him back. But as the evening unfolded and he and Gloria made small talk, he came to understand that it was nothing more than a friendly smile.

Gloria wished him well. That was all.

His memory was interrupted. "Excuse me, Arthur, but I can't seem to find the new Danielle Steel novel. Could you help?"

Standing before him was Florence Arbitrage. Florence, as she would tell anyone who would listen, was from Charleston, South Carolina. Every sentence that came out of the woman's mouth got stretched to its utmost length.

Arthur didn't particularly like Florence, but when it came right down to it, he didn't like many people outside his immediate family. It had been this way for as long as he could remember. Maggie and Jess teased that he was a modern-day misanthrope, but Arthur knew better. He liked people in general, just not in particular. There was a difference. A subtle distinction, but a distinction nonetheless.

"Sure, Eleanor. Do you know the title?"

She regarded him strangely for a minute. *Did he just call her Eleanor?* "Oh, I don't know," she said, her voice twanging on *know*. "Something about friends, I think?" People's inability to remember titles always amazed him, which was why he spent countless hours coming up with memorable ones for his own books.

They headed back over to the circulation desk, where Arthur typed "Danielle Steel" into the library's search engine. *Friends Forever* was the first title to pop up.

"*Friends Forever* sound right?" he asked.

"That's it!" She slapped her hand on the desk, delighted that Arthur had been able to seemingly conjure it out of thin air. "Now where can I find it?"

Arthur eyed the inventory list on the computer. Two copies supposedly sat on the New Fiction shelf out front, making him wonder if Florence had even bothered to check in the first place. He headed for New Fiction, Florence following behind him like a porch dog.

"How are your girls?" she asked. The other thing about small towns, Arthur thought with a modicum of chagrin, was that everyone knew everyone else's business.

"They're great," he said. "Ah, here it is!" He pulled out the novel, displayed on the front shelf plain as day. "I'm going down to the Cape house on Saturday, in fact."

"Oh, isn't that wonderful," Flo said with a purr and took the book from his hands, brushing them lightly with her fingertips. "Family is the most important thing, isn't it?"

She said the words with a hint of wistfulness, enough so that Arthur was nearly prompted to ask her what she was doing for the Fourth, but he stopped himself. He didn't want to be put in the awkward position of inviting her over if she didn't have any plans.

"Will that be all?" he asked as they headed back to circulation.

She hesitated. "Yes. Thank you. Unless you have a recommendation for me? You know how I love to read. Widowhood can be so lonely." She drew out the *o*'s.

"I'm afraid I haven't been reading much lately. I've a got a deadline for the new book." He quickly scanned the novel into the computer and slipped the due-back receipt between the pages.

She laid her hand on the book. "You do? That's wonderful. I can't wait to read it. You're so very talented, Arthur." He felt a shiver pass through him, as if he should be doing a better job of hurrying Florence along.

"Well, back to work!" He excused himself and headed for the small room where they housed shipments of new titles. He pretended to do a quick inventory until he heard Florence shout "Ta-ta!" After a few minutes, he returned to the desk, relieved that there was no Florence in sight. A small line had formed, and he scanned each book so that it prompted the machine to print out a crisp receipt. How he missed the days of stamping a yellow card at the back of each book! It made such a triumphant sound, that stamp. Funny, how much a person could miss the tactile sensation of sliding a card back into its little pocket. It had taken several years for their sleepy town to catch up with new technology, but once it had, there was no turning back.

Arthur was wistful not just for the old checkout system but for the days when newfangled computers didn't encroach upon every aspect of life. Technology was forever messing up his writing. He would type sentences such as, "Rita Wigglesworth turned the car window handle, and the summer breeze streamed in," only to have his editor write in big red letters in the margins: "Arthur, people have *automatic* windows now!" Once he wrote about Inspector Larson helping himself to a few ice cubes from the tray in the freezer, and his editor picked up the phone to call. "Arthur, you realize that the majority of Americans have refrigerators that *make* ice now, right? Do they even make ice cube trays anymore? You're dating yourself."

Arthur disagreed with her about that one. He felt it to be more a matter of class. To his mind, rich people had automatic ice dispensers. The rest of America still used ice cube trays. One day, he was at Target on an errand, and there, in aisle seventeen, was the most magnificent assortment of ice cube trays he'd ever seen. Red and blue, trays shaped like stars, fish, the alphabet. He'd been so thrilled to be proven right that he stuffed his cart full with them. When he got home, he realized he'd bought more than he could fit in his freezer, so he sent six to his editor, trays with smiley faces, hearts, and pineapples. He wrapped them up as a gift and mailed them to her with a note, saying: *Some of us still like our rocks the old-fashioned way!* He thought it was clever, but his editor had never acknowledged it. Hadn't even sent an e-mail ribbing him for his gag gift. Perhaps, he thought now, she hadn't seen the humor in it.

That was another reason he liked going to the summer house: everything remained more or less the same, even as his family changed, grew up. While Maggie had replaced the refrigerator and stove a few years back, they were nothing fancy, just run-of-the-mill appliances that fit the rest of the house's unassuming décor. No fancy ice machines. Only recently had his eldest daughter insisted on tossing out their ancient black rotary phone. If ever they needed to dial 911, it would take them half an hour to twirl the numbers around the plastic dial, she argued. They had their cell phones. Arthur agreed she had a point.

He combed through the various newsletters and announcements pinned to the library's bulletin board. He'd come to think of the board as the town crier, the place everyone gathered for breaking news in their little haven. He pulled down the flyers that had expired—ads for rummage sales two Saturdays ago, a puppy for sale, a lost cat, piano lessons, sign-up for swim lessons, Irish step dance classes. Some flyers he tossed, but a few he stuck in his briefcase to take home. Even if the event had passed, he liked having the information at his fingertips if anyone were to ask him, *Say, whatever happened to that ad for cleaning services or dance lessons?*

Eventually, the sun began to tilt in the late-afternoon sky, and only a few patrons remained, including a man who'd been perusing magazines for more than an hour. Arthur didn't mind. He was accustomed to vacationers who came to the library to escape their noisy families, in search of an hour of peace and quiet. A handful of women from the Wednesday knitting club were still gathered in the conference room. As far as Arthur could tell, they only read trashy romances, but it was better, he supposed, than not reading at all. He switched on the front desk microphone to make the "Fifteen minutes till closing" announcement and felt the small rush that traveled over him each time he heard his voice magnified in the hallowed halls, as if he were the Wizard of Oz standing behind deep red curtains.

In time, the solitary man and knitting club gathered up their things and waved good-bye. Arthur did a full sweep of the library, shutting off the lights and making sure no one was lurking in the corners. The building became shrouded in darkness and quiet.

It was peaceful here, he thought, as he let himself out the door and locked it behind him. Peaceful like a tomb. He shook his head, as if to shoo the image away. The thought of a tomb came unbidden like so many thoughts these days; try as he might, metaphors of life and death kept flinging themselves at him. Was he unnecessarily preoccupied with his own mortality? He didn't think so. When a man reached a certain age, it was hard to stop thinking about it. And now that Gloria was gone . . . He felt a stab of pain in his side. Well, he thought about dying, more particularly about dying alone, quite a lot.

When he got home, he pulled out the minute steaks from the fridge. He found a bag of frozen peas and dumped them in a pot of boiling water. He pushed aside mail piles, magazines, bills, and set the table for one, always for one, and placed the steak sauce next to his plate. These were the meals he used to make for himself when he was a bachelor in his own apartment in graduate school. How odd that he'd come full circle, even after having a life full of family. Here he was in his kitchen, alone, eating the same meal he'd eaten nearly fifty years ago.

When the steaks were done, he flipped them onto his plate, drained the peas. He pulled a hunk of bread off the French loaf in the bread box and poured himself a glass of scotch. He considered saying a small prayer before lifting his fork.

Did he even believe these days?

He wanted to. He really did. Because if there were no God, that meant there was no heaven. And then what? What was left for a person to look forward to? A box set in dirt? No, he wouldn't go that way. If he went, he wanted to be cremated, his ashes scattered offshore, perhaps dropped from the cliff where the library sat. That would be appropriate, he thought. He could drift on the sea next to the place that housed his books. All twelve of them, though only one had amounted to anything, two weeks on the local bestseller list.

What on earth had he been doing with his life?

He folded his hands, bowed his head. "God bless my family. Please watch over us. Keep us safe. Keep us healthy. Keep us happy.

Amen." It was succinct, hardly eloquent, but it was the best he could do. He knew if he continued he'd start asking God for miracles, pleading for Gloria to come back to him. And when she didn't return, his faith would be shaken further.

He cut into his steak. Arthur knew he owed Maggie a call to confirm the details of his trip. He hoped to leave around five in the morning on Saturday and arrive in time for a late breakfast. He'd tell Maggie how much he was looking forward to seeing them all, and then he'd place his breakfast order: a ham and cheese omelet. What had started as a joke between them was now a tradition. He and Maggie had always been the breakfast lovers in the family. Not so with the others; Gloria, Jess, and Virgie snatched their breakfast on the way out the door, a granola bar, a banana, a cup of dry cereal. But he and Maggie enjoyed a square meal, pancakes soaked in syrup with sausage on the side, fluffy blueberry waffles, eggs Benedict. Whenever they got together over the summer, they easily rediscovered their father-daughter bond. Arthur was grateful for this one small thing.

Soon, he'd call Maggie. He got up, cleared his plate, and went to search for one of those microwave bags of popcorn. Maybe there would be something good on television tonight. He knew he'd bought a case of microwave popcorn at Costco a few months ago. Now if only he could recall where he'd put it.

9

Maggie

Above them, fireworks popped, huge, magnificent plumes of color darting across the night sky. Like s'mores on the beach, peach and rhubarb pie, or the feel of sand across the hardwood floors, fireworks were synonymous with summer in Maggie's mind. She wouldn't miss them for the world.

After a slightly crazed start to the week, vacation had settled into a languid pace. Jay had fixed the window, the refrigerator was stocked, the linen closet organized, and now, ever so slowly, Maggie could feel herself letting go, unwinding. Virgie had arrived yesterday, a hot little tamale in her Mini Cooper, and taken the kids for hair-raising rides on the back roads. Lexie, she could tell, was completely charmed by her aunt. Maybe, Maggie hoped, some of Virgie's enthusiasm would rub off on her.

This Thursday morning, at the crack of dawn, like every Fourth of July since Maggie could remember, the family had set up their folding chairs on Main Street to watch the annual parade of fire trucks, antique cars, and clowns. Luke, Teddy, and the girls chased after red licorice whips and Tootsie Rolls while the adults sat on the sidelines, pulling sodas from the cooler. Maggie spied Gretchen and her kids sitting further down the street and gave a small wave. The parade was loud, noisy, bordering on obnoxious—everything a good holiday parade should be. When the floats with homecoming queens and Little League teams drove by, the crowd cheered, blowing their plastic horns. Even the local dry cleaners had a float, and they tossed inflatable beach balls to the kids. But when the Minutemen shot off their muskets, the boys scurried back to their mothers' laps like skittish puppies.

"Don't be such a scaredy-cat," Lexie chided. But Maggie didn't mind. She was glad that Luke still needed her to comfort him on occasion.

"You used to jump, too, you know, Lex," said Maggie. Her daughter rolled her eyes. "You did. When you were Luke's age." It was enough to make Lexie lay off her brother. Maggie understood that the only thing worse than being forced to play with her younger brother was being *compared* to him. How could two sisters be so different, she wondered, when Sophie appeared to be the easiest, most carefree child in the world? Maggie and Jess had had their differences growing up, for sure, but they'd always been bound together by the twin thing, often finishing each other's sentences. If Lexie and Sophie weren't identical, no one would guess they were twins.

Now, following an afternoon of swimming, all the kids except Luke were crashed on the beach, watching the fireworks. Maggie crouched down next to him, helping him roast a marshmallow over a flickering flame. "See, you turn it like this, so you get all the sides," she coached, holding the stick above a narrow gap where the flames licked up. "You have to be patient."

"I've got the chocolate bars," Virgie called out from the deck. Still in her red-and-white bikini, she approached their group. Well, Maggie thought, at least her sister had had the decency to wrap a blue sarong around her waist.

"If you're not the Star-Spangled Banner, I don't know who is," Mac teased. Maggie swatted at him.

"Shut up, honey." She was glad, however, that Virgie was her sister, forbidden fruit.

"It's not fair that you look so awesome," Jess said petulantly from her perch near the bonfire. "We're supposed to share the same genes. Honestly, how do you keep so skinny?"

Virgie settled herself into a beach chair and smiled. "Starvation?"

There was a wave of laughter, but Maggie pressed. "C'mon, Virgie. You must do something to stay in shape."

"Oh, I run all the time," she confirmed. "And my best friend is Botox."

"Who's that?" She'd caught Luke's interest now.

"Oh, nothing, Lukie. It's just another way of saying that your aunt Virgie takes good care of herself."

Mac chuckled, but Maggie thought she detected an undercurrent of bravado to her sister's comment. Something about Virgie seemed off this vacation. Was it just the first flushes of love with this Jackson guy that made her more cavalier than usual, more reckless? Virgie had always been the one to push the envelope in the family, staying out past curfew, dating boys with earrings, smoking a random joint. But ever since she'd landed her *Verbatim with V* show, she'd been more grounded, less likely to take chances. Which was why Maggie couldn't believe that just a few hours earlier she'd been yelling at her baby sister to get off the deck railing.

Virgie had been walking across it like a tightrope walker, *as if there weren't a good twenty feet to drop off the other side onto the beach,* Maggie thought when she opened the deck door.

"Get off of there before you kill yourself!" she shouted. "Before the kids see you."

"Naggy Maggie," Virgie parroted her nickname from years ago. "Can't you let a girl have a little fun?" She teetered for a moment, then righted herself, her arms outstretched.

"Honestly, Virgie. What's gotten into you?" Maggie held her breath as her sister reached the end and jumped down onto the deck, landing as gracefully as could be expected with a loud thump.

She flashed a smile. "Just having a little fun."

"Well, I have enough kids trying to give me a heart attack," Maggie said. "Don't you go joining them. You are firmly in the *adult* camp," she reminded her.

"Aw, you're no fun," Virgie whined. Still, something about the whole incident bugged Maggie. A few times at dinner Virgie's words had slurred just a touch, and Maggie wondered if her sister was drinking too much. Again. There'd been an episode after college, and another after that, when, after tumbling drunkenly from a bar tabletop, Virgie had ended up in the hospital with three cracked ribs. The family had called a mini-intervention. And while Virgie hadn't exactly sworn off drinking, she appeared to at least have gotten it under control. When Maggie wondered aloud to Jess and Mac if maybe Virgie's "problem" had returned, they told her she was being paranoid. *Virgie's fine,* they reassured her. *Probably more sane than the rest of us put together,* Jess said.

Maggie sighed. Why was it so hard for her to stop worrying? She just wanted things to be like old times. Everyone happy, sound of body, sound of mind.

"Mommy!" Luke yelled, interrupting her thoughts. "I think mine's ready."

She grabbed the stick from him and carefully slid the crispy brown puff off, leaving the gooey center intact. She watched as Luke fashioned it into a s'more and took a gigantic bite. "Awesome," he said with a grin, before running off to join the circle of other kids. *So easy to please,* thought Maggie. She looked over at the children's eager, upturned faces. They might as well have been watching Neil Armstrong land on the moon, so great was their fascination with the night sky. She was glad her kids would have evenings like this to remember.

She could still conjure up the fireworks on the Cape when she and her sisters were little. Gloria had always turned it into an elaborate production, packing rare treats like egg salad sandwiches, miniature hot dogs, and fruit tarts. She'd pretended they were royalty.

When Gloria had begged off joining them for the Fourth this summer, saying she was going to the concert on the Esplanade in Boston, Maggie had been surprised, slightly hurt. Now those plans included someone named Gio. *Gloria and Gio.* If nothing else, it had a nice ring to it. Leave it to her mother to date a man with an alliterative name! But, honestly, the thought of Gloria's being with someone other than her dad made Maggie's throat tighten.

When Maggie had talked to her mom the other night, Gloria insisted on staying at the B and B and confirmed that she was bringing along a "nice young gentleman." Maggie reminded her that Arthur would also be visiting that week.

"Oh, don't you worry, honey. We'll be fine. Your father and I are grown-ups. We're just friends now."

But when Maggie broke the news to her dad later that night, it was obvious that the visit wouldn't be as easy for him. There was silence on the other end of the phone. "All right, then," he finally said. "I guess I've been warned." Maggie was trying hard not to think about it. *Que sera, sera.*

She joined Mac on the blanket near the fire. Jess and Tim excused themselves to take a walk along the beach.

"There she is," Mac said, pulling her close and kissing the top of her head as she nestled into his arms. *I could get used to this,* she thought. *Having Mac all to myself.* No precinct to call in to, no buddies needing help with their cars, nothing to distract him, save the beach and the kids. Would they grow old like this? she wondered. Still in love, hungry to snuggle into each other's arms? When the kids were out of the house, would the two of them be enough? She thought so, hoped so, but how could anyone really know?

For a moment, Maggie wished they could all flash back to twelve years ago, when she was first pregnant with the twins and Jess and Tim had started dating. That summer had been sublime. Mac was the doting daddy, even with the twins swimming in her big belly, and Jess and Tim could barely keep their hands off each other. Or when all the kids were still little. Maybe the summer right after Teddy was born, four years ago. Jess and Tim were still good then, weren't they? Everyone was happy—and together. Even Arthur and Gloria.

"Hey, look." Mac nudged her and pointed in Virgie's direction. "Looks like your sister has a new admirer." Sal had shown up a few minutes earlier carrying a cooler. After saying a quick hello, he'd planted himself next to Virgie and the kids. Maggie watched while Virgie said something and flipped her hair.

"Sal's not really new," she corrected. "He's been in love with Virgie since we were little girls." Maggie suspected that, as with each passing summer, Sal hoped he could persuade Virgie to be his love interest for the time that she was here. Maggie was curious to see if her sister would mention Jackson or if she would she play it coy. It was difficult to know with her baby sister; Virgie was accustomed to having her cake and eating it, too.

"Where's my s'more?" Mac asked now.

"Sorry, honey, it's every man for himself tonight." Maggie reached into her jacket pocket. "But I did manage to score us this." She held out the Hershey's chocolate bar, its tinfoil shining in the moonlight. He dove for it, but Maggie was quick. She broke off a small piece and passed it to him.

"This," he said, plopping the chocolate in his mouth, "is all I need to make my life good. You, the kids, fireworks, a cold beer." He paused, stroking her hair. "The only thing that could possibly make it better would be that entire Hershey's bar." She laughed, took another bite, and snuggled in closer.

Just then, another big boom exploded overhead. Maggie watched the bright tendrils of color drift down to the water like streamers.

"Good one!" Luke shouted, and the kids whooped in unison.

The scent of woodsmoke hung in the air. She could taste the bittersweet mix of beer and chocolate on her tongue. This was summer. Sticky fingers. The smell of mosquito repellent. The wind whipping up, then settling down again. Her husband's arms around her. The sound of the kids laughing. *Yes,* thought Maggie. *You're right.* Now, if she could just work up the nerve to tell Mac what she'd been dreaming about for the family.

But she stopped herself. Right now she wanted to enjoy the moment, take it all in.

10

Jess

It was Friday night. Already. How on earth did the first week of vacation pass by so quickly? she wondered. Jess climbed the stairs and poked her head into the kids' room before getting ready for bed. After a full day of swimming, Lexie and Sophie were sprawled out on the top bunks, zonked. Teddy had crawled into bed with Grace, his warm body pulled into an S. On the other bunk, Luke snored softly, surrounded by his army of stuffed pigs. She honestly didn't know how her nephew managed to keep track of them all. She blew them kisses, then shut the door behind her and went to grab a fresh towel from the linen closet. When she pressed it to her face, she was hit by the familiar scent of lavender.

Jess was trying to relax, soak in the summer, but it was proving difficult this year. The fact that she and Tim had had a fight this morning wasn't making it any easier. Two days into vacation, when he asked her how old the milk was in the fridge, she'd refrained from snapping that milk had an expiration date like anything else and why didn't he just check the carton? And they'd had a decent Fourth last night, hanging out with Mac and Maggie to watch the fireworks. They'd even gone for a walk and *talked* about things, remembering summers past. It almost felt like old times.

Almost.

She told herself she couldn't expect Tim to perform a 180-degree reversal, going from hardly present in their marriage to a devoted husband in a week's time. But she didn't expect him to further piss her off either. And that was exactly what he'd done this morning.

They were sitting out on the deck drinking iced coffees. It was hot for so early in the day, the heat sending off shimmering waves above the sand. The kids were busy building sand castles a few yards down the beach. She and Tim talked casually about the usual stuff. *Did the kids have enough sunblock on? Wasn't it great to have some time to kick back? What should they do for dinner?* Jess allowed herself to think for a brief moment, *This is good. This is what we should be doing every day.* And then somehow the conversation tumbled disastrously into free fall. She mentioned that when they got back to Boston she would need to go into work for a week in August and did he think his mom could help cover with the kids?

"Do you really think it makes sense to ask my mom to help out over the summer?" he asked.

"What do you mean?" Jess asked, thinking perhaps he was implying it was time to hire a nanny, something she'd suggested over a year ago, when she started her job.

"I don't know." He gazed out over the water. "I'm just wondering if it's a fair trade; you have to give up a week of your summer with the kids so you can go into a job that drives you crazy and hardly pays anything."

She couldn't believe she'd heard right. "Excuse me?" She was still willing to give him a chance to explain himself. Give him an out.

"I don't know. I've just been thinking. With your job, we've brought in some extra money, and I'm not saying it's not important. It is. But, do you really think the stress is worth it?"

Jess licked her lips, trying to parse her words, to understand the motivation behind Tim's sudden second-guessing of the one job in the world she loved, where she felt she was making a difference. Sure, it was crazy, but all jobs were crazy to some extent. Was he implying that her job wasn't important or that the kids were missing out on mommy time while she toiled away at her little *hobby*?

She felt her blood pressure shoot up, her heart thumping in her chest. She spoke carefully, not wanting to say something she would regret, words that would irretrievably damage their marriage.

"Yes, Tim. I think it's worth it," she finally spat out. "It's the whole reason I went back to school. You might even say it's my passion, after the kids. I think it's important for them to see their mother engaged, doing something valuable and that it trumps any inconvenience it might create during the month of August. Plus, that little bit of money you refer to isn't like our pin money. That money helps pay the bills, like groceries and heat and clothes for the kids."

He held up his hand. "Whoa. You don't need to go ballistic on me."

"Well, sorry. I feel like you kind of did on me. Is this what you've been thinking my whole first year as a principal?"

"I'm sure you're great," he said tightly. "I just happen to think our kids need you more than the punk kids you work with at that school. How many of them end up dropping out anyway?"

She couldn't believe it. He was more or less insinuating that her job was one big hideous joke. "God, you're patronizing!" she cried and jumped up from her seat. She flew into the house, up the stairs, and hid in the bedroom. For an entire hour, while she lay on the bed and wiped her tears, she felt zero regret for her fling with Cole. Tim deserved every little heartbreak he got. How he could be such a consummate asshole astounded her. As if the responsibility of raising their kids was hers and hers alone. It wasn't like he was bringing in huge sums of money either. It worked because there were two of them!

It took every ounce of willpower she had not to call Cole at that moment. How she wanted to! But she knew it wouldn't solve anything. It would only make things worse. So, instead, she popped two Xanax and sank into a deep sleep, one that she didn't wake up from until later in the afternoon.

Not until after dinner did Tim apologize. "I'm sorry," he said, sneaking up behind her when she was reading a novel on the couch. "I didn't mean to upset you. I was just thinking practically. You know, the economics of it all."

"Mm-hmm," said Jess, unconvinced.

"Let's not let it ruin our vacation, okay?" He sat down beside her and took her hand, his fingers lacing between hers. Had he sensed, like she had yesterday during their walk, that they both still wanted this marriage to work?

"Don't worry. I don't intend to let it ruin *my* vacation," she huffed. She took in his small eyes behind the glasses. *Squinty eyes,* she thought. Somehow they made her even angrier.

"Jessie," he said softly. "Come on. I was stupid to say anything, but don't make it worse than it was."

"Belittling my entire career is pretty low, Tim. It's like . . ." Her voice trailed off while she searched for the right word. But there was no single word. "You don't value me beyond what I do for the kids."

"That's not true," he argued. He cast around the room nervously, as if making sure none of the kids was in earshot.

"Well, that's how it sounded. I mean if we're talking about the *economics* of it all," she snapped. "It kind of negates all that intangible stuff, right? Like helping kids who otherwise wouldn't have a chance of going to college?" She knew she was entering dangerous territory, where their ideologies on larger issues sometimes clashed. But if it was truly how he felt, she needed to know.

"Jessie, you know that's not what I meant," he ventured again. "What you do is amazing. It helps a lot of kids. It's just that I see how stressed out you get. And when it starts to affect our own family life, I guess that's when I start to wonder if all that stress is worth it."

When he put it that way, it sounded marginally better. She decided not to point out how the long hours he logged at his office "affected their family life" as well. It was true that her job was stressful for nine months of the year. But it was the adrenaline rush that she craved; it made her feel important, needed. How could she make him understand that?

Now, with the passing of a few more hours, she could see how her reaction might be construed as a bit much. After all, here she'd been craving honesty and open conversation with her husband over the last year. At least they weren't trading Post-it notes. But if the dam had splintered, well, there was a lot of emotional wreckage waiting behind it. Tim's words smarted.

She hung the bath towel over the rack and flipped off the bathroom light. Quietly, she tiptoed down the hallway that was lined with pictures from summers past, many of them shots of the family posing on the dock. Everyone was getting so big! Even Teddy's face had shed the fat baby cheeks she'd loved to kiss a hundred times. She traced her finger across those cheeks. Where had the time gone? How had things gotten so confused?

At the bedroom door, she could make out Tim's body already in bed. She slipped in next to him and felt the rough sand at the bottom of the sheets, an unavoidable hazard of sleeping at the summer house. She kicked it down further toward the end of the bed. Tim rolled toward her and circled an arm around her. She was surprised that he was even half-awake. She felt him inch his way closer, pressing his body up against hers, and for a second, her mind darted to Cole. It startled her, the way he wormed his way into her head even when she was doing her level best not to think about him.

She hadn't returned any of Cole's texts or messages, and in fact, after fifteen missed calls, she'd finally blocked his number entirely. If she'd quit caffeine cold turkey (as she had when she'd gotten pregnant with Grace), then, her reasoning went, she should be able to quit Cole cold turkey, too. Cole wasn't the reason her marriage was in the pits. She'd read enough self-help books to understand he was a mere symptom of her troubled marriage. That she had allowed herself to fall for him in the first place and return his kisses was further testament to the fact that her marriage wasn't working. She wasn't *in love* with Cole. He was practically a kid, for goodness' sake, eight years younger.

But she couldn't remember the last time Tim had snuggled up to her, when the atoms between them had buzzed with attraction. It hadn't always been this way. It used to be that he would want to be intimate as soon as he got home from work, before she could even get dinner on the table. He would sidle up behind her, running his hands under her shirt and over her waist while she stood at the stove. But with the kids, first Grace, then Teddy, sex had taken a backseat. Never like this, though. Never for months at a time.

"Jessie, come here," he whispered into her hair. He pulled her closer and nibbled on her ear. Her husband smelled of beer, sunblock, and something sweet—honeyed peanuts, perhaps? Slowly, he kissed her hair, her cheeks, her lips. His lips were chapped. She worked to conjure up the boyish image of him when they'd first met in an Irish pub in South Boston—flashing dimples, brilliant green eyes, straight white teeth. The boy she'd fallen in love with. He was here, somewhere in this same skin.

"You know what the best part of making up is, right?" he asked. But it was Cole's soft lips, his tanned skin, his muscled arms that flexed when he opened a bottle of wine that kept swimming through her mind while her husband kissed her.

"Tim," she began, then hesitated. How on earth could she broach the subject? Did she really want to confess her history with Cole? Would it help things or only make it worse between them? If she didn't tell but got her husband back, would the ends justify the means? She weighed the various scenarios in her head while Tim kissed her gently, then, gradually, more forcefully.

"Hey, you didn't answer," he whispered.

It was an old game they used to play after they'd had a knock-down fight, usually over a girl whom Tim had flirted with. Funny how times had changed. Jess's answer was always the same: "Yep, the best part is that you admit I was right."

"You got it," he said. He squeezed her and rested his head next to hers. Jess waited. His arm, wrapped around her, grew heavy. And then the sound of her husband's snoring drifted across the twisted sheets.

Jess listened to the night. She could hear the crickets singing outside the window. Someone in the kids' bedroom rolled over, causing the bed to squeak. Beyond the open window, the waves rolled in and out, in and out. She lay there for a few minutes, thinking not of her husband but of a man ninety miles away. A small tear slipped down her cheek, the salt stinging her pinked skin. *What was she going to do?*

11

Virgie

On Saturday at the stroke of noon, Gloria arrived, riding in on a wave of perfume. Colorful gift bags with tufts of tissue paper fanning out from the tops dangled from her hands. Virgie couldn't help but think all that was missing was an entourage. Well, there *was* one person who followed on her mother's heels, she saw now: a handsome Latino man, who appeared delighted to be carrying their mother's bags.

"My darling, Virginia," her mother exclaimed as she came up the walkway and kissed Virgie on both cheeks in a cloud of gardenia perfume. "It's been *forever* since I've seen you. How *are* you?"

Gloria had a way of making a person feel as if she really had been missing her, a feeling soon eclipsed by the realization that she handed out this greeting to everyone she saw. Virgie turned her head to receive her mother's kisses, then peered over her shoulder to better focus on her companion.

"Gio, meet Virginia, my baby," her mom announced with a flash of pride. "She's the news reporter."

"Ah, Virginia. Virgie, yes? I've heard so much about you."

Virgie smiled. "Only good things, I hope."

"Yes, yes, of course," Gio said hurriedly, taking her hand and kissing it. "But you don't look like a baby to me." He winked and Virgie thought, *Gross.* Her mother's boyfriend hitting on her? But that was ridiculous. Even if Gio was young for Gloria, he was no spring chicken. If Virgie had to guess, she'd say he was in his mid to late fifties. He was dressed in neatly pressed navy shorts, brown loafers and little white socks, and a pink golf shirt. A small gold chain looped around his neck. She supposed this was the way men of a certain generation handled themselves. She supposed it was debonair.

"Nice to meet you." She ushered them into the hallway, and this time got hit by a blast of cologne. Gloria and Gio set down their bags as Maggie rushed in from the kitchen, still clutching a dish towel.

"I thought I heard someone!" she exclaimed. "Mom!" She gave Gloria a once-over. "You look . . . radiant," she said finally and hugged her.

"Oh, honey, you've always been such a good liar," Gloria said, but her face beamed as she pulled away.

"And you must be Gio." Maggie extended her hand. Her sister was always good with names, not that any of them would have trouble remembering their mother's boyfriend's name. But it was more than that. Maggie made everyone feel welcome, no matter what she might be thinking. Virgie knew her big sister was less than pleased to have Gloria and her lover here the same week as their father. Even if Gloria was staying at a bed-and-breakfast fifteen minutes away. But she'd never guess it to look at her sister. Maggie's blond hair was pulled up in a loose ponytail. Her cheeks shimmered with a light pink. Her tanned face was relaxed, happy, as if she'd been waiting her whole life to meet Gio.

"A pleasure, my dear." Gio took her hand and kissed it.

"My kittens!" Gloria squealed all of a sudden, the grandchildren running in and collapsing in a heap around her. For some strange reason Virgie couldn't recall, her mom insisted on calling her grand-kids kittens. "Look at you all! You're just gorgeous, girls! And you boys—handsome as ever." She grabbed Teddy's face in her bejeweled hands, while he squirmed to get free.

"Come on in." Maggie led everyone into the kitchen, where Mac welcomed his mother-in-law and Gio. Gloria set the party bags down on the table. "Can I get you something to drink?" Maggie asked. "Maybe a glass of lemonade?" She held up an ice-filled pitcher and began filling glass tumblers before anyone could answer.

"That would be lovely," said Gio.

"Well, aren't you going to open your presents?" Gloria demanded.

"Yes!" yelled Lexie, snatching her gift from the table. Everyone knew that Gloria never visited her grandchildren empty-handed. Virgie's snarky side couldn't help but think, *Typical Gloria, co-opting her grandchildren's love with gifts.* It was small of her, but it had an element of truth to it, she thought. Ever since her mother left Arthur, Virgie had come to see Gloria as selfish, an insecure woman hungry for approval and affection. Virgie had always been closer to Arthur, but with each passing day, she felt as if Gloria pulled farther away from the family. As if she were a distant aunt coming to visit rather than Virgie's own mother, who had kissed her scraped knees and rubbed her back when she was little.

Gloria pulled a chair up to the table, and Virgie studied her more closely. Maggie was right: their mother looked radiant, even young. Instead of wearing her signature Talbots top and shorts, she was dressed in a pink Indian print shirt and a long teal skirt. Her usual mauve lipstick was missing, and her hair was held back by a twisted, bright pink head scarf. Remarkably, she'd said *nothing* about the sand the kids had tracked in on the kitchen floor in their rush to see her. Was it possible, Virgie wondered, that her mom had mellowed since she'd last seen her? Maybe had a personality change?

But when Gloria regarded Maggie and said, "Honey, you look

bloated. Have you put on some weight?" Virgie realized her mother was the same as ever.

Maggie blushed beneath her pink cheeks, while Mac coughed into his hand. "Thanks, Mom. Not that I know of."

Gloria waved her hand as if she must have been mistaken. "But you, missy"—she turned to Jess—"look positively skinny. Are you eating enough?" It was part criticism, part concern—her mother's particular brand of caring, a hug delivered with an upper right hook.

"I'm fine, Mom," Jess said before disappearing into the other room.

"Well, I guess someone's in a happy mood." Gloria clicked her tongue.

Virgie and Maggie exchanged glances. A guest in her own home, Gloria could still fell them like giant oaks with a quick swipe of words. It always flabbergasted Virgie when her mother seemed surprised by other people's reactions to her. Was it possible she was truly unaware? The rest of the family had been here for nearly a week, falling into its own rhythms, with tomorrow unspooling pretty much the same way as yesterday. Virgie prayed that Gloria, around whom the world seemed to orbit without ceasing, wouldn't throw everything off-kilter.

"She's fine, Mom," Maggie said now and passed her a glass of lemonade.

Thus far, Maggie had admirably played the role of cruise director, righting the ship anytime it got rocky. In fact, Virgie thought the whole gang had done a commendable job of establishing their personal boundaries. She knew, for instance, she couldn't mention anything about microwave dinners (a staple in Virgie's diet) to Jess or she'd fly off the handle, citing the evils of preservatives. And if she asked Maggie one more time why Gloria, Gio, and Arthur couldn't all crash in the summer house together, there'd be no turning back. Mac and Tim were easier—there wasn't much that upset them unless she started talking trash about the Red Sox. But with Gloria's arrival, it was as if they'd hit a snag in the smooth fabric of summer.

"A Lego guy!" Luke shouted as he ripped open his present, piercing the momentary awkwardness.

Gloria glowed. "I *knew* you'd love it." Gracie and Teddy let go similar squeals over their gifts. Virgie watched while Lexie and Sophie worked to rearrange their faces into something like delight as they pulled off the wrapping paper from theirs—elaborate cosmetic cases with multiple tiny drawers and trays. They were ridiculous presents for two girls who couldn't be more sports-oriented, but her nieces did an excellent job of pretending they loved them. "Thanks, Grandma," said Lexie.

"Yeah, thanks," repeated Sophie. "It's awesome."

"You're so very welcome, my kittens," Gloria cooed. "I thought you girls might be at the age where you were getting interested in boys and wanted to look pretty."

Hug, hug, jab, thought Virgie.

"Where's my other son-in-law?" Gloria asked now, searching the room.

"I think he went for a run," said Jess, who had rejoined them. Virgie hadn't even noticed Tim was missing. "I'm sure . . ." Jess continued but then stopped. Virgie followed her eyes to the doorway.

There stood Arthur in the kitchen archway. He'd arrived promptly at ten this morning, and the family had already shared a breakfast of omelets and bacon. The room fell quiet while he cast about the kitchen, as if trying to get his bearings. He reminded Virgie of a bird with a broken wing in search of a place to land, and she nearly held out her arm for him. *Here,* she thought. *Land here and I'll protect you.* His thinning hair, combed carefully to the side, revealed the pink scalp underneath.

"Hello, Gloria," he said softly and stepped forward. Her mother got up and went to embrace him.

"Arthur, how *are* you? So good to see you."

"Fine, just fine, thanks." He took her elbow and leaned in awkwardly to receive his ex-wife's kisses. Gio approached as well. The king of debonair just moments ago, he appeared flustered to have his flame's ex-husband in the same kitchen.

"Gio?" her dad asked now, offering his hand, while Gloria stepped back.

"Nice to meet you, Arthur."

Maggie shot Virgie a glance as if to say, *Could this be any more awkward?* But Virgie shrugged. So long as Arthur didn't get hurt, somehow they'd have to all learn how to get along this week. The old kindergarten assessment *plays nicely with others* darted through her mind. Who would pass? Who wouldn't?

"Well," tried Maggie, "shall we all go out on the deck?"

"Great idea." Mac slid open the deck door and they followed him outside, where a slight breeze fought to cut the humidity.

"Ah, ocean. How I've missed you!" their mother exclaimed and plunked down in a chair. Arthur, then Gio, performed an awkward little dance before Gio settled into the chair next to their mother. Arthur sat down across from them. The noonday sun was already scorching. Virgie couldn't wait to get in the water and wondered how long she'd have to sit here and pretend to make small talk.

She could feel a bead of sweat begin to work its way down her chest. If Jackson were here, she would have whispered in his ear that she was hot, needed cooling off, and he would have jumped at her cue. *Jackson.* She let herself fantasize for a moment that he *was* here. Earlier this morning they'd traded texts: *I miss you,* he wrote. *I miss you more,* she texted back. She felt as if she was in high school all over again. What would he think of this crazy family of hers? Would he laugh with her later, tell her all families were bizarre in their own way? Maybe he had a deranged aunt or an uncle who smoked Cuban cigars. She realized she had no idea what his family was like. She'd met no one in it.

When she got back to Seattle, she'd make a point of finding out.

She knew his parents lived an hour outside of Seattle. Why hadn't he introduced her yet? Was it a bad sign? She stopped herself, sipped her lemonade. *Of course not.* They'd been dating only a few weeks. She couldn't expect Jackson to have considered formal introductions yet. After all, they were still feeling out whether they liked each other.

The thing was, Virgie knew she liked him. He was funny, smart, and *kind* in a way that her previous boyfriends never were. The fact that he was a male nurse probably had something to do with it. And while the whole male nurse thing was a bit of a mystery to her (she typically dated men who were slick, quick with the pickup lines, in general, *bad* for her), she reminded herself that if Jackson hadn't been a nurse, she would have never met him.

She'd sprained her thumb and was worried it was broken. It was such a stupid thing, but she'd driven herself to the ER in the middle of the afternoon to get it checked out. She had been walking, yes walking, on her way to the sandwich shop for lunch when she managed to stumble. For a brief second, the world had tilted, not taking Virgie with it, and she lost her balance. Any normal person would have twisted her ankle, but not Virgie. She fell as ungracefully as she could, catching herself on the sidewalk, her hand scraped and bloodied, her thumb swelling by the minute. A nice woman helped her up and asked if she should call 911, but Virgie declined. It wasn't necessary. She was fine. It was only a few scrapes and bruises.

But by the time she got back to the office and washed the blood off her hand, her thumb was throbbing. It didn't look broken, or dislocated, but what did she know? She told Larry she was going to get it checked out. "Damned high heels!" she said, trying to make light of the fact that the pain was so bad now she wanted to cry. She drove herself to the ER, where she waited what felt like hours to see someone. It was Jackson who'd come to her rescue. By then, she probably would have fallen for anyone willing to help. He ushered her into a room, offered to get her a drink of water, and gazed at her with those understanding eyes while he ticked through his checklist of questions.

When the X-ray revealed no broken bones, the doctor came in to wrap the sprain. It was still painful as hell. But Jackson returned as she was leaving, handing her a prescription.

"These should help with the pain," he said, pressing the small paper into her palm. "I wrote instructions for when to take them on the back."

She hadn't connected the dots, but eventually, while she waited in line at the pharmacy to hand over the prescription, she flipped the small white paper over. On the back, Jackson had written: *I think you're beautiful. Call me? 206-555-0882.*

Virgie hadn't considered that such things happened in real life. She assumed things like guys leaving personal notes on the backs of painkiller prescriptions happened only in the movies. Plenty of men hit on her when she went out to the bars with her girlfriends. But a telephone number on the back of a prescription? That was a first. She was intrigued. She called. "How's the thumb?" Jackson asked, as if they talked every day.

"Much better. Thanks." A few days had passed, and it *was* feeling better. The painkillers, though, were making her a bit loopy. She blamed it on the medicine that she had the guts to call in the first place. "You were very kind," she said.

"It's what I do." An awkward pause followed.

"So, will you have dinner with me?" he asked. She thought of his dark, wavy hair, his blue eyes, his gentle touch on her hand.

"Um, yes?"

"Right answer," he said and laughed. "Tomorrow night? I'll pick you up at seven?"

And from there, she handed over her address to a perfect stranger, though he didn't feel like a stranger. That night she tossed and turned, wondering what she'd just done. What if he was a stalker who watched her on the news and now she'd given him her home address? What was she thinking? She should have asked him to meet her at the office.

But when the night actually arrived, Jackson showed up at her door with a dozen pink roses.

"For your thumb," he said. And Virgie knew he was all right.

"Earth to Virgie?" someone was saying. Virgie pulled her eyes away from the ocean. Maggie was looking at her strangely.

"I was just telling Mom and Gio how amazing your last segment on homeless kids was." Virgie had sent her sisters and Arthur the clip. She was proud of the piece, which spotlighted a group of Seattle children who often went without breakfast before school. *How can we expect these kids to focus on their schoolwork when their stomachs are growling and they've had next to no sleep? Could you do your job?* she asked the camera.

The show had garnered a shower of praise, and as a result, the station had raised nearly ten thousand dollars for the local shelter. It was those types of stories, Virgie thought now, that made her job worthwhile. It seemed almost silly, sitting on the deck with a glass of lemonade, how important the Liz Crandle case had been back in Seattle. Here on the Cape, Virgie couldn't care less that Liz had told her story to Thomas. It wasn't going to be a life changer, any way she sliced it. The firm would most likely settle, and Liz would go her merry way with a boatload of money. Where was the inspiration in that?

"It sounds amazing, honey," Gloria said and patted her hand. "I can't wait to see it." Virgie braced herself for her mother's follow-up punch. Something along the lines of *Well, isn't it wonderful that you're finally doing some* real *reporting?* But she'd already moved on.

"How's the book coming, Arthur?"

Virgie realized with a start that none of them had thought to ask her dad that very question. They'd all been so focused on getting the house presentable for Gloria, taking marching orders from Maggie after breakfast—that they'd completely forgotten to inquire about Arthur's writing. She felt a pinch of guilt.

"Good," said her dad. "It's coming along. Due in a few months."

"That's wonderful! Arthur is an author," her mother explained to Gio. "He writes mysteries."

"You must be a very smart man," Gio said. Virgie could feel Maggie and her dad exchange glances, as if to say, *How cute. He thinks you're smart.* But no one said anything, only nodded their heads. It was, Virgie thought, a bit of a conversation killer.

"So, Gio, do you like to fish?" Mac asked, breaking the quiet.

He laughed. "If only I knew how."

"We'll have to get you out on the pier with a fishing pole," said Mac. "Fishing is one of the easiest things in the world." And the way he said it, Virgie almost believed him. "We've got some great bass around here."

"I look forward to your lessons," Gio said just as the kids appeared at Virgie's side.

"Aunt Virgie, want to go swimming?" Teddy asked.

"I wondered where you all disappeared to. Absolutely," she said now and got up from her chair to grab a towel off the deck railing. "Mom, Gio, we'll see you later?"

"You bet, honey." Her mother winked. "We'll be around all week. Besides"—she drained the rest of her lemonade—"we were just leaving. We need to check in before they give our room away to someone else."

"That's smart." Mac stood as well. "You never know, this time of year. Those New Englanders can be sharks." Gloria laughed and patted Mac's arm.

"We'll see you kids tomorrow, then?"

"You bet," Jess said.

"Can't wait," said Maggie, as she got up to follow her mom and Gio to the door. Virgie had to hand it to her sister as she headed down to the beach. Maggie actually managed to sound sincere.

12

Jess

"So that was weird," Jess said when she walked into the bedroom. She was referring to the introductions between Arthur, Gloria, and Gio. "Mom and Dad with another guy in the mix?"

Tim, freshly showered after his run, appeared to consider it for a moment. "I don't know. Your parents have been divorced for what? A year and a half now? It doesn't seem so strange that your mom is moving on."

He tossed his sweaty socks in the laundry basket and slid his flip-flops from underneath the bed. Neither of them had talked about last night, when Tim had kissed her eyelids, run his hands along her body before falling asleep. Jess wondered if he even remembered. Perhaps he'd been too drunk.

She slipped out of her shorts and top and pulled her swimsuit off the drying rack. Tim paused to look at her. "What?" she asked.

He shook his head. "Nothing. I just haven't seen that in a while."

"That?"

"Yeah. You. Almost naked."

"Oh," she said. "That." She felt strangely awkward, like a teenage girl being checked out.

"It's nice." He offered a small smile and pushed up from the bed. He walked over to her as she pulled up her suit, her breasts still revealed, white discs against her newly browned skin. His fingers grazed her nipples and he gently began to kiss her neck.

"Tim," she whispered. "The kids."

"So what?" he mumbled. "They're all outside with Virgie. Can't we have a little fun?"

It was one-thirty in the afternoon. Jess couldn't remember the last time she'd fooled around with her husband in the middle of the day. Maybe the day that Teddy was conceived? It was quite possible it had been that long ago.

She held his head in her hands as his lips made his way down to her breasts, circling her nipples. Jess waited. She waited for something to spark in her. It seemed she'd been waiting for months for her husband to realize she was in the same room. But there was nothing.

"Honey, come on." She shrugged him off and tugged at her bathing suit straps. "What's gotten into you?"

He gave her a hangdog look. "Never mind," he said brusquely.

"Hey, don't be pissed."

"I'm not pissed. Just because my own wife doesn't want to fool around with me." He grabbed his sunglasses off the bedside table without looking at her. "I'm going to take the kids for a bike ride."

"Tim, come on. It's not the best time, you have to admit."

He opened the bedroom door, his hand resting on the handle. "Yeah? Well, when is the best time, Jess? You act like you don't even want to be in the same room with me anymore. Am I really that bad?" His voice trembled with anger, and she watched his free hand clench into a tight little ball.

"Tim, not here. Not now," she tried, looking past him down the hallway, worried someone might hear.

"When then, Jess?" He unfurled his knotted fist. "You're the one who's all about 'open' communication." She watched him hook little sarcastic apostrophes in the air. She sighed. He was right. But she didn't feel like airing their dirty laundry for the whole house to overhear. He gestured around him. "Don't worry. There's no one around." His voice was laced with judgment, as though that was all that mattered to her. *The appearance of normal.*

His eyes locked with hers, and the way he looked at her, she almost told him. How easy it would have been to say that there was someone else. *Had* been someone else—someone who cared deeply about making the world a better place and who gave out-of-this-world back rubs. Or to say that Tim had been missing in their marriage for so long he couldn't just expect her to turn it on at a moment's notice. But his voice carried a dare, a threat even, as if everything that had happened in their marriage the past year—the breakdown in communication, the thwarted trips to the therapist, the lack of touch—was her fault. She was the one, he seemed to imply in his simple stare, who had made things impossible for them.

"Jesus, Tim. You can't pretend that you're not part of the problem here—" But he cut her off.

"You think I don't know?" His face was beet red. "You really think I'm that big of an idiot? Like I don't notice how Cole is at our house every time I get home late from work? Like I don't see the empty wineglasses on the counter?"

She was struck silent, speechless. *He knew? He knew.* Here she'd thought they'd been so secretive, so careful. What a fool. "What did you say?" She needed a minute to recover, to process the accusation freshly delivered.

"How far did it go, Jess? Is it *still* going?" he demanded, the words shooting like tiny arrows.

"Tim . . ." Her voice escaped her and she collapsed on the bed. "How did you know?" she asked, almost a whisper.

His arms dropped by his sides. "I didn't for sure. Until now."

"Oh," she said. Then, "Oh, no." She swallowed hard, her throat cottony. "I never meant for it to go anywhere." She paused, grasping for a way to explain. "He kissed me . . . and it just sort of happened. But it's over." She felt tears well up. "Completely, totally over."

Her husband stared at her, as if willing himself to believe her. "When?"

"Right before we left for vacation. I broke it off."

He inhaled, turned away. "And what exactly do you mean by *it*?" She could tell it took every ounce of strength in his body to ask this question. She owed him an honest answer.

"We didn't sleep together, if that's what you're asking."

He waited. "We kissed," she explained moronically. "He gave me back rubs. We talked. It was pretty innocent, actually."

Tim made a coughing sound. "Innocent? Really?"

She realized how absurd she must sound. There was nothing innocent about it. It was duplicitous, deceiving, unfair. Wrong. She'd betrayed her husband. How to explain? "He made me feel attractive, Tim. He *talked to* me. He listened. When you went missing from our marriage. Where *did* you go, by the way?"

For a moment, she was seized by a fit of righteousness. She wasn't the only guilty party here. Tim had contributed to this whole mess that was now their lives.

"Um, work?" he countered. "Trying to provide for my family. You know, that whole business?"

"Hey, that's not fair. I work, too, you know."

"Don't you," he said, lifting a finger, "Tell. *Me*. About. Unfair." He punctuated each word with a pointed finger, and his face pulled into an ugly sneer. Jess burst out crying.

"Honey, I'm so sorry. I never meant for anything to happen," she said. "What about us? Can we get *us* back?"

She watched as his body seemed to almost physically deflate.

She tried to think of the word to describe it. Then it came to her: *defeated*. Her husband appeared totally, utterly defeated.

He shook his head. "I don't know, Jess. I used to think so."

It was a truthful answer. How had they gone from the couple who used to giggle at the ridiculous line "You complete me" in *Jerry Maguire* to the couple who no longer knew what the other person was thinking? Her stomach clenched and she thought she might be sick.

"Can we at least try?" she asked, swallowing the bile in her throat. She hated the tremor in her voice, the desperation.

But Tim was already heading downstairs.

Jess sucked in big breaths of air between sobs, trying to gain control. So, they'd done it, had it out. Finally. Had she irretrievably destroyed her marriage? She'd been such an idiot! She reached for a tissue, then stopped short when she thought she heard a noise coming from the hall. She got up and tiptoed toward the sound, like little mouse squeaks, down to the kids' bedroom. Behind the door, she found Gracie. Her dear sweet Grace, kneeling down, her head bent in her small hands.

"Gracie, honey?" Panic shot through Jess's heart. Had Grace heard them fighting?

Grace peered up at her, her cheeks wet with tears. "Mommy, are you and Daddy getting a divorce?" Her bottom lip quivered.

"Oh, sweetheart." Jess bent down to take her in her arms, welling up again herself. "Of course not. No." She whispered "Shush" while she rocked her daughter and wiped her tears. How did a seven-year-old even know what divorce was? Then she remembered one of Grace's friends, Kelsey, had watched while her parents went through a bitter divorce. Kelsey had gone from an energetic five-year-old to a fragile seven-year-old. "We just had a little argument, like you and Teddy do sometimes." She kissed Gracie's sweet-smelling hair.

"And you're going to make up?" Grace asked, her voice threaded with hope, her innocent hazel eyes framed by thick, wet lashes.

"Yes, we're going to make up," Jess said and squeezed her tightly. "Of course we are. That's what moms and dads do. That's what families do. We always make up. It's all gonna be okay." She whispered the last sentence over and over.

Over and over again, until Jess convinced herself that she was speaking the truth.

Jess lay on the beach, the scent of coconut floating by anytime the wind decided to send a breeze her way. There wasn't a soul within a hundred yards. As soon as Gracie had stopped crying, Jess had poured her a glass of water, wiped her face with a cool cloth, and coaxed her back outside to play with her cousins. They were heading out on a bike ride, and soon enough, Gracie was back to her old self, goofing around and ready to go. Tim wouldn't look at her, though. Jess would tell him later, she decided, about what Gracie had said.

She lay looking up at the bright sky, a flotilla of misshapen clouds floating by, and considered how she would save her marriage. If there had ever been any doubt in her mind that she and Tim should stay together, it had dissipated the moment she saw Grace dissolve into tears. Jess realized with a racing heart that she'd done more damage to her family than she could have imagined. What had she been thinking? That Cole was just a lark, an easy shot in the arm of self-esteem? Other people—people she cared about deeply—had been hurt. She'd been selfish, foolhardy, all those things that mothers weren't supposed to be. Guilt as sharp as a blade cut through her.

It was Saturday, nearly a week since she'd texted Cole back. *Please leave me alone. I'm with my family. It's for the best.* She'd deleted all the texts he'd left before she blocked his number. She'd read each and every one of them, some twice, three times: *I miss you,* he wrote. *I can't sleep. My head's a mess. I know it's wrong but I can't help it. I'm in love with you.* The phrase *in love* jumped out at her, as if to underscore how ruthless she'd been to cast aside her marriage for someone who didn't even love her. Cole had a crush. She felt sad, guilty, tricked all at once.

She flipped over onto her stomach, resting her head on her arms, and felt the tears start again. How could she fix this? She'd never done anything so wrongheaded, so self-centered in her entire life. Tim had every right to be furious. Even if he wasn't the most helpful husband. Even if they hardly talked. Just because they'd had a rough year did not justify her kissing another man.

Of course, Jess hadn't meant to fall for Cole Wakefield. One night, she'd been working long hours at school, finishing up grant proposals and trying to keep her most troubled juniors on track for college. That evening, when she pulled into the driveway praying that she was home early enough to read the kids a story and tuck them in, Cole introduced himself. Actually, it was Gretzky, Cole's golden retriever, who introduced himself, racing over to the car and leaping on her as soon as she stepped out.

"Whoa, boy! Gretzky, get back here!" Cole shouted from the sidewalk.

Jess was momentarily stunned and dropped her briefcase, but she quickly regained her composure.

"I'm really sorry." Cole walked over to hook Gretzky's leash on his collar and jerked him away. "Usually he's better behaved."

"No worries," she said, laughing. "I think that's one of the best welcome-homes I've ever gotten. My kids might be right about us needing a dog." She picked up her briefcase and brushed off her suit. It was an unseasonably warm April evening, and Cole, dressed in tan shorts and a yellow-and-white striped polo shirt, looked as if he'd just stepped off the golf course.

She knew him well enough to say hello at the corner store. Unlike Maggie's neighborhood, where acres of rambling green grass separated the neighbors, in Jess's neighborhood, triple-deckers abutted other triple-decker homes. When they'd moved in, Tim had joked that he could reach out the kitchen window and touch their neighbors' house, which wasn't far from the truth.

Jess considered Cole to be friendly, hardworking, a diligent taker-out of trash. All valuable traits in a neighbor. Once in a while she would catch him sharing a glass of wine with a young woman on his front porch, and Jess would wave a quick hello, returning home from the corner market with a gallon of milk. The women appeared to rotate in quick succession.

Sometimes she would fantasize about Cole's life. Did he go out to the bars every weekend? Did he sleep with a different woman each night? Or was he as lonely as she had been before she met Tim and they'd started a family? She pondered such things when she was soaking in the tub late at night, the kids in bed and Tim watching sports on the television downstairs.

The night that Gretzky ambushed her, something made her invite Cole in for a beer. She realized they'd never asked him over for dinner, despite the fact that they'd lived on the same block for a few years. She suddenly felt unneighborly. She had no idea what he did for a living. When the kids saw the dog, they ran downstairs in their pajamas. Tim shot her a look from the top, as if to say, *What are you doing? I was just getting them into bed!* But she didn't care. She'd been hoping the kids would be awake.

After tuck-ins and kisses, she stepped out onto front porch, where the men were enjoying the lingering warmth of the day. The azaleas that framed the porch on either side exploded with purple, star-shaped blooms. Cole and Tim were engaged in easy conversation, cool drinks in hand, and Jess hesitated to interrupt, glad to see that her husband's initial icy welcome had melted into cordiality.

Gretzky lay at Cole's feet. She went inside to pour herself a glass of wine and rejoined them.

It was then that she learned Cole worked with special needs children at the local elementary school. It was challenging work, he said, but rewarding. It shocked her that this young, handsome man was devoting himself to something as noble as helping children. She'd assumed he worked in finance or real estate, like so many of the other young professionals in the neighborhood. From that night forward, an easygoing friendship evolved. Cole would join the family for an occasional barbecue, ribbing the kids about when they were going to get a dog. Grace was a little in love with him, Jess thought. But when she considered Cole's kind face, his ruffled sandy blond hair, his easy grin, she was proud that her daughter had such good taste in men. She hoped that one day Grace would marry a guy as solid as Cole.

And Cole was sweet to them, bringing the kids little gifts of candy, playing baseball in the yard, roughhousing with Teddy. Sometimes she imagined what it would be like if Grace and Teddy had a father like Cole. Tim would rather that the kids entertain themselves. When Grace was just five and Teddy two, Tim had told her he was relieved that they had each other to play with now. Jess supposed it was true enough, but it made her a little sad that her husband felt this way, as if he'd been sprung from the shackles of parenthood.

But then, as the days grew warmer, the tilt of their friendship shifted. Cole began dropping by more frequently, bringing with him the first harvest of cherry tomatoes from the small plot of land that doubled as his garden and backyard. At first Jess thought nothing of it. When May came and the school year began to wind down, she enjoyed his company on the nights when Tim worked late, reviewing accounts at his office. She would get the kids into bed, and then she and Cole would talk on the front porch till Tim's headlights danced in the driveway.

Occasionally, Cole would bring over a bottle of wine, coaching her on the importance of letting a red wine breathe in a wide-rimmed glass, and other things. She did not know, for instance, that Chardonnay was the name for the actual white grape used to make the wine. Wasn't aware that Viognier, a dry, floral-scented white wine, came from Virginia's official state grape. Such were the things that Cole taught her. It made her feel sophisticated. She thought he was cute, good-hearted, knowledgeable for someone so young. Eventually she began to look forward to his drop-bys, the anticipation sneaking up on her like a slumbering bat startled awake in an attic.

One night she'd been cleaning up the kids' dinner dishes when Cole leaned across the sink and kissed her, his lips still sweet from a sip of Cabernet. She hesitated at first, surprised. But then she kissed him back. She couldn't blame it on the few sips of wine she'd had. She wanted him. He drew her into his arms and kissed her some more, light little butterfly kisses around her ear, down her neck. Jess felt a stab of surprise; she hadn't known that kisses could be so intimate. Somehow, Tim's kisses always felt perfunctory. Cole worked his way back up her neck, to her lips.

When he pulled away, she brought her fingers to her lips. They tingled and felt swollen, as if from tiny bee stings.

"I'm sorry," he apologized. "I couldn't help myself."

She was torn between wanting to slap him and wanting to kiss him again. She backed away. His face clouded and he took a step back.

"Uh-oh," he said. "Did I misread the signals?"

She laughed. *Signals?* Did Jess even know what those were anymore? Did she know how to send one?

"Sorry. I wasn't aware I was sending them."

"Oh, shit. I feel like such an idiot." He started to turn, but she grabbed his hand in hers, still soapy with dish bubbles.

"No, wait. You just caught me off guard." He raised his eyebrows, which were thick and dark like caterpillars. He waited. She stepped toward him and leaned in. "I liked it," she whispered before pressing her lips against his.

Was it possible to fall in love in the span of three months? She didn't think so. And, if it *was* love, then she was intent on making herself fall out of love again. Her practical side told her that she could. *I miss you,* Cole had texted again and again.

It's over, Cole, she thought. *Please go.*

When she woke, bright pink bands circled her arms, delineating where a curtain of hair had fallen. Her hands, hidden by her hair while she slept, were pale by comparison.

"Oh, shoot!" She quickly sat up and pulled on her cover-up. She dug her watch out of her bag: 4:00. Asleep for almost two hours! Her head felt groggy and thick with the threads of half dreams, her face puffy from crying. She folded up her towel and began the trip back to the beach house. Would she be able to face her family again?

When she got to the house, Tim, Mac, and the kids were sitting on the deck playing Uno, as if nothing had happened. Arthur stepped out of the house and made his way to a wicker chair with a glass of iced tea. "Ouch," he said when he caught sight of her. "Looks like someone got a little sun today."

Everyone turned to look when she crossed the deck. "I fell asleep," she explained.

"It looks good, Mom," Grace said.

"Thanks, honey." Jess walked over and raked her fingers through her daughter's hair, a long tumble of snarls and knots. She would have never guessed that a few hours ago Grace was huddled in a corner, worrying about divorce. "Did you guys have a fun bike ride?"

"It was awesome," Teddy piped up. "Mommy, do you think Cole and Gretzky could come here tomorrow to swim?" She heard a noise escape from her husband, and her eyes darted to Tim. She felt as if she'd been punched. But Tim didn't look up. His hands gripped his cards in an angry little fan.

"Oh, buddy, I think Cole has to work." She tried to sound surprised by the request and convincing at once. *Did Teddy know, too?* She was panicking and went over to the railing to shake the sand from her towel, buying herself time, pretending her little boy hadn't just suggested that they invite her lover, her *ex*-lover, to the summer house. She flung the towel over the railing, her hands trembling.

"It would be so much fun, Mommy!" Teddy persisted. "Cole could sleep in the tent with us." The kids had all been begging to camp out in the front yard. This was her punishment, she thought. She deserved every little dagger her son unwittingly threw her way.

"Oh, honey. I'm sure Daddy would love to camp out with you guys. Right, Tim?"

"Please, Daddy, can we camp out in the tent tonight?" Teddy's focus shifted just as quickly. Forget about Cole and Gretzky. It was really the tent he was lobbying for.

"Sure, buddy," Tim said, still not lifting his eyes. Jess watched as a bright crimson crept up her husband's neck.

Her heart was banging in her chest. She needed to escape before any other little volcanoes erupted on the deck. "I'm going to go get cleaned up," she announced over her shoulder as she headed inside, but no one seemed to hear.

In the living room, Virgie sat on the couch, reading a book.

"Where's Maggie?" Jess asked. The back of her neck was sweating. Somehow Maggie would talk her down, make this all right. Jess had done something terrible. Even her son was picking up on her chemistry with Cole, as if he were a natural part of their family who belonged at the summer house. Had she forgotten she was a mom first?

Virgie shrugged without looking up. "The computer, maybe?"

Jess headed straight for the stairs. There was no time to waste. She needed to hear Maggie's advice. Needed to know what Maggie would do in her shoes. Of course, her twin would never cheat on her husband in the first place, but Maggie was good with these sorts of crises. As if they fueled her blood. She would set Jess on the right path. And, suddenly, Jess realized this was what she'd been hoping for this whole vacation. To confess her sins to Maggie. To, in some strange way, earn her sister's forgiveness. Once she'd heard from Maggie that what she'd done was terrible but not unforgivable, she would be okay.

And then she could focus on the work of getting her marriage back.

She stood outside the bedroom door. Her sister's back was turned to her. "Mags?" she called out. "I need to talk."

13

Maggie

After she slid the birthday cakes into the oven (they were having a little celebration for Arthur tonight), Maggie promised herself she'd only peek. Quickly. She knew it was crazy, but the idea had snuck into her head a few months ago. She'd been talking with the other moms at the playground one spring day while the kids whipped down the slide. Life was crazy; everyone was overwhelmed. But what was going to happen once their babies went off to kindergarten? they wondered aloud. "We'll finally have some time to ourselves!" her friend Kit joked. Maggie got that part—she looked forward to her freedom as much as the next person. But if she was being completely honest with herself, she also missed Luke's snuggles and baby coos, the warmth of a little body being rocked to sleep in her arms. "So, why don't you have another?" Kit asked.

"Not physically possible," Maggie said. In a rush to get into the world, Luke had arrived in a way that made a hysterectomy a necessity. "We're done."

"Oh," Kit said. "I'm so sorry. I didn't know."

Maggie waved her hand in the air as if it were no big deal.

"It's just that you're so *good* at it," Kit struggled to explain. "I mean, I watch you with Luke and your girls and you're a natural. You make it look so easy."

Maggie laughed, but she felt a twinge of recognition in Kit's words. She *was* a good mother. She loved playing and making fairy dresses and reading *Bedtime for Frances* a million times. What on earth would she do once everyone was in school?

"There are other ways, you know," Kit said, a lilt in her voice. "Like adoption or foster care?"

"Oh," said Maggie, right before yelling at Luke to stop climbing up the slide. "I suppose, though I don't think Mac would be into it."

"Why not?"

Maggie shrugged. "I don't know. I think he likes seeing little replicas of himself running around," she teased. "Seriously, though, I guess we've never really discussed it."

"Well," Kit said, "there are plenty of children who need someone to love them. Henry and I researched it when we had such a hard time getting pregnant with Sam."

"Really?" Maggie was shocked. She'd had no idea that getting pregnant had been an issue for Kit, one of those moms who always had a nutritious snack and an organic juice box at the ready.

They watched while Sam ran and flung himself belly-first onto a swing. "Of course, now that Sam's here, it's impossible to imagine our lives without him."

"Yeah, I know what you mean," Maggie said. She couldn't imagine their family without Lexie, Sophie, and Luke. They were all integral parts of the whole McNeil clan. But what had snuck up on her that day at the playground was that she *did* want another. Which took her by complete surprise. Because she felt as if she'd just crossed the finish line of the baby-toddler years. She'd somehow managed to usher all her children through their first years of life relatively unscathed, and it gave her a rush of accomplishment. *Look at how beautiful they were! How successful! How well adjusted* (well, she still had some work to do with Lexie). She had imposed order on the messiness of their lives. And now perhaps she and Mac could get some of their old life back—dinners out, nights at the movies with friends. They could hire a babysitter without endlessly worrying that one of the kids would be inconsolable until they got home.

And yet.

Maggie craved having another little one around. If not a baby, then a toddler. Luke was growing up so fast! Just once more, she wanted to nuzzle a small body against hers. To give love where it was needed. She thought back to a test she'd taken in college that matched her personality with careers. Every match that popped up for her involved helping others: nursing, teaching, mothering, social worker. "I guess you're a natural-born giver," the counselor had said with a hint of condescension. Now, while Maggie watched all the kids at the summer house, the longing was palpable. It was almost as if a phantom child was following her around.

She didn't know the first thing about foster care, but the faces, their expressions! Children of all ages gazed out at her from the screen, their enormous eyes begging her to take them. *Pick me!* they seemed to cry. She scrolled down and clicked on "Frequently Asked Questions." She learned that in Massachusetts, the average age for a child in foster care was eight, but that babies and toddlers were also looking for homes. She wouldn't mind skipping those first few sleepless months with a newborn, she thought. Perhaps there was a toddler in need of a family. Luke was so good with little kids, and Sophie was already like a second mother to him. Maggie loved the idea of expanding their family by one, of giving a home to a child who might not otherwise have one. "There are plenty of children who need someone to love them," Kit had said. She was right.

Maggie's thoughts were interrupted by the sound of footsteps on the stairs, and she quickly clicked off the site, her fingers trembling. She didn't want to get caught. There would be plenty of time to research foster care once Luke started kindergarten. She debated when would be the best opportunity to mention it to Mac, though. It should happen at the summer house, of that much she was sure. Here she had Mac's full attention. But when? Should she suggest a romantic dinner, just the two of them? Or should she try to sell the idea to the whole family at the risk of making Mac feel ambushed? She knew the kids would be on board, and if it were a boy, Luke might even want to share his bedroom. But she was getting ahead of herself.

"Mags?" She spun around in her chair. Jess stood in the doorway, looking as if she might have come down with a bad case of sunstroke. "I need to talk."

"Jessie, honey, what's wrong?" She got up and went to put her hand on her sister's back, guiding her to the bed.

"I'm a terrible person," Jess said and burst into tears.

Maggie felt herself pull back just a touch. "What do you mean?" She couldn't imagine Jess of all people—dear, practical, smart, caring Jess—doing anything terrible.

"I had an affair," she choked out between sobs. And, at that moment, the timer for Arthur's cakes went off in the kitchen.

The adults sat at the table, waiting for Arthur to make a wish. The double-chocolate cake dipped ever so slightly in the middle (Maggie had been a little late pulling it out, understandably so, she thought), but the seventy-two candles burned brightly. The kids were gathered around Arthur, their cheeks puffed, waiting for their grandpa to say "Blow!" Maggie would bet a hundred bucks she already knew her dad's wish: that Gloria would drop Gio and come back to him. She hoped, though, for Arthur's sake, that it was an entirely different wish. Perhaps to see the Galápagos Islands before he died. Maybe to learn how to scuba dive. Bucket list kinds of things. Those were appropriate wishes for a seventy-second birthday.

"Go!" Arthur shouted, and the whole gang blew.

"There's no question there's some spit mixed in with that," Tim said, prompting laughter.

Maggie shot Jess a look, but her sister was preoccupied plucking candles from the cake, her eyes still swollen from crying. *An affair.* So that was it, although technically Maggie wasn't sure it counted as an affair since no actual sex was involved. An affair of the heart. Maggie knew things were off between Tim and her sister, but another man? She would have never guessed it. Where on earth did her sister find the time?

She should be angry with Jess. *Herington sisters didn't cheat!* They were loyal to a tee. And, though she hated to admit it, a small part of her was hurt that Jess hadn't confided in her sooner. Didn't they share everything with each other, sometimes even before they told their husbands? Maggie worked to set aside her pride and consider the bigger problem. The way she saw it, Tim was at fault, too. It sounded as if he'd gone missing as a husband for the last year.

Maggie cut generous slices of cake, chocolate frosting dripping from the sides, and slid them onto festive little party plates. As she did so, she found herself sneaking looks at her sister. Jess was undeniably pretty, with soft brown hair and eyes that were almost black; it was no surprise that another man had swooped in. What Jess needed to do, Maggie recognized, was precisely what her sister had already done. Break things off with this Cole guy and focus on getting her marriage back. Tim might be a wet towel, but he was Jess's husband. He had his strengths, Maggie, of all people, found herself reminding her sister. In fact, he'd been downright solicitous and helpful this vacation. A pleasant surprise. Maggie had seen marriages in much worse shape rebound from the grave. If other couples could do it, Jess and Tim most certainly could salvage theirs.

And she'd told Jess as much, once she'd recovered from the shock of it all. "Okay, so you've done something wrong. Pretty awful, actually," Maggie counseled her. "But it's not the end of the world. For heaven's sake, it's not like you murdered someone!" She ran through a quick mental list of acts that would be worse but had difficulty coming up with much. Cheating on your husband was pretty bad. Still, it wasn't as if Jess had slept with the guy. There had been some kissing and groping, a few heart-to-heart talks. Why, it was practically a teenage romance!

"The important thing is that you've ended it. No more hanging out with this guy. You need to focus on Tim now. And your family."

Jess nodded.

"And I have to say, Tim's been a really good guy this vacation. He's been helping out and doing a lot with the kids."

"I know," Jess said, wiping her nose. "That's what makes the whole thing even more awful. It's like Tim is making this concerted effort to be a dad again, to be my husband again."

Maggie considered this. "Who knows? Maybe if he hadn't gotten jealous over Cole, he wouldn't have been so eager to get his act together."

Jess crinkled her eyes at her in surprise. Had Maggie really just suggested what she thought she had? That in some ways, Jess's wandering heart could be the wake-up call her sister's marriage needed? Thank goodness Maggie hadn't gone into psychiatry. She would have lost her license years ago.

She passed Arthur his piece of birthday cake. "Happy birthday, Dad!"

"How old am I again?" he asked.

She laughed, but Arthur stared at her with such a wondering look, she was caught off guard.

"Seventy-two!" Sophie shouted. "Do you feel wiser, Grandpa?"

Arthur shook his head. "Seventy-two. I am getting *old,* aren't I? And no, can't say I feel any wiser. A little balder maybe, but definitely not smarter."

"Grandpa's going to make a really cool trap for Roger," Luke said, as if compelled to point out that Arthur still had his wits about him.

"Who's Roger?" asked Mac.

"The raccoon, Daddy," Sophie explained.

"That's right." Arthur took another bite of cake. "We're going to get Roger, aren't we, kids?"

Teddy bobbed his little head with crisp, affirmative nods.

"Roger's a good name," said Mac. "I hope you hurry up and catch him, though, because he's making a mess of our yard." Roger had paid them visits the last two nights, strewing trash across the front lawn in unsightly heaps.

"Luke, honey, why don't you give Grandpa his present?" Maggie suggested now.

He jumped up from the table, disappeared into the kitchen, and returned with a gift in hand.

"Why, thank you." Arthur took the present from him and began to peel back the wrapping paper. "Holy smokes. Would you look at that?" He held it up for everyone to see. "My very own flat-screen TV."

The girls laughed. "It's an iPad, Grandpa!"

Arthur winked, pretending to play dumb. "An I-what?"

"Here, I'll show you," and before anyone could stop him, Luke ripped the computer out of his hands and ran to the couch with it.

"Luke, let Grandpa have a look," Mac scolded. "It's his present, right?" But the other kids had already joined him. Mac turned to Arthur apologetically. "Well, at least they can help you set it up. Just don't ask any of us adults."

"It's wonderful, but you shouldn't have," Arthur said with a laugh. "I'm an old man. I'm not sure I can learn new tricks."

"You're going to love it, Dad." Jess went over to give him a peck on the cheek. "Happy birthday, you old man." Maggie got up to do the same.

She cast around for Virgie. "Hey, where did Virgie go?" She and Jess began tossing the soggy plates into the trash.

"I think I saw her head upstairs." Tim stood to help clear the table, and Maggie felt a jolt of sadness hit her. Instead of angry, she felt sorry for her brother-in-law. It was an odd, unfamiliar sensation.

When Mac tossed the wrapping paper and candles into the trash, Arthur said, "Now hold on there," and fished the paper and candles back out of the bag. "You never know when you might be able to use these again." He folded the wrapping paper into a neat little square and placed the used candles on top. Maggie glanced at Jess, who shrugged.

"I'll check on Virgie," Maggie said and took the remainder of the cake out to the kitchen. She snapped the cover on the cake tray and grabbed the dirty kitchen towels for the laundry. *Yes,* she decided, as she climbed the stairs. *I'll tell Jess my plan for Operation Marriage Rescue.* Jess and Tim weren't beyond saving. Sometimes it took a lightning bolt to stoke the old flame. They simply needed time to talk, maybe a date night.

"Virgie?" she called at the top of the stairs. "We gave Dad his present." She couldn't believe her sister had missed it all.

She headed for the laundry room. When she passed the kids' bedroom, she tapped on the door. "Virg?"

She pushed lightly on the door and dropped the towels. There was Virgie. Lying on the floor, facedown, not moving.

14

Virgie

When Virgie opened her eyes, the first thing she saw was light. A bright white light. She thought, perhaps, she had died. She squinted, trying to focus, but it hurt too much. She closed her eyes.

"Virgie? Virgie, honey?" She could hear Maggie's voice above her. Maggie was in heaven, too? She tried to think. Had they been in a car accident?

"She's coming to. Thank heaven." That was Gloria. "Virgie, dear, can you hear us? Squeeze my hand, if you can."

Why was her mother giving her orders in heaven? Virgie wanted to know. Gloria had followed her all the way to the other side and she was still bossing her around.

She tried to say, "Mom, stop it," but the words wouldn't budge. When Virgie worked to move her lips, her throat burned.

Then Maggie's voice found her again. "Virgie, you fainted. You're in the hospital. The doctors are running some tests to make sure you're okay. Then we'll get you out of here." She felt her other hand being patted. "You just rest now."

Virgie tried to nod, but a sharp pain shot through her neck. "My neck," she managed to get out.

"Yes, you twisted it a little when you fell. It's going to be okay, though. Nothing's broken. Just a few bruises."

"What day is it?" she asked. She couldn't figure out how long she'd been in the hospital. Why was everyone in Seattle? She needed to get back to work!

"It's Saturday, honey. We were celebrating Dad's birthday, remember? You fainted. At the summer house."

At the mention of the summer house, Virgie felt a flash of recognition. *Oh, right.* A wash of warmth spilled over her. *Vacation.* She was on vacation. She didn't need to go to work today. Relief flooded her. But she was oh, so very tired. She heard the beeping of machines, then an unfamiliar voice.

"Time to check your vitals, honey." She felt someone take her arm and wrap a cuff around it, followed by a squeezing sensation. "Just a few minutes, and I'll be out of your way."

"Sure," said a gruff voice. Arthur's?

Man, she couldn't remember feeling this tired in a long, long time. If she could just nap for maybe fifteen minutes, she'd be better. She'd catch up with everyone then. Find out what their news was. She was sure they would understand.

When she woke the next time, the bright lights had faded. She willed her eyes to open, but the ceiling above her was gray. She heard snoring. She tried to turn her neck but felt a jab of pain. *Oh, right.* There was something about her neck. Her mouth felt like cotton. She desperately needed water. "Hello?" She tried to get the word out, but it sounded more like a squawk. Somewhere on the periphery, there was a shuffle.

"Virgie?" It was Maggie. She'd recognize that voice anywhere.

Her sister's face appeared above her. "You're awake. Oh, that's good, honey. That's very good. Here." She felt cold ice chips against her lips, and never in her life had ice tasted so delicious. She sucked and let the cold dribble down her chin. She struggled to push herself up in bed.

"Easy, there. Let me help you." Maggie reached for the pillows and fluffed them behind her so that Virgie was semi-upright.

Virgie raised her hand to her neck and fingered the scratchy brace around it. "Yeah, that's to help with your neck. You took quite a fall," Maggie said. "Obviously. Doctor said you'll probably need it for a few days."

Virgie raised her fingers a few inches higher and gently touched the area around her right eye. It was bruised, tender, and she could tell that her eye was swollen. The view through it was narrower, at about sixty percent of what it should have been.

"Here's some water." Maggie handed her a plastic cup. Virgie drank slowly, the water soothing her parched throat.

"Thanks. What happened?" she asked now, as her brain struggled to clear the cobwebs.

Maggie sat down next to her and furrowed her forehead into little lines. "You don't remember?" She put her hand on her sister's knee.

Virgie shook her head as much as she could.

"Well, you fainted. *Why* you fainted is a little less clear. The doctor thinks you were dehydrated. That plus too much sun and a glass of wine with dinner."

"Ah," Virgie said. "Right." She'd forgotten the wine. Was it one or two glasses she'd had with dinner? She tried to think. *Arthur's birthday party!* "Oh, no!" she said with a start. "I ruined Daddy's party."

"Don't worry about it," Maggie said. "We're just happy that you're all right."

It was starting to come back to her now. They'd had steaks on the grill and fresh asparagus. The kids had been fired up to give Arthur his present, an iPad. But Virgie couldn't recall her dad opening the gift. "Did Daddy get his gift?"

"Yeah," said Maggie. "He loved it. Opened it right before I found you on the bedroom floor."

"Oh." Virgie tried to think. She remembered going upstairs for something, but what had it been? Then she remembered: Arthur's birthday card. She'd wanted to give him a card just from her. And it was upstairs that she first noticed the world seeming to shift around her, as if the ground tilted one way while she went the other. It was a similar feeling to the one she'd experienced in Seattle when she tripped and sprained her thumb. And then one of her eyes had seemed to go momentarily blind. She reached out for the bedpost to balance herself, but she must have missed. *Well, clearly she'd missed.* Her face was a car wreck; she could feel it.

"Was there an ambulance?" She remembered nothing right after the fall.

"Yup. Lots of sirens and whistles. You gave us a good scare, but I think the kids kind of loved it. Teddy and Luke wanted to ride with you in the ambulance."

Virgie grinned, then stopped and groaned. Even her lips hurt. "You split your lip in the fall," explained Maggie. "No stitches, though."

Virgie closed her eyes. It hurt to think. "Where's everyone else? What time is it?"

"Mac and Tim stayed with the kids at the house. Mom and Dad were here but they just stepped over to the cafeteria for a cup of coffee. It's around ten o'clock, I'd say. Still Saturday."

"Jess?" Virgie asked.

"Ladies' room."

She nodded slowly. It was all she needed to know right now. The day, the time, everyone's whereabouts. What had happened. She was so tired. Exhausted. If she could just sleep a little more, she was sure she'd feel better. She closed her eyes and, ever so gently, drifted off to sleep.

15

Arthur

The next morning, Sunday, Arthur was peering out the window, drinking his coffee and thinking about Virgie, when he saw him. *The rascal!* There he was, his beady little eyes staring out from behind the mask, his paws raised as he chewed on a corncob he'd dug out of the trash. Arthur slammed down his cup on the counter and hurried out the front door.

"*Shoo!* Go on! Get out of here, you big rat!" he yelled, waving his arms. Roger scurried off behind the shed, and Arthur chased him, banging on the shed to scare him as far away as he could. He saw the flash of a ringed tail in the bushes. Already, the varmint had ransacked the trash can, despite Arthur's sealing the top with a bungee cord last night. They were surprisingly clever animals—he'd give them that. Maybe he'd try duct tape next.

He started back into the house, then stopped. Today was as good a day as any to start building a trap. He'd promised Luke they would. If they actually caught the bugger, they could drive Roger out to the woods, far, far away, and leave him. *Let him bother someone else.*

Arthur headed for his car parked behind the shed and began searching for any gadgets he might use. From the backseat, he pulled an
assemblage of things: a spool of wire, an old box, box cutters, an old
plate, some plastic grapes. He dragged it all out to the front yard.

"What are you doing?" Luke snuck up on him and Arthur
jumped.

"You scared me," he said and dropped back down on his knees.
"I was about to come find you. I thought we could start building a
trap for our friend."

"Roger?" Luke rocked back and forth on his toes, a move, Arthur
had noticed, his grandson did whenever he got excited. "We're going
to catch Roger today?"

Arthur shook his head. "I doubt today, but maybe tonight. Or
the night after that." He snipped a piece of wire and began attaching
a makeshift tripod to the bottom of the box. "I think I scared him
away pretty good this morning."

"Roger was here already?" Luke asked, his voice threaded with
disappointment.

"Yep, made quite a mess, too." Arthur pointed to the litter that
lay scattered across the grass. Corncobs, fish bones, coffee grinds. A
stinky, smelly heap. "Why don't you go in and grab a trash bag. Oh,
and some shiny tinfoil, too. We'll be needing that."

"Okay." Luke bounded up the stairs, letting the screen door slam
behind him.

Arthur chuckled to himself. "Guess everyone's up now."

Soon Luke returned with the other children in tow, and they
worked together for an hour. Arthur figured the trap was a welcome
distraction from the events of last night. He still couldn't believe that
Virgie had fallen over, *kerplunk!* The doctors had run some tests, and
for the most part, everything seemed fine. But Arthur didn't want
the kids to worry. This morning Gracie and Teddy had snuck in
from the tent to ask if Aunt Virgie was going to be okay. "Of course,"

he'd told them, pulling the covers back and making room for them in his bed.

Now Arthur measured a long string and handed Sophie the scissors for cutting. Next, he showed Lexie where to attach the string to the upside-down crate that would act as their trap. "See," he explained to the kids. "When the raccoon pulls on the corncob attached to this string, we've rigged it so that the crate will snap down." He demonstrated the box falling to the ground with a yank. "Gotcha!" Arthur shouted at the imaginary raccoon.

"Cool!" Luke exclaimed.

Grace and Sophie regarded him skeptically. "You really think that's going to catch him?" pressed Grace. The girl was preternaturally smart, so much so that Arthur found it a bit unnerving at times.

"You bet. Roger won't know what hit him. Then we'll take him to the woods and set him free."

Sophie furrowed her little eyebrows. "But he's not going to get hurt, right?"

Arthur rested his hand on the child's soft blond hair. *Like corn silk,* he thought. *And such different personalities!* "Don't worry, Soph. Roger's going to be just fine."

"I'm going to tell Mom that we're gonna catch Roger!" Luke raced back into the house.

Moments later, Maggie stood on the front porch, surveying their handiwork. "*That's* supposed to catch my raccoon?"

Arthur shrugged. "I know it doesn't look like much, but yes, it ought to do the trick."

She sighed and shook her head. "So long as it doesn't catch one of the kids instead." She turned and headed back inside. She looked weary. Last night had given them all a good scare. *But Virgie was all right,* Arthur reminded himself. The doctor had said so. Just wanted her to do a couple of little tests in Boston, and then she could be on her way. Arthur had seen a lot worse when the kids were little. When blood was involved, for example, or when Maggie had knocked out a tooth, or the time that Jess needed thirteen stitches on the back of her head after colliding with a coffee table.

The best thing was to let her rest. And keep the kids distracted.

At that moment, Mac and Tim appeared on the front steps, their golf bags slung over their shoulders.

"Care to join us?" Mac asked. "It's a beautiful day to hit the ball." He wore a Red Sox cap and a striped blue and white golf shirt. Tan pants and wingtip golf shoes. Tim was dressed similarly, though his pants were a wild checkered pattern.

Arthur grinned. "Aren't you fellas looking sharp? But no thanks. I'm going to hang around. Make sure Virgie's feeling all right. Do some swimming with the kids."

"Suit yourself, Grandpa." Tim headed for the SUV and loaded his clubs into the trunk. Arthur smarted ever so slightly to hear this particular son-in-law refer to him as Grandpa. He still hadn't gotten used to it.

"Thank you, I will. Have fun."

He gathered up the remaining parts of the trap project and headed for his car. The trunk was starting to resemble a squirrel's nest, and Arthur struggled to fit in even more. He leaned on the top, giving it all his weight, until at last he heard the latch click. When he got back inside, Gloria was sitting at the kitchen table, cradling a cup of tea.

"Good morning, Arthur."

"Gloria," he exclaimed. "I didn't see you come in."

"I didn't," she explained. "I slept over." Maggie leaned against the counter, and Arthur thought he detected a faint smile at the corners of her mouth.

"Yeah, Mom slept in Virgie's room last night to play nurse. Sorry, I thought you knew."

Arthur glanced from his daughter to his ex-wife and back again. "No, I did not. But that's very nice of you."

"I'm her *mother*," Gloria said, as if that one word explained everything, her rights to the situation and, by extension, Arthur's subordinate role. Was there judgment in her voice? Arthur thought so but decided to push forward.

"So, how's the patient doing?" He helped himself to a cup of coffee.

Maggie and Gloria exchanged looks. "Oh, she's fine," Gloria said. "Just a little sore. Bruised her ego more than anything else, I'd say."

Arthur sipped, considering. "What a shocker, huh? One minute she's up and fine and the next minute she's lying facedown on the floor."

There was another look exchanged between the women. "What? What aren't you two telling me?"

"Nothing." Maggie turned and traced a crack in the countertop with her thumb.

"What is it?" Arthur set down his cup and held up his hands, as if in surrender. Streaks of grease from the trap building project ran along his fingers, and he went to the sink to wash them.

"Nothing, it's just that the doctor got us thinking, you know, a little worried about what might have caused her to black out like that," Maggie said, stepping out of his way.

Arthur turned on the tap and scrubbed. "I thought he said she was dehydrated from the sun. Add a glass or two of wine, and presto, you're down like a fallen tree."

Gloria studied her hands, which were freckled with sun spots. She pushed her wedding band up and down her ring finger. Arthur had noticed she'd moved it onto her right hand after the divorce. Still, it gave him some smug satisfaction that she continued to wear it, a vindication that forty-six years of marriage counted for *something*. He wondered for a moment if it made Gino uncomfortable. *Gio,* he corrected himself.

"You're probably right," she said. "Let's hope that's all it was. Too much sun and wine."

"What?" he persisted. "Do we think Virgie has a drinking problem again?" If pressed, he'd have to admit he'd been wondering the same thing himself over Christmas at Maggie's. Every so often his youngest daughter would slur her words or knock into something. But he decided to chalk it up to general clumsiness. Virgie, arguably his most striking daughter, could also be ungraceful. She was tall, ungainly occasionally. So what?

"No, no, no," Gloria tsked, as if he were indelicate for even raising the topic.

"Well, then, tell me, please. Because I'm confused. What are we talking about here?"

Maggie eyed the stairs. "The CT scan," she whispered.

"What about it? The doc said she was fine."

"Right," Maggie said nodding, as if willing it to be right. "But he said there were some slight shadows. Probably nothing, but what if it's that other thing he mentioned? You know, MS?"

Gloria coughed and held her hand to her mouth.

"Oh," said Arthur. He hadn't given that part of the doctor's report much thought. The doctor was young, probably thirty-five, and a Cape Cod doctor at that. Not to be dismissive, but how much could the fellow know? Arthur hadn't taken him too seriously. "I doubt that it's anything to worry about. I'm sure he was just covering his bases. You know how they are these days. They have to tell you that you could die of six different things so they don't get sued. It's all a bunch of baloney—"

"But, Daddy," Maggie interrupted. "*Something's* not right." Her brow was knitted in worry. "And I've been looking online. A lot of the symptoms of MS could describe Virgie." Gloria tugged at a cuticle.

"Well, that's why she can get it checked out in Boston. Make sure."

Maggie rolled her eyes. "Like Virgie's going to stick around for that. She's headed back on a plane a week from today. You know her, it's all about work and ratings."

"Gloria?" He turned to his ex-wife. "What do you think?"

She folded her hands and lifted her eyes. "I'm concerned. I won't lie. Maybe she just got a little concussion from the fall, but I do think she should get it checked out. Maggie and I have been talking, and she doesn't think Virgie seems like herself."

"Huh." Arthur tried to think. Did his favorite daughter—because let's be honest, everyone knew he had a soft spot for Virgie—seem different to him? Just because he thought she might be sneaking some drinks on the side didn't mean she suddenly had a serious diagnosis, did it? "How so?" he asked.

"C'mon, Dad," said Maggie. "Don't pretend you haven't noticed. She's acting weird, even by Virgie standards. She's slurring her words, she seems to search for the right word sometimes. She keeps testing her balance."

In an odd way, Arthur thought Maggie could be describing him. He'd worried himself that one of them would call *him* on his recent memory problems. The fact that they hadn't made him feel better—it was just typical old age, nothing to be concerned about. "Still, that doesn't mean there's something wrong with her," he said now. "And it most certainly doesn't mean she has multiple sclerosis." Hearing these words sent a stitch through his heart. His grandmother had suffered from MS.

At that moment, they heard footsteps on the stairs. "Jess?" he asked quietly.

"No." Maggie shook her head. "She's watching the kids outside."

"Ah." Arthur hadn't noticed the relative quiet in the house till now.

At the bottom of the stairs stood Virgie, her auburn hair tousled around her face and a deep purple bruise ringing her right eye. A clunky brace circled her neck. She wrapped her arms around herself. "Hi, everyone."

"Oh, honey." Gloria rushed to her side. "You poor thing. Come sit down." She led Virgie to the table. "How are you feeling?"

"My head hurts. And my neck. I could use some of those heavy-duty ibuprofen pills."

Maggie checked her watch. "Sure, you got it. You haven't had any for six hours. You're due." She hurried to grab the prescription bottle from the upstairs bathroom and returned to hand her sister a glass of water with the pills. "I'm so sorry, Virg. What a rough night. Did you get any sleep?"

Virgie took the pills and swallowed. "Yeah, funny enough, I slept like a log, except for the times Mom woke me."

"Sorry, honey," Gloria said. "Doctor's orders. Every two to three hours."

Virgie turned to Arthur. "Sorry to ruin your birthday party, Daddy."

Arthur went to give her a hug. "Don't worry about it, sweetie. I'm just glad you're okay. You certainly made it a *memorable* birthday." They all laughed uneasily.

"Can I fix you some breakfast?" Maggie asked. "Maybe some eggs? Toast?"

Virgie shook her head. "No thanks. I'm not hungry. Juice maybe?"

Arthur struggled to remember if Virgie had been awake when the doctor revealed his concerns to them. She must have been, but would she even recall Doogie Howser's mention of the CT scan? Probably not.

"You know what's funny?" she asked when Maggie set down a glass of cranberry juice. "I remember thinking in the hospital that I needed to get back to work. That they were going to be mad at me. How crazy is that? That the first thing I think of is work?" She sipped her juice.

"That's the sign of someone who's *over*worked," Maggie offered. "Have you called Jackson yet?"

"No." A smudge of juice hovered above her lip, a faint crimson ribbon. "Not yet. I will later today. I don't want him to worry."

"From what you've told me about him, I think he'd want to know," said Maggie. "Being a nurse and all . . ."

"I know, Sis." Virgie held up her hand. "I'll get to it." She was quiet for a minute, then laughed. "Ouch." She touched her lip. "Aren't I a vision? I nearly fell over when I saw myself in the mirror this morning."

"I still can't believe we didn't hear you fall," said Jess, joining them now.

"I *thought* I heard something—" Maggie began.

"Yeah, it's comforting to think about," Virgie interrupted. "Your family helping out in times of crisis. . . . You guys were eating *cake* while I was passed out upstairs."

Maggie and Jess exchanged guilty glances, then laughed. "We're sorry," said Maggie, trying to stop. "It *is* a little funny, if you think about it."

Virgie smiled despite herself. "Frickin' hilarious. Well, if you'll excuse me, I think I'll head back up. My head's still hurting."

"Of course." Maggie gripped her by elbow. "Here, let me help you."

As they made their way upstairs, Jess eyed Arthur, then Gloria. "Ouch. That looks pretty painful. Do you think she's okay?"

"Time heals all wounds," said Gloria, but Arthur thought even his ex-wife sounded unmoved by her own mantra, one she'd recited hundreds of times when the girls were young.

The next day, after he'd gone swimming with the kids, Arthur headed back to the house to invite Gloria in for a dip. She could probably use a break, he thought, from playing nurse. But when he walked into the house, his trunks slightly dripping, there sat Gio on the couch (*his* couch, Arthur's bed!) doing a crossword, his little loafer tassel bobbing up and down.

"Hello, there. Have a nice swim?" Gio smiled at him.

Before Arthur could answer, Gloria drifted into the room, wearing one of those long summer skirts she'd been so fond of lately. She was a vision in yellow, an angel.

"Oh, Arthur. Those grandkids are so happy to have you around. You're such a good grandpa." She sat down beside Gio and patted his leg, smiling up at Arthur.

He was taken aback for a moment and shifted from foot to foot as he considered Gloria's compliment, his dripping trunks, and how to get Gio off his couch. "Thanks. They're a good bunch," he settled for. "Gio, you might want to try the other couch," he suggested while he made for the stairs. "It's really much more comfortable."

Upstairs, Arthur couldn't change out of his bathing suit fast enough. *This was not the vacation he'd been bargaining for!* He could be expected to tolerate only so much. Gio and Gloria might as well move in for the week. Perhaps Arthur should be the one to get a hotel room!

After he found his glasses ("Need these?" Maggie had asked, holding up his wire-rims with a quizzical look. "They were in the fridge."), Arthur decided to head into town. A walk would do him good. He'd pick up the mail and a few things at Sal's. They were almost out of milk.

When he got downstairs, he heard Gloria yell, "*Resplendent!* That's got to be it. Another word for *wonderful*. Write it in, honey. R-E-S-P-L-E-N-D-E-N-T." As if Gio weren't sitting right next to her. On Arthur's couch. Arthur let the screen door slam behind him. *Let them do their crossword! See how far they get,* he thought. When he and Gloria used to solve the *New York Times* Sunday acrostic, they would time themselves. He bet Gio didn't even know what *acrostic* meant. It was only a matter of time, he thought wickedly, before

Gloria grew bored with her little friend. Poor man didn't even know how to spell *resplendent*.

Arthur remembered to double-check his pockets for his wallet (*yes, still there*) and started into town, feeling slightly better about things. As the path took a sharp turn to the right, he came upon one of those lending library hutches, where a person could take a book in exchange for leaving another. Arthur liked the concept of the thing. They had them back home in Maine, too. This one sat atop a thick wooden post and resembled a birdhouse with glass doors. He walked up closer and pulled open the little doors. Usually, he found a bunch of romance novels, though every once in a while he'd discover a thriller or mystery. In the rare instance when he took a book, he promised himself he'd leave one another day. Of course, he never did. When he opened the glass doors today, however, he took in a sharp breath.

There, wedged between the mysteries and romances, was a familiar title. *Fatal Faults,* the tenth book he'd written. He remembered the number exactly because his publisher had thrown a lavish party in Manhattan to commemorate his ten-book anniversary. Buckets of champagne, bouquets of balloons, a toast by the publisher. Gloria by his side. As he sipped expensive champagne, Arthur told himself that he must remember this moment, *the taste of success*. It felt like a million years ago.

The publisher had put them up at the Ritz-Carlton, where dapper men in black top hats opened the door and exquisite paintings lined the lobby. In their suite, he and Gloria marveled at the miniature cans of macadamia nuts arranged in a neat row on the cherry credenza. In every room there was a vase of fresh flowers (purple irises, if he remembered correctly), and a telescope at the window that focused on the lush sweep of Central Park. *Frederick Law Olmsted designed it,* Gloria read from the hotel's brochure. *Wasn't he the same guy who designed Boston's Emerald Necklace?* Arthur remembered thinking how lucky he was to be married to a woman who could retrieve a piece of knowledge like that on a whim. The day after the publishing party, they'd shared frozen hot chocolates at Serendipity 3.

Now he was lucky if his editor remembered to send him a copy of his own book. And here in the woods was a battered paperback of *Fatal Faults* for the taking. For goddamned free. He slammed the glass doors shut. Like a child, he kicked the post, a sharp pain shooting up from his foot to his knee.

If discovering his book in a lending library in the middle of a thicket didn't sum up his entire career, he didn't know what did.

He kept walking. His throat was burning. He cursed himself for forgetting to bring along a water bottle. At last, the post office with its blue shutters and white brick façade came into view. He supposed he could buy a book of stamps as well. The kids might want to send postcards to their friends.

Arthur knew that having both Gloria and him on the Cape at the same time had his eldest daughter on edge. He felt bad about that. But really, what could he do? It wasn't as if he'd told Gloria to come early. He'd had his time at the summer house scheduled months ago with Maggie, penciling in his vacation at the library. Unlike his ex-wife, Arthur had an employer (well, technically, a volunteer position) to answer to, not to mention a pending deadline for a book. He wasn't about to upend his vacation plans just because Gloria had decided to come early.

The path met up with the sidewalk, already shimmering in the late-morning heat. Arthur climbed the stairs to the post office and mopped the sweat from his forehead with a handkerchief. The mail, what there was of it, he pulled from the slender metal box and tucked under his elbow. For so early in the day, the line for stamps was surprisingly long, but Arthur took his place at the end.

He hated lines.

He fidgeted from foot to foot, looking about, searching for details that he might work into his writing. But there wasn't much around to get the old wheels spinning. A wooden shelf for writing labels, an assortment of padded packages for purchase, a display of the latest stamp collections available. He helped himself to a few brochures about updates to the U.S. postal system. You never knew when that kind of information might come in handy.

He noticed a poster highlighting new commemorative stamps available. Musicians like Miles Davis and Ray Charles. Artists worth remembering and listening to again and again. He didn't suppose *their* records showed up in any lending libraries along walking trails. He could listen to Billie Holiday, one of their contemporaries, sing "The Very Thought of You" a million times and never get sick of it. It had been their wedding song. Every time he heard it, he'd picture himself twirling Gloria, his arms held out, as if he were still embracing her.

The line inched forward, and eventually a moonfaced young man peered out at him, interrupting his thoughts. "What can I get for you today, sir?"

"A book of stamps, please. The Miles Davis ones." Arthur tapped his fingers impatiently on the counter. He wondered if this guy even knew who Miles Davis was. If he could name a song by him. It was an outrage how little the next generation knew about music, about art. He'd have to remember to make another donation to the local arts program at the high school when he got home. Something that would make a difference. Maybe a check for five hundred dollars.

He was about to ask the clerk who his favorite jazz musician was, but the melody of "The Very Thought of You" traveled over the intercom. *Their song.* He cleared his throat and said, "Thank you," his voice unsteady, as the young man handed him his stamps and change. On the edge of his vision, Arthur thought he caught a flash of a white dress, a ball gown, a hint of blond hair. He turned toward it, but there was no one there. Just a long line of restless people trailing behind him. He slipped the change and stamps into his pocket and once again gathered up his mail bundle. He was mad at himself for forgetting to bring his satchel. It would have made the journey home so much easier.

Arthur stepped out into the bright light of day. He could feel his shirt sticking to his back. He hoisted the mail higher under his arm and set out for home, forgetting all about the groceries he'd meant to pick up at the store.

16

Virgie

It was Wednesday, Crazy Trivia Night at Grouchy Ted's, and Virgie needed a drink. That, and she needed to get out of the house.

Yeah, yeah, yeah, she said, when Maggie warned her she didn't think it was a good idea. "It's only been a few days since your fall," she scolded. "You should be resting!"

But Virgie pointed out that she didn't even need her painkillers anymore. Her neck was feeling much better (she'd shunned the horrid neck brace), and while her purplish bruise had turned to more of a yellow-gray, a little makeup went a long way to cover it. If she spent one more hour cooped up inside, her head would positively explode. Besides, Sal had promised he'd meet her at Grouchy Ted's and be her official chaperone.

Yesterday she'd called Jackson and told him what happened. She didn't want him to worry.

"Well that's easier said than done," he said. "Should I fly out?" She liked the way he took charge, didn't hesitate to offer to help. But, no, she'd declined and said it wasn't necessary. *Again!* What was the matter with her? Would it kill her to graciously accept help once in a while?

The thing was, she couldn't get past the feeling that having Jackson there would mean *more* work for her, not less. She'd feel compelled to introduce him around, take him to the beach, impress him with this world that was dear to her. And she didn't think she had it in her right now. Nor did she want to hear what her sisters might have to say about him, even if it was all good. No, having Jackson nurse her back to health while her entire family watched was a decidedly *bad* idea. As much as she would love a hug from him. As much as she would relish him lying beside her, his arms wrapped around her.

Maggie and Gloria had been nagging her about seeing the specialist in Boston, coaxing her to go *just to be on the safe side*. The ER doctor had already arranged the follow-up appointment at MGH (*squeezed her in,* he'd said), but Virgie was reluctant to go. It seemed an unnecessary hassle. She would check back with her regular doctor in Seattle. The ER doctor had diagnosed a slight concussion. Even he'd said it was unlikely that MS was the culprit for her blacking out. Nothing time wouldn't heal. She chose to forget about it. At least for tonight.

When she stepped into Grouchy Ted's, the familiar scent of beer and peanuts washed over her. She breathed in. *This* was summer, she thought. *Her summer.* As she headed for the bar, her sandal landed on something hard. When she lifted her foot to check the sole, she discovered a stray peanut shell. Well, she had to hand it to Ted—he'd kept the place classy as ever. She shook it off and scanned the room, trying to make out the faces through the dim light. Rascal Flatts's "Life Is a Highway" played, and the crowd chanted along, drunk and off-key. Apparently, the trivia announcer was taking a break. Finally, Virgie saw Sal sitting at the bar, talking with a handful of friends.

"Hiya, pretty lady," he said as she sidled up to him. "I saved you a seat." He pushed one of his buddies off a barstool and wiped it clean with the back of his sleeve.

"Thanks," she said as Sal gave her a tiny kiss on the cheek. Then, "Sorry" to the guy whose seat she'd just stolen.

"How're you feeling?"

"I've been better," she said and raised her finger for the bartender. "Coors, please."

"Well, you sure look better than you did the other day," Sal said and threw back the rest of his beer. On Monday, he'd appeared at the house with pints of ice cream from the local creamery. "Ambrosia," Virgie said and bowed her head, taking the cartons from Sal. "Nectar of the gods." While the men took the kids fishing, Virgie and her sisters had gathered up spoons and devoured strawberry, butter pecan, then chocolate straight from the cartons. It felt like old times, lounging around in their pajamas, sprawled out on the bunk beds, and talking about nothing.

"Thanks, again, for the ice cream," she said now. "It was the perfect get-well present. Those pints work pretty well as ice packs, too."

Sal grinned and locked eyes with her. His eyes were a warm brown, familiar and kind. His reddish blond mop of hair was soft to the touch. She knew this already. She traced his square jawline with her finger, then stopped herself and looked away. Sal was her good friend. He didn't deserve to be led on. He deserved to know there was someone else.

The bartender set the beer down in front of her. "Start a tab?" he asked.

"It's on me," Sal said. "And anything else the lady wants tonight."

"You got it." The bartender thwacked the counter with his wet bar towel, and Virgie jumped.

"Whoa," said Sal, catching her. "A little edgy, huh?"

She laughed and settled herself back down before hoisting her drink in the air. "To old friends," she said.

"To *good* friends," he added. *Well, okay,* she thought. She could drink to that.

Virgie swiveled on her stool to survey the bar. The place was better in the off-season, she thought. Less crowded, fewer sketchballs waiting in the wings. Since she could remember, Grouchy Ted's had been the local watering hole, and on more than a few Thanksgiving weekends, she and her sisters had gotten blasted here. She couldn't recall much about those nights, though she was pretty sure Sal factored into a few. A couple of the waitresses Virgie had known when they were teenagers, back when they'd all gone skinny-dipping near the lighthouse. Except now they were wives with husbands, a few kids.

Still, she considered Grouchy Ted's their place (as in the *Herington girls'* place) as much as anyone else's. Usually, after a few drinks, everyone was friends again (and Ted was infamous for turning a blind eye whenever the bartender slid an occasional shot across the bar to a waitress). The wide-planked pine floors that sloped toward the back, the weathered bar counter studded with multiple glass ringlets, the dingy mirrors lining the top half of the walls, the tables with their red-and-white check tablecloths, even the occasional stray peanut shell—all of it said *home* to her.

"Virginia!" her mom shouted, waving from a corner table. Virgie nearly fell off her stool again. There were her mom and Gio, apparently hamming it up at trivia night. She knew that Arthur, Mac, and Tim would be in as soon as they parked the car. Maggie and Jess had volunteered to stay home with the kids tonight (though frankly Virgie thought Maggie was staging her own little protest over Virgie's going out; and, as far as she could tell, Jess and Tim were barely speaking to each other). From the glossy look on her mother's face, Virgie guessed that Gloria had already tied on a few. She was in a flouncy pink skirt and an orange, ruffled top with a plunging neckline. There was a hint of the Caribbean to her outfit, and Virgie found herself wondering again if her mother was consulting a new stylist or if she just didn't give a damn about the way she looked anymore. Her wardrobe was beginning to seem positively cruise-worthy.

"Hi, Mom," she said, after she'd wound through the crowd to her table. Gloria stood up to hug her, then patted the empty space next to her on the bench to sit.

"How're you feeling, honey?"

"Okay," Virgie said, scooting in beside her. She couldn't entirely lie to her mom, who had returned to her B&B only yesterday after playing nurse. Virgie's head still hurt, though nothing like a few days ago. "Hey, Gio."

"Glad you're feeling better," Gio shouted over the din.

Virgie nodded. When her cell vibrated in her jeans pocket, she assumed it was Sal; texting her from across the room and telling her to hurry back. But it was Jackson. *Whatcha doing?* Goose bumps popped up on her skin. *Nothing. Hanging out at Grouchy Ted's,* she texted back. *Sounds like a fun place!* he wrote. She grinned. *Not as much fun as if you were here.* Jackson wrote back: *Aww. I miss you.* Her fingers tapped. *Me, too. Not much longer till I get to see you. Xoxo.* She waited for his sign-off: *Can't wait. Have a good night. And take it easy!—J*

When she glanced up, Arthur and the rest of the gang had materialized at the front door. Her dad stared in their direction. How was it that he could still pick her mother out of a crowd? Perhaps that's what happened after forty-six years of marriage: it was as if your spouse carried around a little black box that emitted sound waves that only you could detect, particularly in areas of danger.

Mac appeared to be taking drink orders and set off for the bar while the rest of their group, Virgie realized with a pinch of dread, was now headed directly for their table. She couldn't abide more small talk, pretending they were all just one big happy family. The whole thing was getting too weird. She'd left the house to *escape* the family drama tonight. She certainly wasn't going to sit here and listen to Arthur and Gio struggle to be civil to each other.

During the past few days, Jess had paid frequent visits to Virgie's bedside, updating her on the various dramas playing out downstairs—Gio being her mother's toady, Arthur taking subtle jabs at Gio, and their mom reveling in all the attention. It was, after all, what Gloria did best. Virgie shuddered to imagine it. Maggie had probably been caught between runs to the fridge for Gio, to the liquor cabinet for Arthur's scotch, and to the medicine cabinet for Virgie's ibuprofen. Add a few kids to the mix, and her überorganized big sister was likely on the verge of a nervous breakdown.

Virgie didn't necessarily want to see Maggie fail, but *the idea of it,* of her sister falling apart as her perfect little world at the summer house spun out of control, was just a little bit amusing. It would be nice for once to see that even her big sister couldn't sew everything neatly back together.

Yes, Virgie had come out tonight to *get away* from the madhouse that Pilgrim Lane was turning into. One more plaintive look from Arthur to Gloria and Virgie was going to lose it. One more terse exchange between Jess and Tim (*and what the hell* was *going on between those two, anyway?*) and the whole house might erupt. And frankly, Maggie's Florence Nightingale routine was starting to wear on Virgie's patience, too. What she needed was a good ol' night of fun. Drinking, dancing, and kicking up her heels. Sal would provide that. She wasn't going to feel guilty about having fun with an old friend.

She pulled herself away from the group and breezed past Arthur and Tim. "Hi, guys." She gave a little wave and pointed in Sal's direction. "Gotta get back to Sal," as if that explained why she would not be joining them tonight. She grabbed Sal's hand and pulled him onto the dance floor. "C'mon!" she yelled over the music. It was Depeche Mode. How could they *not* dance to Depeche Mode? The band had

had as big a hand in defining her teenage years as big hair, acne, and lip gloss.

"Are you sure you're okay to dance?" Sal leaned in to ask.

Virgie rolled her eyes. "I am," she said, shouting into his ear, "so sick of everyone asking me if I'm okay. Just please stop for the next few hours," she pleaded.

Sal pulled his head back and watched her. She noticed that his hands had shifted to her waist and his fingertips softly tapped to the beat of the music. "Okay, Virginia. I think I can manage that."

"God bless you," she said. Sal smiled his earnest, good-guy smile, right before he dipped her to the sticky, salty floor. It felt like heaven.

17

Maggie

Maggie was distraught. Her entire world was on spin cycle, like when she threw a bathroom rug in the washer and the whole thing went off-kilter, thumping and bumping until the machine had traveled a foot across the floor. When that happened, she would ask Mac to shimmy the washing machine back into place. No harm done. But life was so much more complicated.

What a fool she'd been to think that this summer would be like summers past! She should have switched the QUE SERA, SERA sign to one that read ENTER AT YOUR OWN PERIL.

She was embarrassed by her mother's overtures toward Gio and her seeming inability to sense when she was making Arthur uncomfortable. Or perhaps Gloria knew full well the strength of her powers and didn't care. Maggie wouldn't put it past her. Gio was *awkward*—there was no other word for it. He didn't belong at the summer house. He acted more like her mother's porter.

Then there was Virgie, who couldn't seem to care less about her medical condition (for that's how the doctor had referred to it: *a possible medical condition*). Was it denial? Or was Maggie overreacting? When she asked Mac, he told her it was Virgie's business. But, honestly, what could her sister be thinking? Going out drinking only a few days after her fall? And then there was Jess, who clearly needed to get the burden of cheating off her chest and whose marriage was evidently in trouble. When Maggie broke the news to Mac, he hadn't been nearly as surprised—or judgmental—as Maggie. "Tim's a better guy than you give him credit for," Mac said. "He'll get over it. I'm sure his pride is just a little wounded, that's all." All these worries, and that was without even *touching* upon Arthur, who appeared to grow more absentminded by the minute.

"Haven't you noticed?" she asked Mac in the privacy of their bedroom. "Something's off with Dad."

"Oh, honey." Mac sighed. She was wearing him out with her constant fretting, she could tell. "I love that you want to help everyone in your family, to make things right, but sometimes you just have to let people live their lives. Arthur's not getting any younger. I'm sure some of what you're seeing is plain old age."

"No, that's not it," Maggie insisted. "There's something wrong. Like he's forgetting things. And I don't just mean the window. The other day he left his glasses in the refrigerator!" She was propped up on her elbow, staring at the tiny red hairs sprouting from Mac's chin.

"Old age. People lose their glasses all the time."

"But in the refrigerator? Next it will be the microwave."

"Well, that would be an interesting science experiment, wouldn't it? Bet the kids would enjoy that one."

"Mac, this isn't funny. I don't think you're taking me seriously."

"Oh, I'm taking you seriously, all right," he said and pulled a loose strand of hair behind her ear. "Just not as seriously as you'd like me to, maybe."

"C'mon. You're a cop." She was growing annoyed. "You spend

your life looking for clues. Don't you think there's something suspicious about Dad's behavior?"

He held up a finger. "First of all, my job is not nearly as interesting as you make it out to be. Second of all, Dad's getting a little dotty in his old age. So what? He's still writing books, isn't he? He's still building raccoon traps."

Maggie clicked her tongue. "Yeah. Like *that's* going to catch anything. And then the other day . . . " She paused. She wasn't quite sure how to describe it. "I was putting folded laundry on top of his suitcase, and I found this old trash bag sitting by the couch. I thought someone had forgotten to take it out from the night before, but when I went to throw it out, Dad nearly took my head off. Said it was stuff he was collecting. He had his birthday candles in there and some other junk—mostly rocks and shells and, well, trash to be perfectly honest." She traced little circles on the sheets with her index finger.

"And that upsets you?" Mac asked. "That's just further evidence that the apple doesn't fall far from the tree." Maggie sighed. Maybe her husband was right. She *had* been on everyone's case about recycling their plastics and glassware this summer. Who was she to point a finger?

"So, aren't you going to tell me about Lexie?" Maggie had been dying to hear. Mac and Tim had spent all day with the kids out on the boat, and when they got back, Mac told her he knew a secret about their daughter. Her mind raced with the possibilities: an eating disorder? As far as she could tell, Lexie was still eating all her favorite foods, but maybe she was bulimic. Maggie had read somewhere that bingeing and purging could start as early as ten. Nothing was beyond her worry zone.

"Lexie has a boyfriend."

"What? You're joking." Maggie shook her head. It wasn't possible. Lexie wasn't even *interested* in boys. Every time Maggie brought it up, her daughter made a retching sound. "How do you know?"

"Lexie was texting on the boat and I took her phone away from her," Mac said. "When I read her texts, I saw they were from some guy named Matt."

Maggie's mouth dropped open. If she had done such a thing, Lexie would have refused to talk to her for weeks, maybe months. Such an invasion of privacy was unthinkable. "What did she do? Mutiny?"

"Not quite. There was lot of yelling, but eventually she recovered. Thank goodness we were in the middle of the ocean." Mac was grinning now. This was classified information worth millions, and he knew it.

"No wonder she's been moping around here," Maggie exclaimed. "She's heartsick. All for a little eleven-year-old boy named Matt. That's so sweet."

She leaned back on her pillow. "Wow. And to think I never saw it coming."

"I know." Mac grinned and wrapped his arms around her. "With all the worrying you do, you'd think you would have picked up a bleep on the radar."

"It's this house," Maggie said and smoothed the sheets over her. "I can't keep track of everyone's problems. Maybe if I had my flow-charts back home . . ."

But Mac was holding a finger over her lips, shushing her. "That won't be necessary."

"You don't think?" Maggie asked in all seriousness.

"Don't you know," he said, kissing her softly, "there are other ways to relax?"

After they made love, she drifted off, but a bang downstairs startled her awake. Maggie struggled to place the noise in her half sleep. Was someone knocking on the front door? Maybe one of the kids (they were all now sleeping in the tent) needed to use the bathroom. Then her mind flashed to Virgie. Of course. Virgie was home from the bar and locked out. Probably drunk, she'd forgotten they left the side door open at night.

Maggie stood up and wrapped her robe around herself. Mac snored, fast asleep.

She hurried downstairs and flicked on the porch light. When she saw who was standing on the front porch, she inhaled sharply. Gloria and Gio.

"Mom, what's going on?" Maggie asked as she pulled open the door. Gio was holding their suitcases. "I'm so sorry to bother you, honey, but a pipe burst at our B and B and they've evacuated the whole house. Would it be too much trouble for us to crash here? It's just for tonight." Maggie studied her mother for a moment. Her mascara was blurred in dark half-moons beneath her eyes, and her blond hair stuck up in messy tufts.

Jess came up behind Maggie. "What's going on?" Maggie could feel her carefully constructed house of cards tumbling down around them.

"Oh, nothing," Maggie pronounced with false cheerfulness. "Mom and Gio can't stay at their inn tonight, so they're going to crash here." She willed herself to open the door wider. "Come on in, Mom. It's your house after all." Maggie hoped the words would encourage her feet to move out of the way.

"Thank you, honey." Gloria snaked around her, Gio following behind.

From the living room, Arthur called out: "Maggie, is everything all right?"

They froze, four deer caught in the headlights. "It's fine, Dad. We've got it covered."

"It's just us," Gloria piped up.

"Gloria?" Arthur asked. Maggie groaned. The hallway light

flicked on, illuminating her dad's face, a pale, hungering moon. "What on earth is going on?"

"Oh, a silly little pipe burst at our hotel, so Gio and I are going to sleep here for the night. Don't mind us. Where would you like us, honey?" She turned to Maggie. "In the living room? On the pullout?"

Maggie yanked out her ponytail holder and smoothed her hair. She pulled it up again and looped the elastic band around while contemplating sleeping arrangements. That scenario wouldn't work, of course, because Arthur was sleeping there.

"I guess you could sleep in my bed," she offered, though her voice sounded reluctant even to her.

"Nonsense," Gloria countered. "We're absolutely not kicking you out of your own room. Besides, I'm sure that husband of yours is already asleep. Am I right? Mac was always such a sound sleeper."

Her mother had a point. Maggie's thoughts somersaulted.

"Gio, be a dear, and go get the rollout bed ready, would you?"

"But . . ." Arthur began and shot Maggie a worried look.

Suddenly, Jess began to giggle until she was full-out laughing. "I'm sorry," she got out between breaths. "I can't help it. This just all strikes me as hysterically funny."

Gloria looked at Maggie. Maggie looked at Jess. "Wait a minute!" Maggie nearly yelled. If she'd had a whistle around her neck, she would have blown it. *This was not happening.* "Dad's already sleeping on the pullout. You guys can sleep in the bunk room. All the kids are camping in the front yard tonight anyway." Why hadn't she thought of this obvious solution in the first place?

She glanced at Gio, her mom, and Jess, who all appeared to be digesting the new sleeping arrangements. "Look, people, this isn't rocket science. We can make it work. Just keep an eye out for Virgie whenever she decides to roll in. That's her bedroom, too."

"All-righty then," said Gloria. "We'll head on up."

"Here, let me help you with that, Gio." Jess grabbed a bag and followed them upstairs while Maggie checked to make sure she'd left the porch light on for Virgie. Maggie felt a tiny burst of satisfaction that she'd saved the night, one that only moments ago had disaster written all over it. They all had sleeping quarters, and Arthur and Gloria were nowhere near each other.

But when she got back upstairs, Maggie couldn't fall back asleep. She tossed and turned while Mac slept beside her. Noises emanated from all corners of the house. The dehumidifier clicked on and off at odd intervals, and the ceiling fan hummed above her, interrupted by the occasional shuffle of feet down the hallway or a toilet flushing. Doors opened and closed, and at one point, Maggie thought she heard the stairs creak. She willed herself to stay in bed, to let the house and its inhabitants fall asleep at their own pace.

But her mind wouldn't stop spinning. Her dad, she realized with a swift certainty, needed Gloria. Without her, he was orphaned, heedlessly making his way in the universe. As curmudgeonly as he could be, he still loved his wife and had come to depend on her all these years. He still did, a fact that was dawning on Maggie only now. The thought saddened her. He must be so lonely in the house in Maine. She flipped onto her side. *She would do better by her dad,* she resolved. She would make frequent trips up to Maine to check on him. They'd invite him down for the holidays and make a point of helping him feel more included, a part of their family.

The last time they'd visited Arthur, it had been over Thanksgiving. They'd picked him up at the house, where he'd been waiting in the front yard, and then gone out for dinner at the Sea Shack. Their Thanksgiving dinner was a buffet of clam chowder, fish, lobster, and French fries. The meal was rushed, slightly forced, with the kids complaining about the lack of gravy and turkey. Luke kept insisting that Grandma would show up any minute, and each time he mentioned her, Arthur would look up expectantly, as if he, too, were waiting for his former wife to appear.

Maggie flipped her pillow, fluffed it, and squinted at the clock: 12:30. She climbed out of bed and crept down the hallway to the bathroom. As she passed the kids' room, she nearly bumped into someone.

"Oh, hi, honey," Gloria whispered. "You startled me."

"Sorry, Mom. You go ahead first," Maggie said in the dim glow of the hallway night-light. She gestured to the bathroom.

"Thank you, but I'm all set. Nighty-night." Gloria turned in to the bunk room and shut the door.

In her half fog, Maggie realized her mom had been coming up the stairs. Was she getting a glass of water? Saying good night to Arthur? Maggie tiptoed to the top of the stairs and listened, but all was quiet. She went to use the bathroom, then threw back two Tylenol and prayed they'd help her sleep, stop her mind from whirling.

When she got back to bed, Mac had yet to stir an inch. She crawled in next to him and lifted the sheet over her. At last, the room had cooled down. She listened. The house had quieted as well. Only the whir of the fan and Mac's breathing. Somewhere beyond the window she could hear the familiar trill of crickets punctuated by the croak of a lovesick frog. She remembered Lexie, heartsick and mopey. She would try to talk to her in the morning.

Maggie was starting to float into sleep again when a tremendous crash jolted her awake. *Again.* She sat up, wide eyed, her heart racing. Then she remembered: *Virgie. Home from the bar at last.* She stood and crept downstairs, where she flung open the door, expecting to see her sister hanging on Sal's shoulder. But what she witnessed instead made her lift a hand to stifle her laugh.

Because there, in the light of the full orange moon, sat Roger. On top of the overturned crate, nibbling away on a corncob that Arthur and the kids had jerry-rigged to the crate. His yellow eyes glowed out at her in the night, as if mocking every well-intentioned thought she'd ever had.

18

Jess

It was Thursday—four excruciating days since her husband had spoken to her, really talked to her. While she waited to see if he would forgive her, she was simultaneously fuming that he was making her suffer so. She knew she was in the wrong, but wasn't Tim a little bit, too? If, say, Jess was seventy-five percent guilty, couldn't Tim assume the remaining twenty-five percent of that guilt? He'd suspected something might be going on between her and Cole and had done nothing to stop it. Was that somehow worse, she wondered, than if he had? Was he truly invested in their marriage, or would he use Jess's betrayal as a way out?

Her nails were bitten down to the quick, something Gloria was fast to point out. "I've never understood why you just can't let your nails be," she carped over breakfast that morning.

"Mom, let it go. Jess is a grown-up. She can do whatever she wants with her nails," scolded Maggie.

"I know," Gloria said, then exhaled heavily, as if Jess's raw fingernails were among the biggest disappointments of her life. "It's just so unsightly." She paused. "Or do I mean unseemly?"

Jess had had enough. She grabbed her coffee and headed down to the beach. The kids were still asleep. It was while walking along the beach that she ran into her husband, returning from the other direction. She'd wondered where he'd gone when she woke up this morning, the bed vacant beside her. She approached him tentatively, hesitantly, as if he might be a con artist or a thief. He slowed when he saw her. Eventually, he headed her way.

"Hey, there," he said. Dark aviator sunglasses hid his eyes. Jess recognized the prescription glasses that Tim had paid a small fortune for last year.

"Hi." She dragged a flip-flop across the sand, forming little parallel lines. Where to begin when so much had happened? For a brief moment, she considered dialing their therapist on her cell phone. Then she remembered how much Tim disliked their therapist.

"So, this has been quite the vacation, huh?"

"Yeah," she said, looking out over the water and trying desperately not to cry. "I came here with my husband and my kids," she said softly. "Now I'm wondering: Will I be leaving with them?"

Tim pushed his sunglasses up on his head, and she saw the green eyes she'd fallen for in a bar in South Boston. Little lines fanned out from them now, but his eyes were still beautiful. His face was tanned, and for the first time, she noticed he'd also lost some weight this vacation. He was, she realized, looking more like his old self.

She wondered what he saw when he looked at her. A cheat? A reminder of his struggling marriage? Or did he see her for what she was? The hurt, the exhaustion, the worry and regret, and, yes, the love. She could feel all those emotions radiating from her every pore.

His hands were stuffed in his pockets, and Jess was all too aware that this was where they remained. She waited for what felt like an eternity for him to respond.

"I've been thinking," he said finally, casting his view out over the water. "We've both had a lot going on this year." He cleared his throat, and she couldn't help but wonder if he was about to leave her. She listened, as if trying to decipher the code her husband was tapping out on the sand for her. She felt a sob beginning to travel up her chest.

Oh, God, no. Tim was going to say he wanted out. What would she do? Poor Grace and Teddy! She pinched her sides and inhaled.

"And I don't think I've really been paying attention."

"What?" she asked. She coughed, caught off guard. "What do you mean?"

He sat down on the sand, and she dropped down next to him. "Well, it's easy to get caught up in stuff. You know, the speed of life. The busyness of everyday stuff. It's easy to forget the big picture— like it's all passing us by so quickly."

She hadn't expected Tim to get philosophical on her. She waited. "I thought a lot about what you said," he continued. "How I don't listen, and I think you're probably right about that." He paused, cleared his throat. "I feel like my mind is going in a million different directions, so I'm always half hearing what people are saying. It's not just you."

He stopped. She watched as he picked up a stone and ran his thumb over its smooth edges. "Okay," she said softly. "Thanks." It felt like a small victory when she'd been expecting outrage, ultimatums delivered. She felt her diaphragm drop back into place.

"I'm not saying that what you did is okay."

"Honey, of course not! I wouldn't expect that. It *wasn't* okay," she jumped in. "There's no excuse for it. You have every right to be furious with me—"

"And I was. Trust me," he said, interrupting. "I think I might still be. But I've had a few days to cool down and think more rationally." He threw the rock out on the water, where it skipped three times. "When I think about Cole kissing you . . . well, I get kind of crazy."

"Tim, don't." She rested her hand on his arm. *That must mean he cared, right?* Jess worked to be quiet, to let her husband talk.

"And I'm pissed with myself for not saying something sooner. I think I knew something was going on between you two—or that at the very least, it was *about* to go on. I should have spoken up. I didn't. That makes me a little bit of an idiot."

She laughed softly. "Just a little bit?"

"Hey, I'm trying to apologize here. Don't push your luck."

"That's ironic." She was more than willing to extend the longest olive branch. "Because I'm the one who should be doing all the apologizing."

"Maybe," he said, dropping back into seriousness. "Probably. But, really, it takes two to create the mess we're in."

Jess couldn't believe it. Her husband was speaking the very words she'd thought thousands of times in the past year. Perhaps some small kernel from their counseling sessions *had* registered.

"And, I don't know," he continued. "But seeing everyone here at the summer house—all the generations, the kids, us, your parents— it kind of brings it home that we're all family, and well, it might not always be this way."

"What do you mean?"

"Just that we might not always be around. I look at Arthur, and he seems so *old* to me this year. Like he's aged ten years since last summer. I don't think he's fared well without Gloria. And then I look at Mac and Maggie, who seem so happy and perfect, and I think to myself, why not that for us? Why can't *we* have that? And then I watch the kids, and sometimes I want to cry they're so incredible—I can barely stand the thought of them growing up, of us growing up."

Oh, thought Jess with a surge of relief. *Okay, we're talking about growing old, not divorce. I can handle that.* She didn't think she'd heard Tim say so much at one time during their entire marriage.

"Sometimes, I'm running my hands through Grace's hair—have

you ever noticed she has the softest hair?—and I'll think there is nothing better than being able to hold your little girl. Or, I'll be swinging Teddy around, and he'll be squealing, and I'll get a flash, like *this is it*. This is what it's all about." He stopped. "I'm sorry. Am I making any sense at all?"

She nodded. "Yes, yes. Absolutely. I know what you mean, I think. We might be in the thick of our midlife crises. *Life is short. Enjoy it while you can* kind of thing."

"Right." He lifted her hand to his lips now and kissed it. "And I realized that what that means for me is enjoying it with you and the kids. Making a point to take *time* to enjoy it."

Jess exhaled audibly. Her husband wanted to stay. He wanted to make things better. She would still have a family. She hadn't ruined their lives forever. She felt like she could breathe again, even though she was crying.

"Come on, don't cry." He wrapped an arm around her and pulled her close. But Jess couldn't help herself. For four days, she'd been sick with worry over what she'd done, over what Tim would do. Now he was giving her absolution. He wanted to carry on with them, with her.

"I'm sorry," she managed to get out finally. "I'm just"—she searched for the word—"so grateful. Grateful that you can forgive me."

He kissed her, a soft, gentle kiss. "I love you, Jessie. That never changed."

"Do you think we can start over?" she whispered.

Tim pulled his face back and studied her, as if considering. "Yeah, I do."

Wouldn't it be strange, she thought, to be able to go back in time and gaze forward? If only she'd known then what beautiful, amazing children they'd have, she would have been giddy. She would have been delighted with a playbook that showed her, yes, one day you will marry this handsome man with green eyes. One day you will have two lovely children. She would have signed up for her future in a heartbeat, probably suspecting all the while that it was impossible. Good things always happened for her sisters, not Jess.

But what if the playbook revealed that there would also be sadness, some heartbreak, a pulling away by her husband, followed by a brief affair by her? Would she still sign up for this life, this man? She thought of Grace and Teddy. She thought of all the good days their family had shared, of all the love—*yes, love!*—that they'd had.

Yes, Jess realized, even if the playbook had revealed all these things to her, she would have chosen this life, this man, most certainly her children. Life wasn't perfect. Why had she thought it might be, if only for a minute? The feeling began to sink in for her as she sat there, leaning against her husband. How naïve of her. How very spoiled of her to think that she might be spared life's vicissitudes, a lull in her husband's affections, in her own. She suddenly felt foolish, embarrassed, humbled. Tim was an adult. He'd bucked up under the circumstances, had done what needed doing, while she'd wallowed in self-pity, thinking there should be more.

It wasn't all her fault, she realized. But nor was it his. She wanted desperately to keep the love they had alive, stretching between them, like the woman and the man she'd seen in a photograph in an old book, standing on opposite sides of a bridge. The woman clasped a bouquet of red tulips. The man gazed at her from afar, his hand outstretched. The love, the palpable longing in that single picture, that moment. That was what she aspired to have in her own marriage. She hoped for the bouquet one day. For now, she took her husband's hand while her heart stretched inside of her.

19

Arthur

Arthur wrapped his toes around the edge of the dock. He wasn't sure what he was doing out here at night. In the moonlight, he studied his feet, threaded with thick veins and speckled with age spots. His toes had turned knotty, arthritic, the nails slightly yellowed. How strange, he thought, to mark the passing of time by the way one's feet appeared on the dock each summer.

It was Thursday night. He couldn't honestly say that everything was right with his family, but he sensed that Jess and Tim had reached some kind of détente, making it bearable for them to be in the same room. He would talk to Virgie about sticking around next week for her specialist appointment; ask her what the hell she was thinking coming in late with Sal last night and crashing in the tent with the kids. She needed to take better care of herself! And Maggie, well, the poor girl was chasing around like a mother hen who'd just lost her chicks in a fox raid. Arthur felt bad for her. She only wanted the best for everyone, but her carefully orchestrated peace at Pilgrim Lane had been disastrously upended.

He supposed when you lived to a certain age, you were bound to see a certain amount of heartache. Divorce, a child's thorny marriage, various ailments. Why he'd assumed he would be impervious to such hardships, he didn't know. But he found himself surprised by the circumstances that surrounded him this summer. And for once, he was at a loss for words of advice to parcel out. It felt as if the Herington clan, while making the best of things, was falling a little bit apart.

He still wasn't accustomed to thinking of his wife as his *ex*-wife. Even if Gloria called out of obligation, they had continued their conversations about the girls and the grandkids, like a scarf they'd started knitting long ago and added to each month. *Knit one, purl two*. Last night at Grouchy Ted's, he'd felt like his old self again. After watching Gloria and Gio fox-trot like teenagers on the dance floor, he'd joined them, inserting himself into their circle like an extra stitch. His feet had fallen into the cadence of the music, which had turned from rock 'n' roll to bluesy melodies. When the DJ played "At Last" by Etta James, he gripped Gloria's hand and led her away from Gio to a corner where he twirled her on his hand as he had on their wedding day so many years ago.

And then Gloria had tiptoed downstairs last night and found her way to his bed. She sat down and rubbed his back, knowing just the places that cried out for extra kneading, as she used to. When he rolled over and whispered, "Gloria?" in confusion, she shushed him and kept massaging.

"I've missed you, Arthur," she said. "I didn't realize how much until tonight. I'd forgotten how much fun we used to have together."

"Yes, we did, didn't we?" he asked.

It was quiet for a few minutes while they both swam in their thoughts. "What about Gio? Are you two serious?" He was afraid to ask but was more afraid that he'd lose the nerve to ask later.

She gave a small laugh. "Oh, I suppose we are. As serious as you can get when you're a sixty-five-year-old broad. But we're not in love, if that's what you're wondering."

Arthur found her answer perplexing. They were serious but not in love? What did that mean, exactly?

"Oh," he said while she continued kneading.

"Do you think the girls are okay?" she asked. "I'm worried about Virgie. And Jess. Even Maggie seems a bit off."

Arthur agreed. Something was going on with their family. He was tempted to cast blame, to say everything had been fine with the Heringtons until Gloria decided to leave. But he knew that would be unfair. The girls were grown-up now. They carried a certain amount of responsibility themselves for how they led their lives. "I know," offered Arthur. "It's a little crazy. What about Jess and Tim, huh?" Maggie had sketched out the details for him.

"They've been having their problems. But nothing they can't work out, I'd imagine." Her fingers pressed firm little circles into his back. "I hope Virgie will slow down. She's literally working herself sick."

"Yes," he said. And it struck him: no matter what, he and Gloria would always share the bond of parenthood with their three incredible girls. The bond of being grandparents to their grandchildren. It was a comforting thought.

And then she'd gone back upstairs. To Gio.

Now Arthur stood on the dock watching the stars blink on in the night sky. The moon was just shy of full, and a soft breeze tumbled off the water. Behind him, the house shone like a tiny cathedral, a handful of lights flickering downstairs. He was trying to remember what had brought him out to the pier in the first place when there was a large splash and holler about ten feet away, causing him to jump. He was close enough to the edge that he lost his balance and fell straight into the bracing cold. The dark water engulfed him, shooting into his ears and mouth, and when he came up gasping for air, he spotted Gloria—hooting and laughing—out of the corner of his eye. "Sorry, Arthur. Didn't mean to scare you!" she shouted.

Arthur coughed and coughed, treading water till he got his bearings. It wasn't deep where he'd fallen, and now he remembered to lower his feet, which blessedly touched the bottom. His toes searched for a foothold in the squishy sand. He banged on his chest, cleared his throat, and wiped the water from his eyes. His T-shirt was soaked, his shorts waterlogged. *Ah, right.* He remembered now: Gloria had invited him for a late-night swim.

When he peered in Gloria's direction, however, he caught two silhouettes. *Gio.* The two swam over as Arthur made his way closer to shore. When he glanced back, they were both standing in waist-high water. It was then that Arthur realized neither one wore a bathing suit.

"Good Lord, Gloria! Where are your clothes?" he asked.

Gloria put her hands on her hips and said, "What? You see something you don't like?"

He was speechless. Of course, he liked it. What he didn't like was the picture of Gio standing next to her, naked as a jaybird.

"Come on, Arthur. Lighten up. It wouldn't kill you to take your clothes off once in a while!" she shouted, as if he weren't standing just a few feet away from her. He watched mesmerized, while the moonbeams danced across her chest, her breasts like two pale melons laid out on a fabulous table. He knew those breasts well. Gio, on the other hand, was covered in chest hair, lots of dark, spiraling hair. How odd that Gloria was attracted to such a hirsute man, Arthur thought. Arthur's chest was practically hairless. Gloria had always admired his smooth, unblemished skin.

Even in the dark, he could feel his face flushing. "Wow, you two kids have fun." He suddenly felt a hundred years old. He felt himself shriveling. Yes, he'd gone skinny-dipping with Gloria at the summer house when the kids were little and tucked into their beds. But that was light-years ago. Now their daughters were grown and quite possibly watching them out their bedroom windows. He backed out of the water, unable to turn away as much as he wanted to. "I'm going to go in and dry off."

"Suit yourself, Arthur," Gio said and slapped at the water. Arthur thought he detected an edge of bravado in Gio's curt dismissal. *As if Arthur weren't man enough to skinny-dip!* For a brief moment, he was tempted to charge back in, leap on top of Gloria, and claim her as his own.

Gloria still cared for him. He knew she did. Why else would she have snuck downstairs last night? Just to talk to him about the girls? She missed him. They were made for each other, just as they had been more than forty years ago. He wanted to ask her, *Why? Why did she leave?* Right there in the living room last night while the moonlight danced through the blinds. But he suspected he wouldn't get an answer any more satisfying than the one he had the first time. *She needed a change. People outgrew each other. She wanted time to think, to be on her own. Maine didn't suit her anymore,* which Arthur had interpreted as *Arthur* no longer suited her.

But a person couldn't cast all that history, that love aside. Arthur had lobbed these salient points at her when she first requested the divorce, but Gloria had dodged each one like an errant tennis ball.

He smiled and waved now, but the gesture came off halfhearted. Arthur turned and climbed out of the water onto the beach. His clothes felt as if they were made of armor, and suddenly he was overcome by a terrible tiredness. Steadying himself, he walked unevenly across the sand. His toe snagged on something in the dark, and he crouched to see what it was. *Gloria's bra strap*. He reached down to pull it off, a lavender frilly thing, and flung it back onto the sand before climbing the deck stairs and nearly losing his balance.

The sound of Gloria's and Gio's laughter followed him as he entered the house and slid the glass door closed behind him. Perhaps it was for the best, he reflected, that Gloria and Gio had managed to book a room at another hotel, thanks to a last-minute cancellation. Arthur didn't think he could trust himself to sleep under the same roof with his ex-wife for another night. Nor did he trust himself to refrain from inflicting bodily harm on Gio if the man continued to share a house with them. It wouldn't be a bone-breaking kind of harm, but Arthur had written enough mysteries to know a few ways to exert force without leaving behind any evidence.

20

Maggie

It was Friday night, and Maggie's hair was pulled up with elegant Japanese hair sticks. Each July, Gretchen hosted a fund-raising party for a cause dear to her heart. Last year it had been Rosie's Place, a homeless shelter in Boston. The year before, Children's Hospital. This year it was the Boys & Girls Club. Anyone who wanted to be known as a dedicated philanthropist made a point of attending her annual summer gala, which had garnered accolades over the years. *The Boston Globe* called it "a slice of the Hamptons on the Cape." Gretchen found it amusing that the paper ascribed such a lofty title to her "little event," but Maggie didn't. She thought the *Globe* got it right. She, for one, anticipated it every summer.

She shifted in her white dress that had a thin black ribbon circling tightly under her breasts (a fact she was only unfortunately realizing now). Her feet were wedged into a pair of impossibly high heels. Maggie felt fashionable—and slightly uncomfortable—in a way she hadn't in months. The past two weeks had been crazy, but tonight she was going to enjoy herself. Gloria and Gio had found another hotel room, so she didn't have to worry about their sleeping under the same roof as Arthur. And they'd left Arthur in charge of the kids at home tonight.

She, Mac, Jess, Tim, and Virgie all climbed out of the car as Mac handed over the keys to the valet. Before them, Gretchen's house twinkled with hundreds of tiny white lights. Tiki torches lined the walkway, and elegant paper lanterns hung from the porch, fat, luminous globes suspended in the night. A familiar song—was it Hootie and the Blowfish?—floated out from the house. Maggie smiled; Gretchen was so old-school. At the front door, they were greeted by a swarm of people, women in sequined gowns, men in tuxedos, and a waitstaff parading around. Maggie suddenly felt underdressed, and her eyes flashed at Mac apprehensively. He took her hand and squeezed it.

"Maybe they'll think we're part of the help," he whispered. She batted at him, saying, "You're terrible," but it made her laugh. To hell with it if they weren't as wealthy as half of the people here. Gretchen was her friend. Maggie belonged here as much as, even more than, anyone else.

At that moment, the hostess ran up to greet them. "Maggie! Mac! You made it. I'm so glad. Hi, everyone," Gretchen said, shaking all their hands. She was stunning, her hair done up in a loose twist, long diamond earrings dangling from her ears. Her face glowed with a healthy tan, and her blond hair seemed more natural in the evening light. Or perhaps it had faded to a subtler hue over the summer. Either way, Maggie's friend was a knockout in a long blue shimmering gown.

"You look fabulous," Maggie said. "I'm afraid I didn't get the memo about it being a black-tie event this year. Sorry."

"Pshht. Pleeease," said Gretchen with a roll of eyes. "I'm only dressed this way because I'm hosting the thing." She leaned in closer to Maggie and Mac. "You know this is just a chance for the millionaires to show off who's got the most money."

Mac chuckled. "Don't mind us. We'll go hang with the kitchen help."

Gretchen smiled and elbowed Maggie. "That's why I love your husband. A man who knows his place. Now scoot! Go eat some of this outrageously expensive food before it's gone. And don't forget to put your names in for the raffle." And she was off, grabbing other guests' hands, telling them how fabulous it was to see them.

Maggie and Mac wound their way to the back of the house, through the living room that was layered with Oriental rugs and leather couches, to a deck with stunning views of the water. She and Mac found a small pocket of uninhabited space on the deck and planted themselves there. Maggie leaned against the railing and studied the handsome young waiters who darted in and out of the crowd, carrying trays of spinach and goat cheese crepes, pigs in a blanket, Chinese dumplings, and prosecco. Maggie grabbed two bubbly glasses off a tray and handed one to Mac. "Cheers," she said and clinked glasses.

"Cheers, my love."

"Here's to hoping the rest of the month is a bit calmer," she said.

"Aw, it hasn't been that bad, has it?" Mac asked. "I was kind of enjoying having everyone around."

"You're joking, right? All the drama? It's like *One Flew over the Cuckoo's Nest at Pilgrim Lane.*" Mac laughed.

Virgie swept up beside them, a crepe in hand. "Have you guys tasted these? *Seriously* good," she proclaimed. "Your friend knows how to throw a party. Oopsies! Excuse me," she said and dashed off to chase a waiter carrying a tray of dumplings.

"Stop fretting," Mac whispered into her ear. "Did I mention how beautiful you look tonight?"

Maggie tilted her head back and smiled. Her husband was right. Virgie seemed to be feeling better. Jess and Tim had been casting each other furtive looks all day and holding hands, as if they were young lovers again. Even Arthur had been his old irascible self today.

And there were no kids handing her their wet towels or their trash. She reminded herself that this was her night to have fun. "You're absolutely right," she said. "I need to let it all go. And thank you. You don't look half bad yourself."

When a waiter passed, she nipped a dumpling off a tray, dipping it in the small bowl of sauce proffered, careful not to dribble any on her dress. She took a bite, a savory blend of pork, cabbage, and carrots. *Divine.* She reached for another before the server flitted off to another group. She struggled to remember the last time she'd been offered an appetizer and could only recall Gretchen's party last year. Of course, there had been the occasional "date night" with Mac, but those were more often places like Chili's or the 99. Restaurants that required a mere dash of lipstick or eyeliner, if that. Certainly not Japanese hair sticks.

It occurred to her that there were likely a lot more nights of frozen pizza and chicken fingers in her future if she and Mac went ahead with her foster care idea. Was she really willing to give up the new-found freedom they'd have once all the kids were in school? There was the possibility she'd be able to get back in shape, read again, have casual lunches with her girlfriends. Adding a new member to the family would, of course, change all of that. But, as she sipped her prosecco, she knew she wasn't ready to give up on the thought of raising another child. She wanted this. She would tell Mac. Soon.

She watched as guests gathered themselves into small circles, suggesting an intimacy that she suspected no one really felt. The downside to these events, Maggie considered, was that, despite the goodwill propelling them along, they always carried a whiff of being forced, the rich strutting about to better establish themselves in the pecking order. That she and Mac were so far removed from this world, as if in another galaxy altogether, made it all the more interesting. She felt like a voyeur, spying on how the other half lived.

Tim and Jess had disappeared somewhere, but Maggie glimpsed

Virgie off in a corner talking to an older man and, presumably, his wife. The man, with a head of thick gray hair, bore a striking resemblance to Walter Cronkite. His wife had a snow-white bob that highlighted her ruby red lipstick. She was exaggeratedly thin, like so many women in these opulent circles. Maggie watched while her sister talked, admiring Virgie's ability to charm a crowd wherever she went.

Maggie was grateful that her dad had offered to babysit the kids tonight. They'd left him with a pile of G-rated movies and detailed instructions on how to make the microwave popcorn, though he'd waved them away. "For God's sakes, I'm not a small child, you know," he said. This past week, she'd watched her dad come to life around Gloria and then just as quickly shut down when Gio appeared. Virgie had even caught Gloria and Gio skinny-dipping the other night. *Imagine!* Two people of their age whipping off their clothes on the beach.

Just then, the Stonehills swept up beside them to say how lovely it was to see them, hadn't the children grown, and how was their father doing? Local year-rounders, the Stonehills made it their business to know everyone else's business in their tightly knit community. Both were retired now, but they had amassed a small fortune in the restaurant business. Tonight, Susan Stonehill was dressed in an elegant burgundy sheath with a ballet neck and cap sleeves. A large ruby necklace rested on her freckled chest. George wore a tuxedo with a bow tie and pulled uncomfortably at his shirt collar, as if eager for the chance to escape. Maggie had always liked Mr. Stonehill, a Vietnam vet. He projected a judicious air, as if he'd seen everything he needed to in life and nothing could surprise him now. His shock of white hair and dark, horn-rimmed glasses suggested that he might have been a college professor, an intellectual in another lifetime.

"How is your dad doing, honey?" Susan leaned in toward Maggie, concern etched on her face.

"Oh, he's fine," Maggie said. "He's hard at work on the next book."

Susan took Maggie's hand in hers. "You let us know if you need us to do *anything*. I know you've got Jay looking in on the house, but if there's anything else we can do, don't hesitate to ask. We adore your dad."

"You bet," George said. "Happy to do anything for your old man. I love that guy. Speaking of which, where is he tonight? You didn't make him dress up in a penguin suit?"

Maggie snickered. "We left him at home with the grandkids. Figured he'd have more fun there than at a fund-raising event."

George offered a knowing nod. "Smart move. The old man's bound to say something to embarrass you here. You know how he hates rich folks."

And they all shared a laugh at her dad's expense before George clapped Mac on the back and the Stonehills plunged themselves into the next wave of benefactors.

"What was that all about?" Maggie asked.

Mac shrugged. "They're the friendly type. They consider themselves mayors of their little inlet. And they like Arthur."

"I guess." She suddenly felt in need of sustenance, something to clear her head. The prosecco was shooting straight to her brain. She grabbed Mac's hand to go in search of more dumplings. Eventually, they found their way to the main table and bar, an extravagant spread laid out in the dining room. Succulent pink shrimp hung by their tails from crystal bowls, a pool of tangy sauce in the center. There were trays of roasted vegetables, miniature crepes, and an assortment of chilled hors d'oeuvres. Maggie took a small plate and helped herself to the shrimp and vegetable skewers.

On an adjacent table sat posters highlighting stories from the Boys & Girls Club. There were pictures of kids of all ages from various Boston communities, including Roxbury and Dorchester. Above the photos was the heading ENGAGED. INVOLVED. ENVELOPED BY LOVE. WHY NOT DO YOUR PART TODAY? Maggie peered over Mac's shoulder at the shots of kids rock-climbing, hiking in the Blue Hills, cruising

THE SUMMER OF GOOD INTENTIONS

on a whale watch, painting a mural. Seeing so much goodwill on display made her bubbly. Here were people who cared deeply about mentoring children, about building a better world. Perhaps it was the prosecco, but Maggie felt herself among like-minded souls. The do-gooders, the givers, for whom helping formed the crux of their lives. She wanted to get involved, volunteer somehow. She'd have to ask Gretchen. And, of course, if she and Mac took in a foster child, they would be an extension of this world.

"Oh, honey," she said, leading Mac into a corner with their appetizers. "I have something to tell you."

Mac was caught in mid-chew of a shrimp. "Uh-oh," he got out around a mouthful.

"No, it's good!" She set down her plate on the fireplace mantel. "I've been thinking about it for a while now."

"Double uh-oh." Mac swallowed and grinned. "What's up?"

She took a deep breath and plucked a piece of lint off his jacket lapel. Then she slid her arms around his waist. "I've been thinking," she said, looking up into his eyes. "With Luke starting kindergarten in September, and the girls practically teenagers, well, maybe we should look into adding another member to our family."

Mac's face blanched slightly in the dim lighting of the room. "Like a dog?"

"Not like that," she said quickly. Mac was allergic. "I mean foster care. You know, helping a child who wouldn't otherwise have a home."

"Oh?" He raised an eyebrow and then coughed into his hand.

"I've been researching it a bit, and there seem to be plenty of kids who could use a loving family."

"And by 'loving family,' I assume you're describing ours?" Mac joked. "Wow, Mags." He paused. "Where did that come from? That's a pretty big commitment, don't you think? It's not like you have the kid sleep over a few nights and then send him back home."

"Of course not!" she exclaimed. She waved at the table with the pictures of all the children in the Boys & Girls Club. "But look at all the good this organization is doing. Doesn't it make you want to be a part of something bigger?"

Mac eyed her skeptically. "I'm happy to volunteer on weekends, but actually signing up to be a foster parent? That's something else entirely. Don't you want to enjoy the fact that all our children are finally out of diapers? Signing up for another one? I don't know, Mags. I kind of thought we were done." His voice trailed off doubtfully.

"I know, but this would be different. Most of the kids who need homes aren't babies. They're older. Toddler age, even five or six. He or she could be a playmate for Luke." She clapped her hands together, as if adding an exclamation point to her idea.

"Don't you have to get approved by the state or something, prove you're worthy?" continued Mac. "We might be shooting ourselves in the foot, inviting a stranger to evaluate our parenting skills."

Maggie laughed. "Something tells me we'd pass. Look, I get that it's a big deal. You don't have to answer now." She picked up her drink and let the prosecco sweep over her tongue. "Just promise me you'll think about it, okay? And in the meantime, I'm going to talk to Gretchen about volunteering for the organization. You know, something different. For me."

Mac sighed. "I'll think about it, honey, but that doesn't mean I'm going to give you the answer you want to hear."

She shrugged, trying not to let on how very important this was to her. She would give Mac time. He always needed time with big decisions—this one was no different. Eventually, she was confident he would come around.

She turned on her heel and scanned the crowd, which appeared to be expanding by the minute. *Poor Gretchen,* she thought. *She must be going crazy trying to glad-hand all these guests.* She was about to seek out her friend to see if she could help when the Shania Twain tune that Sophie had picked for her new ringtone played on her phone.

She shot Mac a smile, as if to say, *Our girls,* then pulled the cell from her purse.

"Hello?" She held a finger to her other ear. "Hello?"

"Is this Mrs. McNeil?" She moved to a corner, away from the noise of the party.

"Yes?" *Telemarketer* she mouthed to Mac.

"Mrs. McNeil, I don't want to alarm you, but this is Fire Chief Souter. There's been a small fire at your residence on Pilgrim Lane but—"

"What?" She shot Mac a look. "Is everyone . . . ?" She struggled to hear and headed for the front of the house. Mac followed her out to the front porch.

"Everyone is fine. It was a small kitchen fire." She put the phone on speaker so Mac could hear, too. "We got it out, but I think your dad and kids are pretty shaken up."

"Can I talk to my dad, please?" She could hear the pleading in her own voice, the crackle in the phone, a bad connection.

"Mommy!" It was Lexie. She was bawling. "Mommy!" Maggie heard her daughter gulp for breaths of air. "There was a fire!"

"Lexie? Are you okay?" Her voice was panicked, and Mac wrapped his free arm around her.

"Lexie, honey, listen to me," Mac began, but suddenly the phone switched over. "Maggie, Maggie is that you?" It was her dad, coughing, rasping into the phone.

"Dad, what's going on?" she cried.

"Maggie, I'm so sorry. I left the kettle on. We're all okay. I think it's out. The fire."

"Dad, it's Mac here. Are all the kids with you?" Mac was shouting, and a small group was beginning to form around them.

"Yes, yes. I've got them right here," Arthur said. Suddenly, Jess and Tim were by her side. They could hear sirens in the background, more shouting across the phone lines.

"Count them, Dad. Just count them for me please, okay. There should be five kids," Maggie pleaded.

They waited as her dad counted aloud. "*One, two, three, four, five.* Yes, we're all here. Everyone's safe."

"Oh, thank God," Jess whispered.

Maggie remembered to breathe. "They're okay," she said as much to herself as to anyone else.

"We're on our way, Dad," Mac said now. "We'll be right there. You guys sit tight." They were the words she needed to hear to remind her that she could get to her children and hug them. *They were safe.*

Mac grabbed her hand as they careened through the small throng, Tim and Jess following. Somewhere Virgie was calling out Maggie's name. Gretchen rushed after them. "Maggie, my God! I just heard. Are the kids okay?"

"Yes. They're out of the house. I'll call you when I know more." It was a jumble of words, but it was all she could manage as they piled into the car.

"We'll follow you," Gretchen said.

When they pulled up to the house, flashing sirens circled the front yard. Two fire trucks and a handful of police cruisers were parked at jagged angles on the lawn. Maggie leapt out of the car, her eyes searching for the kids. Pillows of smoke billowed from the kitchen window. The air smelled acrid, the singe of smoke lingering. To the left of the house, a good twenty yards away, stood Arthur and the children.

"Mommy!" shouted Luke. He ran toward them, the rest of the kids racing behind him. Arthur slowly began to make his way over.

"Oh, honey. Are you okay? Let me look at you." She cupped Luke's face in her hands, checking for any burns or scrapes. His cheeks were streaked with tears. Lexie's and Sophie's eyes were wide with fear. But each one was okay. Maggie kissed their sweet, angelic faces. Jess did the same with Teddy and Grace. "Are they all right?" Maggie asked, and her sister nodded, tears of relief leaking from her eyes. A fireman brought over blankets and wrapped them around Arthur and the kids, still in their pajamas.

Arthur collapsed on the hood of the car, rested his head in his hands, and began to weep.

"There, there, Dad," Mac said, coming over to rest an arm on his back. "It's all okay now, everyone's safe."

"But it could have been so different," he said between sobs. "I just forgot about the kettle. It must have steamed up all the water. My kettle at home has a whistle," he said, as if it explained everything. "And the house! Look at the house! It's ruined." His breathing was labored, his face streaked with soot.

"No, no. Come on now. All of that is fixable. Don't you worry about the house. What's important is that you're all okay."

Two paramedics walked over to check her dad's pulse and breathing. "Sir, your oxygen levels are a little low. Do you mind if we put a mask on you for a few minutes?"

Her dad shook his head, as if not hearing, while the paramedic was already slipping a mask over his nose and mouth.

Maggie studied her dad, her emotions tumbling inside her. He seemed so frail sitting there, the mask strapped to his face, the tube trailing out one side to the oxygen tank. She worked to tamp down the fury that was starting to color her overall relief. Didn't Arthur understand that she'd entrusted him with her children? That Jess and Tim and Mac had done the same? It wasn't just about him anymore—it was about his grandchildren! And he'd failed to keep them safe. She felt her stomach lurch, and she ran to the bushes, where it emptied itself. She wiped her mouth with the back of her hand, trying to squelch the sour taste at the back of her throat before Mac was at her side, propping her up and helping her to the car.

Maggie took a water bottle from Mac and rinsed her mouth. The scene before her was a montage of fire engines, swirling red lights, and firemen lumbering around in heavy jackets and boots. She wanted to erase it away, a whiteboard made clean again. Somewhere on the periphery Gretchen and her husband had arrived and led the kids to a safe spot at the end of the driveway. Maggie watched while her friend handed out water bottles and rubbed her children's backs.

She felt her body begin to shiver, then shake. Mac took off his sports coat and wrapped it around her, rubbing her arms vigorously. "Ssh, honey, it's okay now. Everything's okay."

But she couldn't stop her body from quaking, her teeth from chattering. Somewhere in the last ten minutes she'd lost her shoes, and she rubbed her bare feet against each other, as if trying to spark a flame of warmth inside herself. The hem of her dress was torn, the white sheath streaked with dirt and soot. She watched while, one by one, firemen exited their home and placed their tools back in the truck. The chief walked over to brief Mac.

"You guys were lucky," he said. "It's a good thing you had that extinguisher handy. Your dad put out most of the fire with it. Not too much damage. The fire's bark is bigger than its bite."

"What does that mean?" asked Tim, joining them.

"It means it looks worse than it is. The flames mostly got the cupboards above the stove and the drawers right next to it. You should be able to save the rest."

"Thanks, Chief. Do we know for sure what started it?" asked Mac.

"Looks like a teakettle that ran out of water. It's melted right into the stove; you'll see. You'll want to invest in a new stove. And a kettle. Maybe one with a whistle next time."

"Thanks, Chief," Mac said again, shaking hands. "We're grateful for what you've done for us tonight."

Maggie searched for her voice, but it came out as a squeak. Her throat burned. "Yes, thank you." She uncapped her water bottle and drank.

"Can we go back in the house?" Tim asked. No one had thought to ask yet. It seemed they were all still in a state of shock. Maggie fixed her eyes on her dad, the oxygen mask still in place.

The chief glanced over his shoulder and regarded the house. "Once the smoke has cleared, I don't see why not." He tipped his head toward Arthur. "Want me to have my guys take him to the hospital? Just to get him checked out?"

Mac studied Maggie, then Arthur. "I don't know. Let's ask."

They walked over to her dad, who was pulling off the mask. "I don't need this thing anymore," he declared stubbornly. "I'm just fine."

"Dad, how about a quick trip to the hospital? Make sure you're okay?" Mac asked.

"Do I look like I'm okay?" Arthur's voice was tinged with anger. Maggie was about to say, *No, not really,* when Arthur answered for himself. "Of course, I'm okay. I don't need to go to the hospital, for goodness' sake."

"I guess we have our answer then." Mac smiled at the chief. "Thanks, anyway."

The chief shrugged and nodded before traveling back to his squad car, the squeaks and clicks of the officers' radios piercing the night air.

Mac returned with an extra blanket and wrapped it around her. Gradually the fire engines and police cruisers began to pull away, and Maggie and Mac joined the kids at the end of the driveway.

"Oh, honey, I'm so sorry," Gretchen said, pulling her into a hug.

"Thanks," Maggie said softly. She took a few steps back and dropped to the ground, where Luke crawled into her lap. She stroked his hair and kissed his head, whispering, "It's all right, honey," while the last retreating cruisers blinked by them. "It's all right," she said, looking at their emptied house, the lights still glowing upstairs. But she couldn't stop shaking.

21

Virgie

All Virgie wanted to do was sleep, lose herself in a world where she wouldn't have to think. Not about the fire. About the persistent, nagging feeling that little bugs were running across her legs and, more recently, the sense that every so often the ground shifted beneath her feet, forcing her to grab on to a wall for balance. She needed to quiet the voices in her head telling her that something wasn't right. Stop googling MS, that other thing the ER doctor had mentioned in passing as a "possibility." *This is what happens,* she told herself, *when you have too much time on your hands.*

She pulled the fluffy comforter over her head, leaving a little pocket of air to breathe. The house was quiet. Earlier this morning, Mac had gotten a structural engineer to come out to ensure the kitchen was safe, and he'd given it a thumbs-up. Fortunately, the fire hadn't spread much beyond the cupboards above the stove. Later this afternoon someone else was coming to give an estimate for repairs and a new stove. Mac had been on the phone with the insurance company for most of the morning. *But the smell? What about the smell?* Maggie had asked. *What about it?* Mac asked. *Will it ever go away?* To which Mac replied, *Let's hope so.*

And then there had been the wail from Sophie. "Mommy, the notebook! *The Book of Summer!*" Everyone had raced into the kitchen to find Sophie clutching the singed spiral notebook, its pages flaking at the touch. The top waxy cover, once blue, was now gray, with the words *The Boo of Su* forming a jagged line across what was left of it. "It's ruined," she wailed and broke into tears.

"Oh, honey, come on now. I'm sure we can salvage it somehow."

"No, no, no!" Sophie stomped her foot and threw the notebook to the ground before running out of the room.

Maggie bent to pick it up. "This breaks my heart," she said quietly. "It was in the top drawer by the stove. It's all the kids' milestones and quotes over the summers. Eleven years' worth." She turned to Mac, tears budding at her eyes. "The stove is replaceable. This is not."

Lexie gently took the battered journal from her mother's hands. She turned what was left of the pages, searching for anything she might be able to read. "Look, here's something, Mom." It was the first time Virgie had seen Lexie try to make her mother feel better, and Virgie felt her heart lift. "You can just make out the date; it's from two summers ago." Lexie began to read: *"Luke says he 'thinks he'll wear his* (I can't read this part) *instead.'* "

"His feet," Maggie echoed. "He said he'd wear his feet when Daddy asked him if he wanted boat shoes before going in the water. That was when he was three." Her eyes traveled around their circle. "How we laughed at that." Mac came and circled an arm around her.

"I know it's sad, honey, but I bet we could re-create a lot of this book from memory. It's the memories that make it real."

Maggie let out a deep sigh. "I know you're right, but it feels as if we've lost the best part of the summer house." She removed Mac's arm from her waist and walked out of the kitchen.

"Look." Grace broke the quiet and pointed. "*The Boo of Su.* It rhymes."

"Yeah, sounds like a creepy ghost story," said Lexie. "The Boo of Crazy Sue."

"Maybe let's not share that with Mom," Mac advised. "She probably won't find it funny."

But Maggie was right, Virgie thought: *The Book of Summer* was irreplaceable. This vacation was a disaster. Virgie needed Jackson, needed to hear his voice. She emerged from her air pocket to grab her cell off the table and saw that Larry had left five messages while her phone was on mute. But she didn't feel like talking to Larry. She punched in Jackson's speed dial number. All she got was his voice mail, telling her to leave a message.

"I miss you. Call me. You won't believe what happened last night."

She tossed the phone on the floor and buried herself deeper under the blankets. She was also a little upset with herself for hanging out with Sal so late the other night. When he'd invited her back to his place, he was surprised that she said no. Then she confided in him about Jackson, about how much she liked this guy. That he might be the One, which was completely ridiculous because they'd been dating for only a month and a half. Sal had been gracious. "If that's the case," he said, kissing her lightly on the cheek, "then I'm really happy for you." When he dropped her off at home later that night, she told him, "You're such a sweet guy, Sal. You're going to find an amazing woman someday." And he gave her the saddest look. "That's what they tell me." She crawled into the tent with the kids, too tired to trek upstairs, and only then did she wonder who "they" was. All the women he'd dated over the years? She felt a twinge of guilt for letting Sal down.

Of course, now Sal was the least of her problems. Maybe, she considered as she dug deeper into the sheets, she'd never go back to work. Maybe she could live at Pilgrim Lane. She could be like one of the kids, except slightly more mature, able to help out on occasion. And Jackson could visit her on the weekends. It was an appealing thought. She imagined herself reading books all day, lounging on the deck. She wouldn't have to report to work! Wouldn't have to earn a living. All the pressures of the crazy world she'd jumped into with two feet would fade away. She'd been running and running on the success wheel for years. And she was exhausted.

Maybe it was time to get off.

She flipped onto her side. It was no use. She wouldn't be able to nap now. Not with all that had happened. Even Jess had thrown her for a loop, pulling her aside on the beach earlier and admitting that she and Tim were having problems but were working on it. *No surprise there,* Virgie thought. But then her sister confessed that she'd had a brief "flirtation," for that's what she'd called it (not a fling, not an affair, but a *flirtation*) with a guy in the neighborhood. Virgie didn't think it was such an appalling sin. What was the big deal? she asked Jess, if the two hadn't even slept together? In Virgie's book, a few kisses didn't necessarily make a person a cheat.

She threw off the covers and checked the clock. Already two in the afternoon. Half of Saturday gone, wasted. She pushed out of bed and tiptoed downstairs, still in her sweats. The house was eerily quiet. When she walked into the living room, she found Arthur sitting at the dining room table, his eyes closed.

"Daddy?" she asked, hesitating.

He cracked one eye open. "Oh, Virginia," he said and opened both eyes. "Come, come sit with me."

She sat down across from him. His face was ashen, his eyes puffy, as if from crying or lack of sleep.

"Virgie, honey, I'm so, so sorry," he said softly.

"Daddy." She put her hand on top of his. "It's not your fault. It could have happened to anyone." She knew Arthur was feeling bad about the events of last night. But Virgie didn't think the blame fell squarely on him. In fact, she felt her own twinge of guilt: she'd wondered last night if they weren't leaving Arthur with too many kids. Was he really equipped to handle five by himself? But when Virgie had asked, Maggie shushed her, saying that Lexie and Sophie were big enough to help out with the little ones. Arthur was simply there to play chaperone.

And, so, Virgie had let it lie. She wondered if Maggie remembered the conversation now. Not that things would necessarily have turned out differently if someone had stayed behind. But who knew?

That was when she noticed Arthur was crying. "I'm so sorry," he said again, as if she'd been waiting for an apology all day. He swiped at his tears with heavy hands. "I don't know how it could have happened. I keep replaying it and replaying it in my mind." Virgie cast about for her sisters. *Where had everyone gone?* "One minute I put the kettle on, and the next minute the kitchen was on fire."

Virgie wanted to reassure him that it was all okay. The protective instinct swelled up in her again. *Land here,* she thought to herself. *I'll help you, Dad.* Everyone was all right. It could have happened to any of them. Virgie hated to think of how many times she'd forgotten to take the kettle off, chatting away on the phone or wrapped up in a movie, only to have the whistle holler at her.

"Daddy," she tried again. "People set kettles on fire all the time. I've almost set a few on fire myself."

"You have?" he regarded her with such earnestness that it was all she could do not to invent a story, as if confirming her own shortcomings would absolve his own.

"Sure," she said. "It happens to the best of us. It's no big deal. What's important is that you put the fire out quickly and you got everyone out of the house. I'm not sure I would have even thought to grab the fire extinguisher. If it had been me, I probably would have chased everyone outside and the whole house would have gone up in flames. We most definitely would not be sitting here at this table, talking."

A small smile played across his lips. "Virginia," he said softly. "How do you always know how to make your old man feel better?"

"It's a gift," she said gently. "I got it from my dad. Remember that thing called empathy you once taught me about? You said no writer could amount to anything without it."

"I said that?" he asked. She laughed at his surprise. "That's pretty good advice, I guess." He paused and pushed a small pile of toast crumbs around on the table. "Do you think Maggie can ever forgive me?"

"Forgive you?" Virgie's head was throbbing again. "What for?"

He gestured widely, a sweep of the dining room and kitchen. "For this! For starting a fire when the kids were in the house!" His voice rose and broke. "For not keeping them safe," he whispered and swept fresh tears from his eyes.

"But you *did* keep them safe, Dad. That's what you're forgetting."

"You think?"

"Yes, Dad, I think."

He sighed and patted her hand. "I suppose you're right. Thank you, Virginia. I needed to hear that. Thank goodness everyone is all right." He pulled out his handkerchief and blew his nose loudly. "Now, tell me all about you," he said, tucking the bandanna back in his pocket. "We haven't really had a chance to talk this vacation."

And so she launched into everything—about her job and how she thought she was being treated unfairly even though she loved her show, about Jackson and how much she liked him, about her doubts that she was the marrying type. Her dad had heard much of this before, during their weekly telephone check-ins. He nodded as she ticked through her mental list. It was nice to have him listening to her. Someone who really understood her. It occurred to her that maybe there was some truth to the saying that every girl wants to marry her daddy. Would she ever find him? Could it be Jackson?

Arthur sipped an iced tea while she talked. Every so often he'd glance off to the side, as if looking for one of the kids. She even got him to laugh a few times.

Then he stopped her short, slamming his hand down on the table. "I'm sorry, Virginia," he interrupted. "But would you excuse me? I think I forgot to turn the kettle off on the stove." His watery eyes looked at her in alarm.

And that was when Virgie knew.

22

Maggie

Maggie tossed the salad with the vinaigrette and shouted out the window to give the kids their five-minute warning for supper. They were playing Red Light, Green Light in the front yard. Lexie was in charge, tagging anyone who dared move when she turned her back. Did she look like she was having fun? Maggie wondered. Her little brow was furrowed, her hands on her hips. Maybe she was still thinking about that boy Matt. When Maggie had pressed for details, Lexie had predictably shut down. Even Sophie, Maggie's usual source, claimed to know nothing. Maggie sighed. It had been a long day, the contractors visiting the house to give estimates on the kitchen repair and the electrician checking to make sure all the wiring was safe, which, fortunately, it was.

The good news was that it didn't look like the cost would be too terrible (insurance would cover almost everything), but the contractors wouldn't be able to get to the repairs till the last week in July. Their final week at the summer house. Maybe, Maggie thought, they could extend their stay. Mac needed to get back to work, but there was no reason she and the kids couldn't remain a little longer.

At the moment, though, the smell of smoke permeated everything. Even the couch seemed to release an invisible puff each time she sat on it. She grabbed all the linens from the kitchen—towels, curtains, rugs—and threw them in the wash, dousing them with fabric softener. Earlier in the day, the contractors had hauled out the stove, leaving behind a square grid of linoleum covered in grime. There was still the charred cupboard to look at, of course, and the outline of the stove chalked in black along the wall. Maggie filled a bucket with warm water and ammonia and spent the rest of the afternoon scrubbing down the kitchen.

"You're like Lady Macbeth," Mac teased. "Just say, *Out, damned spot!* once for me. What are you trying to hide, Maggie McNeil?" She shooed him away. When she finished, she could still detect a whiff of smoke beneath the ammonia, but it was a noticeable improvement, bearable now.

Cleaning usually helped her feel better, but she knew she was being short with everyone today. She might as well be tossing her emotions while she dressed the salad. Earlier she'd scolded Luke for a minor infraction.

"Honestly, Luke, can't you pick up your own socks?" she'd asked when she was doing a sweep of the living room. "I don't know how many dirty socks I've picked up this vacation. There's a hamper— conveniently located in your bedroom, I might add—that you can toss them into at the end of the day." She was sick of tidying up after everyone. And the water glasses! How many glasses could she be expected to wash a day? They were constantly running out, no matter how many times she ran the dishwasher.

"Yeah, Luke," Lexie said. "You're such a slob."

That got her. "And, you, missy!" Maggie pointed an accusing finger. "Don't pretend you're not a culprit here, too. Dirty clothes in the hamper, wet suits on the deck. I shouldn't have to remind you girls, you're old enough now. And when you open up a box of cereal, please, *please* reseal the package. Otherwise everything goes stale." She was a wrecking ball, picking up speed. Why did everyone expect her to magically take care of everything with the wave of her wand? *Because it was what she'd always done.* "I swear you kids think we're your maids. Someday this house will be yours and you'll be responsible for keeping it clean, yelling at *your* kids!" She'd meant it as a threat, but she realized she'd spoken out of turn. This wasn't her house to give; it was her parents'.

And then Lexie and Sophie had gotten into an argument over whose turn it was on the hammock. Between two white oaks on the side of the house stretched a rope hammock where the kids liked to read and nap. Maggie had been hauling out the trash, wondering why she hadn't assigned this chore to one of the kids, when she caught sight of the girls. Sophie appeared to be hanging on to the hammock for dear life while Lexie swung it as high as it would go. Maggie was about to yell at them to stop fooling around when Sophie screamed, "Lexie, stop it! I was here first!" Only too late did Maggie realize it was a full-blown fight, one that ended with Lexie slugging her sister with a tight little fist.

"Ow!" Sophie wailed, grabbing her arm, and fell off the hammock.

"Alexandra Ann McNeil!" Maggie dropped the trash and raced over to grab her daughter by the shoulders. "Don't you ever hit your sister like that again!" She searched for the words. "What were you thinking? Unacceptable!" She dragged Lexie into the house and hauled her up to the kids' bedroom, where she slammed the door, her hands shaking. She leaned against the wall, her heart racing, and tried to slow her breathing. Where was Mac? She could hear Lexie bawling. She needed reinforcements here.

"Honey?" Mac called up the stairs. "Everything okay?"

She almost laughed. "Um, no? Everything is most definitely not okay. Your daughter just punched Sophie." She heard Mac thunder up the stairs.

"Let me talk to her," he said, and she could tell by the look on his face that it was a conversation they both might live to regret. He reached for the door handle.

"Hold on a sec," Maggie said, thinking, buying time. "Let's pull ourselves together before we go in there. I think we're all on edge after last night's debacle."

"What the hell was she thinking?" For a man whose job demanded violence, Mac was intolerant of any in his own home. "Is Sophie okay?"

"I think so," Maggie said, but she couldn't really be sure. Her focus had been trained on Lexie. As if she'd heard them, Sophie stormed up the stairs. "I hate her!" she yelled. "I really hate her!" She darted into their room, threw herself on the bed, and burst into tears.

Maggie shook her head. "Well, there's your answer." She waited. "You want to take Soph and I'll try Lex?"

"Really?" Mac eyed her. "You sure you don't want me to be the heavy here?"

"Let me try first," Maggie said and let herself into the girls' room, pulling the door closed behind her. She sat down on the bed next to her daughter, whose head was buried in a pillow. Maggie ran her fingers through her hair. "Lex?"

Lexie rolled over, revealing a splotchy red face soaked in tears. "I'm sorry, Mom. I didn't mean it. Is Sophie okay?"

Maggie handed her a tissue. "I think she'll survive, but honestly, Lexie, what were you thinking? Why are you so mad?"

"I don't know." She sniffled into her Kleenex. "It just kind of happened."

"But, honey, it's not like you to slug your sister. What's going on? Is there something else? Is it this Matt boy? You haven't been yourself all summer."

She shrugged. Maggie combed her daughter's hair behind her ears with her fingers. "Do you really miss him that much?"

Lexie shrugged again. "Not anymore, I guess."

Maggie searched her daughter's face. "Not anymore? What does that mean?"

Lexie started to cry again. "He broke up with me!" She buried her face in her pillow again. "In a text." Maggie's heart tugged for her daughter. Her thoughts raced from *What a jerk!* to *Poor Lexie.*

"Oh, honey, I'm sorry." She rubbed between her daughter's shoulder blades. "Any boy who breaks up with you doesn't deserve you." She wondered how many more conversations like this they would have. She wished her daughters could be spared the kind of heartbreak that left a girl desolate, feeling as if she couldn't bear to fall in love ever again. Maggie didn't think Lexie had been dating this boy very long, maybe a couple of weeks? Though she understood all too well that in tween years, a few weeks could feel like months.

Eventually, Lexie calmed down. She found her way to her sister, who was still lying on her parents' bed, and apologized. "Your punishment, young lady," Mac said, "is to make your sister's bed for the rest of vacation." Lexie groaned, but within a matter of minutes, the girls were back to being friends and headed downstairs to hunt for shells on the beach. Maggie marched down to the kitchen and posted a new hammock schedule on the wall by the door. Why hadn't she thought of it earlier? From now on, people would need to reserve their hammock time in half-hour increments. She hesitated a moment, then wrote her own name in the first slot for today.

Upstairs she tugged off her smoky clothes and pulled on a bathing suit.

"Mommy!" Luke shouted, need laced in each syllable, when he spotted her coming down the stairs.

"Sorry, honey. I'm going for a quick dip before I rest on the hammock. Ask your aunties or daddy to help."

"Mommy, can I come?" His words trailed after her as she edged out the sliding door and onto the deck. She pretended not to hear.

There it was. She could see her spot of tranquillity on the edge of the dock, beckoning in a slant of late-afternoon sun. The water was a steely blue, the waves lapping up on the beach leaving little eddies behind before rolling back out to sea. She tiptoed around the beach toys littering the sand. Behind her, she overheard Mac coaxing Luke back inside: "Let's give Mommy some alone time, okay?"

She crossed their small private beach and walked onto the dock, the steel planks hot beneath her feet. Now that the crisis with the twins was resolved, she could turn her attention to what was really bothering her. She knew what they had to do: they needed to arrange an intervention for her father. Virgie had sought her out in a panic earlier this afternoon. She'd had a weird conversation with Arthur, almost as if he were stuck in time, replaying the teakettle incident in his mind. It appeared that the fire had jostled his confusion even further. He was ailing, and Maggie had known it. But she'd put on blinders, trying not to see. The teapot incident had been her wake-up call, Virgie's secret conversation in her bedroom the final straw. They'd all been in denial. No one wanted to admit that Arthur was getting old, needed their help. And Maggie felt responsible. Even Mac had agreed with her last night, when they spoke privately in their bedroom: Arthur shouldn't be left alone with the kids, maybe shouldn't be left alone at all. The man was seventy-two, Mac gently reminded her. Maybe after the summer, Arthur would consider moving in with them in Windsor.

Maggie felt a small shudder at the idea. She'd felt sorry for her dad this vacation, resolving to do better by him and include him more in the family. But inviting him to live with them? She wasn't sure she could handle it. Her dad hadn't been the easiest person to live with growing up. What would make her think it would be different now? It could, quite possibly, be worse. And the clutter that seemed to follow him wherever he went these days was enough to give her pause. One day, when she'd gone to retrieve a ball behind the shed, she'd stumbled upon his car. Upon his arrival, Arthur had parked it there out of sight, but Maggie was stunned to see the back-seat swimming in newspapers, tools, clothing, empty pizza boxes, all sorts of things that appeared to be, frankly, junk.

"Dad, how about we clean out your car after supper?" she asked one night at the dinner table. "We could help," she offered.

Arthur set down his hamburger and swallowed. "I think," he said, regarding all the adults at the table, "some people should mind their own business." He helped himself to more corn. Mac tele-graphed her a look, as if to say, *Best to let it lie.* But it irked her. Her dad could at least *try* to keep up appearances. She and her sisters all exchanged glances, while Gloria rolled her eyes. Maggie had meant to revisit it, but here they were, the house practically burnt down. She cast her eyes out over the water and dove in, the cold stroking her skin. Slowly, she surfaced and breathed, then began to put one arm in front of the other, cupping the water as she'd done thousands of times before, ladling up all the courage she could.

Maggie glanced down at the salad she'd been tossing in her stupor. The green leaves appeared wilted from overdressing. She set down the tongs and carried the wooden bowl to the dining table. Someone had already laid out plastic plates and silverware. Mac had suggested they eat out for dinner tonight, but now she was glad she'd insisted on staying in. The rest of the kitchen was still functioning, after all, and she was reluctant to leave the house alone so soon, as if it were a child in need of watching. So, they'd compromised, ordering the family fish fry.

There was the crunch of gravel as the car pulled into the driveway. A door slammed, then another. The husbands carried big brown bags filled with their supper, the children following them like puppies. Everyone scrambled for a place at the table. The scent of fried fish mingling with the earthy smells of sweat and suntan lotion wafted up. It had been a difficult twenty-four hours, Maggie thought, but they'd made it.

Arthur came to the table, and she watched while he slowly lowered himself into a chair. He'd been quiet all day, as if he suddenly didn't belong here, even declining her offer of a freshly squeezed lemonade. Maggie had pulled him aside at one point to reassure him that it was all right, he needed to let the whole incident go. But he claimed he wasn't feeling well and retired to a room upstairs.

"So, I was thinking," Virgie began, passing a plate of French fries, "that I might stay another week if that's all right with everyone. See that Boston doctor after all." Maggie gave her a smile. She and Virgie had already discussed this plan. Virgie would keep her appointment in Boston next week, and Maggie would drive her up. In the meantime, they'd try to schedule an appointment for Arthur as well.

"That's great." Mac was the first to jump in.

"Good for you," Jess said. "Get a clean bill of health while you're here. Besides, you should take a little more time for yourself. You work way too hard." There was a pause while everyone ate. A bittersweetness flavored the evening. Jess, Tim, and the kids were headed back tomorrow, as well as Gloria and Gio. The old gang was breaking up for another summer.

"I've been thinking, too," Jess continued. "What if the kids and I stayed on a little longer?" She studied the rest of the table. "Tim and I were talking. He needs to get back to work, but there's no reason Grace, Teddy, and I couldn't stay a bit longer. Assuming that's okay with you, Maggie?" She fastened her gaze on Maggie.

"Yes!" shouted the kids. "Can we, Auntie Maggie?" Grace asked.

"Can they?" her daughters pleaded. As much as she wanted everyone to stay longer, Maggie felt slightly trapped. Why would Jess ask her in front of the kids? She knew it would be impossible to say no.

"Well," she began, but Gloria interrupted her.

"Hey, don't forget about us old fogies," she said. She reached across the table and patted Maggie's hand. "Gio and I might prolong our stay, too. Turns out our hotel has some openings next week. Guess it pays to stay at the middle-of-the-pack places."

Tree Pose, Maggie thought. *Calm breezes off the water. Breathe.* This was precisely what she'd been hoping for, wasn't it? Everyone vacationing on the Cape for the entire month of July. Then why was she feeling stressed, as if she was about to sign up for more heartache, more babysitting, more worry? She glanced at Mac, then her dad. A veiled silence hung over the table while everyone waited for her to speak.

"Of course," she said finally. "It would be wonderful to have you all stay for as long as you like. Besides, you hardly have to ask. It's everyone's house. It's the *summer* house."

Cheers went up from the kids, and Virgie clapped. Luke and Teddy exchanged high fives. Mac grinned, and Maggie smiled back, hoping like hell she hadn't just made the worst mistake of the entire vacation.

23

Virgie

After dinner, a group started up a game of Clue on the deck while Virgie retired to the living room with her sisters. Jess flipped on the television, and Maggie leafed through a pile of magazines. The night was still warm and sticky, and a much-needed breeze drifted in through the windows. Virgie fanned herself with a magazine. She'd been meaning to call Jackson all day, and now seemed as good a time as any. She snuck upstairs and grabbed her cell. "I wish you were here," she told Jackson when he picked up. It was the first time she'd admitted it out loud, but she wanted him to know. It felt important.

"Me, too." She heard him exhale into the telephone. "It feels like you've been gone for months, and it's only been a couple of weeks. What time does your flight get in?"

"Oh." She hesitated. "About that. I was thinking of extending my stay."

There was a pause. "What? Why?"

"Well, my dad hasn't been doing so great. I think he needs to get checked out at Mass General. And then, I can follow up with that specialist in Boston. Make sure everything's okay with me." She hadn't even mentioned the fire yet, but she didn't want to overwhelm him in the first breath.

"All right." He sounded as if he was considering it.

"Don't you think that's the right decision?" she pressed. She was slightly annoyed that Jackson hadn't immediately jumped on the bandwagon with the idea. Everyone else in her family had practically threatened to handcuff and deliver her to the specialist in Boston. And, honestly, at this point, Virgie just wanted to know what was going on with her. The not-knowing was becoming more excruciating than knowing.

"It's not that," Jackson said, backing down quickly. "Of course, it's the right decision. I'm just sorry to hear about your dad. Disappointed I won't get to see you sooner."

She threw herself down on her bed. "Me, too. That part sucks." She twirled her hair around her finger, staring up at the ceiling. "Oh, and I didn't even tell you." She paused. "We had a fire in the kitchen last night. When it rains, it pours."

"What do you mean?" Jackson asked, sounding alarmed. "Is everyone okay?"

"Yes, thankfully, everyone's fine. The kitchen just doesn't look so great." She gave a small laugh.

"Jesus."

"I know. My dad forgot to take the kettle off the stove. Melted right into the burner. That's part of the reason why I need to stay out here. Maggie and I are worried he's having some memory issues." She snorted. "Well, I guess that's pretty obvious."

"Wow. Okay. Yeah, he should definitely get that checked out. Do you want me to call work for you or anything, let them know you'll need another week?"

She was touched that he would think of such a gesture. He

really *was* a good guy. "You're so sweet, but no thanks. Larry is my next call."

"Sounds like you've got everything covered."

"I try."

"I miss you," he said again, his voice gentle, longing.

Virgie knew she had to get off before she said anything she might regret, like *I need you* or *I think I might be in love with you.* "I'll call you tomorrow, all right?"

"All right. Bye."

Her next call was Larry. She checked her watch. It was 7:30, which was 4:30 Seattle time. He was probably crossing the last Ts for the 6:00 newscast, but if she was lucky, she'd catch him.

"Hallo?" He picked up on the first ring, and at the sound of her boss's voice, all the pressure of work came flooding back to her.

"Larry. Hi, it's Virgie."

"Virginia!" he yelled. "Where the heck have you been? I've been trying to reach you all day for a story that's right in your neighborhood. At least I think it is. Nantucket?"

So that explained all the missed calls from Larry today. She'd simply deleted them, not yet ready to talk. She ticked through the list of probable Nantucket stories: A shark sighting? A celebrity visit? Hadn't Jess mentioned that Princess Kate and Prince William were vacationing around here?

"Oh," she said. "Actually, I was going to ask you if—" But Larry cut her off before she could say more.

"Listen, have you heard of a fellow named Howard Isaacson? He's supposedly a business tycoon and word has it that he's gotten himself into a boatload of trouble. Some kind of wild party he had on his yacht down there. Anyway, he's got ties to Seattle money. I don't have time to get into it now, but could you do some sleuthing around, check it out while you're there?"

She felt the familiar surge of adrenaline. A Nantucket tycoon involved in shady dealings on his yacht? The story had *tantalizing* written all over it. Virgie knew Larry was trying to make up for the Liz Crandle piece. She knew she should jump at the opportunity.

"Sounds intriguing," she said carefully. "But I'm sorry I can't do it right now."

There was a pause. "What?"

"I just can't, Larry. The timing is bad. My dad isn't doing well, he almost burned the house down yesterday, and well, I think we need to get him checked out or something." She couldn't help it. The run of sentences that had been playing in her mind spilled out. "I need some more time. Vacation time. I'm sorry to have to ask. If I need to take it in personal days, that's fine."

She waited, her heart racing. "Geez. I'm sorry to hear that. Okay. Yeah, sure. Take whatever you need. Let us know when you're coming back." He clicked off as soon as Virgie thanked him. When she set the phone down, she realized she'd been digging her fingernails into her palm, little pink half-moons popping up on her skin. She'd expected resistance from Larry, possibly a veiled threat of losing her job. That he hadn't offered any made her wonder if she could breathe easily or if, to the contrary, she should worry more. She'd just passed on a potentially huge story, one that she would have leapt on a month ago. Maybe she *was* the one who needed to get checked out.

When she got back downstairs, both sisters were absorbed in their magazines. "Honestly, do you guys read anything other than *Good Housekeeping*?" she asked. "Whatever happened to *Vogue* or *Redbook*?" Jess volleyed her a look, her forehead pulled into little furrows.

"When you're a mom, you'll understand," she said.

"I sincerely hope you're mistaken." Virgie wandered through the living room, picking up stray toys and abandoned flip-flops. She felt anxious after her talk with Larry. She wondered whom he'd pass the story to. Probably Thomas. Well, she honestly didn't care. For the first time in her life, she didn't care.

She sank into the couch, a mystery novel in hand. What was the matter with her?

24

Arthur

Arthur was working on his manuscript, urging Inspector Larson to make a discovery, but nothing was coming to him. Why did he think he could write another book? He'd nearly burned down the house the other night, had probably emotionally scarred his grandchildren for life, and now here he was on Sunday morning pretending to care about a fictional world that perhaps only a few other people would ever care to read about.

He got up to pour himself another cup of coffee, his eyes fluttering to the undisturbed trap beyond the kitchen window. Roger must have had a quiet night. Maybe he'd found another family to harass. Even the house was blessedly hushed, everyone else still asleep upstairs. The kids had slept in the tent again last night. He walked over to the bookcase in the living room and skimmed the titles. All his books were there, his life's work. Funny how slim and insignificant so many paperbacks could look on a shelf.

When he saw *The Things They Carried,* he pulled it out and blew the dust from the top. It was one of his all-time favorites. Arthur thought it the most astonishing depiction of war ever written. The weight, the heft, the burden of those soldiers' packs brought so vividly to life. He could almost feel the pack on his own back. The weight of worry. The burden of his own stuff that he carried around with him day after day. Missing Gloria. Worrying about the girls. The stress of trying to meet another deadline. He was getting too old to cart around so much.

He thumbed through the yellowed pages. Someday he'd like to have a talk with Tim O'Brien, ask him if he thought Lieutenant Jimmy Cross's emotional load got any lighter, or did he truly spend all that time missing Martha and feeling bad about Ted Lavender's death? He and O'Brien could share a whiskey, maybe even a laugh or two, over the things a man was meant to carry during a lifetime. He could ask O'Brien what he thought of Gloria's ending their marriage of forty-six years. He bet O'Brien would have some choice words to offer.

He put the book back on the shelf and checked the clock. Only 6:30, a tad early for his morning walk, but so what? He went to fetch his trash gator, tucked in behind the couch, and the trash bag that he'd been gathering his things in. He'd nearly had to rip it out of Maggie's hands the other day when she'd been in the midst of one of her cleaning frenzies. "That's mine," he yelled, feeling like a stubborn child.

"But it's trash, Dad." Maggie gave him a bewildered look.

"What's one woman's trash is another man's treasure," he explained and snatched it from her. She shook her head, not understanding. And how could she? He didn't expect her to covet the things he'd been gathering on the beach over vacation, a hodgepodge of intricate shells, recyclable cans, a child's lost sneaker, some loose change.

Now when he picked it up, the bag emitted a faint pungent odor. Maggie wouldn't approve. He'd have to start hiding it outside, maybe under the deck. He let himself out the sliding doors and jumped to see two turtles, each no bigger than a dinner plate, scratching about in a plastic pool. He'd forgotten about the turtles. Yesterday, the boys had discovered them in the marsh grasses and lugged the swimming pool out from the shed, filling it with water and rocks and a handful of cape plums. It was a moving gesture, trying to make the pool a more hospitable place for the tortoises. What had the kids named them again? Something silly, like Mister and Thomas.

"Good morning, fellas," he said as he stepped around the pool. "Pretty crappy way to start the day, huh?" He watched while one, perhaps Mister, scrambled up the side, then slid back down again. Arthur imagined the poor thing up all night hatching his escape plan. The other turtle had climbed onto a small rock in the middle of the pool where he sunned himself. When the kids searched through the yellowed guide to Cape wildlife last night, they'd determined that these were boxers, their yellow blotches being the identifying marks. Arthur was tempted to set the creatures free, but then thought better of it. Luke and Teddy would be spitting mad if he did.

Down on the beach, gator in hand, he could see that it was shaping up to be a beautiful day. The weekend had been trying. All he wanted was for it to be over, for the kitchen to be fixed, for the girls to stop looking at him from under hooded eyes. He knew there'd been some discussion about him that he hadn't been privy to. He could see it on their faces all day yesterday. What were they going to do with him? he wondered. Did they think they'd just put him in one of those homes, where old people who couldn't remember what day it was wandered around with their walkers? Where the halls always smelled sour no matter how much disinfectant they used? Where bland, glutinous vegetables were served in the hopes that they would eventually be eaten? Where he was supposed to get excited about placing fall leaves in a wreath with a glue gun?

Being in a place like that would kill him just as surely as a bullet to the head.

He didn't know how many times he could apologize to Maggie and Jess, but he suspected it would never feel like enough. He'd been watching their children, his grandchildren, and he'd dropped the ball. Hell, he'd kicked the ball right into the ocean. He told himself that anyone could forget about a kettle. He'd been absorbed by the Monopoly game. But what he hadn't told anyone was that he was on his second glass of scotch and had decided that a stiff cup of tea would be just the thing to help him concentrate on the miniature boardwalk. All those tiny plastic houses started to look so alike! He wasn't drunk. He'd never get drunk when he was in charge. But he'd had a few drinks, just to ease the way into the evening hours, like he always did. Regardless of the scotch, he would have forgotten the kettle. He knew this, felt sure of it in his old, rickety bones.

But he couldn't imagine confiding this fact to his daughters, ever. Especially Maggie. Then, there would be absolutely no hope of forgiveness. As it was, he didn't know if his daughters would ever exonerate him. The one saving grace was that everyone was fine. And the kitchen could be fixed without huge expense. He'd offered to pay for it all, insisting the girls pick out a fancy new stove with lots of bells and whistles. It was the least he could do.

But Arthur was worried. He'd always promised himself that if ever he felt his mind going, he would end it, take his leave of this world before anyone was forced to help him or, worse, pity him. And he'd gotten confused about the teakettle yesterday, thinking he'd left it on again, until Virgie (poor Virginia!) had reassured him that it wasn't possible. He'd done it the day before. How could he have mixed that up?

Maybe he really was losing it. He couldn't stand the thought of one day looking into a daughter's face and not remembering her name. Couldn't bear the thought of forgetting that he had grandchildren or that he had shared forty-six wonderful years with his wife. Losing his mind, his faculties, was akin to a life sentence behind bars.

Perhaps he would schedule an appointment when he got back to Maine. Check in with the doc to make sure all the pistons were firing.

He removed his shoes and stepped onto the sand. He hated to admit it, but the vacation that he'd been anticipating for so long was not shaping up as he'd hoped. Seeing his daughters and grandchildren was supposed to reinvigorate him; the slower, expansive time on the Cape would allow him to write without interruption. Secretly, he'd dreamed, too, that Gloria would see the error of her ways and return to him. Of course, nothing had gone according to plan. His grandchildren didn't trust him, might even be scared of him now. His novel was in shambles. And Gloria, who at first had been invitingly flirtatious, had basically betrothed herself to Gio. What the hell was he doing here anyway? Arthur wondered. He had another week left, but he'd just as soon head back to Maine now. It would be best for everyone.

His eye landed on a piece of metal, glinting in the sun, and he retrieved it with the gator. A chewing gum wrapper. He tossed it in the bag anyway. It was shiny; Roger might be tempted by it. He thought back to a wonderful interview he'd watched on television the other day. Who was it again? Oh, yes, Delia Ephron, the writer. The sister of Nora. Arthur had always liked Nora Ephron's comedies, even if they had a romantic bent to them. Perhaps *because* they had a romantic twist. Over the years, he and Gloria had watched *When Harry Met Sally* about twenty times. The montages of the old couples who recounted how they met and fell in love made him tear up each time. But Delia had said something that struck him as fabulously, ineffably true in that interview. She spoke about how close she and Nora were and then went on to characterize their relationship as "a collaboration on life." Arthur thought it one of the most beautiful sentiments he'd ever heard. *A collaboration on life.* And as soon as she said it, his mind fastened on Gloria. That's what they'd had.

That was exactly it.

Since she'd left, he'd been without his collaborator. No wonder he was getting nowhere on his novel, in his life. Gloria had given him some of his best material. Helping him on plot twists, inventing red herrings, pointing out where his logic was flawed or where Inspector Larson was being dense. She'd been his best reader. Without her, he was lost. Perhaps these were the words she needed to hear to come back to him. *I'm lost without you.* It occurred to him that he'd never told her these exact words. How dense could he be! He couldn't expect her to read his mind, to know how he still rolled over in bed to lay an arm across her and was jolted to discover only empty space where her warm body used to lay.

As the sky began to brighten, Arthur resolved to tell Gloria this very thing. Today. Gio wasn't her collaborator in life. Arthur was. Perhaps, he thought, shaking his head, she'd only been waiting for him to say these very words before returning to him. Could it be that simple? He started to laugh out loud at how preposterous the whole thing sounded. He was lost without Gloria and she was lost without him. But, true to form, she'd been waiting for him to admit it first. Once he did, her face would reveal her relief and she'd say something like, "I was wondering how long it would take you to realize it. Now, come on, let's go home."

Sometimes life was so simple, and here he'd been making it unnecessarily complicated. The whole kitchen incident had derailed him, but now he saw it was the very thing to shake him awake. To reunite him with Gloria. And he wanted that so very, very much. He wanted back their walks together along the Maine coast, dinners sitting across from each other discussing the latest book they'd read, a wife who would replace the cap on the toothpaste tube for him, who would lovingly turn the glasses in the cupboard rim down, instead of leaving them haphazardly up as he always did. Someone who would switch the radio to a favorite song and offer her upturned hand, waiting to be led across the living room floor, the fire flickering in the background and music playing, perhaps "Let It Be Me" by the Everly Brothers. He could hear it, even taste it, the sweet flavor of Gloria's companionship folded back into his life.

A yawning stretch of dark blue, the ocean beckoned to him. Arthur set down his shoes, gator, and bag and pulled off his shirt, suddenly feeling like a younger man. He rubbed his hands together briskly, thinking of Gloria. *Always of Gloria.* Yes, a dip would be just the thing to mark a fresh start, his resolve to embrace life anew. After a few recent scares, it was dawning on him that his life as he knew it might be flying by faster than he'd bargained for. He was going to make the most of his time left. With Gloria back in his days, the rest would fall into place. His girls would visit more often with the grandkids, his writing would flow, his bed would no longer be empty.

He wouldn't take no for an answer.

He walked to the water's edge, letting the icy waves lap at his toes. He braced himself for the cold, walking in knee-deep, then waist-deep. When he glanced down, he realized he'd forgotten to remove his belt. Too bad. He would swim until his arms started to tire, then return revitalized. His heart was hammering with excitement, and at last his impatience for it all to begin—the rest of his life—shot through him. He dove into the water, ducking his head underneath, and began to swim.

The cold, bracing at first, eventually enveloped him in its soothing embrace. Then, the water lifted him up, buoying his body along, a silver streak in the wide-open sea.

25

Maggie

When the police car pulled into the driveway, Maggie already knew. Three days had passed, too long for a seventy-two-year-old man to survive on the open beach against the elements. It was unlikely there was any good news behind the stiff wrap of knuckles on the door, which came on Wednesday morning at 11:20. Maggie was fixing herself a glass of iced tea when Luke yelled out, "Mommy, policeman's here!"

On Sunday morning, when Arthur had been gone for a few hours, she grew curious. "Has anyone seen Dad?" she asked a silent house. She went out on the deck with binoculars and searched the beach, but only a few families were scattered about so early in the day. Maybe Arthur had set off for a morning walk into town, she theorized, and decided to grab breakfast at the Blueberry Bagel. She sent Mac off to check and, after that, to the library, to Sal's, anyplace that might be open on a Sunday.

But Mac returned shaking his head. Sophie was the first to notice that Grandpa's trash gator was missing from its usual spot behind the couch. "Then he must have gone for a walk along the beach!" Maggie felt herself flooding with relief: Arthur had gotten preoccupied with his search for rubbish and was taking a longer-than-normal stroll along the ocean.

They all rushed down to the beach, including Gloria and Gio, who'd arrived shortly after Maggie called to see if they'd heard from Arthur that morning. About a half mile from the house, Luke, who had run ahead, called out that he'd found Grandpa's shirt, his boat shoes, and the trash gator and bag. They gathered around the small heap of items, then circled the area, expecting to find Arthur bent over investigating a crab or a crane's nest in the sea grasses. Mac snatched the binoculars and cast his eyes out over the ocean, while Jess wondered aloud if Arthur might have fallen along the rocks closer to land. They separated into smaller groups and searched the shoreline. But when, after a few hours, there was still no sign of him, Maggie began to worry in earnest. She could read the look on Mac's face; he was beginning to think something wasn't right, too.

He pulled out his cell and dialed the local precinct. "Hi, it's Officer McNeil here from the house at Forty-two Pilgrim Lane." He paused. "That's right. The one with the fire. Listen, I realize it's early to file a missing person report, but my father-in-law has been missing since early this morning. It's not like him and we're starting to worry." There was a pause. "We just found his shirt and shoes about a half mile from our house down on the beach." Another question. "He's seventy-two. Uh-huh, good swimmer." He paused. "Well, I guess you could say he's been having some memory issues." He leveled his eyes at Jess, who nodded, and Maggie felt her stomach pull into knots. *This is serious* was all she could think. "Thank you, I'd appreciate it," Mac said. "We'll do that in the meantime."

"They're on their way," Mac confirmed. "They want someone to stay at the house in case Arthur comes home. Everyone keep your cell phones on. Why don't Maggie and I head back to the house?

You guys want to keep looking out here?" Jess and Tim nodded and pulled the kids closer.

"I'll stay here, too," Virgie confirmed.

"Us, too," announced Gloria, taking Gio's hand.

But by the time evening fell, there was still no word of Arthur. They'd gone knocking door to door along the beach with a picture, but no one had seen him. Any plans anyone in the family might have had to head back to Boston were scratched. They turned in for the day and left the porch and deck lights burning into the night.

"It's like he disappeared into thin air," Maggie whispered as she crawled into bed.

"Don't worry, we'll find him," Mac said softly, and they fell into a restless sleep.

The next day, Monday, was gray and stormy, and the officers returned to the house with more questions. "Is there any chance he might have gone into the water?" one asked.

Maggie shook her head. They'd already been through this yesterday. "Sure, there's a chance, but my dad's a good swimmer. He wouldn't do anything stupid."

The officer clicked his pen and studied her. "He's familiar with the undertows? They can be pretty powerful down here."

"Of course," she said, angered by the question.

"Sorry, I have to ask," he replied, as if reading her mind. By nightfall on Monday, there was still no word of Arthur. Maggie understood after years of being married to a cop that the first forty-eight hours were critical in a missing person case.

"What about his shoes?" Jess pressed. Maggie nodded. The shoes bothered her, too. She had a difficult time imagining her dad wandering off without his shoes, unless of course he was headed into the water. But Maggie struggled just as much to imagine her dad, a lifetime lover of the ocean, meeting harm in the water. How many times had he gone for morning walks and morning swims in the

Atlantic, both here and back home in Maine? The water was like his second home. For him to simply wander in, ignoring high tide and a strong current—all things he'd warned them about constantly when they were children—struck her as implausible. Had he wanted his life to end? The thought snuck up on Maggie as she sorted through the various scenarios, but she tamped it down just as quickly. They just needed to keep looking.

The next morning, Tuesday, the house struggled awake, reinvigorated by fresh coffee and a call from the station that someone had seen an older man ambling around town, looking confused and lost. Maggie felt her hopes surge. The kitchen buzzed with activity, with second-guessing and stories about what they'd say to Arthur once he arrived home safely. Maggie and Mac would insist he move in with them; he'd have no choice. Within the hour, though, the police had located the local man, an Alzheimer's patient who'd wandered from his senior housing facility. Maggie collapsed in a dining room chair and burst into tears. Gloria came over and laid a hand on her shoulder. "Don't worry, honey," she said. "Daddy's out there, I can feel it."

The rest of the day was even more excruciating. Where else could her dad be? Maggie wracked her brain, but the only scenarios she came up with were bad ones. She went for a run on the beach, cooked pasta and meatballs, and set a place for Arthur at the dinner table, as if calling him home. Later, she stood on the deck and gazed out at the ocean, as if she could coax her father's whereabouts from its rhythms. "Please, please find him," she whispered into the night, even as she felt her hope dwindling.

So, when the police cruiser pulled up on Wednesday, there was a piece of her that already suspected the truth.

"Mac," she called softly. "They're here." She waited for him to join her before opening the door. She took in the young officer, no more than twenty-five, who stood with his hat in his hands. "Maggie McNeil?" he inquired. She nodded and squeezed Mac's hand. "I'm so sorry, ma'am," he said. Maggie fell back against Mac while the officer continued to speak. The rest of the family filed in around them. "A family found your dad washed up on the beach this morning, just a few miles down. He was wearing tan shorts and a belt. Officer Mc-Carthy, who knows Mr. Herington, identified the body."

And at the words *the body,* Maggie let out a wail, a sound almost inhuman, and dropped her glass, sending iced tea, ice cubes, and shards of glass scattering across the floor. The officer jumped back, and only when Maggie lifted her eyes did she notice his hand resting on his pistol. His eyes met hers, and he slowly pulled his hand away.

"Sorry, it's instinct," he explained.

"Kids, go in the kitchen," Jess said, shooing them out of the hallway. She returned with swathes of paper towels, a broom, and a trash bag.

"But, Mommy." Gracie came up beside her. "Is Grandpa okay?"

"Hush," Jess said and led her back to the kitchen. Max helped Maggie to the deacon's bench in the entryway.

"Where's Virgie?" she asked as she settled on the bench, but she could barely get out the words. She realized she was struggling to get air, sucking in quick, short breaths. She placed a hand on her chest. "Can't breathe," she wheezed.

Tim appeared with a paper bag. "Breathe in and out. Long deep breaths. That's it," he encouraged while she worked to deliver suffi-cient air to her lungs. Before them, Jess swept up the glass and ice. Nobody spoke.

"Someone," Maggie began, then held the bag back up to her mouth and inhaled. She pulled it away, exhaling. "Needs to call Mom." Gloria and Gio were still at their hotel.

"Why don't I go get her and bring her here?" Tim offered.

"Good idea, honey." Jess glanced up from the floor, where she was now wiping up iced tea, and when her gaze met Tim's, her eyes filled with tears. "Thanks." Maggie knew that when Tim showed up at

Gloria's door, as anomalous as thunderclouds on a perfect summer day, her mother would understand immediately what his presence meant.

"Where's Virgie?" she asked again, resting the paper bag in her lap. Mac scanned the entryway.

"I'll go look." He left the room while the officer stood by the front door and stared down at his hat, worrying the brim with his thumb. Maggie wondered if this was the first time he'd had to deliver such news on his watch. An odd numbness dropped over her, as if the scene playing out before her was from a surreal film and not her very real life. "Officer . . . I'm sorry, I didn't catch your name."

"Olsen," he confirmed. "Todd Olsen."

"Officer Olsen," she tried again. "Do we know anything else?"

He looked at her searchingly. "There doesn't seem to have been any foul play, if that's what you're asking. On the face of things, it looks like a drowning. An autopsy report would confirm that for you, of course." She nodded, and her gaze settled on the kids, who hovered in the kitchen just beyond earshot. When Lexie caught Maggie's eye, she spun around and coaxed the other children outside.

It felt like only a matter of minutes—though it couldn't have been, that wasn't possible—before Gloria burst through the front door. "It's just like him!" She rushed to Maggie and collapsed beside her, grabbing her arm. "Leaving us like this with a dramatic exit that we have to figure out for ourselves." She sounded angry between sobs, wronged. "How could he?"

Maggie was momentarily stunned. Her mother was faulting Arthur somehow? As if his death were a personal slight against her? She blew into her bag again, then rested it in her lap. "Mom, I don't think Dad planned this."

Gloria turned to her, her bright blue eyes wide and rimmed with pain. Tiny red lines wove across the whites. Maggie could see eddies of wrinkles underneath. "Of course not," Gloria said now, and shook her head as if she'd been in another world and was only now settling back down to earth. "Of course not," her mother's voice repeated, falling to a whisper.

Mac stepped back in the room. "I found Virgie. She's okay. She just wants some time alone. Taking a walk on the beach." He rested his hand on Maggie's shoulder. "Why don't we all move into the living room? Wouldn't that be more comfortable? Officer, can I get you something to drink?"

And with that, they filed into the room that would become the headquarters for all things Arthur over the next two weeks. There was a police report, an autopsy that confirmed drowning, and several phone calls with insurance companies and Arthur's attorneys back in Maine. There was also the heartbreaking work of letting the kids know. Luke and Teddy were too young to understand, really, but Maggie and Jess tried to explain that Grandpa was in a better place now.

"But where is heaven?" Luke demanded. "Can we see it? How did Grandpa get there? On a rocket ship?"

So many questions, and Maggie didn't think she was equipped to answer them. But she tried: "Far, far above the clouds. No, we can't see it, but Grandpa can see us from heaven. He might have taken a rocket ship. No one really knows how you get to heaven." She thought they were fair, honest responses. She liked the image of Arthur traveling to heaven on a rocket, red flames streaking across a star-studded sky.

The thing that nagged at her the most, though, was the autopsy report. She still had a difficult time believing Arthur had drowned, no matter what his clogged lungs might suggest. He was a strong swimmer, he knew the ocean's currents. It didn't add up in Maggie's mind. But Mac had told her to let it go. Her dad hadn't exactly been himself the last weeks. Who knew why he waded into the water that day? Perhaps something had caught his eye. Maybe an undertow had wrapped him in its waves and caught him unawares. What Maggie really wanted to understand most was this: Had Arthur willingly given himself up to the sea? Had he known his mind was going and, thus, wanted to end his life? The thought dogged her, and, of course, on its heels came a swift kick of guilt. If she'd been more attuned to Arthur's situation, if she'd listened more carefully, she might have been able to prevent such a tragedy from happening in the first place.

"Maggie, girl," Mac said to her the night before they would close up the summer house. "Why do you insist on carrying everyone's troubles around with you?" He cupped her face in his hands and stared into her eyes, like she did when she wanted something to register with the kids. "This is not your fault; you understand that, right?"

She nodded slowly, reluctantly, big tears pooling in her eyes.

"Repeat after me," Mac ordered. "Arthur's passing is not my fault. It was his time."

She swallowed, hard. "Arthur's passing is not my fault. It was his time."

Mac dropped his hands and hugged her. "There, now, my sweet girl. Let it go."

They both knew, of course, that it wasn't so easy, but for the time being, she let her husband hold her tightly while she remembered what it felt like to be loved deeply, without judgment.

Maggie pulled the front door shut, turned the key, and handed it to Sophie to return to its hiding spot behind the shed. A shudder swept over her. Coming back to the summer house would never be the same. Would it hold too many sad memories, she wondered, for them to return next year? The kids piled into the car with their iPods and pillows, and Virgie, who'd already returned her Mini Cooper on the Cape, climbed into the passenger seat. Mac had already headed back to Windsor in Arthur's old Buick this morning, and Jess, Tim, and the kids had packed up a few days ago. Maggie studied the house one last time as they backed out of the driveway, as if trying to memorize its every detail. "Good-bye, house," she said, a mantra they'd recited each summer since the kids were little. In the back of the car, Arthur's ashes were safely collected in a blue ceramic vase that was cradled between towels. Though they'd had a small ceremony at the beach house, her father had requested in his will that his ashes be scattered out to sea in Maine.

And so it would be.

They'd dismantled the pier, emptied the pantry, drained the pipes, and turned off the water. The raccoon crate sat empty in the shed. *Maybe next year,* Luke said wistfully. Maggie had thrown sheets over the furniture and drawn the shades. She wondered momentarily if her dad's ghost would haunt Pilgrim Lane. Would Arthur continue writing mysteries, even in death? Perhaps, she thought, she should leave at least one chair open for him, one with a view where he could sit and write. She knew it was silly, but in the master bedroom, she'd pulled the sheet off the armchair that faced out on the ocean. It was a lovely spot to write.

As they pulled off the dirt road onto the highway, Maggie peered over at Virgie, who was already fast asleep. Arthur's death had been particularly hard on her baby sister—she'd been closest to him. But in the last week, Virgie had settled into a quiet, moody place, not unlike that of a teenager, and so now Maggie tiptoed around her as well. She reminded herself that Virgie was dealing with a lot, not least of which was her own upcoming doctor's appointment in Boston. Fortunately, they'd been able to reschedule it for the first week in August.

Maggie sighed. She was trying so hard to do right by everyone. Everyone wanted a piece of her, and the lengths she would go to for each and every one of them were impossible to measure. Her family was her whole world, her orbit. And yet, increasingly, she felt as if she were letting them all down. As if what she were equipped to give would never be enough. Maybe she was crazy to consider bringing another child into their home. She could barely manage with the ones she had.

She was beginning to understand, though, that all her love couldn't protect the ones she loved. Not forever. Not always. Perhaps that was what the summer house had been trying to tell her with its creaks and groans this year. Each time Maggie attempted to negotiate a truce between the kids, between Jess and Tim, or Gloria and Arthur, it was as if the house was laughing at her. *You think you can fix* this? *Think again!* Every time she picked up a stray flip-flop, a forgotten towel, an empty glass, the house knew her attempts at order were for naught. *Just wait till you see what happens in the kitchen!* It seemed to smirk. *The Book of Summer* was lost forever. Arthur was gone to them forever.

Life is about change, Mac had said at one point during the week, and Maggie had brushed him off. *I don't need platitudes,* she'd quipped. But her fervent desire for this summer to be like every other one had gone up in flames. Maybe her husband was right: maybe change didn't necessarily mean disaster. Maybe the mess of life was the very thing she was supposed to enjoy instead of always fighting it, trying to impose order. The universe was trying to tell her something—was it, perhaps, to let go? She bit the quick of her fingernail as she drove along, debating her own battling emotions. When *The Book of Summer* was destroyed in the fire, she'd felt as if her own right arm had been lopped off. But really, wasn't it just a silly book? The memories on paper were the same ones that she, Mac, and the kids carried around in their hearts already. She could re-create the book, maybe even start a new one.

She rolled down the window, letting the Cape air fly through her hair, *feeling* summer. It had been a long, difficult month. And it occurred to her that yet another thing was different about this summer: for once, Maggie couldn't wait to get home.

AUGUST

26

Jess

Jess sat at her desk, wading through the piles of paper that had long ago outgrown her in-box, an inevitable consequence of taking vacation time. Much could be tossed, but some, such as special requests from parents for the new school year, needed attention. When she'd asked her mother-in-law if she could watch the kids for several days in August, Eleanor was more than happy to oblige. "I've been wondering when I'd get my grandkids back," she teased, as if Jess and Tim had stolen them away from her for the month of July. Jess wanted to get through as much as possible before she left for Maine in a few days to help her sisters pack up Arthur's house.

On her desk were scattered piles of thank-you cards and little gifts from students. Things had been so crazy at the end of the school year that she hadn't properly had a chance to sort through any of them before leaving for vacation. There were funny cards (Bart Simpson, in particular, was popular among the boys this year), heartfelt notes, and even a few cards from parents, thanking her for taking a particular child under her wing. Jess flipped through a few more until she saw one addressed in a familiar cursive: *Ms. Herington, Best Principal, Mentor, Friend Ever!!* The exclamation points were dotted with hearts. Jess's own heart lifted when she saw the handwriting. She ripped open the yellow envelope and pulled out the card, an exquisite Chinese symbol hand-painted on the front. Over four years, Jess had watched Tamara grow from a hesitant, soft-spoken teenager into a thoughtful, dedicated young artist. She was the first girl in their school to be admitted to the Rhode Island School of Design, and on a full scholarship.

Jess ran her finger over the design, delicate black shoots of ink on white parchment paper that reminded her of two stars suspended in the night. She opened the card and read:

> *Dear Ms. Herington,*
>
> *I painted this design for you because it's the Chinese symbol for Friendship. You're a best friend, a mentor, and like a mom to me. Thank you so much for everything you've done—without you, I wouldn't be on my way to college!*
>
> *Love, Tamara*
>
> *P.S. Come visit me at RISD! You can sleep on my floor!* ☺

Jess felt herself well up with emotion, then laughed when she read the postscript at the bottom. She propped the card up on the shelf behind her desk. Perhaps she would frame it. It was a good reminder of why she was in this job, even on the toughest, most frustrating days. She turned back to open a few of the colorful gift bags dotting her desk. There were an assortment of new mugs (always mugs!), framed pictures with students, summer scarves in cheery prints, and a beautiful Pandora bracelet with a small cupcake that made her smile. She'd shared a love of cupcakes with the president of the student council; this was the girl's token of appreciation. Jess wrapped the bracelet around her wrist and fastened the clasp.

It felt odd to be sitting at her desk now with the distance of a few weeks. Last she was here, she was rushing to finish everything she needed to before vacation: filing last-minute teacher evaluations; trying to confirm hires for next year; listening to teachers' concerns about everything from a lack of supplies to lack of parental involvement. At the time, she'd half listened, wondering if, when she returned to this place, her marriage would still be intact. A few weeks ago, she honestly couldn't say. But now, she felt as if she could look across her desk with fresh eyes. She was here because she believed in herself; and now she knew with certainty that her husband did, too.

On the morning that Arthur had set out for his walk, she'd been curled up against Tim in bed while he slept. She was looking out the window, thinking about how strange the past month had been. She'd gone from not wanting to share a room with her husband to wanting him by her side all the time. It was a little like noticing the boy you thought was a nerd sophomore year returning in September, tanned, no longer wearing glasses, and suddenly a catch for junior year. The summer sun, the long conversations they'd had since that day on the beach, had all worked to melt the icy ball that had formed between them during the past year.

It wasn't perfect, but it wasn't awful either. They were drifting on calmer seas. Even Grace and Teddy seemed to have noticed.

Tim forgave her, and so how could she not forgive him? They'd both strayed from their marriage, but they also both realized that they wanted it to work. Over the last days at the summer house, Tim conceded that he'd thrown himself into work, not wanting to face the troubles at home. He wanted to try harder, he said now, be more present in their marriage. And Jess acknowledged that the more Tim had insisted everything was fine between them, the more she'd retreated.

When they got back from the summer house, the first thing Jess had done was to toss every single Post-It pad into the trash. From now on, only talking was allowed. *Don't think it, say it!* they joked, even though it was the complete opposite of what they counseled Grace and Teddy to do (*think before you say something you'll regret*).

Now she wanted to hold her husband, run her fingers through his hair. And that's what she'd been doing the morning Arthur set out for his daily walk on the beach. A knock on the bedroom door was the first inkling that something might be amiss. The night before, the sisters had discussed an intervention. They were worried. Worried Arthur wasn't safe living by himself up in the house in Maine. Even Gloria offered to chime in, wield her influence and convince him it was time to move closer to the girls. They wanted him to see a doctor to make sure everything was all right. They'd gone to bed that night with a game plan in hand: they'd approach Arthur after lunch. The trick would be not to alienate him. He could be so stubborn and might dig in his heels further, insisting he was perfectly fine living by himself.

But, of course, all those plans were derailed.

Jess's office line lit, and she picked up her desk phone. "Are you ready?"

She looked at the wall clock: 12:30 already. Lunchtime. "Yep, let's go," she said to her husband, tossing another sheet of paper into the trash. They had a lunch date downtown. The significance of those three words twined together did not escape her. Jess rarely found time for lunch in her days, for dates in her life, or for downtown in general. The fact that she had all three scheduled on her calendar today made her feel unusually lucky.

She felt a stab of pride. She knew it was silly, but she and Tim had endured a lot. They'd earned every hard-won moment that they got together. If someone had asked her six months ago if she believed in reincarnation, she would have laughed. But now, she wasn't so sure. Her own marriage had undergone a metamorphosis. Second chances weren't necessarily second-rate. Sometimes, in fact, they could be quite wonderful. She grabbed her purse off the desk and went to meet her husband.

27

Virgie

Virgie watched as one patient, then another was called into the warren of corridors unfolding behind a large beige door. She checked her watch. She'd been at the hospital for four hours already, wheeled in and out of an MRI. Her blood had been drawn from both arms and multiple veins. She'd postponed her appointment to the first week of August after they'd discovered Arthur's body on the beach. There was simply too much else to deal with. Now here she was, remembering her dad's advice that she should get checked out.

Maggie pumped her foot next to her, pretending to read a magazine, but Virgie knew her sister was as nervous as she was, if that was possible. She'd insisted on coming to the hospital and leaving the kids with a babysitter. When Virgie first met with the doctor this morning, explaining her symptoms, he'd asked her to do the Romberg test, which required her to walk along a straight line. "Isn't that what they do to catch drunk drivers?" she joked. "Yes," he said. "But it's also a good test for general balance." Virgie was surprised that when she tried to put one foot in front of the other, she wobbled off course several times. That got her heart racing.

"Virginia Herington?" a nurse dressed in light blue scrubs asked now, emerging from behind the door with a clipboard.

"Yes, here," Virgie said and stood.

"I'm right behind you," Maggie whispered.

"Hi, there. How you doing, honey?" The heavyset nurse, who had startling green eyes, smiled warmly at her.

"I guess I've had better days," Virgie offered.

"You and me both, honey," said the nurse. "Isn't that the truth?" They followed her down a long hallway lined with paintings of the sea to an office on the right, where Virgie had begun her day.

The nurse gestured them inside, saying, "Have a seat, ladies. Dr. Reynolds will be right with you."

"Thank you." Two leather chairs faced the desk, and she and Maggie settled into them, their skin making squeaky noises against the leather.

"Nice-looking family." Maggie nodded to the pictures on the desk that showed Dr. Reynolds with his dark wavy hair and mustache, his wife with a blond pixie cut, and two beautiful girls. "That's a good sign."

"Really?" Virgie asked. "How so?"

Maggie shrugged, then giggled nervously. "I have no idea. I just find it comforting that your doctor has such a beautiful family."

At that moment, Dr. Reynolds walked in. "Hi, Virginia."

"Hello." She waited. She'd always been an intuitive person, and Virgie was confident she'd be able to tell if the news were good or bad by the intonation of his voice. But he sounded noncommittal. He nodded at Maggie and extended his hand. "You must be Virginia's sister."

"Yes." Maggie took his hand. "Nice to meet you. I'm Maggie."

As he positioned himself in his chair, a manila folder in his hands,

Virgie waited for the doctor to look at her. When he lifted his eyes and met her gaze, she knew.

"So, as you're aware, we've done some tests, and I think we have a pretty good idea of what's been going on with you lately." He paused and pressed his fingers together.

"Yes? What is it?"

"Well, your guess about multiple sclerosis turns out to be a good one."

Virgie let the words sink in. Multiple sclerosis. MS. Her great-grandmother had it. Now she did. Maggie reached across the space and squeezed her hand.

"I'm sorry. I know it's not the news you were hoping for," he said quietly. Virgie shook her head.

"No," she struggled to say. "Are you sure? Is there any chance it could be something else?"

He set down the folder on the desk and flipped it open. "I'm afraid we're pretty sure. As sure as you can get in the world of medicine, that is. Many of the symptoms you mentioned are indicative of MS. The tingling sensation, the fatigue, blurred vision, slurred words. That's why we did the MRI." He paused, waiting for her to take it in.

Virgie thought back to all of the incidents that had begun to add up, like mile markers pointing the way to a final destination. Shortly before she left for vacation, her vision had gone blurry on the air one night, and she'd had to wing it, making up the introduction to her piece on a local Seattle bakery that baked only gluten-free goods. It unnerved her, not being able to read the teleprompter, but she chalked it up to fatigue and congratulated herself on making it through her segment. Then there had been the creepy-crawly feeling along her legs, the balance problem, and, of course, the night she'd blacked out on the bedroom floor.

"So, we performed the MRI," Dr. Reynolds continued. She

worked to focus on his words. "And the results . . ." His voice trailed off. "Well, see for yourself." He scooted his chair over, close enough that Virgie could detect the scent of stale coffee on his breath. With a pen, he pointed to little white beads resembling a string of pearls that traveled along her brain. "If you look here and here along your corpus callosum," he said, highlighting an area in white, "you'll see some lesions. These are typical for patients with multiple sclerosis." He paused, waited. Virgie studied the picture before her. "*Sclerosis* means 'scarring,' he explained. "In MS, the body's immune system attacks the coating that surrounds the nerves and then scar tissue forms. When that happens, the nerves can miss signals or miscommunicate. Which explains the tingling or numbness you've been experiencing in your arms and legs."

"Uh-huh," she said, but she could feel herself fading. *Lesions. Scarring. Missed signals.* The world was slipping away from her. *Oh, no, not again,* she thought. And it just kept slipping and slipping until it was no longer there.

When Virgie came to, she was lying on a table, a sheet of scratchy paper underneath her. A vaguely familiar face appeared by her side.

"There you are," she said, as Virgie's eyes blinked open. "We were wondering when you'd come back to us."

Virgie struggled to remember where she was. A doctor's room. What had happened right before she passed out? Oh, right. *MS.* The doctor had given her a diagnosis of multiple sclerosis. She shut her eyes again. She didn't want to wake up. She wanted to go back to sleep, to dream until she could wake up in a world where she was healthy and Arthur still alive.

"Your sister's here," said the woman, who Virgie now recognized as the kind nurse who'd shown them to the doctor's room earlier.

"Hi, honey." Maggie's concerned face hovered above her. "Do

you think you can try to sit up?" The nurse helped Virgie up and handed her a paper cup filled with water.

"Whoa," she said, feeling suddenly queasy. She waited a minute, then took the cup and sipped. "That's better," she said. "Thank you." Virgie struggled to recall what the doctor had said about MS. Would she be okay?

"You fainted," Maggie said now, rubbing her back while the nurse checked her vitals. "At least this time you were sitting down, though."

Virgie began to smile, but at that moment, Dr. Reynolds knocked and entered the room.

"Feeling better?" he asked.

"I'm sorry," Virgie began, but he held up a hand.

"No need to apologize." He sat down on a swivel stool across from her and folded his hands. "It can be quite a shock."

"Her vitals are fine, Dr. Reynolds," the nurse said as she ducked out of the room.

"Good. Thank you." His kind eyes studied Virgie. "Are you feeling up to a few more questions?" She glanced at Maggie, then nodded.

"Okay. Good. So, tell me what you do for work." Dr. Reynolds listened thoughtfully while she explained she hosted her own show on a Seattle news station.

She stopped herself. "Wait. Will this interfere with my job?" The diagnosis was still too new, too raw.

"Probably not," he offered. "It's hard to say. It's early. It's quite possible you won't have a relapse for another ten years and you'll lead a perfectly normal life in the meantime."

He pulled a prescription pad from his white jacket pocket and began scribbling. "We've made some remarkable advances in medication that can help reduce the number of exacerbations and even slow the progress of MS." As he wrote, Virgie struggled to understand the meaning behind his words.

"Wait. Are you saying this is a life sentence?" She could hear the stitch in her voice. "There's no cure? It will eventually get me in the end?"

She watched as he ripped multiple white sheets of paper off his little pad. "I'm afraid we haven't found a cure for MS, per se, but many people with MS go on to live long, happy lives, often with minimal relapses. In the end, something gets us all, doesn't it?"

She knew he was trying to be supportive, but Virgie didn't want to hear it. She was accustomed to dealing in blacks and whites; there was the truth and there was not-the-truth. She wanted time lines, promises that she would continue to lead a long, productive life with, perhaps, a few minor setbacks.

He handed over the prescriptions. "I'm prescribing Avonex for you to start. It's a shot that you'll need to take once a week. You can administer it yourself. Leslie, our nurse, will show you how. There are other drugs available on the market, but let's wait and see how you do with the Avonex. Many of my patients have had good luck with it, meaning it's helped delay or even stop the onset of further lesions. There's also a prescription here for Prozac. Some of my patients find it helps them deal with the initial diagnosis."

His delivery was so matter-of-fact that Virgie found herself wondering how many times a day he gave this little speech. "Does it work immediately?"

"What, the Prozac?" he asked. She nodded.

"Usually it takes a few weeks before you'll start to notice a difference. But again, if you don't feel like you need it, you shouldn't feel compelled to fill the prescription."

"Oh, I'm pretty sure I'll need it." She folded the prescriptions over and stuck them in her purse. "What else could happen?" she pressed. "There are other scenarios you're not telling me about." She felt the silence sit between them as he pondered her question.

"The disease progresses in different ways for every individual," he explained delicately. "For the kind you have, relapsing/remitting, most patients do quite well for many years before they notice any significant impairment, like having to rely on a cane for balance."

"A cane?" She felt her eyebrows shoot up involuntarily. "I can't use a cane! I'm only thirty-five."

"Whoa. Let's not get ahead of ourselves." Dr. Reynolds held up two hands. "I didn't say that you *would* need one, only that some people do, and not for quite a long time. Physical therapy can be helpful, too. But let's explore that possibility later, if we need to."

Maggie reached across for Virgie's hand. "Thank you, Doctor. You've given us a lot to think about," she said.

Dr. Reynolds nodded and stood. "I know I have, and I'm sorry it's all so overwhelming. Why don't you review the materials that Leslie will give you and we can set up a time to talk later, once you've had a chance to digest everything?"

Virgie nodded, but she hoped Maggie was listening. Because the doctor's words were spilling over her, great, crashing waves of information.

When he left, Maggie leaned in and hugged her. "Oh, Virg," she said gently. "I love you. We all love you. We're going to get through this, okay?" Her big sister's words were all it took for Virgie to break, great sobs wracking her body for the first time since Arthur's body had washed up on shore. She was crying for herself, for her dad, for Gloria, for all of them. Life was so short. You never knew how good you had it.

Until you didn't.

28

Maggie

Maggie drew a warm bath for Luke and tested the water with her hand. She swirled around the bubbles that clumped together like tiny islands. "Perfect," she declared. Luke lowered himself in, sinking his entire body into the suds until only his face peered out. "I'm going to throw in some laundry while you soak," she told him.

"What?" he pulled his head up slightly, unable to hear underwater.

She laughed and repeated her words. "Okay." He sank back down.

They'd arrived home yesterday, though frankly it felt like minutes ago. Maggie had intended to head up to Maine today, but then Virgie's little doctor's appointment had turned into yet another crisis. As soon as they came home, her sister closed herself off in the guest bedroom. Maggie brought up a cheeseburger for dinner, Virgie's favorite, but it sat untouched outside her door. She hadn't even opened the door for Lexie or Soph when they knocked.

What would her sister do? Maggie hated the thought of Virgie going back to Seattle by herself. Even if the progression of MS could be halted, Maggie didn't think anyone should have to bear the weight of an illness by themselves. *We're family,* she told Virgie on the ride home from the hospital. *Families take care of each other. Why not think about sticking around longer? Maybe get an extended leave of absence until you figure out what you want to do?* Even if Jackson were as terrific as she said he was, she'd known him for a total of what? Maybe eight weeks? Could Virgie really count on him if she needed help?

You know, Virgie, Maggie counseled, *sometimes even the most fabulous people need help. And, it's okay. People* want *to help—you only have to ask.* Virgie nodded, but Maggie could tell her mind was a thousand miles away. When they got home, Maggie went online: *An estimated 2.5 million people suffered from multiple sclerosis worldwide. It often went undetected for many years. Approximately 400,000 people in the U.S. had it. About 10,000 new cases were diagnosed each year. There might be a genetic factor.* She read that line twice, three times. Were they all carriers of an MS gene?

All their lives had taken a free fall the last few weeks with Arthur's passing. And now this. She liked to imagine that Arthur was hovering up above, watching out for them. But if he was, he was doing a pretty lousy job of it so far.

She got up to leave and found Mac, standing outside the bathroom door.

"Oh, hi, honey. I didn't know you were there."

"Sorry." He took a step back, sank onto the bed. He was quiet.

"What's going on? Everything okay?" She walked over to him and rested her hands on his shoulders. "Tracy will be here at seven tomorrow morning, if that's what you're worried about. She's great. The kids love her. You guys will be fine while I'm away."

He nodded. "Thanks. I know we will." He reached up and took a strand of her hair. He twirled it around his finger. "So, you know that thing we talked about earlier?"

Her mind wound through the litany of things they'd discussed lately. Virgie's diagnosis. The summer house. The possibility that Virgie might stay with them longer. The matter of Arthur's house and what to do about it. She arched her eyebrows.

"You know, about being foster parents," he said quietly.

"Oh, that," she said, dialing back her surprise. She'd had little time to give it more thought lately.

"I know it's important to you." He hesitated and wrapped his arms around her waist, not looking at her.

"But?" she asked, her chest tightening.

"But." Mac lifted his eyes and met her stare. "I'm still not sure."

"Oh." His uncertainty lay between them, a stretch of unfamiliar territory. She studied his face to see if he were talking in euphemism, another way of saying he *was* sure but didn't want to hurt her. Just not now, when she was already fragile. "Okay," she said, her heart winging in her chest. " 'Not sure' doesn't mean no, though, does it?"

"No." He dropped his eyes. "It doesn't."

She ran her hands through his hair. "It's not like we have to make up our minds today. Besides, we still have to get approved."

He exhaled. "Right. Thank you."

He leaned toward her and rested his head on her stomach. "I just don't want to disappoint you. And with everything that's been happening lately . . ."

"Shh." She didn't know what else to say. "We can discuss it later." She felt a sliver of something—disappointment? anger?—but it was dulled by her own increasing weariness. "Keep an eye on Luke, okay? I'm going to throw in a load of laundry." She pulled away from him and headed downstairs.

In the laundry room, six piles of dirty clothes greeted her. Even though she could have sworn she'd washed four loads before leaving the summer house. Had the kids simply dumped their suitcases here without any regard to what was clean, what was dirty? She picked up a T-shirt and sniffed, the fresh scent of fabric softener wafting up.

"Sophie, Lexie!" she called out. "Report to the laundry room, please!"

She heard groans from the family room, then dragging feet. "What is it, Mom?" Sophie poked her head around the doorway.

"Did you girls even check to see what's clean and what's not before emptying your suitcases on the floor?"

They exchanged looks. "I thought it was all dirty," said Lexie.

"No!" Maggie understood her anger was disproportionate to the crime, but she couldn't help herself. Honestly, how much more could she be expected to do around here? "I told you girls that your clean clothes were folded on your beds before we packed at the summer house. Obviously, no one listened."

"Here." She threw them all back into the laundry basket. "Take these upstairs and sort the clean from the dirty."

"But, Mom," Sophie whined. "How can we tell?"

"Do the smell test," Maggie advised. "If it smells fresh, like fabric softener, odds are it's clean and I don't want to see it again until it's been worn."

They lumbered up the stairs, baskets in hand, while she began to sort a load of darks for herself and Mac. She tossed in sweatshirts, Mac's boxers, sweaty T-shirts, towels that still carried the smell of the ocean. So, Mac didn't want another child in their lives. *Possibly* didn't want another child, she reminded herself. *Okay,* she thought. *Breathe.* That didn't mean he wasn't happy with the life they'd created. To the contrary, he was content with three kids and didn't want to tip the scales further. "We're already playing zone defense," he'd told her one night at the summer house, referencing the fact that, as parents, they were outnumbered in the Herington family. Two to three. Add another child in the mix and the ratio would be four kids to two adults.

Then why did Maggie feel so certain that this was the next step for her? That helping another child who might not otherwise have a home was what she was meant to do? She drew in a long breath and sighed. Maybe Mac was right. Their lives were crazy enough right now. Maybe she was nuts to think about signing up for more. Right now, she needed to help Virgie and get Arthur's affairs in order. The rest could wait.

As she neared the end of the dirty laundry pile, she spied a single sock at the bottom. It wasn't one of Mac's tube socks, and it was too big to be one of the kids'. She picked it up, turning it over in her hands. Maybe it was Tim's? It looked familiar. Then she realized where she'd seen another one like it. In Arthur's suitcase at the summer house. It was thick and woolly, and she'd remarked on it when she'd gone through his suitcase. What had he been thinking bringing such warm socks out in the hazy, humid days of July? She'd tossed it, along with almost all the other stuff that had been crammed into his suitcase and car. And now, here was its match.

She sank to the floor and kneaded the sock between her fingers. She lifted its scratchy texture to her face and ran it along her cheek. It was clean, but it still carried a scent, something else familiar. Then she realized what it was. Her dad's favorite aftershave that he wore on occasion. *Old Spice*. It had pervaded every item in his suitcase. And at the scent of her father, Maggie's eyes filled with tears. As hard as she tried, she couldn't stanch them.

29

Virgie

Virgie sat on a bench in the Boston Public Garden, watching the swan boats drift by in the shimmering heat. It was a sticky, humid August day, and parents squirted their kids with water guns in an effort to keep them cool. It was Tuesday and Maggie was on her way up to Maine. But she'd persuaded Virgie to stay one more day in Boston, to take some time to think things through and spend the night at Jess's house before the two of them headed up tomorrow. On her way to Jess's, Virgie hopped off the train at Park Street. She wanted to walk through the Common, take a few minutes to get her head straight and figure out what she was going to do.

Even before the diagnosis, she'd suspected MS. After her fall on the Cape, she had googled enough to see that her symptoms aligned with multiple sclerosis. Balance problems: *check*. Vision impairment: *check*. Tingling sensation along the extremities. Slurred speech: *check* and *check*. She'd read until she couldn't bear to read any more and had slammed her laptop shut.

"What do you think, Daddy?" she'd asked Arthur in their last talk, before he hinted that he thought the teakettle was burning again. Before she knew that he wasn't quite right. She wanted his opinion on whether he thought Maggie and Gloria were ridiculous to insist that she see a specialist in Boston. Virgie counted on Arthur, as she always had, to be her voice of reason. She felt as if she were seven again, writing her homemade newspaper, eager to make her dad proud and nervous about what he might say.

Arthur regarded her carefully. "I think it would be wise to get it checked out, honey. You've got some of the best doctors in Boston. Take advantage of them. Work can wait."

Virgie pulled her knees up to her chest and tried not to cry. If her father was urging her to follow up, then he thought whatever was going on with her body was serious.

"You know my grandmother, your great-grandmother . . ." His voice trailed off and Virgie waited for him to continue. He lifted his eyes. "Well, she had MS."

Virgie inhaled sharply and Arthur held up his hand. "Not that I'm saying that's what's causing your problems. It's probably nothing. But they have drugs for all sorts of things these days. It's better to find out sooner than later if there's anything the matter. I think you can even take shots these days, you know, like a diabetic."

She nodded numbly. "Uh-huh. Okay. That's what I'll do." She couldn't argue with her dad. She didn't want to.

"Good, I'm glad," he said and patted her hand, as if that settled it. That had been only minutes before a look of alarm fell over his face and he told her he needed to take the kettle off the stove.

Of course, with everything that had happened since, Virgie had no choice but to go ahead with the appointment. She felt as if she'd promised Arthur. She sensed that he'd be looking out for her, whatever the news might be.

Daddy, what should I do now? she thought. For the first time in her life, Virgie was scared. The thought of going back to Seattle, of being on her own and coping with an illness without her sisters nearby, was daunting. The doctor seemed to think she might be fine for a long time, but what if she weren't? The extra stress of her job couldn't be good for a body that was already attacking itself. And she had no idea, really, how her diagnosis might change things between her and Jackson. Last night, she'd quickly shared the results with him over the phone. He'd been supportive, caring: "Okay, we'll get through this." But Virgie secretly wondered if he would see her now as a patient instead of a girlfriend. He probably couldn't fairly say himself.

A part of her—a *really big* part of her—wanted to ignore her diagnosis, pretend as if nothing had changed. But she knew that would be wrong, cowardly. Her life *had* changed. She needed to take medicine now. She wasn't so much angry about her diagnosis as she was exhausted and scared. And while *relieved* wasn't the right word, she felt some small peace in knowing that she hadn't been losing her mind, that the symptoms she'd been feeling were, in fact, very real. Yesterday, she'd watched while the nurse inserted the needle into her fleshy upper thigh, injecting the Avonex and explaining how it worked. Virgie flinched only slightly. Could she, Virgie wondered, do this to herself every week?

Well, she didn't have much choice, did she?

She watched while two men with a guitar and a violin set up in the shade of a weeping willow. They arranged their folding chairs and pulled their instruments from their cases. The guitarist, a round-faced guy with a beard, laid out his case for coins, and then proceeded to fine-tune his instrument. The violinist, a curtain of dark bangs falling over his eyes, plucked at his strings. They were an unlikely pairing—guitar and violin—but once they'd settled into playing, Virgie was struck by the music, an ethereal classical piece.

Her dad had loved classical music. Sometimes he'd switch on the radio just to have it playing in the background while he wrote. When

Virgie asked how he could concentrate, he explained, "It inspires me to do better." She was only twelve or thirteen at the time. "Listen to it. Isn't it incredible? Listen to all the different instruments that come together to create one magnificent sound. Knowing that an artist, a composer, could produce *that*"—and he poked the air emphatically with his forefinger—"pushes me to reach higher, to do better."

Virgie hadn't really understood at the time, but now she thought back to it. Perhaps Arthur was sending her his own small signal of strength right here, in the form of a scruffy guitarist and violinist. Reminding her that there was beauty in the world. That no matter what life handed her, there was still so much to be awed by, inspired by. "Listen for the different melodies," he would coach, and try as she might, she could never detect the thread of a new melody when Arthur held up his finger in anticipation. She only heard the piece in its entirety rather than as separate strains of music.

Perhaps Arthur had been coaching her for this moment all along. Life was made up of individual lines of music, a person's lifetime a mere collection of moments. But it was what a person did with those moments, those discoveries, how she wove them together, that made for the symphony. MS was but one melody playing in Virgie's life at the moment. In fact, it had probably been playing for some time. She just hadn't been listening.

Well, now she was. Now she had to figure out how to weave it into her own story.

For so long, an anchor spot on Seattle's news station had been all that she'd wanted, she could barely remember wishing for anything else. Could she recalibrate her life without losing the identity she'd worked so long and hard to create for herself? She wasn't sure—and it petrified her.

She kept her eyes closed, feeling the warm sun on her cheeks. She wanted to believe that the injections would help, that her symptoms would fade and she would start to feel "normal" again. Thousands of people dealt with an MS diagnosis each year. She saw herself joining yet another subgroup on a pie chart, a negligible piece of the pie, perhaps, but a significant one. A tiny yellow wedge.

And she realized one startling fact: she didn't want to be alone. For the first time she could she recall, she doubted her ability to take care of herself. The thought of diving back into work and negotiating office politics struck her as laughably petty now. Perhaps, she thought, this was what her dad had meant when he once told her she needed to "get some perspective." She'd been hurt by those words, but maybe Arthur had known all along. Well, MS was a pretty crappy way for the universe to dole out perspective, she thought now. Why did something so valuable have to be so hard-won?

Daddy, can't you help me here? Please? she whispered.

When her cell rang, she opened her eyes and picked up. "Hello?" Her voice sounded small and tired, even to her.

"Hi, it's me. Jackson. I'm coming out there," he said. "And don't tell me no."

30

Maggie

When Maggie pulled up to Arthur's house, it seemed to let out a heavy sigh, as if it had been awaiting her arrival. She climbed out of the car and stretched her legs. It was only early afternoon, but already a chill threaded the air. She hadn't visited since last Thanksgiving, and now the gambrel home appeared to list to one side, as if part of it had sunk deeper into the ground over the winter. The gray shingles were peeling in places, lending it an air of distinguished neglect. While the grass appeared freshly cut (Arthur hired a local boy to cut it each week), the rhododendron bushes lining the front of the house were exploding, in desperate need of a trim. Maggie approached and noticed the curtains were drawn in the front room. Quite frankly, it looked as if no one had lived here in ages.

On the front steps, she searched under the flowerpot where her dad always hid the key but found nothing. Had he moved it to a new spot? She hoisted the terra-cotta pot to one side and searched again until at last her fingers landed on the cool metal. She pulled out the key and blew off the remnants of potting soil. When she cracked open the door, the scent of mildew, rotting trash, and dust overwhelmed her in a malodorous rush. A month's worth of mail had piled up through the mail slot and now blocked the door, as if the house itself were wary of granting her entry. Maggie gave the door a shove with her shoulder and barged in. It took a moment for her eyes to adjust to the dim light, but *packed to the rafters* was the expression that jumped to mind, followed soon after by *Oh*. She felt as if she'd been punched. Arthur's house was overflowing. With stuff. *Junk*. All kinds of it.

She held a hand to her mouth and made her way past piles of what appeared to be old newspapers. To reach the windows, she had to climb around a tower of boxes. As soon as she threw back the curtains, thousands of tiny dust motes went flying through the air. Maggie struggled to push the window open, but the sash wouldn't budge. She thought back to the broken transom at the summer house, the speckled blood on the floor.

"Damn it!" she yelled and pounded on the sash. "Can't you at least give me some fresh air?" At that moment, as if the house had been listening, the window unstuck, the sash rising up. A blast of fresh air blew in, momentarily reviving her. Slowly, Maggie made her way around the tower of boxes and back through what could only be described as a passageway in the living room. The mess was incredible, the smell nearly intolerable. Stacks of papers, magazines, random pizza boxes and KFC buckets were stacked around the perimeter of the room. Her dad, it seemed, had carved out a small space that allowed him to travel from the front door across the living room to his leather chair, which was still worn in all the familiar places. There was also a small square area, probably eight feet by eight, that remained free of debris and provided a clear path to the television.

It was in this space that Maggie stood now, hands on her hips, breathing through her mouth. "Dad, what happened here?" she asked aloud, her voice shaking. Because she couldn't believe the disarray, the sheer mess of what his living room had become. When Gloria lived here, the house was always immaculate. Was this her father's small act of rebellion against her? His way of giving his ex-wife the proverbial middle finger?

Surely her dad had friends over, but how had he entertained anyone? It hadn't been like this last Thanksgiving. Or had it? She tried to think back. But then it dawned on her: her dad had been waiting for them in the front yard when they pulled up to the house. He'd never invited them inside. Maggie didn't think much of it at the time, only that he was upset with them for being late and didn't want to miss the buffet at the restaurant. But perhaps his waiting outside had been intentional all along. A chill brushed over her. Was it possible he'd been living this way for nearly a year? More than a year?

She made her way from the living room to the kitchen, where a similar living area had been cleared amid piles of junk. There was the old maple table, where she and her sisters had shared countless meals. Except now, it was covered in stacks of papers and books, a few random ice cube trays. Only one corner was free of clutter. A place mat with a complete setting—plate, glass, silverware—sat on the cleared space, a chair tucked in neatly as if waiting for Arthur to arrive any minute for supper.

Maggie stepped over to the sink, where piles of dirty dishes spilled onto the counter. When she poked at them, a cockroach scurried out, sending her reeling backward. "Jesus!" she yelled and grabbed a magazine from the table, swatting madly at the counter, where the roach disappeared into a crack.

"Oh, Daddy," she said. "How could you?" Big black trash bags lined one side of room, and when she peeked inside one, she realized it contained more dirty dishes. It appeared that Arthur had simply been throwing away plates once they'd been used, the ones not in the sink, that is. It was some of her mother's best china. She couldn't believe he hadn't run out of dinnerware. But then she realized that paper plates, plastic forks and knives, were also mixed in with the clutter. An odd nostalgia swept over her as she regarded so much that was familiar and comforting, like the family dinner table, her mother's china.

How had it come to this? Because she had three kids, it had always been easier for her dad to make the short trip to their house in Windsor rather than vice versa. Or so she'd told herself.

She braced herself to go upstairs. Could there possibly be more wreckage? The living room and kitchen alone would take them a couple of days to clean out. She would need to buy about a thousand trash bags, rubber gloves, dust masks so they could breathe. And a professional cleaner. There was no way they'd be able to cart out the rubble *and* clean the house in a week, which had been Maggie's original plan. She'd assumed it would be a matter of packing up Arthur's clothing and furniture for Goodwill and divvying up his books among them. Then they'd roll up their sleeves and start cleaning, readying the house for sale. But she could never have anticipated the hovel that would welcome her. Not in a million years.

As she began to climb the stairs, she was amazed to see that even the steps were littered with junk: piles of old tax forms, a box of winter hats and gloves, a couple of bottles of scotch with the holiday ribbons still knotted around them, a pair of dirty socks, stacks of books. It was as if Arthur couldn't be bothered to find a home for such mismatched objects. At the top, she was confronted by a continuing path of rubble. Large stains marked the beige hallway carpet that led to a bathroom that might as well have been condemned. Crap pocked the upper edges of the toilet bowl, and the rusty water inside was rimmed with muck.

At that moment, Maggie realized a certain horrible truth: her dad had been living in squalor. And she hadn't even thought to suggest he hire a cleaning lady. She'd assumed when he explained that a neighbor lady stopped by to help out from time to time, that he was set. What on earth was wrong with her? Her dad had never cared about such things. Why would he when Gloria left? Still, the vision that greeted her was incomprehensible, her childhood home transformed into an unsightly, behemoth dump.

But it was when she opened the door to his bedroom that she fell to her knees. The floral bedspread lay askew across the mattress, the sheets soiled. An acrid smell attacked her senses and she covered her nose with her sleeve, nearly gagging. She felt tears spring to her eyes as she cast about the room, more piles of junk lurking in every corner. *How, oh, how, could she have been so clueless?* There had been plenty of signs—Arthur's absentmindedness, the collection of trash he'd started at her house, his overstuffed car—but she'd written them off as typical for a slightly scatter-brained older man. Clearly, though, what Arthur had been dealing with was much more serious than a handful of quirks. She'd refused to see what was right in front of her. Only when the teakettle lit up like a volcano had it finally dawned on her, on all of them, that Arthur needed help. But by then it was too late.

Nothing, not a thousand Hail Marys, could pardon her from such a sin of neglect, of abandonment. She quickly left the room, closing the door behind her.

Where to begin?

She poked her head into the two extra bedrooms, one her father's study and the other now a guest room, her and Jess's old bedroom. The guest room was relatively free of clutter, but Arthur's office teemed with books and boxes. It could have been an aisle in Walmart or Target. Huge cases of paper towels, toilet paper, and other staples hugged the walls. Near the door sat several cases of fruit punch juice boxes, Luke's favorite, and miniature packages of Goldfish crackers. It was as if her dad had been expecting them to show up any day and wanted to be prepared. She could hear him talking, as if perched on her shoulder. *See, Maggie. I was ready for you. I was waiting for you*. The thought flooded her with despair. She closed the door and slid down the wall to the floor. There was something terribly cruel about the juxtaposition of a life filled with so much junk and a life irretrievably lost. Arthur had died drowning, but he'd been drowning long before that.

She pushed up to her knees and crawled along the hallway, keeping her head down as if trying to avoid fire smoke. Suddenly, she was eager to be free of the house. She hurried down the stairs, knocking over the piles. She rushed out the front door, and then—she ran. Down the road she'd traveled earlier. And on. And on, until finally her throat burned so sharply that she had to stop. She bent over, hands on her knees, and drank in the fresh air like cold water.

She dug in her pocket for her cell phone, but it was in her bag back at the house. She needed to talk to Mac. Somehow he would make this right and explain to her why her dad had chosen to live this way. She gazed up, lovely cumulus clouds wheeled across a bright blue sky. Gradually, she found her way back to the house. The door was still ajar, daring her to step foot back inside. She didn't want to. But she had to. Had to grab her bag and get supplies.

She inhaled deeply, plugged her nose, and darted into the living room, where she'd dropped her purse. She grabbed it, then hurried back outside, closing the door and locking it behind her. In the car, she tried to calm her thinking. They certainly couldn't stay here. Maggie would have to book them rooms at the nearest hotel. And then she tried to remember how to get to Home Depot. She needed supplies, multiple provisions, a whole army of cleaning products. Hell, what she needed was the National Guard.

31

Jess

When Jess and Virgie set out for Maine on Wednesday, something nagged at Jess, though she couldn't put her finger on what exactly. She'd stocked the house for the entire week and had posted the various doctors' and dentists' numbers on the fridge. Tim's mom was on board to watch the kids. The assistant principal could pick up the slack at school. So what was it? Then it dawned on her: the strange sensation was *missing Tim*. The physicality of him. The comfort of him. He'd been remarkable the week after Arthur went missing, helping out at the summer house, talking to lawyers, cleaning out the mess that was Arthur's car. It was almost as if her husband, after a long hiatus, had come back to her and the kids.

And now Tim had encouraged her to go to Maine and help her sisters organize Arthur's affairs. *Everything is under control here,* he said. The old Tim would have never uttered such words. The old Tim would have whined with impatience, demanding to know why it took three sisters to sort through Arthur's things. The old Tim would have sulked the night before instead of making gentle love to her.

The other night, just back from the Cape, she'd spotted Cole sitting out on his porch with another woman, much younger than Jess, with long, thick blond hair. They cradled wineglasses in their hands. Jess walked by briskly, pretending not to see, hoping not to be seen. All she could think was what an idiot she'd been. To have imagined that she was special! She was no different from the parade of women Cole entertained on his deck. She heard him give a deep laugh while he chatted with his date, and Jess thought, *Yep, joke's on me. Good one, Cole.*

What would Arthur have said, she wondered, if he'd known about her brief affair? Would he have read her the riot act or would he have understood? It bothered her that even after all this time, Jess didn't know. *Damn you, Arthur,* she thought. *You were never there for me; why should I be there for you now?* She gasped, the words springing to mind unbidden, as she gripped the wheel.

Because he's our dad. She could almost hear Maggie whispering in her ear.

But it was Virgie, saying, "This reminds me of Dad."

Jess was startled out of her reverie. They'd been driving for hours, listening to country-western music on the radio. The sharp coastal air cut through the car's open windows as they pulled off the highway onto her dad's exit. She'd meant to discuss Virgie's diagnosis on the long drive, maybe encourage her to get a second opinion, but the moment she'd brought it up, Virgie had closed her eyes and said, "Can we please not talk about it right now? I don't have the energy." And so, what choice did Jess have but to crank up the radio a little louder?

Jess's mind had been churning, thinking about how crazy it was that Arthur was no longer in their lives. She hadn't even had a chance to have it out with him, to work through all those issues that daughters were supposed to with their dads before they passed away. What would she have said to him if she'd had the opportunity? *I wish you would have been around more when we were kids. Why did you always seem to like Virgie the best? Did you really think your books were more important than us? Why don't you like Tim?* The thing was, she didn't think any of Arthur's answers would have been particularly illuminating. Perhaps it was enough to know that he'd loved her, loved all of them, even if he hadn't always been able to tell them.

As for Virgie, Jess wanted to grab her sister and shake her, tell her to get her things and move to Boston. *There's no sense in going back to Seattle,* she wanted to yell. *Don't be stupid! Who will take care of you there?* But she'd done an admirable job of refraining, she thought, for the entire ride up to Maine. She and Maggie had talked the night before (*you won't believe the mess that's here!* Maggie warned) and agreed that pushing Virgie to make any kind of decision right now would be the worst possible tactic. *Let's let her sit with the diagnosis a bit,* Maggie advised. *Let her figure out what she wants.*

And now there was this other little wrinkle: Virgie had informed them that Jackson was flying out on Saturday. He wanted to be there for Arthur's memorial service on Sunday. It was a touching gesture, but personally Jess thought that Jackson was only further mucking things up. Virgie didn't need the distraction of romance right now. What she needed was her sisters, who could help her through this stressful time. She needed *her family.*

"What reminds you of Dad?" Jess asked now.

"This." Virgie gestured with her hand. "The air, the smell of balsam mixing with the ocean." They followed a winding road that curved back into a wooded area, limber firs stretching skyward to form a canopy above. "I miss this place," Virgie remarked. "I haven't been here in ages."

"Me either," admitted Jess. "Is that terrible of us?"

Virgie shook her head. "When Dad and Mom divorced, the center of our family shifted to Maggie's house."

"I think you're right," reflected Jess. Though for a brief moment she considered why it hadn't shifted to *her* house. But Maggie's house was bigger, friendlier—the natural meeting place for everyone over the holidays.

They drove by old farmhouses and dilapidated barns the color of smoke, the beams bent and breaking. Silky milkweed pods tumbled along the roadside. Jess thought back to one summer when a population of monarch butterflies had landed in a nearby field, blanketing the milkweeds in orange and black. Arthur woke the girls at dawn to watch as the sun warmed the butterflies' fragile bodies into motion, and then, just as quickly as they'd appeared, they were gone, a thrumming flock suspended against a blue sky.

She was saddened to think that Teddy and Grace would never be a part of this simpler, breathtaking world once they sold the house. She'd forgotten how much she loved it up here.

Eventually, the car wound around the bend leading to Arthur's house.

"Wow," whispered Virgie when the place came into view. "Look at this."

In front of them sat their childhood home. It looked, however, as if it had aged fifty years since her last visit. Paint curled on the front shutters, the walkway and front steps were cracked, and weeds and oversize rhododendrons swarmed at the front. Jess's mind shot back to Boo Radley's house in *To Kill a Mockingbird*. Maggie's old Subaru sat in the driveway.

"Incredible," she said as she pulled the car up next to Maggie's and killed the engine. They climbed out just as Maggie emerged on the front steps.

"You're here!" she exclaimed, running over. Her jeans were rolled up to her knees, and she'd wrapped a pink bandanna around her head. A paper breathing mask hung around her neck. "I can't tell you how glad I am to see you guys." She slipped Virgie's purse strap over her shoulder. "Come on. You won't believe this till you see it. It will blow your mind."

Virgie and Jess exchanged glances. Virgie went first, while Jess grabbed her shoulder bag and followed slowly. Maggie slipped her free arm through Jess's elbow as they walked up the path. As soon as the screen door slammed behind them, Virgie yelped.

"Holy crap!" she shouted. "What happened here?"

32

Virgie

Most of her adult life Virgie had guarded vigilantly against germs, slathering on antibacterial lotion. What a cruel, ironic joke then that her own body had turned on her, attacking her very cells. Still, that didn't mean she was eager to confront the various species of bacteria and mold lurking in Arthur's house. She gladly took the cleaning supplies that Maggie handed her: a bucket, a pair of bright yellow dish gloves, a bottle of Windex with ammonia, sponges, dust masks, paper towels, and a box of trash bags.

She and Jess tackled the kitchen first, where they scrubbed and cleared trash for several hours. It was all Virgie could do not to go running from the place. She'd never guess this was her childhood home to look at it now. She remembered walking down these very stairs to meet her date for senior prom, recalled meat loaf dinners at the kitchen table and watching *Saturday Night Live* with her parents on the old rabbit-eared television. She'd already crept upstairs to her old bedroom, now Arthur's study, and had rediscovered the faint pencil marks where, each birthday, Gloria had faithfully recorded her height along the closet doorframe.

She couldn't quite believe that her dad had let things get so bad. *What had he been thinking?* She'd once done a story about a hoarder in Seattle, the man's house filled with old appliances, like broken coffeemakers and toasters. But unlike Arthur, that man had been a recluse, severing all his ties with family and friends. No one had seen him in years. Arthur wasn't like that. He'd been out and about, socializing, working at the library, traveling to the Cape. He could still entertain a crowd with his stories. And yet, he'd managed to keep his obsession, for that's how Virgie thought of it—an unhealthy obsession—a secret from them all.

It was eleven o'clock on Thursday, and already they were knee-deep into cleaning. Like a drill sergeant, Maggie had woken them at the hotel at 6:30 to drive over to the house. So far, the dent they'd made in her father's mess was negligible. At this rate, it would take them a month to get the house ready to sell. Maggie had called a local company and enlisted a dump truck and the help of a few burly guys to lug out the heavy stuff. They'd filled fifteen overflowing trash bags, carted out her dad's leather chair, the ancient television and its rickety stand, and thrown out a good number of boxes stacked up against the walls.

"Aha! I found it!" Maggie shouted out midway through the morning. It was their parents' floral couch, navy blue with magenta roses running over it that had been hiding under so many boxes and books they hadn't been able to locate it when they first launched Project Clean-Up.

"Oh, I remember that couch," Virgie said wistfully. "Daddy and I used to sit on it and read the paper every Sunday morning."

"I remember all the bad movies we watched on it when we were kids," reminisced Maggie.

"Yes," said Jess, looking over her shoulder. "Remember when Dad rented *The Shining* and neither you nor I could sleep for a month?"

Maggie hugged herself. "I was so freaked out by that movie.

Every time I went in the bathroom, I was sure I was going to see REDRUM written in lipstick on the mirror."

Virgie waved her gloved hand in the air. "You guys are crazy. I never knew you were off your rockers. And here the whole time I was thinking you were my cool big sisters."

"Us?" Jess laughed as she threw old papers into a trash bag. "Well, maybe Maggie. But never me."

"What are you talking about?" Virgie said. "You were the one who always wanted to save the world. Remember when you took all the money in your piggy bank and sent it to the starving children in Africa? You saw some weepy ad on TV."

Jess laughed. "You're right. I completely forgot about that." She thought for a moment. "Grace is the same way. She wants to make the world a better place."

"Good for her. The world could use her." Virgie tossed a pair of brand-new men's sneakers into the Goodwill bag.

"Is all this stuff going?" One of the guys from the dump truck company stood at the front door and gestured to three large trash bags. He wore jeans, a T-shirt streaked with dry paint, and a Red Sox cap turned backwards.

"Yep. All of it," Maggie confirmed. "That's all trash."

They worked in silence for a few minutes. Then Maggie said, "What on earth was Dad thinking, saving all this junk?"

Jess shook her head. "Clearly, he was not well."

"But did you have any idea? Did you, Virgie? You spoke to him all the time."

"No," snapped Virgie. "What's that supposed to mean? That I was the one who missed something because I checked in with Dad?"

"Of course not," Maggie murmured. "But I didn't have a clue. So, I'm wondering if everyone is as surprised as I am."

"Make that two of us," volunteered Jess.

"Three of us," said Virgie.

"I guessed something was a little off," Maggie continued, "when he kept forgetting things, but I chalked it up to old age." Her voice cracked, and Jess stopped cleaning to glance at her sister.

"Hey, don't beat yourself up, okay? None of us knew anything about it. We all thought he was doing fine."

Maggie nodded, but Virgie knew what she was getting at. There had been some signs, like Arthur's car, which was a junk mobile, and, of course, the forgotten teakettle. She'd been feeling guilty, too, as if if she'd just taken the time to fly out and visit him once during the past year, she would have stumbled upon the muddle that his life had become.

"What about Mom?" Virgie pressed. "How could she *not* know? Didn't she and Arthur talk all the time?"

Maggie sighed. "Who knows? I think you really had to visit the house to get any idea of the extent of the damage here."

They continued to cull through beat-up cardboard boxes, a motley assortment of pots and pans, books, Tupperware, old mail, and stacks upon stacks of newspapers. One box housed a bunch of old, rusty tools, probably from another yard sale, Arthur transferring one hoarder's stash to another's. "This is starting to look a lot like gluttony," Jess commented, pulling out a rusty socket wrench.

"Eew, this is what I've been smelling." Maggie winced and held up a moldy white carton at arm's length. "Old Chinese food. That is so disgusting. Honestly, how did Dad stand the stench?"

"Where is Mom, anyway?" asked Virgie. "Didn't she say she was coming to help?"

Maggie rolled down a glove and checked her watch. "Eleven-thirty. She should be here any minute. She's due at noon. You know how Mom likes to make an entrance."

Virgie cackled. "Well, she's going to have a hell of a time competing with this mess, I don't care what she's wearing or driving."

Virgie felt betrayed. She thought that she and Arthur had a special relationship. He was her proud mentor, she, his happy protégée. He'd continued to offer her his advice up until the day before he died. How could he have kept such a significant secret from her? She searched her mind for clues, intimations of a secret life, but nothing came to her. Arthur always sounded like his old self when he picked up the phone on Sunday nights. Yes, he'd been a little absentminded at the summer house, but nothing that struck Virgie as out of the ordinary until the teakettle incident.

No, Arthur knew he had a problem and had gone out of his way to hide it from his daughters and Gloria. Was this, too, hereditary? Was there a little gene for hoarding? If she'd gotten the bad hand in the family cards for MS, why wouldn't she be the one to develop this disorder as well? She was glad Jackson was coming soon. He would stop her mind from spinning. She pulled out a brown package from LLBean, wrapped in packing tape. When she ripped it open, there was a brand-new sweater still in its plastic wrapping.

"So, Dad was ordering new clothes but never even took them out of the bag?" Virgie held up the sweater.

"I know. It's strange, isn't it? I've come across a few shirts like that, brand-new and completely untouched." Maggie wiped a loose strand of hair from her forehead with the back of her glove, leaving a streak of dirt behind.

"I don't get it," Jess said. "It's like he was preparing for Armageddon or something."

"I don't either," said Maggie softly. They continued to work, and Virgie found herself falling into a kind of routine: *Dig, sort, toss. Dig, sort, toss.*

A few minutes later, Gloria arrived, calling out, "Hello, my darlings!" But as soon as she stepped into the house, she clapped her hands over her mouth, scanning the room. "Oh my word! That smell! Look at this place!" She rushed back outside. When they reached her, Gloria was pacing in front of the house.

"Are you all right, Mom?" Jess asked. "Do you want some water?"

Gloria stopped and took the bottle from Jess. "Thank you, honey." She appeared frail in her faded jeans and orange gingham shirt. She'd tried to pull her blond bob into a ponytail, and stray tufts of hair stuck out. Somehow the ponytail made her seem even more vulnerable.

"This isn't my house," Gloria said softly, staring at it.

"We know, Mom." Maggie came over and rested a hand on her shoulder. "We're all pretty shocked."

"It's a pigsty!" exclaimed Gloria. "It looks like a bomb went off in there."

"I'm sorry. I tried to warn you over the phone," said Maggie, "but nothing can really prepare you, I guess."

"What happened?" Gloria asked, her voice sounding like a thin reed.

Maggie shook her head and cast around the group for help. "We're not sure, Mom." Jess stepped forward. "But for the time being, we want to get the place cleaned up. You should make sure there's nothing here that you want."

Gloria grunted. "Fat chance of that. How could I possibly find anything in that mess?" She sipped her water. "Do you girls mind if I sit out here for a few minutes?" She settled onto the grass.

"Of course not. Take your time. It's not like we're going to finish today anyway," Virgie joked. "There's plenty left to do."

When they'd started on the living room, Virgie assumed they would need to sift through everything with care, salvaging family keepsakes. But, sadly, there wasn't much worth saving. Countless catalogs, most months old, were mixed in with random information flyers about town meetings, the dangers of BPAs, and Publishers Clearing House sweepstakes envelopes, still sealed. One corner of the living room appeared to be heaped with rubbish that Arthur had acquired at other people's garage sales: used kids' clothes (as if he might one day pass them along to the grandkids), an old Easy-Bake oven, a collection of *National Geographic* magazines, a transistor radio in need of repair, a set of Ken Follett paperbacks.

The sisters headed back inside and continued to cull through the muck. When Virgie heard her stomach growl, she checked her watch. "Hey, it's one o'clock. Anyone want a sandwich?" She couldn't believe she had an appetite in the midst of such squalor. But they'd bought turkey sandwiches this morning on the way to Arthur's, and her body was famished.

"Yes, please. I'm starved." Jess pulled off her gloves and lowered her mask. "We should probably check on Mom anyway." Gloria had yet to poke her head back in the house.

Outside, their mother sat fanning herself, her eyes trained on her phone. Virgie pulled off her mask, sucked in the fresh air, and grabbed a turkey sandwich and soda from the cooler.

"Mom, can I get you anything?"

Gloria lifted her head. "No thanks." She offered a feeble smile.

"Here." Virgie turned to Maggie. "You take half."

"No thanks. I'm not hungry."

"Mags, you need to eat something." Pale half-moons hung under her sister's eyes, and her jeans were practically sliding off her hips. "Come on, eat." Virgie pressed the sandwich into Maggie's hand. She took it but made no effort to eat.

"Remember when we used to climb this tree?" Maggie asked, settling down next to Gloria under the old oak and looking up at the branches, which still swam with green leaves.

"Mm-hmm," said Jess. "And, Mom, you used to yell at us to come down before we broke our necks."

Gloria laughed lightly. "That's true. I was sure one of you girls would kill herself." Her eyes danced around their small circle. "And now look at you. Each one of you, beautiful and successful. I couldn't be more proud."

"Thanks, Mom," Jess said, patting her hand.

"I never stopped loving your father, you know that, right?" Gloria announced out of the blue. "We just grew apart. I wanted the rest of our lives to be exciting, filled with culture and all the things the city had to offer. Your dad, though, was perfectly content writing his books and taking walks on the beach. That was his world. I grew tired of it."

Maggie shot Virgie a glance but said nothing.

"I'm heartbroken that this is how his life ended." Her eyes, steely blue, turned a milky gray as she stared at the house. "I wish I could have done something to stop it."

"We all do," said Jess quietly.

For a few minutes, everyone was quiet. At last, Maggie broke the silence. "I figure the downstairs is going to take us the rest of the day. Then upstairs is where the real mess begins."

Jess groaned. "You must be kidding."

"Sorry," said Maggie. "The only easy part about the upstairs is that pretty much everything can get tossed."

"Maybe we should hire professional cleaners for that part?" Virgie suggested. She wasn't sure how much more she could take. Not to mention her back was killing her. Though she wasn't about to complain. For a blessed twenty-four hours, no one had asked her about her diagnosis or what she was going to do or how she was feeling. The last few days had been all about Arthur. The shock of Arthur.

"I thought of that," offered Maggie, setting down her uneaten sandwich. "But I don't know that in good conscience we can ask professionals to go in there and clean. We might need to get rid of the first layer of yuck."

"But isn't that what professionals get paid to do?" Jess pressed. "My conscience would be perfectly fine with it."

Virgie laughed. "Mine, too."

"Let's see how it goes," said Maggie.

Her mother let a small sigh escape from her lips. "I had no idea it had gotten this bad."

They stopped and stared at her. "This bad?" Virgie inquired. "You mean, you *knew* Dad was hoarding stuff?"

"Oh, well." Gloria waved her hand as if she suddenly thought better of it. "I didn't *know* know. I just kind of suspected."

"Mom, what are you saying?" It was Jess this time who sounded incredulous.

"Well, it was nothing specific. Just a feeling I got. You know, sometimes when Dad and I chatted, he'd mention a great find he'd discovered at a rummage sale. Or he'd prattle on about how he got an entire set of *National Geographic*s and didn't I think the grandkids would love them? I didn't think there was anything obsessive about it, maybe just a little strange." She shrugged. "He was lonely."

"I still don't get it," Maggie pressed. "Did you or didn't you suspect that Dad had gone off the deep end?"

"Maggie, stop," Jess cautioned. "This isn't an inquisition. Mom was as much out of the loop as we were, probably more so. Arthur didn't tell any of us. He didn't want anyone to know. He was a smart man. He was probably embarrassed."

Virgie watched while Maggie dug the toe of her sneaker into the ground and twisted, making a small indentation in the grass.

"I didn't know. I swear," promised Gloria. "I never imagined anything like this." She frowned and gestured toward the house.

Virgie crinkled up her sandwich wrapper and tossed it into the bag along with the empty soda can. She felt around in her jeans pocket for some gum and was surprised by what her fingers landed on. She'd forgotten she'd grabbed it at the last minute. When she left the summer house, Sal had dropped by one last time to say good-bye. He'd also given her a little memento to remember the summer by. Now her fingers played with the joint in her pocket. Were her sisters too goody-goody to enjoy something like this? Would her mother be appalled?

Virgie decided she didn't care. She could really use a few puffs, and so, it seemed, could everyone else around her. She pulled the tightly wrapped coil out of her pocket and held it up to the group. "Anyone interested in a quick smoke before we head back in?" She grinned.

"Is that what I think it is?" Maggie spun around.

Virgie tilted her head to the side. "That depends."

"Virginia Herington!" exclaimed Gloria. "I can't believe you brought drugs to your father's house!"

And somehow, with her mother's pronouncement, they all broke into laughter. There was something ridiculous about being upset about a little marijuana on the premises, given all the other horrors that lurked inside.

"I'm in," Jess said. "I can't remember the last time I got high."

"Me, too." Maggie glanced around. "Who has matches?"

"Hey!" Virgie called out to the Dumpster guy, who sat in the front seat of his truck with his buddy, eating a sandwich. She held up the joint. "Got a light?"

33

Maggie

It didn't take long to realize that there was no way they'd get through cleaning the entire house in just one week. More like a month. Maybe six months. Jess was the first to point it out, though Maggie suspected they'd all been thinking the same thing. They agreed they would finish what they could by the end of the day, Saturday, and then she and Jess would handle the rest in pieces, coming up on weekends and hiring a professional cleaning crew once the house had been emptied and tidied up.

Arthur's place wouldn't be going on the market anytime soon.

Project Clean-Up had morphed into Project Throw-Out. After they broke through the fortresses of boxes upstairs, they began tossing what they could directly out the window into the Dumpster below. There was no point in saving Arthur's clothing for Goodwill; it all reeked with the overpowering stench of his bedroom. And so they threw pants, shirts, old blazers, socks, shoes, every item of clothing out the window. The larger boxes in his office, filled with fresh supplies of paper towels and toilet paper and such, were easier to tote down the stairs. Jess and Virgie hauled out a few before letting Red Sox Guy and his buddy cart off the rest to Goodwill.

Maggie's back muscles ached. Even her calf muscles smarted. She couldn't remember doing this much physical labor since, well, childbirth. On the way back to the hotel yesterday, she'd stopped at the pharmacy to pick up a couple of tubes of Ben-Gay. A young teenager with a pierced lip sold them to her with a grin. *Just you wait,* she wanted to say. *This will be you someday, so wipe that smirk off your face.* Then she realized he was smiling at the young woman in line behind her. Back at the hotel, she rubbed the cream into every pore of her body, relishing the wonderful tingling sensation as her muscles began to unknot.

They were cleaning in Arthur's study on Saturday when Gloria excused herself to get some fresh air. Maggie glanced over at Virgie. Her T-shirt was wet with sweat. Even with multiple fans blowing, the upstairs felt like a sauna. "You should take it easy, Virgie." Maggie turned to her now. "You don't want to overdo it."

"Thanks. I'm okay, aside from the usual aches and pains of moving all this crap. I honestly don't think I've ever cleaned out such a pit unless you count my apartment in college," she added. "And that was a much smaller space."

"Did you tell Mom yet?" Jess asked as she piled books into boxes. "You know, about the MS?" Maggie noticed that Virgie had avoided discussing her diagnosis since she'd arrived. In some ways, sorting through Arthur's things had been a convenient distraction. At least her sister was *talking,* unlike the glum, withdrawn teenager she'd become back in Windsor. But eventually, her sister would have to face the facts.

"No," admitted Virgie. "I figured she had enough to deal with right now. I will. Eventually. So, what's the plan for Dad's ceremony tomorrow?" she asked in a blatant attempt to change the subject.

"Well," Maggie began, willing to take the bait. She and Gloria had been working to set up a simple memorial service for a group of Arthur's closest friends. "Nothing too fancy. There should be about thirty people. Jay and the Stonehills are driving up from the Cape. Some of Dad's friends from town. Mom, us, maybe Gio?" Maggie paused. "Though I'm not sure about Gio, come to think of it. Mom hasn't really said. And, of course, *Jackson*." Her voice dripped with sugary sweetness. "We can't wait to meet this Mr. Wonderful, Virgie."

Virgie smiled. Maggie knew her sister was excited; she'd been checking her cell every fifteen minutes for messages, up until the battery died, that is. "I hope you like him."

"I'm sure we will," said Maggie. "And if we don't, we'll let you know." Her sister laughed.

"At least the weather is supposed to be good tomorrow," Jess said. "In the seventies."

"Perfect weather for a funeral." Virgie caught herself and giggled. "You hear that, Daddy?" She called in the general direction of the vase with Arthur's ashes that sat atop the fireplace mantel. Maggie lifted an eyebrow, but Virgie just smiled. "What? I feel like he's in the room with us. He kind of is, isn't he?"

"Thank goodness," Jess said. Maggie knew she was alluding to yesterday's scare: they'd been cleaning in the guest room, when Gloria stopped, scanned the room. "Where are Daddy's ashes?" she asked.

Everyone stared at her, as if she were posing the most ridiculous question in the world.

"Downstairs?" Jess had asked. "Right? Isn't that where we left him?"

Virgie giggled. "It sounds funny, like Daddy's sitting downstairs in his chair." Before she'd finished talking, though, both Maggie and Jess were tromping down the steps.

"Where is it?" Jess called out.

"It's got to be here somewhere," Gloria cried as she came

downstairs. "You don't think," she began, then shook her head when everyone looked at her. "Oh, nothing."

"What, Mom? What is it?" Maggie snapped.

"I was just thinking how strange it would be if we happened to toss Arthur's ashes out with the rest of his junk." She motioned around the room, which was now relatively clean.

"Mom, please don't go there." Maggie groaned. "As Lexie would say, 'That is *so* not funny.'"

Minutes later, Red Sox Guy appeared holding the vase in his hands, the delicate blue flowers stitching around it. "Is this what you're looking for?" Jess ran up and snatched it from him.

"Where did you find this?" Her tone carried a mild accusation.

"I put it out near the bushes. I didn't want it to get knocked over when we were hauling stuff out. Thought that would have been pretty bad."

Maggie let out a breath. "Yes, that would have been bad," she agreed. "Thank you, um . . ."

"Ernest," he filled in. "The name's Ernest."

"Thank you, Ernest," Maggie echoed. And since then, the vase had been following them from room to room, carefully placed out of harm's way.

Maggie continued pulling manila files from Arthur's desk and tossing them into the trash. "Junk. Years' and years' worth of old bank statements. Honestly, what did Dad think he'd need these for? Statements dating back to the eighties?"

Jess shook her head. "Who knows? About the only thing we know about Dad at this point is that we didn't know him very well."

Virgie stood and clapped her hands on her jeans, sending grime flying. "I don't know about that," she said. "I think we knew Daddy pretty well, aside from this particular side of him."

"Well, it's a pretty huge side of him, wouldn't you say?" Jess demanded.

"So, his house turned into a mess after Mom left. So what?" Virgie said. "He was still working at the library, still writing books, still had plenty of friends. It wasn't as if he became a recluse. He wasn't *crazy*."

Jess shot Maggie a look.

"Look," continued Virgie. "I know I'm the baby sister, but Dad and I were close. Really close. I'd like to think that the person I knew and trusted and loved was the real Arthur, too. They were all pieces of the same man."

Maggie nodded thoughtfully. "You're right." A silence sat suspended among them. "I was reading a little bit about it last night," Maggie said now. She'd gone to the library and checked out a handful of books on hoarding. Just walking into the place where she knew Arthur had worked only weeks ago had given her goose bumps.

"Really?" said Jess, unable to hide her surprise.

"Yeah. I wanted to try to understand what was going on in Dad's head." She waved her hand in the air as if she were foolish for contemplating the idea. "Anyway, there was some interesting stuff about hoarding. Apparently it's a mental disorder, not just a quirk. Everything I read suggested it has a lot of similarities to OCD."

"Huh? That doesn't make sense," offered Virgie.

"I know. That's what I thought, too," agreed Maggie. "But apparently it's all connected. It's about obsession. People with OCD are obsessed with organizing while hoarders are obsessed with holding on to everything. Whatever part of the brain that helps people prioritize what's important—and what's not—doesn't work right in a hoarder. Hoarders think *everything* is important, and so they hold on to it all. They can't bear to throw anything out."

"Wow," Jess reflected. "So Dad was like totally opposite of you."

"Very funny," Maggie said. "But yeah, I suppose we are linked in some weird way with our obsessions." Maggie remembered learning about the brain in her tenth-grade biology class and how neurons fired across the synapses. She'd been spellbound by the thought of a whole world of biological fireworks operating in beautiful synchronicity. Little did she know then how easily neurons could misfire, how certain parts of the brain could fizzle out. How the scaffolding of a mind could collapse with the simple flick of a switch. What had been Arthur's switch? she wondered. Was it Gloria's leaving that had started his unraveling?

"Hey, check this out," Jess said now. "It's Dad's old music box, remember?" She retrieved it from the bottom desk drawer and turned it over. When she rotated the switch on the bottom, "Singing in the Rain" began to play, and the funny little man with the yellow hat and umbrella spun around on top. Arthur had brought it back from Germany, intending it as a gift for their mother, but the girls had quickly co-opted it for themselves. Over the years, it had gone from housing their little trinkets to holding Arthur's cigars.

Jess flipped the latch and lifted the lid, revealing three portly cigars, untouched. She raised the box to her nose and inhaled. "Now *this* reminds me of the Dad I used to know."

"I thought Dad quit smoking those years ago," Maggie said.

"Apparently not," said Jess. "Or maybe he did and he just forgot about these. It was stuffed in the back of his drawer."

"We should definitely keep it," Virgie confirmed.

Jess dropped the lid and handed it over. "All yours."

Maggie began to sift through another pile of books. Sadly, there wasn't much in Arthur's library that she wanted for herself. She retrieved a few fishing books for Mac, but most of the philosophy books got tossed into the donation box. A few minutes later, the heavy black rotary phone on Arthur's desk rang, startling them all. Maggie reached for the receiver.

"Hello?" She gave Virgie a knowing look. "Oh, hello, Jackson. We've been dying to meet you. One minute, please. She's right here. Virginia?"

"Give it to me!" Virgie yelled, as she ripped the phone out of Maggie's hand. "Hi, Jackson?" Her voice was syrupy, that of a love-struck teenager.

Jess glanced at Maggie, and they erupted in laughter; their baby sister was smitten, totally, completely, head over heels in love. Anyone could tell.

34

Jess

The wind whipped up from the water, sending whitecaps sailing into the shore and crashing against the rocks. A bright, generous sun shone down on the small group that was gathering near the cliffs. While the day was perhaps not the calm, balmy one they'd been anticipating for Arthur's memorial, Jess thought the drama of it was fitting. More important, her dad, she thought, would approve.

Thirty to forty people lingered near a set of white folding chairs that faced the ocean. Earlier that morning, Ernest (who was proving indispensable this week) had helped them load the chairs at the rental shop and then drove them out to Governor's Park in his truck. Almost no one in the assembled group, Jess noticed, wore black. Guests were wrapped in woolly gray and purple sweaters to shield themselves from the wind. Maggie and Virgie wore pretty floral dresses, but even they'd given up and thrown windbreakers around their shoulders. Only Gloria donned a black dress, black jacket, and white pearls. Jess's throat tightened when she saw the pearls; she remembered the anniversary when Arthur had given them to her mom. Their thirty-fifth. The family had supper at the Lighthouse Club, buttery lobsters and crab, and the sisters had written limericks for the occasion. Jess felt nostalgia swell in her; her parents had been so in love then.

Gloria stood at the front, talking to the minister about last-minute details. Their father had always been fond of the Book of Job, and Jess was certain her mom was requesting a passage from it for the service. The sisters had drawn up a quick memorial program on the computer last night and printed out fifty copies at Kinko's this morning. It was hardly a classy affair, but she thought Arthur would have appreciated their nod to keeping it simple. The fact that they'd even assembled a small group beyond the immediate family for the scattering of his ashes was beyond what he had requested in his will. Still, it was fitting, tasteful.

She took in the setting for the ceremony, a pretty little park hemmed in by soaring firs on one side and with expansive views of the water in all other directions. Gloria had suggested the spot, explaining that she and Arthur used to hike along the park's paths. Jess could almost see them now, holding hands and marveling at the seascape. She wondered if her mother was envisioning the same thing while she talked with the minister.

Shortly, Jay and the Stonehills arrived in the Stonehills' black Mercedes. Jess watched while they got out and stretched their legs after the long drive, their eyes quickly landing on Gloria. As she stepped away from the minister, they approached to express their sympathies.

"Thank you so much for coming," said Gloria, clasping Mrs. Stonehill's hands. "It would have meant a lot to Arthur to know you were here."

"We loved him dearly," said Mrs. Stonehill.

"He was a spectacular man," offered her husband. "We're going to miss him." But he had to excuse himself before he could say more, removing his glasses to swipe at tears while his wife hurried after him.

"I loved your dad, but you already knew that," said Jay as he grabbed Jess in a bear hug. "He was one of a kind." Jay seemed different somehow from when she'd last seen him; then she realized it was the baseball hat, or lack of it. Jay always wore a baseball cap. In fact, Jess didn't know as if she'd ever before seen his hair, which turned out to be surprisingly curly and gray.

Off to the side, near a clutch of wildflowers, stood Virgie and Jackson. Despite Jess's initial wariness about Jackson's flying out, she now understood why her sister had wanted him here. He struck Jess as smart, caring, even-keeled, and—this was a surprise—a little nerdy. Her baby sister usually dated only the drop-dead handsome guys. The fact that Jackson's nose was slightly out of proportion to his face, that he was on the thin side, meant that Virgie must really like him. His hand rested on the small of Virgie's back now, as if his lanky frame would catch her should she ever fall again. Dressed in a black blazer and khaki pants, he was perhaps the only man (other than Mr. Stonehill) wearing a tie. He reminded Jess a bit of Dylan McDermott with his bright blue eyes and dark, thick hair. A slightly geeky Dylan McDermott, who happened to have one of the softest hands Jess had ever shaken.

"I like him," Jess had whispered to her sister after dinner last night, and Virgie had smiled, as if she'd been keeping a precious secret from them all this time.

"Me, too," said Maggie, joining them in the hotel hallway.

"I'm so glad," Virgie said.

"You weren't really worried we wouldn't, were you?" asked Maggie.

Her sister grinned. "I thought it was a pretty safe bet. The bigger worry for me was whether he'd like our crazy clan."

Eventually, the minister urged everyone to take a seat so the ceremony could begin. Jess watched while people settled themselves.

Some faces were familiar, like that of Florence Arbitrage, whose children Jess and her sisters had attended grade school with. Or Herbert Langley, the president of the library where her dad had worked and who had been instrumental in suggesting whom Arthur would have wanted at his funeral. There were also a number of faces she didn't recognize, but who came up to her nevertheless to share a particular memory of Arthur.

She fell in step behind her mom, sisters, and Jackson as they headed for the front row. "No Gio?" she whispered to Gloria as they took their seats.

Her mother shook her head. "Oh, no. That's over." Jess nodded, but she was surprised. What had happened? "A passing phase," Gloria whispered in her ear, as if she'd read her mind.

As if on cue, the wind quieted as soon as the minister stood and approached the lectern. Reverend Holmes thanked everyone for coming and began to lead them in an opening prayer. At the prayer's close, a slight man with a black scally cap walked to the lectern, a silver trumpet in hand. The audience held its breath as he proceeded to play a Bach adagio. *The music.* It always got to her. Even when she'd been a little girl, Arthur knew the way to her heart was through music. If Jess were in a foul mood after a bad day at school, he'd put on a record of Count Basie or Chopin or Bach and twirl her around the living room. She'd forgotten that! But now the song, as it flitted across the sea air, brought the memories racing back.

Gloria sniffled next to her. Virgie dug in her purse for a tissue. Maggie squeezed her hands tightly in her lap, folded as if in prayer. Arthur's voice still played in Jess's mind. The funny, irascible voice of his grandfather years, not the judgmental one of her youth. Maggie had mentioned a similar sensation, of continuing to hear Arthur's voice, as if he were an immutable, invisible presence hovering around them. "It's like his energy is still here," she'd said to Jess the other night. "Little atoms bouncing around. I can feel him, urging us to do the right thing." And somehow, Jess had known exactly what she meant.

The memories spooled through her mind until the trumpet player closed on a final, plaintive note. Spellbound, the crowd was silent as he lowered his instrument and returned to his seat. As if in deference to the moment, Jay, who had risen to say a few words, waited at his chair for half a beat. Then he walked over to the lectern, cleared his throat, and began.

"Arthur Herington and I knew each other for at least forty years, though to be honest it might have been longer. I don't remember the exact date when we first shared a beer at Grouchy Ted's down on the Cape. But I knew from the moment I met him, that I liked him. And even though he couldn't fix a thing around the house to save his life"—a small chuckle rippled through the crowd—"I can say that he was a kindred soul. We shared the same views when it came to politics (hate the rich, save the poor), beers (nothing like a good Sam Adams), music (blues and classical), and an appreciation for good-looking women." Here he stopped to nod at Gloria, who blushed even beneath her tears. "Arthur and I especially liked to go out and listen to music together." He smiled. "I have a lot of good memories of sitting in bars with him listening to a musician picking at his instrument. I think he'd be glad to know that."

Jay paused and scanned the crowd for a moment. "Some of you I know, many of you I don't. We're all here because of one person: Arthur Herington. We all knew and loved Arthur. He was a kind soul even beneath his sometimes rough exterior." A few more chuckles undulated through the crowd. "But what some of you may not know is that, for me, Arthur was my unsung hero. I suspect he was for many of you as well, in his own quiet way. You see, several summers ago, I was diagnosed with prostate cancer." Jess breathed in. She'd never known. She glanced at her sisters, who shook their heads.

"I won't lie," Jay continued. "It was hell. I thought for sure the good Lord was going to take me. Not many people knew. Heck, it wasn't the kind of thing you went around advertising. But Arthur knew. He figured out something was wrong as soon as he took one look at me that summer.

"Unlike Arthur, I was never lucky enough to have a family, a wife and children as beautiful as Gloria, Maggie, Jess, and Virgie. But I do have some incredible friends. And do you know who showed up to take me to my doctor's appointments that summer and, after that, my chemo treatments?" He paused. "That's right, it was Arthur." His voice cracked and Gloria shifted in her seat. "He showed up every day, every moment I needed him. And I didn't have to ask. He just did it. *That's what friends are for,* he'd say. And you know what? He was right. I was humbled by his generosity. And—" Here his voice broke and he stopped to collect himself.

"And, he did one thing for me that I'll never forget. I want to share it with you today because I think it speaks to the nature of our friendship and to Arthur's character. When I was sick as a dog after chemo, Arthur said he wanted to surprise me with something when I was feeling up to it. A week later, when I was a little better, there was a knock at my door. It was Arthur. He told me to go sit on the couch, that he had a surprise for me." Jay stopped again and scanned the crowd, seeming to conjure the day once more in his mind.

"And into my living room marches a fellow carrying a violin. And another guy carrying a violin. Then *another* man with a huge cello. And one more fellow with an instrument I didn't recognize at the time, but it was a viola. Can you imagine? They go and set up in my living room without saying a word, as if they did this all the time. And the next thing I know Arthur sits down next to me with a shit-eating grin." He paused, "Sorry, Pastor. And Arthur says to me, 'If you aren't well enough to go out and listen to some music, I thought we could bring it to you.'"

Jess felt goose bumps run along her arms. She'd never heard this story.

"And so there we sat, on a late summer's day, listening to these gifted musicians play the most enchanting music I've ever heard." He gestured to the trumpeter. "I was reminded of that today. Arthur had hired my own private string quartet. We listened to them play Chopin, Bach, a little Beethoven. It was the most divine present a person could ask for. I'll never forget it. I think it sums up Arthur, my friend, your friend, in a heartbeat."

He folded up his paper and said, barely audible, "My, how I'm going to miss that man." And with that he hung his head and walked back to his seat.

Tears streamed down Jess's face. She glanced over at her sisters, who dabbed at their eyes. Gloria cried quietly next to her, and Jess laid a hand on her mother's arm. "Are you okay?" she whispered.

Gloria shook her head. "No, not really."

At last, Reverend Holmes stood and spoke. "Thank you, Jay, for that beautiful memory. I think I can say it spoke to all of us. I can see why it stays with you."

There was more music followed by a reading and then a Maya Angelou poem. As the minister finished the poem, a cloud passed across the sun and then disappeared just as suddenly as it had appeared. Jess shuddered. It was as if Arthur were signaling that he was here, watching them. After a final benediction, the minister invited the group to join them in the blessing of the ashes before casting them out to sea.

He carried the tall vase to an area set off to one side, an enclosure protected from the wind by a scattering of pine trees. The family trailed after him, then the guests. Jess watched while Reverend Holmes blessed the urn and then tapped out a small amount of ashes into Gloria's hands. She closed her eyes, as if in silent prayer. Then, she took a deep breath and shouted, "Rest in peace, Arthur

Herington!" tossing the ashes into the wind, where the gray dust sparkled in the light before spiraling away. Next it was Maggie's turn. She kissed her cupped hands. "Bye, Daddy," she whispered, "Be good up there," and threw her handful skyward.

When the minister poured the ashes into Jess's hands, she was surprised by the texture, how grainy the ashes felt. She could still see bits of smooth bone in the dust. Her stomach knotted. She was holding her father in her hands. Did she have a piece of his heart, she wondered, in this mix of bone and dust? Or was it something less grand, like a toe or an elbow bone? The only way she could get through the moment, she knew, was to focus on his heart. *Yes, there must be a piece of his heart in here somewhere.* And with that silent thought and a prayer that he watch over them, she tossed his dust out to sea. Then she stepped back and waited as Virgie, between jagged cries, managed to send her handful of Arthur sailing. Jess watched the ashes catch and dip on the wind.

It was then that she felt the sobs rush up her body. And it was Jay who stretched an arm around her, leading her away from the cerulean sea, her father's final resting place.

35

Virgie

After the ceremony, they headed back to the hotel for a farewell dinner. Jay and the Stonehills joined them. Virgie and Jess excused themselves to check their makeup in the ladies' room. Virgie was worried that mascara was running down her face in long black streaks, but in fact, her face appeared raw and tender with hardly a stitch of makeup on it. Well, she thought, she'd more or less washed it with her tears at the memorial service.

She reapplied mascara and dabbed her forehead with powder. "That went as well as could be expected," she said, pursing her lips together and reapplying lip gloss.

"I agree." Jess brushed her hair. "Jay's speech pretty much undid me, though."

"Me, too. I never even knew he had cancer, did you?"

Jess shook her head. "That's quite a secret to keep. And the story about Dad and the string quartet? That was amazing."

"I know. Goose bumps." She snapped her purse shut and offered her sister a small smile. "Ready to go back?" Jess nodded.

At the table, Gloria was thanking Jay for his kind words. "Arthur would have loved what you said." She spoke softly. "You captured him beautifully." Virgie slipped in next to Jackson and felt him reaching for her hand under the table. She took it, squeezed it.

"How are you doing?" he whispered.

"Okay." She felt a wash of relief that Jackson was finally here, sitting beside her. When he'd first pulled up to the house, she'd worried that seeing him might be awkward, her diagnosis standing between them like a cement wall. But as soon as he got out of the car and she glimpsed his shock of dark, wavy hair and his smile (*that smile!*), any second thoughts melted away. She raced to him and jumped into his arms, practically knocking him over. He hugged her, hard, then buried his head in her hair, saying, "God, I've missed you. I didn't know I could miss someone so much."

"I know," Virgie said. "It's so good to see you. Thanks for coming. So much has happened these last few weeks, I don't even know where to begin."

"Shh." He held his fingertips to her lips. "You don't have to. You've filled me in on the big stuff." And then she led him back to the house, to her sisters and Gloria, who'd been standing just beyond the front door, she was quite sure, spying on them. Maggie, then Jess, said hello, and Virgie could tell by the way they leaned forward, lingered in a handshake, that they liked him. Even Gloria acted sweetly surprised and pulled Jackson into an embrace. "You're even more handsome than Virgie gives you credit for."

"Go," her sisters ordered. "Go lie in the hammock or something and catch up. We'll finish cleaning up." And so, Virgie offered him a drink from the cooler and led him by the hand out to the back deck, where the ocean breeze felt good on her sticky skin.

"Man, this place is gorgeous," Jackson said. It was the first time that week that Virgie had given a moment's thought to the house's charms. She'd been so focused on the mess, the squalor, the sadness of what they'd discovered inside that she'd almost forgotten the beauty that the place once held. She tried to see it through Jackson's eyes now. He was right. The house had been lovely, could still be lovely.

"It's funny. I'd kind of forgotten, given everything we found inside."

He folded his arms around her while they looked out on the water, dragonflies darting above the sand like tiny sparks of light.

"My dad used to love to take walks along here. And when we were girls, we'd have races on the beach. Jess always had to win, of course—you know, middle sister complex. But sometimes they'd let me win."

"I thought Jess and Maggie were twins," Jackson said, surprised.

"They are. But Maggie was born first, so she always lorded it over the rest of us." Virgie laughed. "In a good way, of course."

"Sounds like my big brother, Adam." It occurred to Virgie that while she was aware that Jackson had brothers, she knew nothing about them.

"I know nothing about your family, while you know so much about mine," she said now, almost apologetically.

He laughed. "Don't worry, there's not much that's interesting to know. Both my brothers are successful businessmen. I'm the big disappointment in the family, at least according to my dad."

"But how is that possible?" Virgie exclaimed. "You're a nurse, helping people every day."

"Exactly. A nurse, but not a doctor."

"Well, I think you're perfect," she said, turning in his arms to kiss him.

"Careful. You don't want to inflate my ego even more."

She realized, as they sat at the table now, that she wanted to know every little thing about this man. Not just the mole that hovered above his right elbow, or the exact shade of blue of his eyes, but the big stuff. What his parents were like, what his best memories of growing up were. They'd talked so much in the first month of their relationship, and yet there was still so much to discover. The thought of it gave her a small thrill. She leaned back as the waiter set down her plate of roast beef, mashed potatoes with gravy, and carrots. Comfort food. Virgie glanced around the table and thought how proud Arthur would be to have all these people, so dear to him, gathered in one place to celebrate his life. Had he been given the chance to write the ending to his own story, would he have written something similar to this? she wondered. She hoped so. But at the thought of her dad sitting there with them all, telling jokes, her eyes swelled again with tears. *Damn it, Daddy,* she thought. *You should be here. At your own funeral.*

She picked at her roast beef, her appetite suddenly gone. Jackson reached over and gently rubbed her back.

"Hey, can I get you anything?" he asked. "Maybe some ginger ale?" She loved that he could intuit her moods, understand when she needed a soft touch, reassurance. She shook her head, then caught Maggie watching them, a smile playing across her lips. Virgie recognized that look: it was her sister's "approving" smile.

Mrs. Stonehill was placing another drink order. "Would you like your Chardonnay oaked or unoaked?" asked the waiter.

"Most definitely *un*oaked, my dear boy," she said. "I prefer oak in my floors, not in my drink."

"Good enough," replied the waiter and turned on his heel. Jackson shot Virgie a puzzled look, but she just laughed. It was better that her boyfriend learn sooner than later the quirks of her family and friends. And she realized with a start that it was the first time she'd actually called him her *boyfriend,* if only in her mind. The talk circled on with memories of her dad.

When it was time for dessert, the decision was unanimous: bananas Foster, Arthur's favorite. The waiter placed a platter on the table—the bananas arranged like daisy petals dripping in brown sugar and rum—and set it ablaze with a huge whooshing sound.

"Arthur always said he wanted to go out with a blast," Jay joked, and they laughed.

Eventually, their table was the last one still seated. They exchanged reluctant good-byes with Jay and the Stonehills, who were staying at a hotel further down the street. Virgie and Jackson headed back to their own room. The emotional and physical drain of the last few days was settling in, and she leaned against Jackson as they walked. Back in the room, she pulled off her heels, changed into her pajamas, and brushed her teeth and scrubbed her face before crawling into bed.

"Come here," Jackson said, gathering her in his arms and stroking her hair. The local news played on the television—some story about a missing dog—but Virgie wasn't listening.

"It's so nice to hold you again," he said.

"It's nice to be held." The scent of Jackson's soap drifted over to her, fresh, comforting, familiar.

He kissed the top of her head. "I missed you so much."

"You already said that," she teased.

"No, like *insanely* missed you," he clarified.

"Oh, well, in that case, I apologize. I only sanely missed you."

"Such a wiseass," he said and kissed her again. She looked up at him and felt the butterflies. It had been one of the strangest, most exhausting weeks of her life. But also, quite possibly, one of the best. Because here was the man she thought she might very well love, holding her and telling her how much he'd missed her. If she told him she loved him, would she risk everything? She was afraid. Afraid that he might not feel the same way. She needed her own place to land, her own island. Was Jackson it? He took her chin in his hand and grazed his lips against hers.

"I love you, Virginia Herington," he whispered. And there it was. Virgie felt her heart jump. There was so much more they needed to discuss. Was he really okay with her diagnosis? What if they got married? What if they had kids? Would he worry they'd be carriers? And the other big question that had been tumbling around in her head all week: she didn't know if she wanted to go back to Seattle.

"Me too," she said. "Me too," she repeated, savoring the words like a sweet liqueur.

The next morning, Virgie called a family conference, texting her sisters to meet her in the hotel restaurant by 8:30. She couldn't postpone her announcement any longer, and she was bursting to tell. She'd shared her plans with Jackson late last night, and now she needed to get the go-ahead from the rest of the family.

As soon as she stepped into the dining room, she spied Gloria sitting at a table across the room, reading the paper. Virgie went to grab herself coffee and said a quick hello to her sisters, who were already waiting in the omelet line.

"Mom, I've got something to tell you," Virgie said, pulling up a chair. Gloria lifted her eyes from the paper.

"Good morning, dear. Are you feeling okay? Yesterday was a pretty dramatic affair, although I think your dad would have loved it." Before her mother could continue, Virgie interrupted. She'd already decided it was best to cut to the chase.

"Mom, I don't want you to freak out, but remember the doctor's appointment I had in Boston?"

Gloria's eyebrows peaked into tight little arches. "Yes? I thought it went fine. No news? Isn't that what Maggie told me?"

Virgie wondered if she looked as guilty as she felt. She'd asked Maggie to lie when Gloria called the night after the appointment. It wasn't so much a lie, she told herself, as it was an omission of the truth. She simply didn't have the strength to weather Gloria's reaction, whatever it might be, to the news that she was only beginning to digest herself.

"Well," Virgie began, searching for words. "Part of it was okay, but the other part, well, they do seem to think it's MS." She was surprised by how easily the acronym slipped off her tongue. She took her mother's hand while Gloria gathered a sharp intake of breath.

"What?" she asked, pulling away her hand and covering her throat, her ringed fingers trembling. "But, I thought you were fine. I thought all the tests were negative."

Virgie sighed. "That's what I'd hoped. I'm sorry I didn't tell you sooner. I needed some time myself to get my head around the news. And with Dad's death and then the house . . ." She stopped. "Well, it just never seemed like a good time to give you even more bad news." While she'd been bracing herself for Gloria's reaction, Virgie realized now that it no longer mattered so much to her. Her sisters had already offered to help however they could, and there was Jackson. *Jackson, Jackson, Jackson.* It was funny—when she'd thought of his name back in Seattle it had been with a shiver of excitement; now the thought of *Jackson* was like a Zen mantra she recited to calm herself. Whether her mom wanted to help or not made little difference in the scheme of things. Virgie was not alone in this.

She watched while her mom worked to rearrange her face into an expression Virgie couldn't immediately identify. "Oh, honey," Gloria said finally and pulled her into a hug. "Oh, my sweet, sweet girl. We'll get through it. Don't you worry. Everything is going to be just fine."

And Virgie felt yet another small piece of her protective armor slipping away. Because whether or not she cared to admit it, weren't those the very words she'd been waiting to hear? She recognized now the expression on her mother's face, one she hadn't glimpsed in a long while: maternal love. She'd almost forgotten. Just then, her sisters joined them at the table, setting down oversize omelets.

"Everything okay?" Maggie pulled out a chair and sat.

"Yes," said Virgie. "Everything's fine. I just told Mom the news."

"Oh?" Jess arched an eyebrow.

"Yes, she did." Gloria patted her hand. "We're going to take good care of her, aren't we, girls?"

"Of course we are," said Maggie.

Virgie sipped her coffee. "That sort of brings me to the other topic I wanted to discuss." She took a breath, then launched in. "I'm thinking of staying."

"Oh, honey," Gloria said, waving a hand in the air. "That won't be necessary. We can take care of things with Arthur's house. You don't need to worry about that."

"No, as in sticking around. I want to move here and"—she paused again—"and live in Daddy's house." She waited. "If that's all right with all of you, of course."

"What?" Maggie asked, her voice catching in her throat. "Really? You're going to come back this way? For good?"

"But what about your job? About Jackson?" Jess, ever the practical one, pressed.

Virgie had been thinking about it all week. "I'm tired of all the stress. I've been wanting to leave the station for a while," she explained. "I e-mailed my old boss at the *Portland-Press Herald*. He wants me to come in and start on a few pieces. Hopefully, it will turn into something full-time. I've got a little savings. I shouldn't have to worry about money for a while." She paused. "I haven't told my boss yet. I wanted to hear what you all thought first."

Maggie jumped up and leaned in to hug her. "That is the most fabulous news! And here you had me thinking it was something awful."

"I'm sorry," Virgie continued. "But the past few weeks have made me realize how much I miss you all. And with MS, well, who knows, but I could probably use a little help down the line. I don't want to be alone. I don't think I can do it alone," she admitted, her voice quiet.

"Finally," Jess said. When Virgie shot her a questioning look, she explained, "I'm just glad you realize you're not alone in this. That's what we've been trying to tell you since you were a little girl." Virgie smiled, suddenly grateful.

"And Jackson?" her mother asked again.

"I'm going to fly back to Seattle with him. I need to arrange for movers anyway." She hesitated, not quite sure she believed the words she was about to utter herself. "And Jackson . . . we're going to try things long-distance for a few months while I get settled out here. But"—she glanced around the table—"he says he's always wanted to come back East. He graduated from Dartmouth, so, maybe . . . " She shrugged. "Who knows, maybe he'll move out this way, too."

"Well, there's certainly plenty of room in that house!" Gloria clapped her hands together. She sighed. "Just think: I'll have all my girls in one place again."

"So?" Virgie's gaze traveled around the table. "It's okay with everyone if we don't sell the house? At least not right now?" It was remarkable to be asking such a thing, given the state they'd found the place in. But it was her home, where they'd grown up, filled with memories. How could she let that go? Arthur had left the house to the girls to dispense with as they pleased, the proceeds to be divided evenly. Virgie understood she was asking her sisters to forgo a possible financial windfall.

Jess leaned back in her chair and nodded, grinning. Maggie rested her elbows on the table and looked at Virgie dreamily. "It's perfect. It's what Dad would have wanted. I'm sure of it."

"Then it's decided!" Gloria exclaimed.

"What's decided?" asked Jackson, who sidled up next to Virgie and set down a bowl of cereal. His dark hair was tousled, his eyes still sleepy. Virgie grinned at him. She couldn't help it. She couldn't stop.

36

Jess

Jess draped her wet towel over the shower rod. As chaotic and crazy and sad as this week had been, it had been a little bit of a break not to have to put dinner on the table or do the laundry or pick up someone else's towel. But she was missing her kids. She was missing Tim.

She packed her brush and toothbrush into the zipper compartment of her suitcase. Checkout time was in fifteen minutes. Tomorrow, Virgie would fly to Seattle with Jackson, but once she had movers set up, she'd be back this way. *Home!* The thought of Virgie—and possibly Jackson—living in Arthur's house made Jess smile. She knew Arthur would approve. And now Grace and Teddy would be able to see their younger aunt. They could visit the house in Maine. Perhaps there would be a wedding! All those memories that Jess had been sad to think the kids would miss out on could become a reality. Walks along the rocky Maine coastline, succulent lobster pulled fresh from the ocean, blueberry picking by the bushel.

She closed her suitcase and zipped it up, set her purse beside it on the bed. She surveyed the room one last time to make sure she hadn't forgotten anything. But aside from a few dirty towels and a missing handful of travel-size lotions that she'd heisted for the kids, the room appeared ready for the next guest. A text popped up on her cell, which lay on the bed, and she grabbed it. A picture of Grace and Teddy playing at the park this morning. They looked so happy. *Can't wait to see you!* Tim had typed underneath.

I love you guys, she texted back. *See you this afternoon.*

Jess checked her pocket for her room key and rolled her suitcase behind her as she closed the door. They'd all agreed to meet in the lobby to say their good-byes. When she stepped off the elevator, Gloria was already seated in a leather couch in the main gathering area. Virgie and Jackson sat across from her, engaged in conversation. Jess walked over to them.

"Jessica," her mother said, "I was just telling Virginia and Jackson that I might fly out to help with Virginia's move. It seems a shame for her to fly back here before she's even had a chance to show me around Seattle."

"Wow, Mom. That's great." Jess didn't add that Virgie had invited Gloria to visit her about a million times in the last few years, and each time, Gloria had offered a convenient excuse for why she couldn't travel. Now she and Virgie exchanged looks as if to say, *See, all it took was your leaving Seattle to get Mom to finally fly there.* "Well, I, for one, can't wait to have you back on this coast," Jess said. "When do you think you'll be able to head this way?"

Virgie glanced at Jackson. "Probably in a few weeks? I'll be driving out with the movers." He nodded and wove his fingers into hers.

"I'm hoping I can join her sooner rather than later," he added. "I've already started dusting off my résumé."

"Did I mention I like this guy?" Jess smiled and headed over to the checkout line.

Just then, Maggie entered the lobby pulling a wheelie suitcase behind her. "Hi, gang." She waved and pushed her sunglasses up on her head. Long blond waves framed her face. She wore a pink sundress and wedge espadrilles. Even after a funeral and a week's worth of housecleaning, Maggie still looked gorgeous. She pulled up next to Jess in line.

"Damn you," Jess whispered. "Seriously, don't you *ever* look tired?"

Maggie smiled and batted her eyelashes. "You should see how many gallons of concealer I have on these bags."

"Next?" The concierge motioned them up to the desk. "I hope you enjoyed your stay," she said pleasantly as she took Jess's room key, then Maggie's.

"We did," said Jess. "Thank you." After they'd paid and Maggie took a package from the concierge, the sisters went to join the rest of the family in the lounging area.

"Well, it looks like this is it." Maggie's voice cracked, and Jess suddenly noticed the tears streaking her sister's face. Maggie pulled a tissue from her purse and dabbed her eyes. "I'm sorry I'm such a softie. I've always hated good-byes."

"Oh, Mags." Virgie bounced up. "I'll see you really soon, okay? I love you." And before she knew it, everyone was embracing and saying their good-byes.

Jess caught Jackson standing off to one side, his hands stuffed in his pockets, looking slightly at sea. "Don't worry. We almost never do this," she reassured him across the group hug, and he laughed.

"Okay," he said. "Good. I think."

After a few more minutes, the family disentangled themselves. Virgie and Jackson were staying an extra night, and Maggie teased that Jackson better look after their sister or he'd have Maggie to answer to. Gloria would drive back to Boston after visiting some friends in town. "Till tomorrow, then," Maggie said. It was an old saying, one she always liked to offer at the end of their holiday gatherings, precisely because she hated saying good-bye. Somehow it made the leaving seem easier. Maggie flipped her sunglasses back down on her face.

"Give those precious grandchildren kisses for me," Gloria ordered.

"We will, Mom," Jess said as she fell in step behind Maggie. They headed for the revolving doors, and Jess gave a little wave over her shoulder.

"See you soon!" called Virgie.

Jess couldn't recall the last time Virgie had looked so happy. Nor could she recall the last time all the sisters had been together outside of the beach house. Odd how Arthur's passing had precipitated everything. What a long summer it had been! And yet, what strides everyone had made. She thought secretly that Arthur was looking down on them, gratified to see that the mess of his life had become the very catalyst to bring them together again, to cast clarity on their own jumbled lives. It would be good to have Virgie closer to home. And in a strange turn of events, thought Jess, in losing Arthur, they'd gotten Gloria back. However loosely, their mother was knitted into their lives again.

Perhaps, Jess thought, she was beginning to understand the conundrum that was her life—at least a little. And she realized with a start that she was happy, too. For the first time in a long time, she was truly, honest-to-goodness happy: she had her husband back; her kids were showered with love; she had a job that made a difference in the world; and she'd shown up for her sisters when it mattered. They were a family who had been tested—and tested again. And they'd survived.

In the parking lot, Jess leaned in to give Maggie a hug before climbing into the car. "Thank you," she said.

"For what?" Maggie asked.

"Everything. For helping me get my marriage back." Jess settled into the driver's seat.

"You did that. You know that, right?" said Maggie.

Jess shrugged, then smiled. "I guess. Well, till tomorrow then," she said. "And I mean it. I'll call you tomorrow."

"I know you will," said Maggie. "That's what makes this okay."

Jess waved to her sister as she drove out of the hotel parking lot. The sun shone down as the car passed the local flower shop and a string of seaside homes fronted by wide porches. When she rolled down her window, a cool, salty breeze washed over her. She wanted to breathe it in, to take it all in, so that she could conjure this moment whenever she might need it at school or even back home. Because she didn't want to be fooled into thinking ever again that life should be a certain way or that marriages should follow a certain path—and that if they didn't, then something was the matter. Because she understood now that it was all necessary, even the heartache. She recalled a quote from a book she'd been reading last night by one of her favorite authors, Annie Dillard. She'd been searching for words to make sense of Arthur's death, but instead she'd found a statement that seemed appropriate to the entire summer, her entire year. She had highlighted the line in bright yellow ink:

If, however, you want to look at the stars, you will find that darkness is necessary.

It had been a long night. But Jess had found her stars this summer, indeed an entire dark sky studded with stars. She switched on the radio, pulled onto the ramp for the highway, and fastened her eyes on the bright road ahead, eager to get home to her husband and kids.

37

Maggie

After breakfast, Maggie carted all the books back to the library. She wanted to understand why her dad had collected so much stuff, but now she realized she probably never would. Not fully. There was a part of her that got it: Arthur had wanted to hold on to every little thing in case he needed it. Perhaps after losing Gloria, he began to worry that it was only a matter of time before he lost all that he cared about—the rest of his family, his mind. He had gathered every piece that might one day be of significance.

She phoned Mac to let him know she was on her way home and offered a quick update: the ceremony had been lovely, but she and Jess would probably need to come back over the next few weekends to help finish things up. There was still work to be done on the house. Oh, and Virgie was moving back! Into Arthur's house. They weren't going to sell after all. Her sister was slowing down and was going to try to figure out next steps in light of her diagnosis.

"Good for her," Mac said, sounding genuinely pleased. "It'll be nice for all of you to be together again. And moving into your old house. How about that?" He waited a beat. "Arthur would love to hear it, I'll bet."

"I know. Talk about coming full circle."

"Did you get our package?" Mac asked.

"Package?" Her chest tightened. "No. Oh, no! Was it something for the memorial service?" She panicked that she'd missed something important.

"No, no, nothing like that. Just a little something the kids put together for you. They thought it might cheer you up."

"Oh, how sweet. I'll have to check. You sent it to the hotel?"

"Yes, should have arrived yesterday."

After she'd she pulled up to the hotel, Maggie was headed for the front desk when she bumped into Gloria, treating herself to the free Danishes and coffee. "Oh, honey, can you help me? I can't seem to get my suitcase shut. I'm afraid I've packed it to the hilt. You know how I am—can never seem to decide what to take and what to leave at home."

"Sure, Mom." She followed Gloria back to her room. When Maggie caught sight of the suitcase yawning on the hotel bed, she burst out laughing. "You weren't kidding!" Shirts, skirts, and scarves stuck out everywhere. A stray shoe sat forlornly next to the bag, as if it had long ago given up searching for its match. Maggie flipped open the top and worked for a few minutes to rearrange her mother's clothing. At last, when it looked as if it might close, she jumped on top and tugged the zipper from one end to the other.

"There!" she exclaimed, triumphant. When she hopped off, she saw the suitcase was slightly misshapen with a raised lump in the corner, but it would do. She yanked it off the bed with a loud thunk.

"Thank you, honey. I could have never gotten that thing closed without you," Gloria said and laughed, tucking her blond hair behind her ears.

"You're welcome. Here to help anytime." Maggie felt the words come out with more meaning than she'd intended, but Gloria drew her into a hug nevertheless.

"I know you are, honey. It means a lot. Especially now with your father gone."

Maggie pulled back slightly. It was the first time she could remember her mother admitting any vulnerability since leaving Arthur. The first time she'd hinted that Arthur had filled a void, even in her single life. Maggie had always assumed her mom still loved Arthur, that a love of forty-six years didn't simply vanish with a snap of the fingers. But she'd also assumed that her mother called Arthur regularly as a way to assuage her own guilt over leaving him. Now, Maggie wondered if Gloria had been equally adrift, missing her husband but too proud to admit it. Would Gloria pick up the phone one night in the upcoming weeks and dial Arthur's number out of sheer habit, expecting to hear his voice? Had those talks been as important to her as they were to him? Maggie felt a knot form under her breastbone. Was it possible that Gloria had been faking her happiness, her joie de vivre for the last year and a half? That shortly after the divorce she'd regretted her decision, and they'd never known?

Of course, her mother would never give voice to those thoughts. But it was shocking to consider that perhaps Gloria had longed for Arthur as much as he had longed for her. Maggie gazed into her mother's soft blue eyes and smiled. She had missed all the signs with Arthur. She would not make the same mistake with Gloria.

"We'll stay in better touch, Mom. I promise," she said now, hugging her back.

"I'd like that," Gloria said, her voice dropping to a whisper.

When Maggie got back to her room, she packed quickly, throwing everything in without any mind to what was dirty and what was clean. It was unlike her, but a lot of what had happened in the last weeks was unlikely. She felt a small sliver of herself ceding control. She'd struggled for so long to keep her world neatly organized, and look where it had gotten her. *Hah!* Arthur was gone. Lexie had spent most of the summer in a funk. Virgie was fighting MS. Jess and Tim were fighting for their marriage. And even Mac, her dear, sweet Mac, wasn't entirely ready to jump on board with her idea of fostering a child.

Maggie was ready to cry "Uncle!" to the universe. "You win!" she shouted as she struggled to zip her suitcase shut. Arthur didn't have OCD, but Maggie feared that her own tendencies in that direction could tumble down a slippery slope. Was there a switch in the brain that could just as easily turn her obsession with neatness into an obsession with stuff? Maggie didn't know, but she desperately did not want to find out.

No, this summer had given her a new perspective. Her battle to keep everything the same had been lost. How silly of her. Of course, the girls and Luke were growing up. That was a good thing. Of course, there would be setbacks in the family. That was life. Certain traditions would be kept; others would be tossed, and new ones would take their place. *Life is change,* Mac had counseled her. At the time, she'd thought it trite, but now she was struck by its authenticity. She couldn't freeze time. Nor, she realized now, did she want to.

She headed for the lobby, where everyone had already gathered in the semicircle of lounge chairs and couches at the front. She waved and joined Jess in the checkout line. When she reached the front desk, she realized she'd almost forgotten. "Excuse me, but do you have a package for Maggie McNeil?" She turned to Jess. "Mac said the kids made something to cheer me up."

"That is so sweet," said Jess. The young concierge ducked his head behind the desk for a moment and returned with a padded envelope the approximate size of a book.

"Is this what you're looking for, ma'am?"

"I believe so. Thank you." She took the package from him and stuck it in her shoulder bag before heading over to the others. Tears began to bud at the corners of her eyes. "I'm sorry I'm such a softie," she said. "I've always hated good-byes." Virgie jumped up to hug her, and suddenly everyone was hugging each other.

Maggie pulled away at last.

"Bye, Mom. We'll talk soon, all right?" Gloria nodded. "In fact, why don't I plan to call you in a few days?" Maggie asked. She pressed her lips together. Hadn't she just promised herself she'd stop planning every minute of everyone's life? But this was important. She wanted her mom to know that she and Mac and the kids were there for her.

"Okay," Gloria agreed. "That sounds good."

Maggie swiveled and turned her attention to Jackson. "Jackson, we like you. Don't screw things up with my sister, okay?" He stared at her uneasily and then laughed when they all broke into laughter.

"She's kidding," Virgie explained. "Sort of."

"Virgie, honey," Maggie said "I love you. We'll see you soon." She cleared her throat. "Till tomorrow then." She offered her standard parting phrase and flipped her sunglasses down as she felt more tears coming. She and Jess headed out to the parking lot.

At the car, they exchanged hugs, and Jess promised to call her tomorrow.

Maggie went over to her beat-up Subaru, a few parking spaces away, and unlocked it. She hoisted her suitcase into the trunk and then climbed into the front seat, dropping her shoulder bag on the passenger seat. That was when she noticed the yellow envelope poking out. She'd nearly forgotten. She stopped and extracted it.

When she ripped it open, a faint cry escaped from her lips. There, in her hands, was a yellow notebook with red and purple flowers twirling across it. Each one had a different little face (the girls' work, no doubt). A small raccoon face that Luke must have drawn peered out from the top right corner. In the center were scrawled the words *The Book of Summer II.*

"Oh," she whispered.

She opened it, and on the first page, she began to read the long list of milestones and quotes from last month: *Luke dove off the pier! Grammy went skinny-dipping!* Maggie raised her hand to her mouth and covered her laugh. There was a whole stream of memories in the girls' slanted cursive, including *Lexie dumped Sophie out of the hammock. Lexie punched Sophie!* Slowly, the tears began to fall as Maggie read on. *Grandpa built a trap for Roger, the raccoon. We got a new teakettle. Aunt Virgie fainted and got to ride in an ambulance! Mom, Aunt Virgie, and Aunt Jess ate three cartons of ice cream in one night!* It was all here, all the new memories they'd created, good and bad.

She turned the page and kept reading until her eyes fell on the very last one: *The McNeils add a new member to the family, a foster child?* It was in Mac's handwriting.

It was listed as a question, but it was there. On the list, for them to decide as a family. Could it be the next step forward, building on all that was precious, on all that they were already fortunate to have? How appropriate, Maggie thought, their new *Book of Summer*. As with the last notebook, this one would document the best, the funniest, the most outrageous of their memories. But as Maggie had also come to understand, the family journal was as much about the *promise* of next summer, of a new year, as it was about the summer before. Each July stitched a bright new color in their family flag. Maggie brushed away tears as she closed the notebook and gently set it on the passenger seat.

She hooked her seat belt, checked her rearview mirror, and slowly began to pull away from the hotel. She was driving away from her childhood town, her old home, from memories of Arthur. From so many things that had shaped her into the person she was. But the hint of a smile played on her lips as she traveled forward, only forward in this sweet journey, this wonderful mess that was her life.

Because she knew in her heart that she was along for the ride. No matter what. For every beautiful mile of it.

Acknowledgments

The list of people to thank seems to grow exponentially with each book. I'm grateful to so many who have encouraged me along the way, including my gifted editor, Trish Todd; my wonderfully supportive agent, Meg Ruley; and the entire crew at Simon & Schuster.

If a girl can't have sisters, she ought to have her own group of best friends: for me, that group consists of my "roomies"—Barb, Katherine, Lisa, and Lora—the best surrogate sisters a girl could hope for, as well as my dear friends Lori and Jennifer. My sisters-in-law—Marian, Lynne, Nichole, and Linda—have also offered great support and much-needed laughter during the past year. A special thank-you to my in-laws, Barbara and Leo Francis, whose own New England home has provided endless summers of good memories and late-night bonfires on the beach (and fortunately, not nearly as much drama as this novel).

To my brother, Pedro: thanks for the invaluable car "edits" to the book. To my amazing stepkids, Michael and Katherine, I appreciate your letting me bounce a million titles off you and appropriately wrinkling your noses when they were no good. And to Mike and Nicholas: no one makes me smile more than you two. Thanks for always being my cheerleaders and for giving me the much-needed quiet time at my desk for writing.

In writing this book, I learned about hoarding and the impulses behind it. Randy Frost and Gail Steketee's book, *Stuff: Compulsive Hoarding and the Meaning of Things* helped to illuminate the life of a hoarder as did countless stories from friends and strangers who confided in me about a relative who'd kept his obsession with stuff a secret from the family, in many cases, for years.

I also researched multiple sclerosis to better understand Virgie's character. While I spoke to a handful of people and doctors, it was a family friend, Susan, who spent large chunks of time talking with me about MS, its onset, and its possible progression. I am awed by her and others like her who struggle with this daunting illness each and every day. While we've made great strides in treatment, we need more: may we soon have a drug that can permanently keep the symptoms of MS at bay. Any medical errors within the story are my own.

For every author, I believe there is someone who inspires her to write; for me, that person was my mom, who passed away from leukemia in October 2014. Though she was never able to read this novel, we talked about it a great deal, and it was her belief in the power of the written word that kept me writing, even during her illness. She was and always will be my "big sister."

About the Author

Wendy Francis is the author of the novels *The Summer of Good Intentions* and *Three Good Things*. A former book editor, she lives outside of Boston with her husband and son.

SIMON & SCHUSTER PAPERBACKS
READING GROUP GUIDE

The Summer of Good Intentions

INTRODUCTION

The Herington sisters and their families come together for their annual vacation at their Cape Cod summer house. Life there is supposed to remain reassuringly the same, but they quickly realize that their relaxing summer vacation is jeopardized by each sister's secrets.

Through poignant and engaging storytelling, Wendy Francis offers a fresh new summer read that takes readers through the complex and emotional web of family relationships.

TOPICS & QUESTIONS FOR DISCUSSION

1. All the Herington sisters, particularly Maggie, think of their summer house as a place of comfort and relaxation. What does the house symbolize for each sister? Do you have a place where you, too, can escape the routine of everyday life?

2. For Maggie, summer is represented by "sticky fingers. The smell of mosquito repellant. The wind whipping up, then settling down again. Her husband's arms around her. The sounds of the kids laughing." Virgie thinks it's not really summer until she steps into Grouchy Ted's and breathes in "the familiar scent of beer and peanuts." What does summer mean to each sister? What makes these memories so significant? What do you think of when you think about the summertime?

3. Describe the relationship between Maggie, Jess, and Virgie. What are their roles in the family? What do they teach you about sisterhood?

4. Jess doesn't think her relationship with Cole is the reason for her marriage troubles: "She'd read enough self-help books to understand he was a mere symptom of her troubled marriage. That she had allowed herself to fall for him in the first place and return his kisses was further testament to the fact that her marriage wasn't working. She wasn't *in love* with Cole." Do you agree with Jess's assessment of her failing marriage, or do you think she's making excuses so that she doesn't have to take responsibility for her affair?

5. How would you characterize Gloria's role in her daughters' lives? Does her elusive and carefree personality put a strain on her relationship with them?

6. How does Tim learn to forgive Jess and move forward with their relationship? Can Jess trust that Tim will now change his attitude toward their marriage? Can Tim trust Jess?

7. Why is it so difficult for Maggie to tell Mac she'd like to have another child? How do you think Mac handles the news?

8. How does the fire Arthur accidentally started bring attention to issues he has been keeping under wraps? How do his daughters interpret the accident?

9. Arthur has an epiphany right before his death. "He rubbed his hands together briskly, thinking of Gloria. *Always of Gloria.* Yes, a dip would be just the thing to mark a fresh start, his resolve to embrace life anew." Describe the irony of this scene. Why do you think the author included it?

10. "MS was but one melody playing in Virgie's life at the moment. In fact, it had probably been playing for some time. She just hadn't been listening." What does Virgie learn from her MS diagnosis? Why had she been ignoring the signs for so long? How has her diagnosis offered her a different perspective on both her career and her relationship with Jackson?

11. Do you think there was an active denial of Arthur's illness in the Herington family? Maggie realizes, "There had been plenty of signs—Arthur's absentmindedness, the collection of trash he'd started at her house, his overstuffed car—but she'd written them off as typical for a slightly scatterbrained older man." How did each family member deny the signs? If they had been able to confront Arthur's illness head-on, would the story have had a different outcome?

12. Arthur's daughters are shocked to discover that he has been living in squalor. Maggie thinks, "There was something terribly cruel about the juxtaposition of a life filled with so much junk and a life irretrievably lost. Arthur had died drowning, but he'd

been drowning long before that." What was Arthur drowning in? Why did he start hoarding? Why do you think Arthur never told his children about his problem?

13. How does each woman—Maggie, Jess, Virgie, and Gloria— move forward after Arthur's memorial service? How do their memories of Arthur inspire each of them to do better?

14. The essence of this story is about strengthening family ties and romantic bonds. How does each Herington sister accomplish this?

15. In the beginning of the story, Maggie remembers that *Que sera, sera* is one of Gloria's favorite sayings—they even have it on a plaque in the house. What does this saying mean? Is this message as relevant at the end of the book as it was at the beginning?

ENHANCE YOUR BOOK CLUB

1. *The Book of Summer* was Maggie and her family's notebook of special memories, funny moments, and important milestones that they collected each summer at their Cape Cod summer house. Create your own notebook to memorialize special times in your life. Write a brief entry, even just a few sentences, for each funny anecdote or exciting moment that you experience with your family.

2. What are your good intentions for the summer? Share with your book club.

3. Visit Cape Cod. The peaceful beauty of the Cape comes to life in the pages of *The Summer of Good Intentions*. Plan a summer vacation to explore the beaches and the history of one of New England's most popular vacation destinations.

4. Read Wendy Francis's first novel, *Three Good Things,* for your next book club meeting. Filled with love, humor, and the scent of the delectable Danish pastry called kringle, *Three Good Things* tells the story of two midwestern sisters, each with a secret. You can even bake kringles as a special treat for your group using the recipe on page 233 of the book.

5. Wendy Francis does a wonderful job introducing two important, serious health conditions to readers: multiple sclerosis and hoarding. To learn more about MS, visit the National Multiple Sclerosis Society's Web site at http://www.nationalmssociety .org/. To learn more about hoarding, visit the Anxiety and Depression Association of America's Web site at http://www.adaa .org/understanding-anxiety/obsessive-compulsive-disorder -ocd/hoarding-basics.

Despite being sisters, Maggie, Jess, and Virgie are very different and very dynamic individuals. Which sister do you relate to the most?

Maggie is probably the sister with whom I identify the most. I'm at that age where my six-year-old son is growing up at rapid speed and I'm wondering what's next. Who else needs nurturing? My husband likes to joke that I'm always trying to fix things for people, and that's probably not far from the truth. Though I hope I'm not a meddler, per se, there's still some of that midwestern girl in me, the one who wants to set things right and make sure everyone is happy. Like Maggie, I also love the beach; summertime; and the slower, languid pace that those things suggest.

Was the setting of the story important to you? Why did you decide on Cape Cod?

As much as I love the Midwest (where my first novel was set), I also love the seaside. Even as a young girl in Wisconsin, I would search out whatever pockets of beach I could find, usually just a slice of sand next to a water-filled quarry. Once I moved east and settled closer to the ocean, I felt as if I'd found my second home. I'm also fortunate in that my in-laws have a house near the Cape, which has become a favorite retreat for all of us during the summer. So the rhythm of the waves, the sound of crickets whirring at night—all those things were familiar to me. What's more, it seemed a summer house would be the perfect setting for the sisters' emotions to percolate and collide.

Each chapter is told from the point of view of a different member of the Herington family, except Gloria. Why didn't you write from Gloria's perspective?

It never really occurred to me to write from Gloria's perspective. She was always a bit of an outsider in the family, and I thought it should remain that way. Besides, Gloria is such an opinionated, zany character, I'm not sure I could have handled going into her head!

Did you plan how you were going to develop each character's journey, or did their stories evolve as you wrote the book?

For better or worse, I'm one of those writers who let the characters guide the story. I've never been able to map out a novel's plotline in its entirety (though I wish I could!). All the sisters, I knew, would be dealing with some kind of conundrum, and once I determined that Arthur had a hoarding problem, all the other elements began to fall into place.

The Summer of Good Intentions **emphasizes the strong bonds between sisters. Do you have sisters who helped inspire this story?**

No, but my mom was my best friend, and in many ways, like a big sister to me. I'm a big believer in the support system that women can provide for one another, whether as sisters, mothers and daughters, grandmothers and granddaughters, aunts and nieces, or good friends.

How was writing this book different from writing your first novel, *Three Good Things***?**

Looking back, I feel as if *Three Good Things* almost wrote itself. Don't get me wrong: it took multiple revisions and drafts! But, as my agent likes to say, first novels tend to live inside an author's heart for a long while. Somehow I felt as if I *knew* Ellen and Lanie in that book, as if they were my neighbors. I wasn't sure I could ever feel the same way about another cast of characters. Also, as a former book editor, I was all too familiar with the curse of the second novel, when authors get stuck wondering if they'll ever write another book—or was the first novel just a fluke? *The Summer of Good Intentions* had some false starts for sure, but eventually, I found myself falling in love with all these women, and Arthur, too.

You tackle very emotional and complex issues in *The Summer of Good Intentions*: divorce; infidelity; expanding a family; and health matters such as memory loss, MS, and hoarding. What literary challenges did you face to properly address these subjects in the book?

The challenges in tackling the various health issues here was to reveal them over time, as the characters' stories played out, and to resist the impulse to infuse the book with research and statistics. I'd done a fair amount of research on MS and hoarding, and at points the book veered into textbook territory—thankfully, those sections were cut! As for the more everyday issues, I really just trusted my own emotional instincts to guide me through the characters' thoughts and reactions. With luck, they ring true in the book.

As a former book editor, how does writing your own book compare to editing someone else's? What's the biggest challenge for you in the writing process?

Oh, my goodness, writing is much, much harder than editing! And I'd had no idea. You think when you're an editor that you have a fairly good understanding of how a book should be written. But when it's *you* staring at the blank page, you realize just how impossible and insurmountable the whole writing thing is. Given that, it's amazing to me how many great books get written. The biggest challenge in my writing is turning off my editor's ear so that I can focus on getting the characters and story down on the page. Otherwise, I'd be tempted to revise every sentence as soon as it's written, and it would take me about ten years to finish a single chapter.

If your readers were to take away only one message from this story, what would it be?

Wow, that's a tall order. Basically, the epigraph at the beginning of the book by Dani Shapiro sums it up: "The mess is holy. . . . There is beauty in what is." She was referring to the writing process in her wonderful meditation *Still Writing: The Perils and Pleasures of a Creative Life* (which, incidentally, every writer should read). When I read those words, they resonated with me on so many levels. My whole life felt like a big mess at the time: my mom was battling leukemia; I was flying back and forth between Wisconsin and Massachusetts, trying to help her and still be a good mom back at home. For me, those words were a potent reminder to live in the moment. Yes, our lives may be messy, and every last good intention we have may get foiled. But remember: there is beauty in our lives *right now,* as cluttered and out of control and crazy as it might seem. That's the conclusion I think Maggie comes to by the book's end and the one that I hope readers will take away from this novel.

Can you share with us any news of upcoming writing projects? What can we expect from you next?

All I'll say is that my new novel involves plenty of family drama once again—and a boat. Stay tuned!